Part One
TRAINING

$3

fiction

DOUBLE EUCHRE

a novel

by

Daniel Luther Olson

"For it is my belief no man understands quite his own artful dodges to escape from the grim shadow of self-knowledge."
—*Lord Jim,* Joseph Conrad

Norway Pine Press
Athens, Ohio

This is a work of fiction. Names, characters, places, and incidents either are a product of the author's imagination or are used fictitiously. Any resemblance to actual persons, living or dead, events, or locales is entirely coincidental.

To Steve Rudolph, Steve Mowrey, Richard Mayer,
and, as always, my wife, Sharon

Cataloging-in-Publication Data

Olson, Daniel Luther.
DOUBLE EUCHRE
by Daniel Luther Olson
"A novel of espionage, romance, mystery & murder."

1. Cold War – Fiction. 2. Espionage, Soviet – Germany – Fiction. 3. Russian Language – Study and teaching – Fiction. 4. Defense Language Institute (U.S.) – Fiction.
5. Americans – Germany (West) – Fiction.
6. United States. Army – Fiction.
7. Male friendship – Fiction.

ISBN 979-8-9870067-0-2
www.daniellutherolson.com

Cover design by Enzo Varrie
First edition

Chapter One

What must it feel like to drown?

Dying to save his life, the best man I ever knew swam out to sea and went under not once but twice. Without a buddy to hold your head above water, you sink like a rock. Eyes open or shut, I still can see him and his fateful lover the way they looked fifteen years ago, but then their memories are burned in my brain like tombstone inscriptions. How improbable that the two should ever meet, much less, fall in love. If the tiniest of circumstances had only occurred otherwise, four people would not have died decades too soon nor would that toll still be rising.

Mornings before breakfast I take bracing walks around the freezing lake beside this cozy cabin here in northern Minnesota. When I stomp through the powdery snow, I ponder what all had to happen just so for a mild-mannered dork like me to end up this outlaw on the run. Evenings I add to the account below explaining how such calamities came to pass, while keeping my back to the scary axe, propped against the wall opposite the crackling fireplace. It won't be long before the sturdy tool at last gets the chance to prove it can chop far more than wood and thereby do me a huge, final favor.

* * *

Nineteen sixty-eight wasn't just a pivotal year for me, but the entire nation. In January, Tet proved the US wasn't winning in Vietnam. In March, for revenge Lieutenant Calley and his men cleared the VC out of My Lai but good. By Easter, James Earl Ray made sure Martin Luther King wouldn't be leading anybody to the Promised Land. In June, Robert Kennedy won the California primary, but didn't survive the celebration. In

August, Soviet tanks brought winter down on the Prague Spring overnight, and we besieged the Democratic Convention in Chicago and pushed Clean Gene, but couldn't Dump the Hump. Our tide was already cresting then, but still felt so strong we didn't even suspect the coming ebb.

That May, I earned my BA in linguistics at St. Olaf College after successfully postponing conscription for a whole year. I moved back home to Madison, Wisconsin, and, fresh diploma in hand, got back my old summer job, packing batteries for Rayovac. Mid-June, the dreaded draft notice landed in our mailbox like a bomb. Like other guys I appealed and used the ensuing reprieve to consult military recruiters and underground advisors on emigration to Canada. "The decision's all yours, son," Dad told me, and teary-eyed Mom did her best to agree. But it was clear once I settled abroad I could never return. I compromised by enlisting for four years in Army Intelligence to become a Russian linguist, a choice a sergeant all but promised would keep me far from Vietnam.

Following Boot Camp at Fort Leonard Wood, Missouri, I flew to Monterey, California to attend the Defense Language Institute, the former Army Language School, located on the Presidio garrison. A taxi dropped me off outside Company D, a three-story, cinder-block barracks, painted an industrial pastel green. At first glance it looked like a nondescript college dormitory.

A passing zoomie in dress blues—every service branch attended the DLI—directed me to the Orderly Room, where I handed the company clerk a copy of my orders. Spec Four Remington accepted them with a genuine smile, just like I was a fellow human being, a first from any GI outranking me. I lugged my bulging duffel bag after him to the laundry room. A sullen private first class issued me army blankets, sheets, and a pillow case. From there Remington led me to the second floor into a cramped room, furnished with double sets of cots, tin wall lockers, utility tables, and desk lamps, and reeking of brass polish and floor wax. "The empty bed's yours," he said and vanished.

A pasty-faced sailor lay on the far cot, staring wide-eyed at the ceiling and clutching a personal letter to his chest. "Hi, I'm Tom Bakken," I greeted.

One glance at my dress greens and my new roommate moaned, "Army." A native of Gainesville, Florida, halfway through a course in Mandarin Chinese, Jimmy Wells preferred writing and reading letters to conversation, and I quickly learned not to mind. So early in my own enlistment, his virulent hatred of the military was more than I could bear.

My Russian course wouldn't begin for a week, so in the meantime the First Sergeant had me report to the Orderly Room for work details daily at oh-eight-hundred hours. At first, I watered ice plant around the classroom grounds by myself. But the fourth morning when I arrived downstairs, a fellow E-1 buck private, his lapels like mine lacking even a single stripe, was seated on the buffed gray tile floor outside the First Shirt's office, holding a paperback copy of Hermann Hesse's *Der Steppenwolf* propped against his thighs and circling what appeared to be every other sentence with a ballpoint. Unlike my squared-away uniform, his fatigues were wrinkled and his combat boots scuffed. ZIELSDORF his nametag read in bold, black letters, looking as German as his ash-blond hair.

We were both gaunt, our cheeks sunken and wind-burned, and pale scalps showed through our temples' bristles in the traditional white-walls style. So he had just been through the same hell I had—ten weeks of Physical Training, Dismounted Drill, and deliberately short nights of sleep made shorter by Fire Watch and Guard Duty, before arising at oh-five-hundred for grueling days of forced marching, bivouacking, and learning to shoot down pop-up silhouettes of men with hot lead. We hadn't neglected the other venerable martial arts either, such as heel-stomping a man's brains out or disemboweling him with bayonet thrusts. They call it Basic Combat Training.

His gaze was hidden behind a reflection of my red hair and freckles off his plastic military-issue glasses, but his grin was kindly. "So you got rooked into the laundry detail, too?" he said and tilted his head, my mirror image disappearing to reveal deep blue eyes.

I managed a thin smile, while his own broadened good-naturedly to reveal slightly crooked canines that had obviously never worn braces. No sooner had I set myself down against the wall across from him than a paunchy, round-shouldered soldier moseyed out of the stairwell down the hall. At the sight of the guy's four stripes we scrambled to our feet and snapped to attention, *Steppenwolf* flopping to the floor. From the subtitle I noticed that the book was in the original German. The NCO gave the novel a kick down the buffed tiles past the duty roster and thrust himself inches from my fellow soldier, the top of his balding head barely reaching Zielsdorf's strong nose. I wasn't short at five eleven, but my buddy was a good two inches taller. "Okay, Alphabet," the Staff Sergeant growled, "I give up. How do you say your name?"

"Just as it's spelled," Zielsdorf said. "Zealz. Dorf." How else? It wasn't strange to me because Germans mostly immigrated to Wisconsin, though Norwegians, like all of my ancestors, didn't lag far behind.

"Call me Sergeant when you talk to me, Troop. Sergeant Hopkins." Spoken with the drawl of almost every Army NCO thus far. "Today you men are comin' with me to Fort Ord on laundry detail. You college boys think you can handle loadin' and unloadin' a truck?"

"Yes, Sergeant!" Zielsdorf bellowed in a voice the drill instructors must have loved.

"Yes, Sergeant," I echoed hoarsely and cleared my throat.

Hopkins faced me with the hard glare of a country sheriff sizing up a shady stranger, and I blinked. To judge from his weathered skin he might have been either side of forty.

"Back-in," he said, reading my nametag BAKKEN. My family always pronounced it "Bahk-kin," but I didn't correct him. "Back-in, keep your shit together, and you and me will get along just fine. But cross me even once, and you'll be one sorry son of a bitch."

“Yes, Sir,” I said, this time more loudly. “I mean, yes, Sergeant.”

Hopkins bared his brown teeth in a semblance of a friendly smile. “Now your buddy, Alphabet, has already fucked up in my book. He’s on my shit list ‘cause he don’t know how to talk to an NCO.”

I gulped.

An hour later, the three of us were riding in the cab of a deuce-and-a-half truck full of dirty bed linen up Highway One toward Fort Ord, and I was watching waves caress the long, sandy beach and wishing I was back in Northfield. “What I want to know,” Hopkins piped up, “why ain’t you privileged college boys humpin’ it in Nam like everybody else? So what if you’re educated?”

I shrugged. Zielsdorf didn’t move a muscle.

“You four eyes deaf, too?” Hopkins said.

“We may end up in Nam yet, Sergeant,” Zielsdorf replied. “You know the Army and its promises.”

Hopkins cackled. “You bet I do. But fair’s fair.”

Instead of heading straight for the base laundry at Fort Ord, Hopkins drove east into the treeless California hills, explaining that he needed to look up his buddy Johnston. On the way, he sang, “I’m Just A Honky-Tonk Man,” with a down-home twang. “Him and me are gonna get shit-faced tonight, “ he said. “And maybe hustle us up some gash. In Seaside for sure, maybe even in Monterey.” He chuckled hard at the prospect. “Hey, men, just do what I tell ya and we ain’t gonna have a problem. I’m working my way up from a court martial in Nam, where the pukes busted me to buck private on a bullshit charge. Hell, everything over there’s bullshit. My CO tore my chevrons off in front of the entire frickin’ company, not that I gave a shit. That fuckin’ Jody was lucky his tour was up or I’d a fragged him. Say, you fellas wouldn’t wanna see my collection of gook ears, would ya?”

Zielsdorf shook his head, and I gasped. Hopkins chortled. “You don’t really believe Americans would cut off ears, do you?”

Why hadn’t I emigrated to Canada when I had the chance I couldn’t help but think.

"That's too fuckin' good for 'em," Hopkins said, "after what they done to us. I'll never forget one night at a fire base near Pleiku. About oh-three-hundred hours my damned platoon was dreamin' away about American gash, when VC sappers slit a sentry's throat and snuck through our perimeter quiet as snakes. Somebody fired a flare and I woke up, grabbed my M-16, and shot the shit out of everything that moved. You ever seen hamburger in black pajamas? Well, it looks better than the shit those dinks eat, let me tell ya." His snaggle-toothed smile was scary.

After an uneasy silence, Hopkins asked, "You know how to make a Viet Cong squeal?"

Neither of us spoke.

"It ain't hard. Just take three gooks up in a Cobra and throw two out." He giggled with a chilling glee, and I began to fear the Army truly might waste our linguistic talents and throw us into the hell of Vietnam, no matter what the recruiters had all but promised. God, would I have to desert?

Hopkins tooled past a half dozen armored personnel carriers parked alongside a gravel road and pulled up behind a bleacher full of troops in helmets listening to a staff sergeant deliver a training lecture. "Take ten," Hopkins ordered with a crooked grin, and we all climbed out. While he chatted with his NCO buddy, Zielsdorf and I stared at the trainees, seated in sullen, rigid obedience.

Upon Johnston's barked command, the troops clambered into the APCs, showing us nothing but the demanded assholes and elbows. The engines kicked on and roared, and at a radio signal the metallic behemoths skittered like cockroaches over a knoll, jerked to a halt below a ridge, opened up their rears, and spewed out GIs, who hit the sand, blasting their M-16s.

"May God preserve us from this," Zielsdorf muttered. "DLI students have been yanked right out of language class and transferred here the same day. The Army can turn a linguist into an Eleven Bravo as fast as it can cut an order. And it cares no more about what happens to us than we do ants underfoot."

"I never consciously step on ants," I said. "Live and let live."

"How noble of you. You care about nature, but of course you realize it doesn't worry about you. If a mine rips your body apart, nature will recycle your molecules without shedding a tear. No problem."

We drove on to the Fort Ord laundry, where Hopkins announced, "You guys got exactly thirty minutes to unload my truck." With that he strolled off toward the PX for a cup of coffee.

Zielsdorf and I worked quickly without talking. "You're from Wisconsin or Minnesota," he finally said. "I hear it in your deep 'o's, clipped syllables, and nasalized a's." His own deliberate English, without any regional accent, was fluent and definitely American, but didn't sound quite native.

"I grew up in Madison," I told him. "And went to college at St. Olaf in Northfield. I've spent my whole life in Wisconsin and Minnesota." The "o" in my "Olaf" sounded so pure 'Sconsin, it made Zielsdorf chuckle. "Where are you from?"

"So I fooled you." His vowels suddenly turning as nasal and Germanic as mine, he said, "I'm from 'Sconsin, too." "Peter" he insisted on being called, never "Pete" or "Petie." His major at UW-Madison had been German, his minor French, and after graduation he had studied a year at the University of Marburg in West Germany before returning to his alma mater and earning a Master's in German the previous May. He had grown up near the Mississippi in "Shootin' Wire"—spelled Chute Noire—and his Upper Midwest accent became even thicker when he talked about it. It was a tiny place I remembered seeing on maps in the vicinity of La Crosse.

His great-grandparents had emigrated from Pomerania, the northeastern arm of the old Reich that stretched along the Baltic Sea toward East Prussia, territory that the Potsdam Treaty of 1945 at Stalin's insistence had partly wrested from Germany and given to Poland. He didn't say what his relatives had done once they reached America, and I didn't ask, but his articulate manner suggested they had done well.

"My ancestors never really looked back," he went on. "Even if they had stayed in Pomerania, the Poles would have kicked them out fifty years later anyway and forced them to resettle. Free will's a funny thing. You choose a fork early and that's the road you take. We're free to keep going straight or turn yet again, but we can never go back and get a do-over."

I told him about my own high school, Madison East, and the street I grew up on in a tract of ticky-tacky Cape Cods built after World War Two. My father taught junior high general science and my mother sold women's wear at a mall. Peter listened with an opaque expression, his deep blue eyes betraying a weird curiosity, as if hearing about Borneo headhunters. At St. Olaf I had majored in linguistics with a minor in Norwegian, I said.

"*Kan du snakker norsk*?" he asked with a passable Oslo accent. Can you speak Norwegian? It didn't equal his German, but it still impressed.

In English I replied I could. My mediocre Norwegian had always embarrassed me, because I should have been fluent. Though my parents were born in Wisconsin—my dad outside Mt. Horeb and my mom near Stoughton—they were both at heart more Norwegian émigrés living here in exile than true Americans. My cousins and I were the first among my kin since time immemorial not to have grown up on a farm.

"What language did you get?" he asked, his gaze hardening.

"Russian," I said. "I start next Monday."

"We're in the same class." His expression was pained.

I almost mentioned my four semesters of Russian at St. Olaf, getting all A's, but refrained. If the treads found out this Monterey course was superfluous for me, who knew what they'd do with me? I also neglected to mention my two years of German in high school and looking up and learning every unfamiliar word in a half dozen novels on my own time.

On the ride back to the Presidio, Hopkins chattered like a robin at dusk, an angry edge undercutting the good cheer. In our shared room Wells was pining over another letter from his sweetheart. That night I slept fitfully between terrifying dreams about cockroach armies chasing me into rearing cobras, every snake grinning just like Peter.

Chapter Two

"First-platoon-all-present-and-accounted-for-Sirrr!"

"Second-platoon-all-present-and-accounted-for-Sirrr!"

"Third-platoon . . ."

Captain Toddhunter's sharp salutes to the candy-striped student platoon leaders, rattling off attendance in the morning fog, set my teeth on edge. Our gung-ho CO, fresh from a tour of duty in Vietnam, was an Officer Candidate School grad a couple of years our junior. Unlike most students at the DLI, he hadn't gone to college, and he resented those of us who had.

The last platoon finished reporting and Toddhunter glared at us like a flinty-eyed streetfighter sizing up intruders. He wasn't going to bother earning our respect. He would simply demand it.

"Everybody-but-the-new-students, fall out!" he screamed. Four-fifths of the formation headed across the street, leaving a few dozen of us scattered on the grass between the horseshoe wings of Company D. Toddhunter sneered another long minute before drawling, "Men, we're at war. Hundreds of Americans are dying every month, sometimes every week. Now this building might look like a dormitory to some of you, but it's a barracks. You're no longer Joe College, you're GI Joe. Which means you count for jack shit. You have no rank, you have no authority. You will obey your superiors' orders without question. And who are your superiors? Me, the XO, the First Sergeant, all the other NCOs, your platoon leaders, and their deputies. Anybody with more stripes than you, and right now that's just about everybody in sight.

"Now here are the company regulations. You will be in proper dress uniform according to your branch of service at all times between oh-eight-hundred and sixteen-hundred hours Monday through Friday, except as otherwise ordered. Your uniform will be clean and pressed. Your shoes, brass, and belt buckle will be polished. You will wear your regulation head cover at all times outdoors and at no times indoors. Your haircuts will be regulation military, which means no longer than three inches on top and tapered shorter on the sides. Sideburns will be no longer than mid-ear and well-trimmed. The only facial hair allowed is a neat moustache that will not extend beyond the corners of the mouth. The penalty for a single gig is weekend duty. Two gigs, two weekends. Three gigs and it's an Article Fifteen." The Captain paused and then screamed, "Do I make myself clear?"

"Yes, Sir!" most of us shouted. There was one sarcastic "Yes, Drill Sergeant" behind me, but Toddhunter didn't let on he had heard.

"Now some of you bolos might need your buddies' help to get squared away. But that's what buddies are for. Sometimes without a buddy to hold your head above water, you sink like a rock. Is that understood?"

"Yes, Sir!" we bellowed, again except for one falsetto "Yes, Drill Sergeant."

"But then what would you lily-livered college boys know about esprit de corps?"

"Yes, Sir!"

I had an inkling of what the CO meant. Without buddies I would have never made it out of Basic Training. By himself, unmechanical Tom Bakken was hopeless with assembling a rifle.

"Did you men hear about Class oh-eight-sixty-seven? After graduation that Russian class got orders for Ord in Infantry. All except for one lucky bastard. He's gonna man the White House Hot Line to Moscow. Now everybody trained at Fort Ord goes to Vietnam, so listen up, men. There are too many lingies around now, especially in languages like Russian. Because we're not at war with Russia. But we are at war. So guess where Uncle Sam wants you to go? That's right—Viet-fucking-nam. And when you end up in that frickin' half-assed country, you'd better be ready to cover your butt. Let your guard down once over there and sure as shit you'll be flying home in a zippered plastic bag."

He gnashed his teeth. "So why am I being tough? When you end up in Nam, I guarantee you'll curse my ass for not being tougher. So don't bitch like a bunch of women. You ain't got it tough here and don't pretend you do. Tough is humping eighty pounds through a three-canopied jungle with Charlie nippin' at your nuts. Tough is being trained as a cook and still having to man the perimeter like any grunt and fighting North Vietnamese regulars overrunning the camp hand-to-hand. There ain't no fixed MOS's in Vietnam, men. My Mess Sergeant forgot how to use his bayonet one night, so we had to zip him up and mail him home."

"That would be even worse than getting a big, fat F," a GI rasped to my rear.

"F, my ass. You mean a B," a deeper voice added.

"So if you college boys think it's tough here, just wait till it gets tougher."

"Don't be embarrassed, Sir," the cocky fellow behind me squeaked. "Go ahead and wipe the foam off your mouth." Muffled giggles on both sides of me.

"Do I make myself clear?" Toddhunter bellowed.

"Yes, Sir!" we screamed except for yet again one "Yes, Drill Sergeant!"

"So study your butt off and keep squared away," Toddhunter said, "and we'll take care of everything else. Flunk one six-weeks period, and you'll be halfway to Fort Ord. Do it twice and you'll befriend an M-16 sure as shit. That means Eleven Bravo, men. That's an infantry MOS for you ignorant college boys. Again, that's not a threat, men. That's a promise. And from Ord you'll go to Vietnam as sure as I piss in the morning. All I can say is if you start flunking now, you had better get in shape. The NCOs at Ord will expect you to be right where you left off after Basic Training, because that's where the other trainees are. And if you're smart, by graduation next year you had better all be ready for Vietnam. Except maybe for the very best student. If you lingies think you pulled a fast one by getting assigned to the DLI, you'd better think twice. You may be stationed here, but you're still in the US-fucking-military."

Like other treads, Toddhunter knew we weren't real volunteers. We had only enlisted to avoid being drafted into combat arms, not because we had any interest in military service. We had only agreed to serve two years longer than a draftee would for the promise of staying far from any action. It was a given that the war in Vietnam was as senseless as Russian roulette, so why risk our lives for nothing?

"A couple more things," the CO went on, "and they're as important as anything I've said yet. The Warsaw Pact intelligence services already have a dossier on each and every one of you." The bold GI behind me stifled a snicker. "They already know your name, where you're from, how you like to spend your free time, even your bad habits. Maybe they even have a photo. So stay on your toes and keep your mouth shut. Nobody needs to know one fucking thing about what you're up to, not your family, not your girlfriend, not anybody. Be security-conscious, men, and you'll get along fine.

"One last thing. The sorry sack of shit who gets busted for dope will wish he had never been born. We had better not even suspect it. Because then you'll wish you was an Eleven Bravo at Ord. Now the slow-learners among you should know the Universal Code of Military Justice is a stacked deck, and trainees always get dealt the shit cards. A court martial isn't a real trial, so you won't stand a chance."

His spiel at last complete, he marched quickly between the ranks with a set jaw—it was a little weak in profile—and halted behind my vulnerable back. "Soldier," he snapped at somebody, "you have one gig for a non-regulation haircut. You *will* get that neck trimmed. You *will* report to the Orderly Room for a detail this Saturday at oh-nine-hundred hours."

Whoever the soldier was didn't respond, and of course I didn't dare turn around. Toddhunter moved back in front, glared at us another minute, and screamed, "Companeeee, dismissed!" The others fell out around me, but I was too dazed to budge. What kind of hell must Vietnam be to turn Americans into Hopkins and Toddhunters? Enlisting for *anything*, even to become a Russian linguist, felt like the biggest mistake of my life. If I hadn't been tough enough for high school football and even sprained my ankle bad enough for crutches in marching band, what was I doing here? That Toddhunter and Hopkins openly hated us, that they actually wished Nam on us, made my knees shake. After no one ever wishing me evil in my whole life. Like my mother, I had always tried to be nice to everybody, and it had mostly worked. But not in the Army.

Finally I turned around. There stood Zielsdorf talking to a swarthy GI with a bushy moustache. I figured he must have gotten the gig. Peter motioned me over, and in an oddly pinched voice introduced Rich Hoffman, who spoke with a relaxed tenor in an East Coast accent I correctly guessed as Bostonian.

"So you got the gig?" I asked Rich. He didn't look the least bit troubled.

"No, I did," Peter said and showed me his shaggy neck. He almost sounded drunk.

"These fucking treads are worse than Daley's pigs," Rich said, the aggressiveness of his words undercut by a light-hearted tone. Chicago police had tear-gassed him in Grant Park only two weeks earlier during leave. "Robert Kennedy, our best bet, was blasted out of the race. Then both McCarthy and McGovern blew it at the convention. So now we're stuck with Humphrey, Nixon or Wallace."

"Humphrey's not really so bad," I replied. "He can work with Congress."

Hoffman made a face like I was nuts. While we strolled across the street to the classrooms, he chattered about his groovy "Summer of Love" the previous year. "I'll be damned if I ever see one day of Eleven Bravo," he said. "A friend in a Czech class ahead of ours told me how to apply for asylum in Stockholm, and that's where I'm going if I have to. You're all welcome to tag along."

It sounded like heaven. But if I hadn't had the guts to emigrate to Canada earlier, I doubted I could summon up the courage to desert now. Not even if the alternative was taking the cowardly way out and dying in Nam for nothing.

A bald, smiling man of fifty emerged from a one-story, cinder-block building painted pastel green like our barracks. "*Gospoda, poidite so mnoi*," he said in Russian and gestured for us to follow. I understood what he had said—Gentlemen, come with me—but I didn't let on I had.

I wondered who had mocked the CO in falsetto, a voice that spoke with Rich's wit and Peter's balls. I would have bet on Rich, but I wouldn't have wagered much.

That evening Peter popped into my room and asked, "You got a Magic Marker? Rich doesn't." Wells glanced up from his stack of love letters.

"What for?" I said, handing him my red one.

"You'll find out."

Did we ever. At breakfast the next morning, the entire Company D mess hall was abuzz over Toddhunter's parking sign. During the night, someone had written on it in big, scarlet letters, "The CO sucks and blows." The thought of such an insult to our nemesis at first exhilarated me but then turned my stomach. Because Peter had done it, hadn't he, and I had been his accomplice. Unwittingly of course, but would the treads care about that legalistic nicety? I gave up on my nauseatingly sweet French toast and raced back to my room. There the offending Magic Marker lay in my desk drawer, the initials "TB" clearly scratched across it, as on all my property to make sure things were returned. I had to get rid of it fast, but where? Not in the trash, not out the window, so where else? But if Wells had seen me give it to Peter, what good would hiding it do? And how did it get back inside my desk? Peter must have sneaked into our unlocked room in the middle of the night.

Recorded bugles signaled roll call. I hurried down the fire escape with a lump in my back pocket. God, if Peter had a death wish, why couldn't he leave me out of it?

Toddhunter glared at us a full minute. "Men," he said with a trembling jaw, "the sorry-assed coward who defaced my sign deserves a court martial and a sentence to hard labor. But if he owns up right now, I'll be lenient and give him an Article Fifteen and immediate reassignment to Fort Ord in Eleven Bravo. You'd better fess up, you fucking coward. I *will* find you out. You have one minute to come forward." He studied his wristwatch while we stood still as gravestones.

My heart pounded and sweat trickled down my ribs in the bracing morning air. If Peter stepped forward, wouldn't I be implicated, too? What if Wells turned us both in? I didn't know him well enough to have any idea what he might do.

The sixty seconds passed without a murmur.

"You goddamned coward," the CO mumbled and then screamed, "Fall out!" My hands shook the rest of the day. Between classes I hunted for a spot to get rid of the evidence, but because of those initials ended up carrying the Magic Marker back to my room and hiding it inside a combat boot.

For the next two weeks, Toddhunter held us after every roll call and threatened weekend details if we didn't turn the perpetrator in. Zielsdorf never brought up the sign himself, and his only reaction when someone else did was a sly grin. I wanted to enjoy my classmates and make the best of my enlistment, but Peter's act of revenge made me feel like I was tiptoeing across a mine field. Overnight, dread had become a sour, metallic taste I woke up with and took to bed and couldn't get out of my mouth no matter how many times I brushed my teeth.

The first language lessons should have been relaxed for me, since all we did was learn the sounds of Russian and form short sentences, but the CO's threats kept me unnerved. We mimicked our émigré teachers by moving our lips and tongues in ways strange for Americans. After five days, all of us knew several simple dialogues *po-russki* well enough to play either role. In the succeeding weeks, the sentences grew more complex. At St. Olaf I had mastered far more complicated vocabulary and grammar, but of course didn't let that on, since what others didn't know couldn't hurt me. Evenings, I skimmed the assigned lessons before slipping my old college grammar inside the introductory DLI workbook and cramming that. I'd be darned if I'd relinquish my head start.

Gospodin Markov and Gospozha Danilova quickly proved themselves the best teachers. He the stickler for perfect grammar and pronunciation, while her irrepressible enthusiasm and minimal correcting first kindled a love for the supple language, which she then fanned into a passion.

One foggy morning on break between classes, Peter, Rich, and I were standing outside, getting some fresh air, when Hoffman launched into a parody of Danilova in simple Russian that perfectly captured her high pitch, merry tone, and stiff posture. Peter managed a laugh, but I couldn't.

A thin, lanky GI in dress greens came running around the corner toward us. MACINTOSH his nametag read, followed by a little "CZ," for Czech, corresponding to the "RUs" on our own for Russian. Rich introduced Dave MacIntosh, a friend from Boston protests. Dave's piercing hazel eyes scrutinized Peter and me.

"Mack, they're okay," Rich muttered.

"I'm fucked, Hoffer," Dave said. "The treads found out about that big anti-war protest I organized last year. A couple of plainclothes agents are going to grill me tomorrow. What about all that other crap I got into?"

"Shit," Rich replied.

"If they boot me over to Fort Ord in infantry, I'm bugging on out," MacIntosh said.

I put a finger across my lips, softly shushed, and nodded toward our classmates, Will Burke and Scott Dickinson, not thirty feet away. "No shit, I'll go to Sweden if I have to!" MacIntosh snapped. "If you guys were smart, you'd go, too!"

Scott and Will turned toward us at that outburst. Rich grabbed MacIntosh's shoulders, spun him around, and pushed him away, whispering, "Get out of here, man. I'll stop by your room tonight."

Burke and Dickinson moseyed over. "Pray tell, who was that gentleman?" Will asked.

"Dave Jefferson," Peter said.

"He's studying Chinese," Rich added.

"Did that guy really say he would be willing to go to Sweden?" Scott whispered.

"No, Salinas," Rich said. "The town just up the road. I hear there's totally nude dancing in a bar there."

Will rolled his eyes. "Honestly, my good man."

I wasn't positive whether Burke doubted our story, but Dickinson's mischievous grin implied he at least did. I looked at Rich and then Peter, waiting for one to ask these other classmates to keep quiet about MacIntosh, but neither did. Because there was no need to, it turned out. From that moment on, the five of us acted as if the overheard conversation had never occurred, and nobody brought up Dave's name. And Will and Scott began joining the three of us on breaks and at meals.

Private Burke and I had already met the Saturday before classes began. I was eating alone in a nearly empty mess hall, when an articulate voice interrupted: "Would you permit me to join you?" Why not? The strikingly boyish man introduced himself as William Burke, or as he preferred, simply Will. He offered me the thick, soft hand of a baseball catcher, his darting, dark-brown eyes averting my gaze. His flawless ivory skin had suffered little shaving, and he frequently bared his large, even, white teeth in false grins.

Scotty Dickinson was a wiry, energetic, little blond with a smile even the treads had difficulty suppressing. A self-styled gourmet from Columbus, Ohio, he loathed mess hall chow, which I didn't mind and Peter actually relished. Several times Rich tried to feel out the Stanford history major's politics, but Scotty shrugged off every attempt and switched the conversation to his greatest loves, the English Renaissance or the novelist J.R.R. Tolkien.

During the brief breaks between periods, I gradually got to know my other classmates. The eighteen of us—fourteen Army privates, a Navy Lieutenant JG, two Marine lance corporals, and a Marine Captain, making for a rainbow of dress greens, browns, and blue—had at first been randomly assigned to three sections of six each. Most of us in Class 0968 were twenty-two or twenty-three, the Lieutenant JG being twenty-five and the Captain thirty-three. With two exceptions, we had all graduated from good colleges with liberal arts majors, and Peter had even earned Phi Beta Kappa. I had only made Phi Kappa Phi, the honor fraternity for those achieving decent grades while also performing public service, in my case tutoring minority students admitted to St. Olaf with deficiencies.

The first month and a half, Peter, Will, and I sat in Section B together with the two officers and a lance corporal. I did my best not to think about the threats hanging over our heads, till one day I started stammering and couldn't stop. The A's and B's I earned in college seemed like mere gold and silver stars glued after my name on a third-grade bulletin board next to the stakes we were facing now. Peter openly conceded my superiority in Russian like he was helping me relax, but I soon came to suspect he was lulling me into complacency while studying fanatically out of my sight.

Already the first week, Will showed an utter lack of aptitude for foreign languages. His American English accent remained thick no matter how many times Markov corrected him, as if Will not only couldn't imitate, but also not even imagine a pronunciation and syntax different from his own. So instead of cramming Russian like the rest of us, he spent his evenings replaying famous chess matches or reading works on Soviet history, his major interest at the University of Washington in his hometown, Seattle. One supper he proclaimed, "Learning a foreign language is a feat of memory and not of intellect." Anger flashed across Peter's eyes, but he didn't rebut. Memory had always been my longest suit in school, too.

Meanwhile, to my dismay, Peter's progress was astounding. While Will couldn't master a single dialogue all the way to the end, Peter never once recited a line wrong, and his pronunciation was perfect from the start. In fact, the third day Gospodin Markov handed Zielsdorf a copy of the novel he himself was reading in the original Russian, Dostoevsky's *Possessed,* and asked him to read it aloud.

"I have no idea how to pronounce these words," Peter replied, blushing. "I don't even know the whole alphabet yet."

Unfortunately, the better he performed, the bleaker his mood became, and this sullenness rubbed off on everyone else. To lighten the atmosphere, Markov tried telling us Russian jokes in English, but following Peter's lead, none of us laughed. "*Shto s vami*, Zielsdorf?' Markov finally asked. What's wrong with you?

"Let's learn Russian," Peter said. "That's what'll save us from Vietnam."

"What do you mean 'us'?" Will quipped, and Peter's smile briefly reappeared.

Much to my chagrin, Markov soon pronounced Peter "student number one" in Section B, and started calling him *nash gordyj prusskij*—our proud Prussian. That made Zielsdorf sit taller, but he still wouldn't relax, and for me mess hall chow began to taste like sand. I couldn't forget for one waking minute what he had done to the CO's sign.

The next Monday morning just before roll call, I was half-asleep at my desk practicing the day's new dialogue, when the PA system clicked on and First Shirt Kelly's voice bellowed, "Private Thomas Bakken, report to the Orderly Room ASAP! Private Thomas Bakken, report to the Orderly Room ASAP!"

That shocked me fully awake. I jerked to my feet. Wells screwed up his eyes. I straightened my half-Windsor knot, tucked in my poplin shirt, buttoned my dress green jacket, put on my garrison hat, and headed downstairs.

Sergeant Kelly was standing at the door, his complexion closer to lurid than its usual ruddy. “Bakken,” he told me, “the CO wants to see you. Take a seat over there.”

I stared at my spit-polished low quarters, while the First Shirt snorted his way through reading a report. I was doubled up with stomach cramps when Captain Toddhunter at last emerged from his office. “You stay put, soldier,” he said with a snarl, aiming a finger right between my eyes. “I’ll nail your ass when I get back.”

“Yes, Sir,” I mumbled, saluting while still seated, an egregious breach of military etiquette. If I was lucky, I figured I faced an Article Fifteen or even a court martial. Meaning I’d either be booted out of the DLI and trucked across the bay to Fort Ord for combat training and eventual orders to Vietnam, or I’d end up in a stockade. Me, Tom Bakken, my whole life a goody-goody and teachers’ pet, never once reprimanded for as little as whispering in study hall.

When Toddhunter stormed back into his office, I just sat there, hunched over, awaiting further orders.

“Go on in, Bakken!” Kelly yelled. “Are you blind?”

I swallowed hard, walked up to the closed door, and gently knocked. No response. I knocked harder.

“Come in I said!” a gruff voice shouted.

“Private Bakken reporting as ordered, Sir,” I muttered and saluted, my heart pounding in my throat.

“At ease,” Toddhunter said without glancing up from a personnel file. Mine no doubt. The parking sign with Peter’s obscene taunt was propped up in a corner.

“Bakken,” he began, “I understand you have a red Magic Marker.” He reached into his drawer, pulled one out, and rapped it against his desk.

“They’re pretty common,” I said. So had Wells turned Peter and me in?

“I didn’t say they weren’t. Do you have one, Private?”

“Yes, Sir.”

"You bet your ass you do. This one, in fact, was found in your combat boot. With the initials 'TB' scratched on it."

My thoughts scattered like a flock of spooked sparrows.

"Well, say something, Private."

"So that's where I must have dropped it," I mumbled.

"Speak up, troop."

"I said I wondered where it had gone."

"Soldier, did you write on my sign?"

"No, Sir."

"Do you know who did?"

"No, Sir."

"Are you lying?"

"No, Sir."

His flinty-eyed glare was relentless. "If I find out you're lying, I'll begin with a court martial. And then I'll really ream you a new one."

"Yes, Sir."

"Do you have anything else to say, shit-for-brains?"

"No, Sir."

"Dismissed, Private."

I moped back to my room, took off my uniform, crawled under the covers, and lay there, worried sick about the horrific fix I now was in. I was edging off into anxious slumber when it hit me that I was skipping Russian class.

By that evening I was so emotionally drained I went to bed early after barely studying. I was just dozing off when Kelly's tinny voice on the PA system jolted me wide awake: "Seaman James Wells, report to the Orderly Room ASAP! Seaman James Wells, report to the Orderly Room ASAP!"

I bolted upright and watched my roommate whip on his Navy dress whites and tie his immaculately polished shoes. He hurried off without uttering a word or making eye contact.

I was at my desk in civvies, staring at my St. Olaf Russian grammar and envisioning myself inside a stockade, when Wells finally returned. Keeping his back to me, he opened his wall locker, removed his uniform, and carefully hung it up. He put on jeans and a blue work shirt and seated himself at his desk and took out stationery.

Was I ever eager to hear what had happened, but feared implicating myself even worse. The rest of that evening I sat braced for an artillery barrage that never landed, eying Russian conjugations till my eyes grew blurry.

Most of that night I lay awake, weighing my bleak options. By dawn I either felt reconciled to whatever fate had in store or was too exhausted to care anymore. The next day Wells still didn't say a word about what had happened, and I kept mum myself, as if our mutual silence were a spell neither of us dared break.

By the third day, it was clear Wells had stood by us and not betrayed either Peter or me. The CO had gotten lucky combing through my room, but without corroborating testimony that evidence wasn't enough. A buddy was your buddy even if you and he weren't friends, and buddies never ratted on buddies no matter what. So it was true that sometimes without buddies to hold your head above water, you sink like a rock. Just ask Zielsdorf or MacIntosh or me. And maybe we did know a thing or two about esprit de corps.

Chapter Three

I was out in the hall on a quick study break to hit the latrine, when MacIntosh popped out of Hoffman's room, tore off in the opposite direction, stopped in his tracks, and hustled back to me. "The best of luck, Tom," he whispered with glistening hazel eyes, grabbed my hand, and squeezed. "I really mean that." His earnestness gave me chills.

Zielsdorf stuck his head out his door. Dave ran over and shook his hand heartily, too, and disappeared down the stairwell. "*Auf Wiedersehen*!" Peter shouted after him. Afterwards, I was too upset to concentrate on Russian. Dave hadn't said as much, but this had to be it for him. Good God almighty.

A platoon of Marines jogged past beneath my window, clapping cadence in perfect step and singing, "Mreeen-Corps! Mreeen-Corps! Number-One! Number-One! On-The-Left! On-The-Left! Women! Women! Mreeen-Corps! Mreeen-Corps! Number-One! Number-One!" They all had on combat boots, fatigue pants, white T-shirts, and squarish baseball caps, the uniform worn by every GI serving in the Crotch.

They had better be number one. Since every last Marine was guaranteed the likes of Hue, Khe Sanh, and Pleiku as soon as they finished their short course in Vietnamese. Who knew how many would be killed over there? My head throbbed at the prospect that I might be joining them unless—unless what? Ending up first in class just might save my skin. But what if it didn't? Fear knotted my stomach.

Later that evening, Rich filled me in on Dave. The treads had gotten wind of Mack's role in a demonstration that had degenerated into a riot. A couple of cops had gotten beaten up, along with a dozen students, not that the treads minded that. A photo they had uncovered showed MacIntosh leading a charge on a police barricade, which by itself blocked his security clearance and guaranteed reassignment to Fort Ord in combat arms. So Dave had gone AWOL.

The news was extremely unnerving, to put it mildly. Who didn't have some skeleton or other in his closet to disqualify them from Military Intelligence duty? Rich had battled Mayor Daley's pigs in Grant Park during the August 1968 Democratic Convention during leave after Basic Training. Peter had participated in violent UW-Madison protests and hung out with German student socialists in the Voltaire Club at the University of Marburg. Scott had participated in anti-war marches at Stanford. Even Will had demonstrated against the draft in Seattle, wielding a subversive placard decrying "involuntary servitude." Me, well, about all I had done in college was study, as if the world going to hell in a basket around me were none of my affair. Though I had witnessed a few protests up close, and who knew how a photograph of that would look to a tread?

Toddhunter's face at at roll call two mornings later was crimson. A tongue-lashing was definitely coming. I hoped and prayed it wouldn't be over his parking sign, which still made me feel like a pop-up target, waiting to get shot down flat. "Men," he began, "Private First Class David MacIntosh is AWOL as of zero-hundred hours today. Private Richard Hoffman, you will report to my office in five minutes. Companeee, dismissed!"

The first break we flocked around Rich. His customary grin stretched a notch wider when he reported, "The pukes don't have a clue. Dave's well on his way to Sweden by now." Scotty and Rich hooted and hollered until Markov stepped outside and shushed us. Zielsdorf blinked and wiped his eyes, while I stood there petrified.

Scotty was the first classmate to begin jogging "to get ready for Fort Ord." The next day Peter joined him. Late the following afternoon I was wheezing and spitting thirty yards off their tails, till they broke into a sprint that Dickinson just barely won. They were both already in the shower when I limped back into the barracks.

My only mail had been a weekly letter from my parents, that is, my mother, till out of the blue Karen Tollefson wrote. I immediately replied, and before you know it she and I were corresponding again like we had as undergraduates in Northfield and Madison. The two of us had dated off and on since high school, and our parents had counted on our eventual marriage, but we had gotten estranged over my stringing out college an extra year to postpone military service. She feared I had lost my ambition.

At first, Karen's letters buoyed my morale, until it became clear she was thriving without me. She was too busy working on a Master's in Linguistics at UW-Madison to have much emotion left over for romance. She was too self-absorbed, too cerebral, too preoccupied. We were a perfect match.

The treads' threats were already souring my stomach, and dwelling on Karen only made it worse. But no matter how much she might learn to love me, she could never save me. Only ending up the best Russian student might.

Mornings, I awoke from pre-dawn nightmares with headaches that pain pills couldn't touch. These only relented in the late afternoons when I ran till I couldn't breathe. I longed to be more like Peter, who never seemed slowed by discomfort and thrived on a strict schedule to squeeze the last drop of production from every day. One trick of his was to keep a cheap alarm clock in view on his desk and let it incite him as a mechanical rabbit does a greyhound. Yet, anywhere near the classroom he had begun to show stress, too, when our robust, natural leader turned tense and aloof. We all admired and respected the student Peter, but he wasn't easy to like.

Early in the second month, I recognized that Peter was closing on me fast, so I redoubled my modest efforts. Still, I figured no matter how much he studied—no one in our class studied harder—I would never lose my head start from St. Olaf.

On the Friday ending the first six weeks, we took both oral and written tests on everything covered thus far and received a mark for each as well as an overall grade. Mine was 98, Peter's 96, Scotty's 94, Rich's 91. No one else was in the 90s, least of all Will. The teachers regrouped us according to these numbers, putting us four buddies good at Russian together in Section A, along with the fifth and sixth best students, the Lieutenant JG and Private Hal Williams, a quiet, baby-faced Atlantan of Southern Baptist persuasion.

The next roll call the First Sergeant announced that our class would be switching to rooms in the Company D barracks wing with a view of Monterey Bay. We also were free to choose roommates as long as both parties were willing. Otherwise, they would be assigned. Peter suggested the two of us pair up and I agreed, so that evening we moved in together. Wells surprised me by shaking my hand in farewell and offering a heartfelt "Good luck." I sincerely wished him the same.

It was oddly pleasing to have my feared rival Zielsdorf so near, and, of course, also flattering. He and I had so much in common–Madison, Wisconsin, foreign languages and literatures, linguistics, and academic ambition–that I hoped he might become the one truly close friend I had never been able to find.

Our second night I was startled awake. "Move it, Zielsdorf!" Peter shrieked. "Get up, shitbird! Get your ass in gear!"

I flipped on my desk lamp.

"Zielsdorf, you sorry sack of shit!" he screamed at himself. "Move it! Get with the program, you buddyfucker!"

I gently shook his shoulder.

Cringing, he shouted, "Yes, Drill Sergeant!"

"Peter, it's Tom Bakken. You're at the DLI. In the Company D barracks."

"Thomas," he said, clutching my arm, "I'm more than I seem! You've got to believe me."

I said nothing while his grip gradually relaxed, the barking of the sea lions a mile away on Monterey Bay resounding through the night. "*bl*" they seemed to say, the peculiar unrounded Russian vowel made low in the throat that many Americans could never master, though Peter imitated Markov perfectly first try. We chatted in the dark about Basic Combat Training. Peter admitted to being a screwup and bolo the whole cycle, especially at Dismounted Drill, and so got assigned shit details like cleaning the grease trap on KP. By the end, he pulled himself together to max the rifle range and hand-to-hand combat, almost aced the final PT test, and so easily graduated.

Shifting our chat to the University of Wisconsin buoyed both of our spirits—till he mentioned battling the Madison police for control of campus streets. That brought MacIntosh's desperate farewell to mind. All of us were so afraid of being dragged down with Dave we were acting like the guy never existed.

"The pigs and their tear gas won't always prevail," Peter said. "And not because we'll take over. Instead everybody will become like us. Remember the Wisconsin springs? The snow drifts don't melt all at once. The piles just get smaller and smaller without anybody much noticing, till one morning they're entirely gone. That's how we'll win." Sounded mighty optimistic.

We both grew still. Across the bay, a Fort Ord night exercise was in progress like a silent movie. Noiseless flares lit up soundless helicopters arcing quiet tracers into treeless hills. I begged Peter not to pull any more stunts like defacing the CO's sign.

"Don't worry," he told me. "I'm harmless. Unless I get screwed over first."

I didn't sleep anymore that night.

With George Wallace's help, Nixon handily won the November election, none of us GIs bothering to vote. Trying to stop Tricky Dick's inevitable triumph felt dumber than joining hands along shore to block an oncoming rogue wave.

Peter's teeth-grinding resolution in studying Russian grew even more intense. Hunched over textbooks and notes, he underlined new vocabulary so hard his pencil sometimes tore the paper. The unpredictable syllable stresses in irregular declensions and conjugations he learned by slashing three-inch accents over the vowels. When he wasn't writing, he leaned forward on his elbows and squeezed his temples, as if pressing more information into his brain, and mumbled phrases. There was no noticeable joy in his learning, but that seemed like asking a Porsche to take pleasure in its torque.

The second six weeks Peter closed on me fast. I was studying harder than I had ever expected, but no amount of effort could perfect my non-native accent, while Peter only had to hear a new sound once to mimic it perfectly. His knack for the alien syntax was equally uncanny. I tried imitating his reading aloud softly, but hearing my own faulty pronunciation so discouraged me I went back to studying in silence, telling myself what I lacked in aptitude I would make up with my secret head start. Did I have any other choice?

Zielsdorf's 97 for the second six weeks cut my lead down to only a single point. We same half-dozen students stayed in Section A, while the other two groups switched four men based on the new scores. Gospodin Markov and the other instructors started saying, "*Molodets*"—Thatta boy—to Peter so often that Scotty took to calling him that in the barracks. Soon Peter was bristling every time Dickinson said anything, especially when Scotty interjected dopey jokes, accompanied by his whinnying giggle, or asked irrelevant questions to ease the classroom tension. No matter how many times Peter glared darts at him, sunny Scott kept up this annoying shtick.

One evening after supper, I was taking a break in place from a new Russian dialogue about self-propelled artillery and camouflaged tanks and staring out the window at Monterey Bay. All of a sudden Peter's stubborn mumbling ceased and he yelled, "Private, what is your name?" An object thumped against our door, and I jerked around to see Peter's workbook flopping onto our polished tile floor. "Bakken, why are we memorizing this goddamned shit?" he screamed. "Let's memorize Pushkin's or Akhmatova's poetry, but not this crap! And where the hell are the fucking treads going to send us? Don't we have *any* say over our own lives? Two hundred GIs were killed in Vietnam last week. For what? For jack shit. Hey, from now on I'm with Dave and Rich. If they give us the wrong orders, I'm bugging on out."

The third six weeks was split in half by a two-week Christmas break. We all were looking forward to flying home to our families, that is, everybody except Peter, whose mood only turned grimmer as the holiday neared. One December lunch, Rich told him, "Maybe going to Nam is better than totally freaking out, Zielsdorf. Loosen up."

"Shut up, Hoffman," Peter said. The rest of that week he ate alone and every night hollered in his sleep. I had never slept more poorly myself.

Over an especially bleak supper, Peter asked, "Did you hear about the latest German class to graduate?"

We shook our heads.

"Every last one is going to Ord. And all as Eleven Bravos."

"If only we'd fight to win in Vietnam, no holds barred," Will said, "we wouldn't be in this predicament. Just obliterate the North with carpet bombing, and the war would end in a week."

"Heil, Burke," Rich said, thrusting his right arm in a Nazi salute.

"Can we please not argue about politics?" Scotty begged.

"I'm not arguing," Rich replied. "I'm simply stating facts. Motherfuckers like Will are holding up the revolution. There's no nice way to say it. It's us against them, and he's on the side of the fucking enemy."

"What revolution, pray tell, my good man?" Will asked. "Surely you cannot mean all this mindless civil disobedience and self-indulgence."

"You fascist, Burke!" Rich shouted. "You know full well we're crushing a popular revolution in Vietnam. And over here we conduct farces we call elections where nobody is worth voting for. And would you cut out your pretentious hear-hear-my-good-man crap, Burke? You sound like a fucking Brit."

“Nixon won fairly,” Will rebutted. “Without question, he was the best choice.”

“If Wallace hadn’t already gotten the award,” Rich said, “Nixon would be a shoo-in for US Fascist of the Year. Too bad Wallace didn’t win. He’d have made such an awful President it would have brought the whole decrepit system crashing down on itself. That way we could start over from scratch and build this society up right.”

“Right on,” Peter seconded.

“What mush,” Will said.

Rich stuck his tongue out a corner of his mouth and, cupping a hand as if holding an imaginary hypodermic, pretended to mainline dope straight into his brain. A moment later he broke into a beatific grin, and we all chuckled.

“We’ve all made compromises to end up here instead of Nam,” Scotty piped up, “so none of us should throw stones.”

“Or sling shit,” Rich quipped, doodling on the back of a Russian worksheet. “Because some of it always sticks. Zielsdorf, was it you who wrote on the CO’s sign? It happened the same day you asked me for a Magic Marker.”

“Do you honestly think I would do such a crude thing to our commanding officer? What has our honorable captain ever done to deserve such disrespect?”

“Don’t worry, man. We won’t tell,” Rich said.

Clenching his teeth, Peter snapped, “Get me another marker and I’ll do it to that asshole again tonight! You should have seen what I did to my Senior Drill Instructor in Basic Training. After forced marches out to the Infiltration Course and back, I was so exhausted I was ready to drop, when the bastard gleefully picked me out of the entire company to wash his coffee pot. I did exactly as ordered, scrubbing and rinsing it in a toilet bowl and letting it drip dry—”

“—Stop,” I pleaded.

“What about you, Thomas?” Will asked me. “What are your political views?”

"I have none," I muttered. "Just live and let live."

"Hear, hear," Will said. "I defer to the wisest among us, young Bakken."

But Rich wouldn't drop the issue. "Surely there must have been protests at St. Olaf, Thomas, and especially once back home in Madison."

I didn't disagree, but that didn't end the badgering. Finally, I owned up to attending several as a sympathetic onlooker. "Close enough," Peter proclaimed, which at last shut Hoffman up.

Rich showed us his doodling, and all of us, especially Will, roared with laughter. He had drawn a parody of the military haircut chart at the Post barber shop. Instead of the six regulation close-cropped styles, he had started with the very shortest and progressed to shaven skin stretched taut across bones and then bare skulls with gaping sockets—and captioned it like the original: "Look your best."

It was a shock to leave Madison's sparkling snowdrifts behind after Christmas vacation for the fog enshrouding the Monterey Peninsula. The whole flight from Minneapolis to San Francisco I sat next to an attractive blonde my age, who wouldn't stop scowling at my dress greens and inching away like I was a leper.

What could I say about seeing my parents and Karen? Her face looked thinner than I remembered—and prettier. Though we enjoyed each other's company at a movie, pizzeria, and concert, we didn't truly relax together until our last night, when she finally told me what was really on her mind—she hated my serving in the military. Because as apolitical as Karen was, she still believed I had thrown in my lot with LBJ and and his babykillers. But was there a person in all of Madison who supported the war? Nobody I knew. Actually, I didn't know anybody anywhere who did except for the treads. "For heaven's sake, why didn't you apply for conscientious objector status?" she asked.

"Well," I said, "mainly because I'm not one. Since I'm not opposed to war in principle. Certainly not World War Two."

She rolled her eyes.

If CO status hadn't been an option for me, emigrating to Canada had been. It tore me up inside that I hadn't done it when I had the chance. Still, that would have broken my parents' hearts. Besides, Karen would have never abandoned her would-be brilliant academic future to follow me.

Peter was long since back from Chute Noire when I returned and refused to say a word about his own visit home. That week Scotty intercepted me on the fire escape and asked me what was bugging Zielsdorf. Whatever Dickinson had said to him, he had meant no offense.

"Peter's always moody," I said.

"He's much worse now."

Scotty was right. I didn't want to pry, but I sensed Peter needed to confide in somebody. The evening of the day our promotions to Private First Class came through like clockwork, a letter from home left him particularly sullen. I took a deep breath and asked, "How's your mother doing back in Wisconsin?"

"She's sick," he muttered, the first personal detail he had ever revealed about his immediate family. I had assumed they were middle class or close, but since he had mentioned winning a series of scholarships, perhaps they were in fact poor.

"Really sick?"

"Yeah."

"You can take emergency leave, you know."

"It's too early. Besides, that'd knock me out of the running in Russian class."

"What's the matter with her?" Again, I didn't want to be nosy, but I suspected he wanted me to ask. Wrong.

"I'd rather not talk about it." So we said nothing further on the subject. I was especially curious about what his father did for a living, but if he wouldn't tell me, I wasn't going to pry.

Peter quickly kicked back into his ruthless schedule, which was so rigid you could predict where he would be every minute of the day. At 6:40 a.m. he slapped off his alarm, hustled to the john, and came back shaven at five till. Next he tugged on black socks, dress green slacks, poplin shirt, and low-quarters and raced out of our room, fastening his narrow, black tie with the required half-Windsor knot as he strode toward the stairwell. In the mess hall he sat alone and devoured an unvarying breakfast of eggs over easy with sausage and dry toast and a half cup of black coffee. Whether I got up in time to join him or not, he finished at exactly 7:20 and hustled back to our room to cram Russian until 7:45 roll call, which he often skipped to study a few minutes longer, letting our Navy squad leader lie to cover his absence. At 7:58 he settled into his seat in the one-story classroom across the street for our eight o'clock instruction.

The rest of the day Peter relentlessly marched through morning classes, lunch, afternoon classes, jogging, supper, and more studying. Instead of ebbing as the day passed, his energy swelled like a flooding tide. So despite no coffee after breakfast, he had trouble falling asleep at 10:45, when without fail he climbed into bed, rolled onto his stomach, and buried his head beneath his pillow.

I always went to bed after him because I functioned better never hurrying, even if I got less rest. I admired Peter's superior self-discipline, but trying to match it upset my natural rhythm and pacing that had worked well enough for me thus far. I preferred edging into new things and growing on people and never doing anything quickly, just the opposite of Peter. I had never met anyone less interested in relaxing.

Rich developed a shtick of setting an imaginary wristwatch to Peter's routines. If Zielsdorf noticed, he never took offense, though Hoffman often rubbed other people the wrong way. Actually, Rich refused to wear a watch as a matter of pride, because to him there was nothing less cool than punctuality or haste.

The second Monday after Christmas break, Toddhunter showed up for roll call looking apoplectic. "Men," he said, "Private David MacIntosh has been AWOL for over a month, so that makes him a deserter. The FBI is on his case now, so his ass is grass." The news about Dave's successful escape cheered Dickinson,

Burke, and Hoffman, but neither Peter nor me. I began chewing Tums to settle my churning stomach.

That day over lunch, Rich asked, "Zielsdorf, would you tell us what's bugging you?" Peter looked unusually drawn and was just picking at his food.

"We're getting orders for Vietnam, no matter what," he said. "I heard the treads even need Russian lingies there now."

"Hey, man, don't sweat it," Rich told him. "None of us have to go to Nam. We can all pull a MacIntosh. You lived in Germany, so why can't you live in Sweden?"

"Forever?"

"You know," Rich muttered, "what we really need for a change is to have some real fun."

"How can a secular monk have any fun?" Burke butted in.

"Who said we were secular monks?" Scotty asked.

"What else with these haircuts?" Rich said. "They make us look like Death Row inmates." We all whooped with laughter at the queer notion of our being monks, but we were in a sense, against our wills. "Do we want any part of chastity and seclusion? Hell, no!"

"Hear! Hear!" Will shouted.

From that day on, the five of us were the Monks–till death did us part.

Chapter Four

The treads were doing their best to make us utterly miserable and succeeding. Learning a foreign language could have been fun, as it mostly had been for me at St. Olaf, but the compulsion to earn top grades under the threat of Vietnam for all but the best Russian student—and even he was guaranteed nothing—kept the classrooms and barracks dreary as a morgue. The more we crammed and schemed to save our hides, the more our idealism, so natural during the late Sixties, was corrupted. But at the same time the more integrity we surrendered, the closer we five Monks became.

Every night, flares across the bay at Fort Ord lit up hills being raked with tracers, and I dreamt of APCs skittering away from their harsh glare like cockroaches to hide in darkness until it was safe to emerge. And a jungle patrol caught enfilade by a VC sniper, the AK-47 bullets tearing my flesh to shreds really hurting. My morning headaches grew more intense.

Nixon's inauguration cheered no one, not even Will, and to our relief Burke shut up about politics. The fourth six weeks ended in late February, and our grades only verified what we already knew—Peter was the best student, and I was only second, just a few points ahead of Scotty and Rich. Not being first was mortifying, since I had taken Russian at St. Olaf, but less so as long as nobody else knew. I simply couldn't let Zielsdorf be the better linguist, not with stakes this high, so I vowed to try harder.

The biggest surprise was Will's plummeting average. A 65 for the fourth six weeks had lowered his overall average to 77, a mere three points above flunking out. None of us academic overachievers could ever swallow a B cheerfully, and fortunately seldom had to, but here Will, a history honor student at the

University of Washington, was facing a threat incomparably worse than disgrace, namely, immediate reassignment to Fort Ord in combat arms.

The rains eased off in March, while the course lumbered on. Every time my complicity with defacing the CO's sign bobbed to the surface of my thoughts, I shoved it back under like a water-logged corpse.

One morning later that month, the last squad leader had shouted the last lie, "All-present-and-accounted-for, Sir!"—Peter for one was still in the barracks cramming—and Captain Toddhunter was glaring at us like a hyena sizing up a herd of antelope. The pair of purple hearts on his chest and the two combat duty slashes on his sleeves screamed, "Vietnam vet." "Men," he began, "I got some good news and some bad news. The bad news is that the Inspector General is coming in three weeks. The good news is that getting ready for him will make you the best damned soldiers there's ever been at the DLI. You *will* get your shit together. I want to see your brass sparkle and your shoes shine. I want to be able to eat off every tile of the Company D floors. You *will* learn what it means to be a real soldier. Some of your haircuts would disgrace a Bangkok whore's crotch. Do you pussies hear me?"

"Yes, Sir," a few of us muttered.

"Do you hear me?" he yelled.

Yes, Sir!" we all screamed back.

Satisfied he had made himself clear, our CO glowered up and down the ranks before bellowing, "Fall out!"

The ensuing treadiness rapidly reached new depths. Not only did we still have to sweat Russian and our eventual orders, but also now weekly inspections every Wednesday afternoon after the last class—either outdoors between the wings or, worse, in our rooms.

In April, the North Koreans shot down a US Navy plane probing their border, killing all thirty-six Americans aboard, including Korean lingies trained here at the DLI. Some luck those guys had in escaping Nam. And then a most unfortunate confluence of events turned Zielsdorf maniacal.

That Wednesday's room inspection fell on the same day as our six weeks' exams. Alas, that Tuesday morning, Peter had to get up at 4:00 a.m. for a grueling stint on KP. Monday night he finished his studying early and climbed into bed, as usual burying his head beneath his pillow, while I stayed up, still cramming. To make it easier for him to sleep, I read by the dim light of my desk lamp and strove not to rustle pages. Peter tossed and turned anyway. When I finally climbed into the rack at 11:30 p.m., he got up to use the latrine, and upon return flipped on his lamp, took out a textbook, and began hissing Russian softly to himself.

At 2:30 a.m. I was startled awake by shouts: "Zielsdorf, you sorry sack of shit! Move it!" When I gently touched Peter's shoulder, he slapped my arm away and refused to speak.

I didn't see him again for sixteen hours, long after his KP duty should have ended, looking so peaked and fierce he scared me. The Mess Sergeant had made him stay late to mop and polish every square inch of the cooking and dining floor twice over. I had already been studying for three hours, so I was eager to prepare our room for the next day's inspection. Still, I tactfully suggested, "Peter, do you want to study first and get ready for the inspection later?"

"Hell, no!" he snapped. "Let's get this damned cleaning over with right now. I'll get the buffer." Unfortunately, everybody needed to buff their gray tiles, and Peter couldn't get us any higher than twenty-third on the waiting list. Meanwhile, he and I swept and washed our floor, straightened the books on our desks, threw away every loose piece of paper, remade the beds, cleaned the windows, and dusted the venetian blinds.

That done, he stormed out for the buffer again and charged back empty-handed. In frustration, he slammed his wall locker open, tore off his fatigues, flung them inside, whipped on black jogging shorts, black socks, black combat boots, a tan poplin shirt, and a thin black tie. Next he snatched paper, Scotch tape, and a ballpoint, and made some sort of armband. When he slipped that on and faced me, there stood a six-foot-one Hitler Youth, giving me the Nazi salute.

The swastika was an insane protest, but he marched out into the hall with it on anyway and came back a minute later with the buffer. And attacked our floor, smashing the appliance against chairs and plunging it beneath his desk and mine. Just like that, our room got squared away. By which point he had so worked himself up I pretended to study some more to spare his nerves the knowledge I already felt so prepared for our six weeks' exam I was ready for bed.

The next morning's written test was the trickiest one yet. In checking my work I changed four answers. The afternoon's oral test I aced with as fluent a spoken Russian as I had managed since a beery class picnic my last year of college by glibly answering Markov's twenty personal questions and ably describing an armor battle in wooded terrain as depicted in a cartoon booklet.

At sixteen-hundred hours, Peter and I hustled back to our rooms to dust and straighten one last time before the inspection. He had just tightened his regulation half-Windsor knot, when we heard the CO and First Sergeant approaching out in the hall. Too late I noticed that his neck was a bit shaggy despite white-walled temples. If we'd had another minute, I would have shaved it for him with my electric razor.

"Ah-ten-hut!" the First Sergeant bellowed, and we jerked to attention. Captain Toddhunter walked right up to me and glared into my face, his coal-black eyes narrowing upon recognizing his nemesis. Leaning past both cheeks, he checked the hair around my ears and on my neck. He scrutinized the polished brass on my shoulders and lapels. "Back-in," he said, "you got your shit together today, but you'd better watch out next time."

"Actually, it's Bahk-in," I longed to say but refrained.

The CO turned to Peter next and stood in silence too long. "Zielsdorf," he said, "you have a gig for your unmilitary haircut. You will report to me tomorrow at oh-eight-hundred hours with a freshly trimmed neck. And you will be in my office Friday at seventeen-hundred hours in fatigues for a cleanup detail. Do I make myself clear?"

"Yes, Sir," Peter replied with a pinched voice.

The First Shirt copied down Peter's last name letter by letter.

The instant they were out the door, Peter said, "Toddhunter is going to regret this big time."

"Please stay away from his sign," I pleaded. "You promised."

The next morning we were shocked by the fifth six-weeks' grades. My 97 was the highest in the class, while Peter's had dropped to 95, moving my overall average one point above his. Will's 75, the lowest possible passing grade, verged on immediate reassignment to Fort Ord.

On Friday, Peter woke up long before his alarm to hiss Russian phrases to himself. That evening as punishment for the gig, he bitterly policed the Company D grounds and swept and mopped the Orderly Room floors.

Then the treadiness plunged into an unimagined abyss. Saturday we arose early and donned fatigues and combat boots for a bite of what the treads wanted to make our steady diet—Fort Ord. Kelly had ordered us there to "Requalify with the Rifle." The sun had just burned off the morning fog when our deuce-and-a-half truck pulled into a sandy firing range. We climbed down, signed out M-14s, and filed into bleachers.

A Staff Sergeant Gonzalez began outlining our day's program in a jolly tone. When none of us sullen GIs so much as cracked a smile, he snapped, "Okay, Monterey bolos, if that's how you want it," and proceeded to rattle off a memorized lecture too fast to follow and hurried us into foxholes along the firing line.

Through a speaker in a wooden tower, he announced he would control our every move. Each of us was paired with an officer candidate, kneeling just behind us, all as unwilling to be there as we were. "Do not fire until I give permission," Gonzalez blared. "Do not even fart unless I give the order. Ready on the left?"

A shot cracked next to me, and Peter's trainee officer scolded him.

"Do not fire, God damn it!" Gonzalez shouted through the speakers. "I did not tell you to fire!"

"Shit, man, why'd they ever give a sorry ass like you a rifle?" the officer candidate muttered to Zielsdorf. Peter's eyes were nervously darting and his hands were trembling. Farther down, Hoffman was chuckling.

What was Peter shooting at anyway? No targets were in sight.

"When I give the order, and only then," Gonzalez went on, "commence firing and continue firing at will." He paused, as I combed the sandy knolls and scattered shrubs for a target. "Ready on the left! Ready on the right! Ready on the firing line!"

A drab green silhouette of a man popped up one hundred meters in front of me, and Gonzalez screamed, "Fire!" On both sides of me a volley of shots blasted away. I took careful aim, held my breath, squeezed, but the target failed to budge. Because I had missed low. I inhaled a pungent whiff of gunpowder smoke, fired again, and once more kicked up dirt too short. To my chagrin, the target dropped from view on its own, when my bullet should have been knocked it down. In random order, figures began swinging up at fifty, one hundred, two hundred, three hundred, and four hundred meters, and my M-14 joined the others cracking in my ears. I'm ashamed to admit I enjoyed plugging the human forms, especially those at four hundred meters outlined against the sky. Guys at that distance wouldn't know what hit them.

Though neither had ever touched a firearm before enlistment, Scott beat Peter by one for the best score, the bullet that Zielsdorf wasted costing him the tie. My tally was so-so, but still better than Rich's or Will's.

After proving that we indeed could still shoot people with commendable efficiency, we marched to a shed to show we couldn't breathe tear gas with impunity and lined up single file outside, Peter to my rear. As Gonzalez eloquently explained, CS was ideal for shutting up demonstrators: "If the fuckers can't breathe, they can't protest." We helped each other fit the black rubber masks over our faces and moved one by one into the hut.

Inside, another staff sergeant had us step forward in turn, salute, and remove our masks, while he kept his own on. Of course. To be perverse, he had us hold our breath a bit before ordering us to state our rank, name, and serial number. Right after saying, "Private First," I must have inhaled, because the sensation of swallowing razor blades cut off "Bakken," and I coughed and choked and went temporarily blind. Buddies shoved me hard outside to join other gasping GIs bent over double there.

My throat and lungs were still raw and my eyes blurry, when Peter stumbled out of the shed, vomited, and fell to his knees. When I ran over to help him up, he punched me viciously in the thigh, and I jumped away from his reach. Ten more guys came out and recovered before Peter rose to his feet. "If I ever get Gonzalez alone, I'll kill him," he rasped.

"Why did you fire early?" Rich asked, wiping away tears, yet still managing a grin.

"My finger twitched, asshole!" Peter snapped.

Sunday morning the CO's parking sign again read in garish, scarlet lettering, "The CO sucks and blows," and Monday the shit again hit the fan. Thank God, the CO still had my Magic Marker. Toddhunter held the formation up after roll call and really let us have it. "You will all learn to hate the sorry-ass coward in your ranks!" he screamed. "If whoever did it has any balls, meet me tonight after dark behind the barracks, and we'll take off our shirts and settle our differences man to man. But if that coward doesn't come forward—or if nobody tells me who did it today by sixteen-hundred hours—then the whole damned company will have hell to pay. This is not a threat, gentlemen. This is a promise."

I trembled in class all day.

Peter and I had just gotten back to our room after 4:00 p.m., when the PA system clicked on and First Sergeant Kelly's metallic voice boomed, "Private First Class Thomas Bakken, report to the Orderly Room ASAP. Private First Class Thomas Bakken, report to the Orderly Room ASAP." With shaking fingers, I reknotted my tie and met Peter's grim gaze. Neither of us spoke.

When I entered the CO's office, Toddhunter returned my crisp salute and glared at me like a pit viper poised to strike. "Back-in," he growled, "do you want to tell me about it?"

My knees almost buckled. "About what, Sir?"

"About writing on my parking sign."

"No, Sir," I whispered breathlessly.

"What, Private? Speak up like you got a pair. This is no way to report to your commanding officer."

"No, Sir."

"No, Sir, what?"

"No, Sir, *Sir*. I didn't do it. The sign, I mean."

"That's not what a classmate of yours told me."

I paused. "You mean Johnston?"

The CO nodded cautiously.

At that reply I silently sighed. There was nobody in my class or wing named Johnston, so Toddhunter was bluffing. "You didn't hear the truth," I said louder.

"Where's your Magic Marker?"

"You kept it, Sir."

"What?"

"You never gave it back to me, Sir."

"Didn't you buy another one?"

"No, Sir."

"A good story, you goddamned liar. Back-in, you'd better be ready for Infantry at Ord any day now. You screw up once more and your ass will land there so hard you won't be able to sit down for a month. I don't like you, troop. Do I make myself clear?"

"Yes, Sir."

His scowl made my pulse race even faster. Finally, he said, "Dismissed." I suppressed a smile, knowing he had nothing on me, Peter, or anybody else. I spun on my heels and marched out past the pair of obscenely defaced signs, leaning against each other like smarmy drunks.

To my dismay, Will was waiting in the Orderly Room when I exited, his fair skin looking especially pale. "Your turn, Burke," Captain Toddhunter barked through the open door behind me. Will avoided eye contact as he stood up. Like me, he knew full well it was Peter who had vandalized our Commanding Officer's parking sign again. Who knew how a student on the verge of flunking out of the DLI like him and therefore facing Fort Ord and Vietnam would respond to the CO's threats?

I was just heading down to the mess hall for supper, when Sergeant Kelly's voice again bellowed over the PA system: "Private First Class Scott Dickinson, report to the Orderly Room ASAP." Ten minutes later I was forcing down a pork chop with mashed potatoes, when the First Shirt similarly summoned Private First Class Richard Hoffman.

Neither Peter nor I said a word the rest of that evening, while studying Russian back to back. Not once did he mutter or hiss his way through textbook exercises as usual. The rest of that week we both stayed braced for the CO's retaliation. None of the other Monks mentioned anything about what had transpired during their interrogations. Whatever they had said, they hadn't ratted on a buddy. Of course not.

Chapter Five

Toddhunter's revenge began that Saturday and continued every weekday at eighteen-hundred hours. Whenever the CO couldn't think up another detail, he held us at attention till our shoulders and backs ached. Still, nobody ratted. Because a buddy never betrayed a buddy. Not a fellow Monk, not Wells, not anybody, not when it was us against them.

We passed the IG with excellent ratings just below outstanding, but the Captain kept up the Wednesday inspections anyway. Any gig, even for the tiniest smudge on brass or scuff on low quarters, meant extra cleanup duty.

The closer we moved to graduation, the deeper my morale plunged and the harder it became to study. One noon news so bad arrived it left my hands shaking–a small Czech class of six Army privates had just graduated, and every last one of them was assigned to Fort Ord in Infantry. Rumor had it that for now the Pentagon had enough linguists in every specialty except Vietnamese. Then my mother wrote that a Vietcong mine had killed Gunnar Onstad, the salutatorian of my Madison East class and a personal friend since kindergarten.

"I'll get us to Sweden yet," Rich muttered over supper. "They have to give us leave before we ship out. That's when we'll bolt." Peter's nod was grim. That day after class he, Dickinson, and I began jogging faster and farther to get in shape for combat arms.

From the start, Zielsdorf had been the most dedicated student I had ever met, but the sixth six weeks he outdid himself. He upped his studying from every evening to all day Saturday and Sunday as well. I forced myself to plow through our workbooks more, too, but I couldn't match his grueling hours. The grammar I had long since down cold, so I concentrated on better slithering and hissing my lips and tongue through the boneless Slavic sounds and on memorizing new words. The clunky military jargon, none of it used in Russia's marvelous literature, so aggravated my migraines that running no longer provided relief.

For Peter, it was easier to study than not, since his conscience tolerated no sloth. He never so much as hinted that all the time spent at his desk was the least hardship. I asked whether learning the military terms didn't at least irritate him. Not really, he said, though he despised every second spent cleaning our room. The way he figured it, if he was going to know all the words in Russian eventually, why not learn this particular vocabulary now while it was being stressed? Besides, all studying was pyramid building.

"Huh?"

"There are two kinds of work in life—the labors of Sisyphus and the building of pyramids. The former, like waxing the floor, are a total waste of time, because there's never any progress. But I can never get enough of the latter."

"With what ultimate goal?"

"Build one high enough to oversee the entire world, and maybe we'll finally come to understand it."

"It sounds like another Tower of Babel."

"No, no. The goal isn't to reach heaven, because that's impossible. I just want to comprehend the nature of reality."

Just? My head throbbed too badly to pursue the argument. Did I yearn to lose myself in the lushness of Brahms' symphonies or Proust's prose. I really missed my beloved stereo safely packed away back home in Madison.

The next Sunday forenoon Peter came up with a novel way to shock us. He disappeared into Burke's room and didn't come out till supper. Why? It turned out he was tutoring Will in Russian to keep him from flunking out as soon as the very next six-weeks exam. The following day Zielsdorf talked Markov into having his wife coach Will evenings at their house for a modest fee.

Helping Will didn't add one tiny block to Peter's pyramid, so why was he doing it? As repayment for Burke's discretion with

Toddhunter, it turned out. Because that's what buddies do. The contempt this showed for my ability at Russian ticked me off, as if he no longer needed to go all out to best me. I resolved to try that much harder.

A special bond formed between Peter and Will that baffled the rest of us, since they were the two most dissimilar Monks. When I asked a Marine in Burke's section how Will was doing, he shook his head and said, "The improvement is un-fucking-believable."

Peter was getting more and more difficult to endure. To escape his constant mumbling at his desk, I took to trotting down the so-called Ho Chi Minh Trail to the Post Library and studying there between peeks at a guidebook to Sweden. I considered just conceding Zielsdorf first place to ease the pressure, but the prospect of Vietnam was too unbearable. If ordered there, Rich was definitely heading to Stockholm, and probably Peter and Scotty as well, so why couldn't I go, too? Because it would shame my parents. Because I was an American. Above all, because I was a coward. I kept seeing myself lying dead in a rice paddy or languishing forever in exile. So what real choice did I have but to beat out Zielsdorf?

That six weeks ended just before Memorial Day 1969. The new grades were alarming. With only twelve weeks to go, Peter had edged ahead of me 98 to 97, while Scott and Rich trailed at 95 and 93. Will had moved up to 78, a passing grade, no matter how unimpressive, but for now it saved his skin. The three months before Class 0968 would end and our dreaded new orders would be cut was enough time for me to surge back into the lead, but how? By sabotaging my relentless rival? In my eighteen years of schooling, I had never once done anything that underhanded, but when had this much been at stake? Still, I couldn't bring myself to do something that dastardly.

Diarrhea began getting me up before my alarm. By then Peter was always already at his desk, studying away. My headaches grew more excruciating, and I dizzily contemplated crazy escapes. Get hold of a hatchet and chop off my trigger finger. Stumble down the stairwell and break a leg. Even swan dive off the fire escape onto the sidewalk. Whatever I did, I couldn't bring myself to desert. But if I didn't, the treads would let me be killed like ants underfoot. Peter and Scott now jogged so fast I no longer could keep them in sight.

The new six weeks I tried to match Peter's fanatical studying hour for hour, and he visibly resented my increased effort. So tense now in class he often stammered, an eyelid of his sometimes also twitched. One morning while we sat back to back cramming at our desks before roll call, he said, "Bakken, why are you studying so damned hard? Did you forget all the Russian you learned in college?"

A tidal wave of adrenaline left me trembling. How had he found out? And who else knew? We spun around and glared at each other. "Don't tell me you didn't know Russian before you got here, Bakken. At first, you weren't improving at all. Of course, your naturally sloppy pronunciation helped with your act." The arrogant bastard.

The next afternoon I took a calculated risk and gave up jogging. This way I wouldn't be ready for Fort Ord, but I could use the time saved to study more Russian—and perhaps not end up in combat arms. Peter quit talking to me altogether and even started stuttering with his English. I was told he now outran Dickinson back to the barracks often as not. Afterwards, both were testy. Scotty began making dumb mistakes during oral exercises, each one making him more prone for another. Our proud Prussian chuckled over every last error.

Graduation was approaching like a scheduled execution. In what other Americans read as a routine report in *The San Francisco Chronicle*, we learned that a communications outpost was overrun in the Central Highlands of Vietnam, and in the ensuing hand-to-hand combat a quarter of the company perished. Instantly it struck us that Monterey grads in Vietnamese must have been involved. Sure enough, two days later our smirking CO informed us at morning roll call that DLI graduates James

Atkinson, Leonard Braun, David Esterhazy, Andrew Nelson, and Lewis Wilson had been killed in action. "Anybody got a spare hand grenade?" Rich muttered.

Affable Andy Nelson dead? It didn't seem possible. Peter and I resumed speaking.

July's big news left us unfazed. Apollo Eleven put the first humans on the moon, and Ted Kennedy negotiated the treacherous waters of Chappaquidick a whole lot better than Mary Kopechne. What did excite us was a postcard to the CO from Stockholm. According to our company clerk, it read:

> Dear Captain Toddhunter,
>
> If I live to be one hundred years old, may I never run into you or a single other puke once. I won't either unless you visit Sweden. You should see how my hair and beard have grown out. Pretty soon I'll be looking human again.
>
> Sincerely,
> David C. Macintosh, ex-private
>
> P.S. It wasn't me who wrote on your sign, but I salute the man who did.

That P.S. sent me reaching for more Tums. Will quit sitting with us Monks in the mess hall, and often as not Zielsdorf joined him at a corner table. The whole course we had seen emotions ebb and flow and friendships warm and cool, often for no apparent reason, but nothing was more inexplicable than this odd new intimacy between Will and Peter—or more irritating.

As the next-to-last six weeks ended in late July and all of us Monks received promotions to Specialist Fourth Class as a reward for a year of military service, our teachers emphasized expanding vocabulary and improving fluency. My biggest worry was that I could never speak as well as Peter no matter how hard

I tried. To sound like a native, you have to use your jaw, tongue, and lips differently, and change your posture and gestures, thus forgetting your American self and assuming another persona. But I'd always had trouble being anybody but me and often play that role poorly. For Peter, it was effortless.

The next afternoon Markov returned the exams, each with three grades in the upper right corner—for the exam, the past six weeks, and the course thus far. Peter's and my overall averages were exactly tied at 97, just ahead of Scotty and Rich at 94 and 93. Will was hanging tough at 77.

The following day Markov held me up after class and asked, "*Chto s Petrom*?" What's the matter with Peter? I shrugged, concealing my pique. Why was it so difficult for others to recognize my talent? I felt doomed.

We all expected the final six weeks of the course to be the worst, and we weren't mistaken. I kept telling myself that if I could improve ever so slightly, I just might not have to desert, but that was scant encouragement. Scotty had the gall to ask the First Shirt when our orders would be cut and was told probably not before graduation. Meanwhile, keep on jogging. Ha, ha. Peter and Scott doubled the length of their runs.

Morning classes we now spent discussing current events in Russian and afternoon periods describing military maneuvers depicted in captionless illustrations. Peter's facility with both exercises dazzled teachers and classmates alike.

In the chow lines Rich did impressions of Toddhunter, and Will took to mumbling to himself that the treads wouldn't kill him, no, not Will Burke. His open admission of fear made him a trifle less obnoxious, if still not exactly endearing. Rich and Scott started debating the best places to live in Sweden. I took to throwing up mess hall chow.

Two weeks before graduation, Markov announced what he called "culmination of course." Trilling his "r's" and hardening his "l's," he explained, "All students must now take your knowledges and informations of Russian language and make speech in front of class about the Russia. All instructors will come."

My heart raced at this opportunity. I could devise a talk better than anything Peter might and memorize it. Because I was the better writer. And if I concentrated enough, my pronunciation just might pass muster.

"Gentlemen," Markov added, "you will give speech in order of alphabet."

My queasy stomach sank. Bakken came first. And Zielsdorf would be last. That would give Peter more time to prepare, but still this was my best shot to outshine him.

For my presentation, I decided on a lengthy synopsis of Robert K. Massie's biography of the last czar and his wife, *Nicholas and Alexandra*, because it flattered our teachers' monarchist prejudices. It took several evenings to compose my text and another to learn it more or less by heart.

The morning my turn came, I was up by 4:00, vomiting and emptying bowels. Unsteady on my feet heading to roll call, I begged Peter just to let me come in first, because he was willing to escape to Sweden and I wasn't. He gave me a long, wistful look before shaking his head.

For thirty minutes, I spoke clear and concise Russian with my best accent, stressing the last Romanov emperor's personal charm and political incompetence. I depicted the Bolsheviks as beasts for their cold-blooded massacre of his entire family—the czar, his wife, the teenage daughters, including Anastasia, and the czarevich.

When I finished, Markov clapped heartily, while no one else made a sound. Had my delivery perhaps been too timid? I hadn't made more than a couple of negligible mistakes, but I apparently hadn't impressed anybody either. In Russian I asked for questions or comments. Rich's hand shot up.

"Did Lenin himself order the execution of the Romanovs?" he asked in Russian.

"*Nyet*," I answered. No.

"Did anyone close to Lenin order their execution?"

"*Ya ne znayu.*" I don't know.

"Gospodin Bakken, why are you misleading us?" Rich said. "You know as well as I do that a local Ural Mountains committee decided on their own to kill the Romanovs."

"Wasn't the overthrow of the czar generally welcomed in Russia?" Scotty added.

"*Dovol'no,*" Markov said. Enough. "You young men have no understanding of the Russian politics. Bolsheviks are uncultured provincials. When they seized the power, hooligans and criminals took over country. Now let me say few things about speech of Mr. Bakken." Markov proceeded to praise my large vocabulary, precise grammar, and adequate pronunciation, but noted little variety of sentence structure and, most damning of all, excessive reliance on notes.

Will tried to praise my insights into the downfall of the Romanovs, but his Russian was too halting. Markov cut off this "return to political discussion" and filled the rest of the period with an account in his beautiful Moscow accent of life in Russia before the Soviets ruined it. Half-listening, I consoled myself that I couldn't have done better, but what solace was that if I ended up in Vietnam?

I wasn't displeased when Burke's speech bordered on disaster, his Russian often literally translated from English and so barely comprehensible. But his remarks on the birth of the KGB from the remnants of the czarist Cheka apparently pleased Markov and Danilova enough to pass him.

The others' talks turned my stomach. Most were far worse than mine, but Scotty's and Rich's weren't at all bad and in some ways better. Both of them were more comfortable performing than I had been, so even if their Russian wasn't always as idiomatic, they were more entertaining.

Finally it was Zielsdorf's turn, and his speech left our jaws hanging. The Muscovite Russian was as good as Markov's or Danilova's, the diction virtually native. And as when speaking

German, Peter assumed a more outgoing, convivial personality that charmed the teachers' behinds off. Of course he was the best student. Hands down.

But the content of the speech appalled us, that is, all except for the teachers and Will. Peter had chosen to report on espionage for the British and Americans carried out by Colonel Oleg Penkovsky, an officer in the GRU—Soviet Military Intelligence. Before the Cuban missile crisis of October 1962, Penkovsky passed on the secret that the Soviet Union's forces weren't strong enough to take the US on in nuclear war, so convincing President Kennedy that if he rattled his sabers and demanded removal of the Russian rockets, they would back down. JFK called Khrushchev's bluff and, as it turned out, we all lived to tell about it.

Peter barely glanced at his note cards the whole speech and repeatedly went off on fascinating asides to describe the KGB and its military counterpart, the GRU. Fifty minutes later, he concluded, "In the end, the Soviets shot Penkovsky as a traitor."

It was all I could do not to vomit. There was no way I could get out of Ord and Vietnam now. Because the better man had won. That by itself was galling.

Before Peter could even ask for questions, Rich blurted, "What do you make of accounts that the Penkovsky Papers are a CIA fabrication?"

"I missed that issue of *Pravda*," Peter quipped, and Markov laughed harder than Will. Rich reeled off a list of student and underground papers that supported his claim. Peter snorted in contempt at these sources. Though he regularly read several of these himself and had personally gotten Hoffman interested in them.

"Saving his ass is no excuse for this horseshit, man," Rich whispered. "I thought we were friends." Then he said aloud, "Why is it fair that the Soviets let us keep massive military forces near their borders, while we risk a nuclear war to keep a few of theirs out of Cuba?"

Peter shredded Rich's argument in extemporaneous Russian that awed us for authenticity of accent and idiom. "Where are we on the Soviet border?" he rebutted. "Not in West Germany or anyplace else. Our troops are at the outer limits of Soviet expansion, far from Russia, and we're holding them at this line. Enough is enough."

Buoyed by his speech's success, Peter walked into the final exam with obnoxious confidence. On the written section, I didn't make a single mistake, but during the interview I accidentally transposed two consonants and changed a saying into an off-color spoonerism and the resulting embarrassment tongue-tied me. Peter was never one to falter under pressure, especially in a test, and the results showed it. His superior final exam grade combined with his brilliant speech rendered him unquestionably "*Studyent nomer odin*"—Student Number One—of Class 0968. His butt at least seemed saved, even if he was prepared to bolt, if the need arose.

Rich was so resigned to getting orders for Fort Ord that he made concrete plans for emigration to Sweden now. He would see his family in Boston first and then fly to Toronto and from there to Stockholm. Scott hedged over joining him, while I flatly refused. Will's reply was quixotic: "The Pentagon won't waste Will Burke's brains on combat arms." As if the treads personally cared about his welfare, the space cadet.

The day before commencement we still hadn't received our new orders, so that evening Scotty talked the company clerk into playing tennis. Afterwards, Dickinson casually popped the big question, "Are our orders in yet?"

"Yup," Remington told him.

"For where?" Dickinson asked, as if only mildly curious.

"Fort Ord, whatever."

"Anyplace else?"

"Maybe. I don't remember."

"Germany?"

Remington didn't think so.

"How many people are going to Fort Ord?"

"Hey, you'll find out tomorrow. You're going where the Pentagon wants you to go, so just do your time, keep your head down, and before you know it, they'll let you go home—if you ain't already dead."

Back in the barracks, Dickinson gathered the Monks together in Peter's and my shared room and relayed the dreadful news. "I hope you guys like blondes," Rich muttered. "Sweden here we come." Nobody laughed.

That night Peter screamed commands at himself in his sleep. Between his nightmares and the sea lions' barking, I barely even dozed between furious debates with myself over whether to join the others in Stockholm. But desertion still terrified me more than Vietnam did. Why couldn't the treads just let us play Russian roulette and if we survived go home? I'd do it.

Friday we all lingered over breakfast in funereal silence, fearing the fateful sheet of paper we would be handed within hours. But first we had to endure the torture of a Mickey-Mouse graduation ceremony.

Students in Arabic, Chinese, Czech, German, Russian, and Vietnamese filled the Presidio cinema and sat together by classes in alphabetical order front to back. The huge group behind us looked even grimmer than we did. Guess where they were going?

Exactly at oh-nine-hundred hours Presidio Commandant Colonel Hirsch, marched to the lectern, greeted us like a proud high school principal—another space cadet—and announced two special awards. The first, for academic excellence, went to a zoomie in Mandarin we had never met. "The highest honor we are bestowing, the Commandant's Award," the Colonel went on, "goes to the individual who has shown the greatest linguistic ability and promise in any class graduating today. This man's department gave him the highest recommendation I've ever seen at the DLI. Specialist Peter Zielsdorf, please come to the stage."

Peter jostled my knees in hurrying to the aisle and bounded to the front. His crisp salute made Rich and Scotty titter, while I gnashed my teeth. I wanted to be happy for Peter, but the joy was undercut by chagrin over my failure and fear of my fate.

Zielsdorf returned with a new watch inscribed with his name, award, and date and passed it around, while Hirsch spoke on. Scotty handed it back, saying, "It's just a Timex," and Zielsdorf bristled. Finally, all the graduates, starting with those in Arabic, filed to the stage, shook the Commandant's hand, and received a certificate.

Afterwards, during our slow climb up the Presidio hill, Peter muttered so that only I could hear, "It's my first watch ever that wasn't a hand-me-down." Nobody else said a word.

Dickinson glumly led us into the Orderly Room, and we lined up abreast against the counter. Typing with only index fingers, Remington refused to acknowledge us.

Scott cleared his throat.

The clerk pecked away.

"Come on, Art," Dickinson pleaded.

Remington kept on working.

"Christ, Remington, can't that damned thing wait?"

"That ain't what the CO said."

"For God's sake, Art, we're dying to learn our fricking assignments."

"The Pentagon cut one set of orders," he told us. "And then canceled them." He slowly reached into a drawer, grabbed a stack of papers, and handed them to Scott.

Dickinson snatched them, tearing the top page, and blurted, "We're all on the same sheet!" Which meant the same fate.

"The first set sent one of you," the clerk said, "Zielbolski, or some weird name like that, to Fort Holabird, Maryland, for MI training. The rest of you suckers were headed to Fort Ord in Infantry. But not anymore."

We pushed and shoved, struggling to look over Dickinson's shoulder. "Where's Knittelstedt?" he said, pronouncing both the "k" and the "n."

"It has to be in Germany!" Peter shouted.

"That's right," Remington said. "Good duty. Every Army member of Class 0968 got West Germany. It's some new classified MOS. You'll learn it over there on the job."

"I, too?" Burke asked in disbelief. Scott nodded.

"Yeah, 'I, too,' you bastard, Burke," Rich squealed and gave Will a quick hug across the shoulders.

We whooped at the fabulous news, like a whole Death Row pardoned at once. Sergeant Kelly came out of his office and told us to settle down. And then flashed a crooked smile and congratulated us.

"What'll we be doing?" Scotty asked him.

Kelly's face went blank. "It's top secret. But I bet you'll be in a windowless building." Suddenly I felt woozy, but Peter's strong grip steadied me. Germany? I wanted to sob.

"Ah-ten-hut!" Kelly shouted as Captain Toddhunter walked in, and we snapped to attention.

"At ease," the CO ordered, but this time we allowed ourselves to slouch instead of standing stiffly relaxed as required. "So it's Germany for you men. But not before your security clearances come through. Till then you're staying here, pulling details for me, the First Shirt, other sergeants, or whoever else needs you. And believe me, we'll find plenty for you to do. I'll teach you yet what it means to be a real soldier."

This tready bullshit didn't faze us anymore. Germany, when it should have been Vietnam? It was like being taken off a train to hell.

"From now on you must be security conscious all waking or sleeping hours," Toddhunter ranted. "Se-cur-ity con-scious. Remember those words. You can't tell your family, your wife, your girlfriend, your friends or anyone else a damned thing about your specialty. You cannot discuss it among yourselves away from work. There you will learn only what you need to know to do your jobs, and not one thing more. And you'll love it, you lucky bastards. If people ask what you're doing, say you're a linguist and shut up. And you, Bakken, I'm still working on who wrote on my signs, and if I find out you had anything to do with it, I'll see to it personally that your orders to Germany are cancelled, so we can court-martial your ass here. Where do you get off, Cowboy, pulling shit like this? Over in Nam I would have just fuckin' wasted ya."

Peter turned away from the CO and gave me a wink. I had to suppress a grin. In a month we'd be free of this crazy asshole—and go to Germany! Tears of joy oozed from my eyes.

What a blunder to believe this was our good fortune.

Part Two
DUTY

Jan. 1, 1970

Happy New Year, Peter. Like everybody used to crow at me back in the States, but here in *Deutschland* it's just been more dismal duty. Some New Year's Eve I celebrated in starched green fatigues and combat boots, where at the stroke of twenty-four hundred Zulu—formerly known as midnight—Sergeant Witless snapped, "Zielsdorf, get off your butt and take over from Burke."

Yeah, right. As if the Soviet troops just across the border in East Germany were up to anything other than drinking themselves shit-faced. No dummies those Russkies, unlike us. I enjoyed West Germany as a student at the University of Marburg two years ago, but it's been hellish now as a GI along the Iron Curtain. Though I am grateful that without a barracks or a mess hall, we're free to lease a room and feed ourselves in Knittelstedt, population twelve thousand. Not that it doesn't get lonely without buddies living cheek by jowl like at the DLI. Except for the hundred or so of us Army guys at this outstation in the British sector, there are no other Americans close-by this far north.

Since my mid ended at 8:00 this morning, I've been shivering beneath a comforter in this rental and struggling to think of something more pleasant than Det Q, better known simply as "the site." Whatever we call the windowless structure, it's the same dreary, one-story building, perched atop a high hill in an extensive beech forest, enclosed by a twelve-foot, barbed-wire fence with a single gate that armed MPs man day and night. Sergeant Whitman insists it's defending freedom from the godless commies, the psycho tread. Though I admit the top secret hidden inside did save us Monks' butts from Vietnam.

If only I could doze off. Hard to do when my pulse races and my head throbs. Bad hangovers have been milder than this. Even if my German landlord, his wife are tiptoeing around the house and whispering. Thoughtful folks, those elderly Schultzes.

This room remains frigid despite the glowing space heater humming all hours that I'm here. Quite a dismal abode with too short a bed for my six-one frame, made shorter by an unforgiving headboard and footboard. Then there's the rickety card table for writing, reading, and eating, and brick-and-board shelves for my books. Still, the place is cheap, allowing me to save most of my paltry Spec Four salary for graduate school later.

7:00 p.m.

Five hours to go before another mid for me. Staying up all night again on this little rest will be torture. Did I get even three hours today? Yesterday it was fewer. It scares me of late to face a mirror. Bloodshot eyes, dark circles, ashen skin—I look like imminent death.

This damp German winter makes everything so much worse—penetrating drizzle and messy slush with highs in the thirties are ten times unhealthier than Wisconsin's dry freeze and powdery snow. It's also why I have a persistent raspy throat here, when I seldom got sick back in the States.

At least I've gotten started on my one and only New Year's resolution— namely, to keep this diary. Because I have so much to say and no one to say it to. I would never whine like this out loud, not even to another Monk, but I have to write some of this stuff down or I'll explode.

The first month of learning our new jobs, Whitman had us pulling straight days, ideal for getting decent sleep, but working midnight to eight a.m. since then has been an ordeal. At least the tread who trained us was easier to take than Sgt. Witless, not that monosyllabic Spec 6 Boudreau isn't peculiar in his own way. It shocked me to discover that Scotty is better at our new assignment than me, even though his spoken Russian sucks.

Tommy's better, too, but that's no surprise. My hearing must be a bit subpar to have any trouble comprehending spoken Russkie, though the intercepts are often static-ridden.

Jan. 2, 1970

Why can't the Monks see that I'm a phony half-farmer, half manual-laborer, pretending to be an intellectual. I'm so not what I seem. It's amazing my buddies are this easy to fool. As a teaching assistant at UW-Madison two years ago, I felt like a pretentious asshole, lecturing on German culture. Who am I to tell undergrad rubes from northern Wisconsin anything about the subject, when beneath this facade, I'm the same hick they are? Even if I made Phi Beta Kappa junior year, was a Fulbright Fellow, and won the DLI Commandant's Award.

So who is the real Peter Zielsdorf? Excellent question.

For centuries my German forebears were Pomeranian peasants, till a great-grandfather emigrated to Wisconsin to seek a better fortune and homesteaded a dairy farm outside Chute Noire. At the age of thirty, he took a younger wife from the same region of Prussia, and together they raised twelve children. The kids kept so busy helping him that none got a chance to attend school. His eldest son inherited the property and in turn passed it on to his own oldest boy. Alas, my father was a middle child and so inherited a pittance and wound up renting forty sandy acres from his brother. Upon his predictable failure, Dad moved us into Chute Noire, and at the age of forty got a job on the assembly line at the local muffler factory.

My dad, a farmer at heart like his ancestors for generations, hated living in town. But my mother pushed for the switch, because country life on their meager income had become too difficult. But if we had stayed, I bet he would have never abandoned us.

Though native-born Americans, my parents were raised like foreigners in a western Wisconsin coulee—as the French voyageurs, the first Europeans to explore the region, christened the wooded river valleys. Where I grew up between Eau Claire and La Crosse, many people spoke German. I didn't really learn proper English until grade school and then with my classmates' accent—the o's too deep, i's too tight, and final s's that hissed where they should have buzzed. At eighteen, I left my hometown for good and at college acquired a neutral Midwestern accent, though I do slip into the broad west central Wisconsin twang of my childhood when excited. Or inebriated.

Foreign languages I've always taken for granted. I learned to speak Polish as a kid—without being able to read or write it—from a Chute Noire neighbor. The Warsaw émigré taught me the names of everyday objects and acts in his native language till Bogdan and I could carry on a simple conversation. Need I mention how much easier this made learning Russian? Polish taught me the roots and syntax of the Slavic family, so unlike German or English, giving me a major head start in Monterey.

If I do survive Det Q, my current plan will be to return to Madison, earn a doctorate in *Germanistik*, and strive to land a professorship at a major university, no matter how much I doubt I'm suited to academia. Anything else would be a waste of talent and scholarship money. What more could a bumpkin from Harrison County, Wisconsin want?

I'm ashamed to bellyache like this, even if only onto paper, but I simply must vent my frustrations. One thing I've never been is a complainer. In fact, my entire life I've always sought others' respect, or even envy, and have never tolerated sympathy. And I don't want it now. But I truly cannot endure this situation much longer. Of course I can't ask to see a psychotherapist because that would quickly cost me my security clearance and get me transferred to a grunt unit farther south to help block Soviet tanks with my carcass.

Then there's Mom and her ailing heart. I'm grateful that I could spend significant time with her on leave after the DLI.

I wonder how Macintosh is making out in Sweden—wait, somebody's at the door.

Jan. 3, 1970

Last evening I was delighted to find dorky Bakken standing there, his red hair freshly trimmed, in one hand holding a half pint of Southern Comfort and in the other two shot glasses. "How about a little drink?" he said with that disarming grin of his.

"Sure thing, Tommy," I replied with a chuckle. "Maybe it'll even help me get through my upcoming mid." Of course I shouldn't have been drinking before duty, but my spirit needed the comforting.

Unlike him, I wasn't circumspect with the booze. The first ounce burned all the way down, as did the second, but the joy juice buoyed my mood. "So what's up? It's not like you to drop by unannounced." Man, did I feel better just having a friendly body in this room, especially Bakken's.

Tommy ran a freckled hand through his crew cut. "Well, none of us have phones, so I couldn't call. I just had a hunch you could use some company."

That I did indeed. Before you know it, we were chatting about the DLI and our favorite Russian teachers, mine being Markov and his Danilova.

Against Tom's kindly advice, I poured myself a third serving, only this one had the opposite effect. Or was the petulance from bringing up my chronic insomnia? In response, Tommy had the gall to suggest I try relaxing "before bedtime," whenever the hell that meant when my trick was staying up all night. "Peter," he said in his gentle tenor, "you should buy yourself a stereo like mine and listen to Mozart while reading one of your favorite authors? Such as Heinrich von Kleist."

"Kleist isn't culinary art!" I snapped. "How could *anybody* read such a master while listening to Mozart? Do you think art is like gourmet delicacies to savor for their 'interesting' flavors? You might as well read escapist best sellers, if you're only going to *consume* art."

"What would art be then?" the dorky Norwegian rebutted. "Political tracts?"

“If you don’t know after all you’ve been exposed to it, you never will. Art assaults complacency. Art unsettles in order to liberate.”

“You don’t enjoy reading?”

“Enjoyment is beside the point. And no criticism ever does the greater works justice.”

Tom’s brow furrowed.

“Literary criticism is to actual literature as the Kinsey report is to sex,” I ranted on.

My mentioning sex shut Bakken up. His face went blank, he said, “I gotta go,” and promptly left.

The very idea of reading Kleist while listening to Mozart makes me want to smash phonograph records. Combining the composer’s sublime transcendence of reality with the writer’s merciless struggle to stare it in the face? Only a philistine could consume them together and not vomit. Kleist, who peacefully shot himself at thirty-three, Christ’s purported final age, because Kant had taught him that we can only experience the world of appearances and never the real world underlying this illusory surface. Kleist, a suicide because he could never achieve his philosophical goal—knowing reality as it actually exists and not just how our limited senses experience it. Now that’s what I call intellectual integrity. But what integrity do I have? Certainly very little as long as I keep doing the treads’ bidding.

Jan. 4, 1970

Okay, I didn’t treat Tommy right. In fact, I behaved like a complete asshole.

I’m too depressed to be upset today. My trick chief never noticed the alcohol on my breath, but then he was reeking of beer himself. I am sincerely grateful for this assignment in West Germany and know I was lucky to get it, no matter how poorly I might be doing, because the alternative was Vietnam.

But gratitude doesn’t begin to solve the conundrums of human existence. Oh, would I love to be the one to solve them. But how?

By sitting here pondering? Hardly. By reading? No. How else? If only the treads and their bosses don't get us all killed first, I may yet come to understand it all. Somebody has to. Otherwise homo sapiens will continue to meander along mindlessly for untold generations till an asteroid or comet smashes the earth to kingdom come and we as a species vanish without any inkling of what life was all about.

My mother doesn't live in such a harsh world—bless her kind, sweet soul. There is certainly no sense of purposelessness for her or an instant's anguish over ultimate ends. Oblivious to her material poverty, she stands firm on a bedrock of faith without the tiniest crack of doubt. She sees herself as immortal spirit fleetingly made flesh in God's own image and the centerpiece of His creation. Through the willing sacrifice of His Son, she feels saved for all eternity, even if the earth should revert to the void whence it came. God, I wished I lived in her world. What sane person wouldn't?

But her beliefs are based on dubious texts of uncertain authorship. Moses parted the Red Sea? God sired a mortal Son? Jesus came back from the dead? Give me a break. Madison professors taught me to spurn all superstition, but what beliefs did they leave me with instead? Only that we humans are an accident of evolution, who as easily might never have come into existence and whom the cosmos won't miss once we're gone.

I'm only beginning to explain what's bothering me. Nearly sixty hours off for me now till the next set of six mids. I may go see another Hollywood flick at Club 69. Admission is only a quarter. On the other hand I doubt I will. The last one I watched was the childish sci-fi flick *Barbarella*. Jane Fonda's sexiness in it only made my involuntary celibacy more intolerable. As badly as I need to get laid, I do believe I miss making out more.

Jan. 8, 1970

I haven't done anything worth recording in the interim other than read lighter fare and sip schnaps. Treacherous ice underfoot outside kept me housebound. Max Frisch's *Homo Faber* as well as Johann Wolfgang von Goethe's *Die Leiden des Jungen Werther* certainly entertained more than weightier tomes on my doctoral list.

Jan. 10, 1970

Today's initial M-16 training session was conducted by Sergeants Wilhelm and Whitman. Wild Willie proved he's as psycho as Killer Whitman. Brandishing the puny rifle lights up these pukes' faces like teenage boys feeling their first bare tit. But when I hold the aluminum-and-plastic spewer of death, I shudder to know I can spray mayhem wherever I point, yet Whitman and Wilhelm caress these weapons like a lover's derriere. What are we humans?

They're both so perky since M-16 training began that I want to vomit. Whitman loves to fondle the gun and regale us with tales about wasting gooks in Vietnam. He brags about needing to build the backs of his foxholes there higher than the front, as if not getting fragged by his own men was an accomplishment. Though for him maybe it was. It's a wonder nobody gags while listening. Too bad Sergeant Witless didn't stay in Nam to kill Oriental civilians and jack up the pukes' body counts, so at least on paper we'd be winning that war, even if in reality we aren't anywhere close.

Keeping the weapons locked up in a shed out of our reach at the site is smart. None of us would live long enough during a Soviet attack to get a key near the padlock anyway. Besides who knows what accidents on purpose we might otherwise have?

The two super-treads passed out booklets featuring a cartoon cutie, squeezing out of skimpy clothes the better to teach us to kill for God and country. That dishy blonde helping us become "M-16 Zapsters" makes me feel like I'm going batshit crazier than the two sarges already are.

I'd love to zap some real woman who looked half as good and I wouldn't use a rifle. And if I don't find her soon, I just might lose it.

Jan. 12, 1970

I just had a dream about a blonde so sexy it's left me pissed off. The contrast between what my life ought to be, and would be without the Army, keeps getting more unbearable. So it's way past time to do something about the problem. But how? I've tried hitting the local bars, but have yet to meet one German woman this way, though I have gotten to know a few local guys who hang out at our NCO club. We call it Club 69 because of its address, Sixty-Nine Bahnhofstrasse—or at least that's what we tell the Germans. It's located inside an abandoned warehouse that also serves as our cinema, library, and laundromat. I especially like Karl-Heinz Schneider, a witty conversationalist whose rapid-fire speech improves my *Deutsch*. Like other natives, he thinks the site is a radar station.

As short-haired GIs at the DLI, we had zero chance of getting anywhere with California women, who couldn't forgive us for joining the ranks of LBJ's and then Nixon's babykillers in Vietnam, as if the draft never existed. But young Germans here don't resent our being soldiers. After duty stateside, this has taken some getting used to. But why shouldn't they like us? We're friendly. We're generous. We enliven this provincial burgh. Knittelstedt isn't nearly so small as my hometown Chute Noire, but it's far from a big city. Still, nobody in our hush-hush unit is permitted to get close to a German woman, which the treads consider "fraternizing with a foreign national." The penalty—the loss of our security clearance and reassignment to a combat unit in southern Germany—is harsh. Casual sex with Fräulein is okay, but don't you dare get attached.

I really need to stop obsessing about women, but it'd be easier to renounce eating.

Jan. 13, 1970

My discipline keeps slipping. I couldn't have won the Commandant's Award in this sorry state. I've tried to speed up the reading of titles from my doctoral list, but I'm stuck on Thomas Mann. He's too long-winded to knock off fast. His essayistic fiction isn't nearly so profound as he thinks. At best a middlebrow intellect. Maybe I should skip over him and try somebody easier.

"So what if your head aches and your eyes burn?" a voice inside my head chides. "Study anyway. Did pain or discomfort ever deter you in Madison, Marburg or Monterey? To achieve greatness, you must knuckle down. And get back to regular exercise." But no matter how many hours I lie in bed staring at the backs of my eyelids, I always feel too tired to jog or do calisthenics.

That's it. No more wasting time. I'll switch to Bertolt Brecht. He's much lighter fare.

Jan. 14, 1970

After twenty pages of Brecht, I had no idea what I had read, so I quit and just lay there in the dark. Getting a doctorate in German feels so wrong. Russian wouldn't be any better nor would Comp Lit. Yet I do love literature. It's the literary criticism I can't stand. It's always so much less than the work itself. Critics tirelessly construct neat Procrustean beds and hack and wrench the works to make them fit. Why not let the novels, plays, and poems speak for themselves? Literary criticism really only sounds profound if you haven't already read the piece. Or if you've read it so long ago, you've forgotten its richness.

So what do I really want? I don't know, but I feel like I've got to have it *right now*. I'm thrashing around like a racehorse, inside a stuck starting gate.

Wouldn't finding a girlfriend here make everything else fall into place?

7:00 p.m.

I gave up on getting more sleep and went for a brisk walk and shopped for groceries—yogurt, Black Forest-style smoked ham, and a loaf of *Heidebrot*—the local sour dough rye. I had reached the Schultzes' gate on the way back, when Karl-Heinz Schneider pulled up alongside in his old diesel Mercedes. He got out and shook my hand limply as he has done every time I've seen him since we first met at Club 69. Germans always greet someone they know this way no matter how often they see that person and consider Americans rude for shaking hands only after significant absences. "*Guten Tag*, Peter," he greeted, giving my name its German pronunciation, close to "Pay-tuh."

"*Guten Tag*, Karl," I said.

"You look a little worse for wear, Peter. Are you sick?"

"I've been sleeping poorly."

"How about a *Bierchen* at my house? Beer soothes the nerves."

I accepted the kind offer, so we drove to his parents' buff stucco house in the New Settlement on the northern edge of Knittelstedt. In his upstairs room, he put on the Beatles' "White Album" and straddled his desk chair crotch to back, a trick he had learned from us *Amis*, while I plopped down on the waxed wooden floor. I relished the friendly company, strong beer, and quirky music.

Karl-Heinz's red beard and long hair don't go far in hiding his pale skin, which is even pastier than Tom's. No matter, his generosity and charm make him as likeable as Bakken. I gather Karl's equally popular with the pupils at the Knittelstedter *Gymnasium*—as Germany calls its college-prep public schools—where he teaches biology and German.

He asked what I thought of Chancellor Willy Brandt's efforts to improve Deutschland's foreign relations with Eastern Europe. I shrugged. I used to care deeply about politics, but I've been too exhausted of late to keep up. Karl went on about how West Germany should pull out of NATO and let the US and the USSR fight their war someplace else.

When I tuned the Beatles out and Karl back in, he was ranting about the Christian Democrats, the opposition party to Brandt and his Social Democrats. Karl-Heinz, like every German university student I've met, is quite a lefty. But then the whole political spectrum here is shifted toward socialism by American standards, which I find refreshing. Even German conservatives take socialized medicine for granted.

A gorgeous young blonde walked in, shook Karl-Heinz's hand, and greeted him with a "*Tag*, Karlchen." She looked ravishing in tight jeans and an even tighter sweater. I stood up, and the beauty faced me with an expectant grin.

"This is my American friend, Peter," he told her in English.

"Charmed, I'm sure," the girl said with an Oxford accent.

"Peter, this is my sister, Dagmar."

"*Es freut mich, Sie kennenzulernen,*" I replied. I'm happy to meet you.

"*Er spricht Deutsch*!" Dagmar blurted. He speaks German!

"As well as you," Karl told her, exaggerating my fluency.

She requested that I use the informal *du* for "you" with her, because the formal *Sie* sounds too stuffy among young people. "Peter, forgive me for asking, but are you sick?" she said. "You look like you should be in bed."

"With whom?" I joked, blushing. I wouldn't have been that bold in English.

She screwed up her sparkling, ice-blue eyes and flashed a grin of mock disapproval. I couldn't decide what I admired most—her snug clothes, fine features, or striking smile. Five-six, leggy, curvaceous, flawless skin—what's not to like? Well, her age, only eighteen. Dagmar won't graduate from the local *Gymnasium* till this spring and next fall plans to attend the Braunschweig Teachers College.

"What have you been eating lately?" she asked.

"Do I really look that bad?"

She listened carefully as I described my diet of ham sandwiches, fruit, and yogurt.

"Where are the vegetables?"

"I don't care that much for rabbit food."

"Nonsense." She proceeded to rattle off which local shops were best for buying what. Much too soon she excused herself to cram for her *Abiturexamen,* the comprehensive tests *Gymnasium* students must pass to graduate and qualify for higher education.

"What are you studying now, Dagmar?" I asked in English, eager to keep her around. Too bad Karl couldn't study in her stead.

"I study English," she said with that Oxford accent.

"I'm studying English," I said, correcting her.

"You, too? But you're an American."

I carefully explained in German what she should have said and what she had misunderstood until she burst out laughing. I offered to tutor her anytime. Glancing warily at her brother, she muttered, "*Danke.*"

"Maybe later," Karl-Heinz snapped.

Without Dagmar's company, I soon got antsy, pleaded having to get ready for work, and left.

Back in my room at the Schultzes, I slept off the mild beer buzz to wild fantasies. Dagmar will turn nineteen in October. That wouldn't be too young for me at twenty-four, would it? Of course not. All right! This is more like it. Getting orders to Knittelstedt might be a lucky break for me yet.

While dozing off a second time, I imagined all the planets and galaxies in the universe becoming aware of what the Big Bang hath wrought through the minds of us humans as the slowly evolving spirit of all this cosmic matter and energy. Before we showed up, it had no idea what it was, but now it at least has inklings, if as yet no overall understanding. Still, that's progress. What we are and where and why now all seem like the same question—we are the beings the universe created so that eventually it might comprehend itself through us, its developing mind. So the grand puzzle will one day be unlocked, and homo sapiens is the key. Life is sweet.

The question is not if I'm going to ask Dagmar out, but when. I've been celibate against my will far too long.

Jan. 15, 1970

This afternoon after seven hours of most welcome sleep I took a long walk in the New Settlement past the Schneiders' house, hoping to run into Dagmar, but no such luck. I keep wondering whether she's too young for me, not that she'll always be. But what about the strict rule that GIs here aren't allowed German girlfriends? Smitty, our gate guard and friendly MP, says a buddy stationed at a Bavarian site was sent to prison practically for life after mentioning a piece of top-secret equipment to a Fräulein, later exposed as a Czech spy. If the dopey GI had only been fluent in German, he probably would have detected that she was a phony. Rich swears Smitty is putting us on. No matter—I would never tell Dagmar a thing about Det Q's top secret mission.

Tom is blessed that he expects so little from life. The monkish deprivation that's driving me nuts scarcely fazes him. We are such different creatures, yet he understands me better than anybody else. But then the fellow Badger knows where I came from, how I grew up, and got where I am.

If he weren't so shy, his Russian would be fluent. His spoken German is awkward, too, but I have to give him credit for using it over here more than anybody else but me. He shops "on the local economy," as the treads put it, while most guys here drive a hundred clicks each way to reach the nearest PX rather than deal with local clerks. And he chats with his landlord's family and even goes to German movies. His love affair with Karen by mail is weird, though better than nothing I suppose. Still, the strangest thing of all about Tommy is that he never complains.

Myself, I'm dying to get my hands on a real flesh-and-blood woman. This weekend I should head down to Braunschweig and hire some flesh and blood on its notorious Bruchstrasse. Now that'd be trick work I could sink my teeth into—literally. I could either take a train or borrow the VW Hatchback that Scotty's dad bought him. But on the other hand, getting my rocks off for money would scarcely beat masturbation. No, what I crave is to love and be loved. If I had the right woman, I suspect everything else in my life just might work out, maybe even an academic career.

I started shivering at the site so badly before dawn I could barely concentrate. Another cup of black coffee just made me more light-headed, so I only pretended to work until trick change at oh-eight-hundred hours. On the ride back to town with a buddy, I had trouble composing a note in German for him, asking his landlord what happened to the hot water.

Once back in this dim room at the Schultzes', I ate breakfast—or was it supper?—my stomach and bowels sure couldn't tell. Next I read the shortest story in a collection by Arthur Schnitzler, the Austrian master of impressionist fiction. By ten a.m. I was close to dozing off to shadowy memories of Dagmar's teasing smile, when sobering thoughts about Mom's poor health welled up. Before long, I found myself folding my hands and experiencing a powerful urge to pray. But what and to whom? Because nothing exists in the entire cosmos that could listen to me except other people, and little good they can do me now.

How can we lead lives whose only meaning is what we humans assign to them? But what choice do we have? Dorky Bakken accepts the world as given as easily as his pasty skin, freckles, and red hair. Doesn't he see that an Auschwitz guard or Jack the Ripper could live by so shallow a credo?

Another M-16 training session this weekend will keep me up late after completing the mid. If only I could teach myself to tune out Whitman, while learning just enough about the deadly toy to skate by. Holding the weapon actually frightens me, but then handling a spewer of death ought to.

Rich says I should have tried for conscientious objector status. I considered it, but I'm no pacifist. I would have gladly fought against the Nazis, as did my father and uncles, and cannot imagine any valid sense of morality that could tolerate a Hitler. But neither side is right in Vietnam, and without a chance of victory we're pointlessly snuffing out lives. And, as Rich keeps saying, we're still waiting to hear one good reason why.

Come on, Zielsdorf, flip these thoughts off like a light switch. Maybe I really could ask young Dagmar out. Somehow I've got to pull myself out of this rut.

Jan. 16, 1970

More M-16 training this morning from Sergeant Whitman. Another good look at the training booklet he handed out and I felt like I was going berserk. Its cartoonist has prostituted himself ten thousand times worse than a woman ever could with her body, drawing that luscious cartoon blonde spilling out of her clothes the better to make us all into "M-16 Zapsters." Exploiting lust to make us into killers is unspeakably evil. Whenever I glance at the sexy pictures, my ears roar and I feel myself hurtling into the gaping blackness of hell.

Fuck the M-16. It's like a Mattel toy, mostly plastic, lacking the heft of a M-14. I bet even strack Sergeant Whitman couldn't keep the flimsy rifle clean enough not to jam in a firefight. Why do we need these M-16s? I dragged my old M-14 through mud puddles during Basic Combat Training and, still dripping, it fired every time. Who wants a new weapon you can't trust? We'll never get to use them at Det Q anyway. A Russian artillery or rocket barrage will obliterate the site the first few seconds of any war, turning whoever is on duty into steak tartare. We regularly overhear Soviet units across the border drawing beads on us, making us the biggest sitting ducks in the Lüneburger Heath.

I keep a suitcase packed in case I'm lucky enough not to be on duty when all hell breaks loose. It's as German as the clothing it holds. Of course they'll only help me escape if the Russkies don't use tactical nukes or nerve gas on us. Or if NATO units don't annihilate Knittelstedt in self-defense after Soviet tanks have overrun us.

It's hard to believe that what saved us Monks from Vietnam was a stolen radio. The Soviet treads must be as dumb as ours for letting that piece of top-secret equipment get away. Rumor has it friendlies faked a truck accident that supposedly destroyed what we had actually stolen. Don't ask me how we get copies of its daily keys. We underlings don't have "a need to know," so we simply are not told.

Soviet SPETSNAZ, i.e. Special Forces, radiomen across the border crawl under groundsheets, sit up on their haunches, and insert matching keys, so they can communicate privately—or so they think—with fellow Soviet commando units in East Germany. But with our stolen receiver and fancy antenna we pick up everything they say within line of sight, which from Det Q's elevation is virtually the entire area between here and Magdeburg, HQ for the Soviet Third Shock Army, an elite tank outfit of five divisions facing the British Army of the Rhine situated to our rear.

Our treads claim that if the Soviets ever move against NATO these SPETSNAZ units will spring into action first. So the mission for us Russian lingies at Det Q is to keep an ear tuned to their tactical communications night and day and stay poised to send a direct teletype to SACEUR—the Supreme Allied Commander of Europe—at the first hint of a threat. This way, if we do our jobs right, NATO's commanding general will at least be awakened before he's killed.

Jan. 17, 1970

What great friends I have! I love Germany! This forenoon I was awakened early by Frau Schultz's shrill, "Peter, you have visitors!" The interruption at first miffed me, because I had at last dozed off after working yet another mid. Was it an alert? Were the Soviets tanks finally attacking?

I tugged on a pair of pants and shirt and opened the door. There stood Rich, Tom, Scotty, and Will grinning like idiots, Hoffman and Bakken in fatigues and field jackets, Dickinson and Burke in civvies.

"Thanks for inviting us over," Rich wisecracked, leading the other Monks inside.

"You could use a bigger place," Scotty said, glancing around.

"And more chairs, my good man," Will added, plopping down onto the foot of my bed.

"You can't beat the rent though," I said, wiping my sleepy eyes. "One hundred marks a month for everything. That's less than thirty bucks."

Tommy descended upon my German literary classics in tiny Reclam paperback editions. "Do you have *Simplicissimus*?"

"It's the thickest volume there. But it's all marked up."

"Good," Tommy said, pocketing the 17th-century picaresque novel. "I'll read your notes, too."

Grinning like a school kid up to petty mischief, Scotty sat down alongside Rich and Will on my cot, leaving me the lone chair.

"You must be saving four hundred bucks a month," Will said. "That's impressive on our meager income."

"Grad school won't be cheap. Come on, guys, what's up? You know I have to get more rest. Working straight mids is killing me."

"You need fun more than you do sleep," Rich said. "Tomorrow afternoon we're all going swimming."

"In January?"

"Yup," Rich added. "Karl-Heinz told us about a big indoor pool at a local power plant that's open to the public."

Despite burning eyes and throbbing temples, the prospect of swimming did appeal. "Did Karl-Heinz send you guys over here?" I asked.

"We ran into him," Scotty answered slyly.

"Actually, Tommy put us up to this," Rich said. "Hey, man, don't forget you're better off over here than any of us. The way you speak Kraut, you should be making out with the Fräulein like a bandit. With a bit longer hair, you could even pass for German."

All of a sudden their concern touched me deeply, and I felt an urge to weep but of course didn't.

"Can I borrow your Gryphius plays, too?" Tommy asked. Bakken was obviously working on the Baroque section of his doctoral reading list.

"Sure," I said with a yawn. Bakken kept browsing. His good-natured Norwegian grin by itself was calming. But then what could ever truly upset Bakken?

My fellow Monks didn't linger long. I climbed back into bed, still feeling lousy physically, but my despairing mood had turned hopeful. Of course I'd meet a special Fräulein here. It was just a question of when.

Late this afternoon, I got up, ate, took a bath, shaved, and put on my favorite outfit—tan brushed denims and a cranberry sweater—and decided to pay an impromptu visit on young Dagmar. Unfortunately, she wasn't home, nor was Karl-Heinz, but Frau Schneider invited me in anyway for a *Bierchen* and a chat. Forty-five years old and well-preserved, she looked more like Dagmar's older, darker sister than her mother.

Pilsener Urquell in hand, I was just describing my great-grandfather's Prussian origins and homesteading in Wisconsin, when Dagmar appeared and lit up the living room with her incandescent smile. To my delight, she joined the conversation.

"Too bad it's so difficult to visit Pomerania," Dagmar said. "Now that most of it belongs to Poland."

"None of it belongs to Poland, Dagmarchen," Frau Schneider replied. "Part of it may temporarily be under Polish administration, but we'll eventually get that back. Let's hope the Polish government gets so sick of these food riots that they return it to *Deutschland* along with Silesia and East Prussia."

"Come on, Mom. That territory is Polish now and will be forever. Just like there'll always be two Germanys."

"*Liebchen*, there is and always will be only one Germany, no matter how NATO and the Warsaw Pact divide us."

Dagmar touched an index finger to her forehead, a gesture implying her mother was nuts. "You'd better not let your father see you do that," Frau Schneider teased, in no way offended. The more I heard Dagmar speak, the better she looked. Sure, she's only eighteen, but mature for her age and by no means a dim bulb. No, indeed.

When Karl-Heinz returned from his teachers' meeting, I begged off a second *Bierchen*, pleading the need to work later that evening, and invited him to join us five *Amis* at the swimming pool Sunday afternoon.

"For sure," he replied in English.

"May I come along?" Dagmar said.

Karl-Heinz replied with an emphatic "N*ein*," but Frau Schneider overruled. "Why not, Karlchen? You won't even notice Dagmarchen in that big pool."

Fat chance of that. My heart thumped at the prospect. As great as Dagmar looked in tight slacks, how would she look in a swimsuit?

Jan. 18, 1970

On the way to the pool today, I doubted that swimming was such a great idea because of a mild sore throat. We five Monks arrived first in Dickinson's VW. I acted as spokesperson to get us in. Admission was two marks each—about sixty cents—and for that we also were given clean towels. After a brief warm-up, Scotty talked us into a one-lap freestyle sprint. Guess who won? Though I came in a close second. Slender Tom swam stronger than he looks for a distant third. Skinny Rich and pudgy Will fought it out not to finish last, and Burke won after Hoffman gave up halfway across. "Man, this is too much like work," was his pathetic excuse.

Irked by the narrow defeat, I organized a contest I knew I could win—swimming the farthest underwater—and beat Dickinson four laps to three, a thrashing that wiped the smirk off his face. Scott was setting up a fifty-lap race, when to my relief Karl-Heinz and Dagmar arrived with two of her *Gymnasium* classmates. Ooh-la-la. Dagmar's pure white bikini was both too brief and too tight, not that any of us objected. No, sirree. Her friends' suits were sexy as well, but they didn't bulge out of their tops and bottoms like Dagmarchen. I feasted my gaze on the girl-woman. Who can blame me as long as I've gone without romance?

When Dagmar knelt at poolside to test the temperature and unwittingly also her top's defiance of gravity, Will and I moaned. Scrawny Karl dove straight in, bless his heart, so I clambered out of the water to greet the three Fräulein, Scotty exiting close behind. Dagmar shook my hand limply like a good European and introduced her two girlfriends. Gitty—light brown hair cut short like Dagmar's, bigger-boned, two inches taller, figure less pronounced. Bärbel—the smallest of the three, jet black hair, milky blue eyes, full lips pursed in a permanent pout. No slouch either.

Scotty shook the trio's hands as well, gripping too hard American style, while Will, Tom, and Rich were shy about leaving the water. Three guesses why? At least for Burke and Hoffman. Dagmar whispered to her girlfriends that the *Amis* weren't being rude—we are naturally lax about manners.

After trying gamely to converse with the threesome and failing, Scott dove back in and showed off his powerful freestyle. Tom's semi-fluent, if non-native, German would have impressed the girls, but he kept treading water fifteen feet away, his dorky face frozen in an outsider's dumb, insinuating smile.

Gitty and Bärbel said they would also be attending the Pädagogische Hochschule, i.e. Teachers College, in Braunschweig next fall like Dagmar. I asked them about their majors, relishing every syllable of their replies and feminine gestures.

When the girls finally lowered themselves into the water, I dove in. For the next hour, we played corner tag and cavorted like otters. I was floating on my back to regain my wind, when somebody grabbed my shoulders and dunked me. I came up sputtering to find Dagmar grinning in my face. I tread water a minute to clear my lungs before slowly pursuing her while she retreated with graceful bobs. When I reached for her underwater, she set her jaw in mock outrage. I delicately grasped the knobs of her pelvic bones, giving her a chance to push me away, but she did no such thing. Man, was I turned on. Without warning I jerked her head under and held it there for a good five seconds.

"Are you crazy?" Dagmar rasped, ripping herself free, swam over to the side, and hung on through my profuse mea culpa, her appreciable chest heaving.

Such shenanigans brought such a thickening to my trunks that I rolled away and envisioned Witless Whitman to calm down. Before long, two strong hands took hold of an ankle and yanked me under. I choked and coughed and swallowed water, but the person wouldn't let go. Until adrenaline electrified my body, and I tore my leg free, thrashed to the surface, and flipped onto my back, gasping for air. The whole while that I recovered, grinning Dagmar clung to the wall, stretching her arms behind her in triumph.

"Excuse me, you two lovebirds," Hoffman shouted from poolside. "The rest of us have had enough fun for one day. Peter, if you want a ride back, you've got to leave now." I indeed had had plenty, but only for the time being. I was already scheming many happy returns. After we both voiced joking apologies, Dagmar and I exchanged *Auf Wiedersehens*, and she pressed herself close and gave me a big kiss on the cheek.

My flirting with his sister left Karl livid. To assuage his pique, I promised to ask a buddy to buy him cheap Marlboros and Jim Beam at the PX. We said goodbye by shaking hands firmly American-style.

All right! This was more like it. Thank God for Dagmar. Germany might be great duty after all.

Scotty dropped the other Monks off, and the two of us drove out to the so-called Newk House three miles south of Knittelstedt. Like every newcomer to Det Q, our first month upon arrival in Germany we had also stayed in the stucco building rented by the Army as a reception barracks, till Captain Slater decided we had passed enough inspections in a row and let us move into town. The two latest Newks had passed muster that morning and needed housing on the local economy, so Dickinson and I took them around to prospective landlords. I did the interpreting, not just translating their polite English, but making them sound downright ingratiating. By the fifth stop, they both had a room with German families in the New Settlement near the Schneiders, the lucky dogs.

Jenkins and Martello thanked me profusely, but the favor I did them was my pleasure. Before we left, I led Marty to a corner public phone booth and, to his delight, showed him how to call his brother stationed with an Armor Battalion near Fulda down south. While the two conversed, I kept an eye on the timer and dropped in coins as necessary to maintain the connection.

Though my body ached with fatigue back in my room, this was still the best I've felt over here. I dozed off to delightful memories of Dagmar's grin and heaving chest and her calling me *du*. Of course I'll ask her out. I haven't given her parents and brother any reason not to trust me. So what if she's only eighteen? I'm not that much older. Ten years from now our age difference will be insignificant. Of course I feel protective toward her. And not just because she's Karl-Heinz's sister and Frau Schneider's daughter. It's silly to feel any qualms since my intentions are nothing but honorable.

Jan. 21, 1970

Late this afternoon on my day off I ran into Dagmar at the butcher shop. She greeted me with a *Guten Tag* and a toothy grin. I purchased my usual three hundred grams of smoked ham and waited for her outside. When she emerged, I popped the big question: "Dagmar, how would you like to go to a movie with me at the local cinema?"

Talk about a smile vanishing instantly. "But I have a boyfriend," she said, namely Bernd, a student at the Federal Research Institute for Physics in Braunschweig. A guy she's known her whole life and her *Freund* of two years' standing. The news hit me like a quick left hook and a right cross. She proceeded to explain that Germans don't believing in casual dating. Either they have a serious partner or they go out with a group of friends, but never do things one-on-one with mere acquaintances. Bernd was why she would be going to the Braunschweig Teacher's College next fall and not the Free University in Berlin, despite her father's heartfelt hopes. She muttered, "*Auf Wiedersehen,*" and traipsed off, leaving me knocked out on my feet.

Who said anything about casual dating?

Jan. 22, 1970

I ran into Dagmar at the bakery today while battling a hangover. She acted embarrassed to be addressing me as *du* and became so ill at ease she turned her back on me, said, "*Tschüß,*" and hustled off. Our cavorting in the pool last Sunday seems like a vivid wet dream best forgotten.

I hear the silence of the cosmos. It doesn't speak because it has nothing to say. We humans are the only beings doing any talking. What are we, where are we, and why are we here? Where do the humanities answer these three questions? The more I steep myself in the liberal arts, the more prepared I feel for a board game testing trivial knowledge. What hibernated in Plato's cave? How did Schiller misconstrue Kant's theory of the sublime? What species of tree fell on the Austro-Hungarian author Ödon von Horvath in Paris and killed him? Which famous American Germanist died of a heart attack during intercourse with a graduate student? Why or why not? Compare and contrast. You may use more than one blue book if you wish.

How is any of this more important than memorizing the World Series lineups for the 1957 Milwaukee Braves and New York Yankees? I used to think that wisdom was the goal and knowledge the path, but now it all seems like a snarl of entrances into an exitless labyrinth.

Three years ago in Madison, I was raging at injustice and relishing every demonstration, whether it degenerated into a riot or not, and sometimes especially when it did. It was intolerable to me that mere accidents of birth made one person grow up to affluence and comfort and another to poverty and squalor. Now all that protesting seems like pushing against a glacier in a vain attempt to slow its advance. Our parents' generation might call my compromises maturing, but it feels like selling out.

Rich keeps saying our generation is transforming the world, but as much as I hope he's right, I fear he's wrong. Are we truly changing things or just blowing off steam? Don't we seek good times too much to make any lasting improvement? What difference have the two huge Moratorium marches of last October and November made? The Vietnam War goes on and on, Nixon keeps lying, the arsenal of democracy still supports a corrupt regime that wouldn't last a month without our aid, and America squares off in a generational tug-of-war, as if striving to tear itself in two.

Rich tells me I've already come a long way from little Chute Noire, Wisconsin, but I still haven't accomplished anything that counts. Except for finding a few great buddies. My desperate grip on their friendship feels white-knuckled.

Jan. 24, 1970

I just returned from a Bundeswehr firing range in the Lüneburger Heath and I'm ready to shoot Whitman. We scared the crap out of the Knittelstedt natives, departing town in four deuce-and-a-half trucks, wearing full combat gear—helmets, canteens, gas masks, and backpacks—and wielding M-16s. Wild-eyed older Germans on the marketplace square looked as scared as I bet they had when General Patton's tanks rolled up in 1945. Natives still can't comprehend why they're occupied by a warlike foreign power over whose policies they have no say, threatening another even more bellicose country over a phony border. I can't either.

Half the site qualified with the rifle today. The other half qualifies next week. I could ask Whitman a million times why Det Q bothers, and every time he would reply, "Orders." What can a person reply to such mindlessness? "Orders" is the kind of answer Nazis gave at the Nuremberg Trials. It's not a valid answer. The Allies should have hanged German war criminals by the tens of thousands, anybody who killed an unarmed civilian or POW face to face, anybody who worked in a death camp, no matter what the orders or who issued them.

Why can't the treads just accept that the Soviet Third Shock Army across the border would blow the crap out of us in seconds if war broke out? We can't defend ourselves, so why try? Besides, we're *supposed* to be a NATO tripwire, i.e. we're expendable. No one expects us to survive. Our piddling M-16s against Soviet APCs, tanks, mobile artillery, and rockets? Come on! Why did I ever let myself become a soldier?

I keep mulling over the same arguments but never make any progress. I'm far from a pacifist or a conscientious objector—of course it was immoral not to fight the Nazis—and I didn't want to emigrate or go to prison or Vietnam, so what was the alternative but to enlist? If accepting this mission in West Germany wasn't the right thing to do, then what was? Still, my expediency mortifies me.

I had been planning my life ever since my fifth grade teacher, Miss Healy, explained what my family's poverty meant for my future. If I was ever going to college, I would have to earn top grades and win scholarships. I promised her I would, starting immediately, and I never let her down. Not yet. After earning my master's degree, I was all set to keep chugging along for a doctorate, when the Vietnam War derailed me. Untold young Americans like me lost control of their lives to feed the Pentagon's hunger for cannon fodder, and so far I've been luckier than many.

Which is more terrifying? Panning out to a cosmic perspective that reduces us humans to miniscule creatures inhabiting an insignificant spot of cosmic dust or zooming in for a close-up? Who can stand either one?

To hell with my reading list. I'm off to Club 69 for a *Bierchen*. Or two or three. After a stiff scotch.

Why do I neglect to mention the perverse joy I felt in emptying two clips on automatic into human-shaped targets at a hundred meters? The first clip climbed on me from the recoil, but the second one I held on a head until I blew it off. I am an M-16 Zapster.

Jan. 25, 1970

I hardly got back to sleep after another nightmare jolted me awake. I dreamt I was in the eighth grade back home in Chute Noire. My junior high classmates and I were anxiously sitting before the judge's bench on the third floor of the unusually stuffy courthouse despite the open windows, awaiting a spelling bee to decide who would represent Lincoln County at the state competition in Madison. "Where are we supposed to go if we miss a word?" I asked.

Rolf Stein pointed out an open, unscreened window.

Nobody laughed.

I lasted until the final three, when I misspoke, giving "foreigner" an unnecessary "h," and had to sit down. Even though I knew the word full well. Some errors can't be taken back.

In the dream our principal, Mr. Wagner, patted me on the shoulder and said I had done my best, bullshit consolation for losers. Even as a kid, I never gave a crap about merely doing my best, not when *the* best is all that counts. Suddenly I sprinted for an open window, dove straight out it, and hurtled for what felt like minutes till I hit a white-capped ocean far below and surfaced in my Knittelstedt bed, soaked head to toe in sweat and gasping for air.

Jan. 26, 1970

Why are we Monks so close? To explain that I'd have to tell you everything that happened in Monterey, where we saved each other's butts again and again. Bakken kept Toddhunter off my trail both times I defaced the CO's sign, even when he nearly got nailed himself. The second instance the other Monks lied on my behalf as well. My Russian tutoring kept Burke from flunking himself into Eleven Bravo and combat duty in Vietnam. Hoffman was poised to get us to Sweden, if the threatened orders for Nam had in fact come down. Each one of us is fricking alive and well today thanks to buddies.

Feb. 1, 1970

I couldn't bring myself to write anything of late, and I've haven't read much either. But I did look up all the unfamiliar German words I had come across the last few months, because that requires less concentration. I had underlined them in texts and written their page numbers on inside back covers. Hundreds of definitions now fill two small spiral notebooks that I carry to the site and review during slack stretches.

Right now I can't find an author that holds my attention, certainly not among the modern Austrians like Hermann Broch, Robert Musil, or Heimito von Doderer. But I can't skip them or any other works on my doctoral reading list.

Feb. 2, 1970

I should be pleased with the special treatment we Russian lingies get. After all, we're just an adjunct to Det Q's main mission as US intelligence support for the British Army of the Rhine—NATO's principal line of defense up north here against the Soviet Third Shock Army. But then again it only takes two good glances there to know whose work counts the most—ours. We can enter anybody else's area, but only sixteen can enter the Green Room that conceals the stolen Russian radio, and that doesn't include every tread, not even Whitman.

Sergeant Witless gets back at us, whenever the SPETSNAZ units are quiet. Then all but a skeleton crew is reassigned to him, and he makes a point of showing us "what it means to be a real soldier." He really seems benighted for screwing us over and then begrudging us our resentment.

If we underlings and the Soviet enlisted men could only frag each other's treads, we'd end the Cold War overnight. Those guys aren't all that different from us. What does Vanya say to his buddy Sasha over the SPETSNAZ radio? "Have I ever got a hangover." Or—"Is your *khui* erect, too?" They're not speaking in code. Such clear-text chatter tells me they're lonely, horny young guys far from home, trained under duress to fight an enemy who's not really a foe. Sound familiar?

Last week those poor Soviet bastards had to don protective suits and trek across a meadow fogged with poisonous gas. Don't even bother asking whether we'd use such an immoral weapon against them. Our treads keep saying the troops we're monitoring are elite soldiers, expert saboteurs, and professional cutthroats, but none of us have heard a thing from the likes of Vanya, Sasha, Kolya or Sergei to back this claim up.

It's foolish of me to write all this classified material down, but no one will ever see this, except perhaps another Monk.

Feb. 3, 1970

Scotty's idea of playing cards at Club 69 was well-intended, because sitting off-duty alone in this room, sipping schnaps and struggling to read, had gotten worse than shifts at the site. It was so cold in the unheated library upstairs that we had to keep our field jackets on, but nobody minded. We were used to the chilliness from watching movies next door. To start off, Rich, Tom, Scott, and I worked on a six-pack of Beck's purchased downstairs and chatted, while Will insisted on finishing *The Scarlet Letter*.

"Your first novel, Burke?" Rich asked.

"Hardly, my good man. Perhaps my one thousandth. I've never counted."

"Can a person win prizes for so much mind-fucking? You know, for mental masturbation? Do you get warts on your brain?"

"Mind-fucking indeed. What does that obscene barbarism mean, young Hoffman?"

"It means you like to fuck your mind. You use your head to play with yourself. How clear do I have to make it, man? You been smokin' some Colombian?"

"I will pretend I did not hear you refer to that which would mean automatic loss of our security clearances and re-assignment to combat arms."

"Refer to *what*?" Rich said. "I never refer to anything. I just say it."

"What, pray tell, was your major?"

"Sociology."

"I should have guessed."

"How about some serious mind-fucking?" I piped up. "Let's choose mindfucker of the year. The award goes to whoever answers these three questions—what are we, where are we, and why are we here?"

"What do you mean by 'we'?" Scotty asked.

"Homo sapiens of course," I replied.

"The answers are easy, Zielsdorf," Will said, looking up from his novel. "Have you forgotten your Christianity?" His mouth was smiling, though his dark eyes gaped like black holes.

"Do you really believe those pat answers?"

"Yes," Will replied without conviction.

"Far out, Peter," Rich said with a giggle. "'Why are we here?' I love it."

"Excellent passage," Will said, starring another paragraph with his ballpoint. "What graceful diction." Burke was cutting a handsome profile that day, except when he bared his upper teeth to deliver another pronouncement. "Don't you agree this is the best American novel, Zielsdorf?"

"It's a good story. With the realism and morality of a fairy tale. I like fairy tales."

Scotty let out a whinnying giggle, and Rich touched an index finger to the tip of his tongue and traced a check mark in the air. Tommy just sat there in solemn silence.

"Are you implying, young Zielsdorf," Will said, "that you prefer carrion eaters like Theodore Dreiser?"

"Yes."

"But Dreiser's diction is dreadful."

"So is Thomas Hardy's. Yet he and Dreiser are far greater novelists than Hawthorne."

"Such middlebrow tastes you have, Zielsdorf."

"Dreiser's far more progressive than Hawthorne," Rich said.

"Pray tell," Will asked, "what do you mean by progress?"

"'Progress' is change for the better," Rich told him.

"Hear, hear. How profound," Will mocked. "Now I know exactly what is meant."

"Our generation will change the entire world," Rich went on.

"I don't accept your definition of 'our,'" Will replied, starring another passage.

"Okay, guys, back to earth," Scotty said. "What are your plans after our discharge? Have you decided upon a career? Tommy, you first."

Bakken tried to beg off, but finally answered, "I want to be a professor. And teach linguistics or Russian. Or comp lit."

"Where? Harvard, Yale? How about Stanford?"

"Hardly," he replied. "At a decent liberal arts college if I'm lucky."

"Me, I want to teach English Renaissance history," Scotty said. "At a great public university. Such as Michigan or Berkeley."

Will put down his novel. "I'd settle for being a Sovietologist at Harvard. Or a newspaper correspondent abroad."

Rich pretended to gag and turned expectantly toward me.

"At the very least," I said, "I want to become a great professor."

"In what field?"

"It doesn't matter. German literature most likely."

Only Scotty laughed.

"What else do you want from life?" Rich asked.

"Everything, except money and power. I plan to pursue knowledge until I can make a substantial contribution toward progress. Then I want due recognition for the achievement. But, above all, I want to experience life. Again and again I want to enjoy moments so beautiful that if I could make any of them last forever I would."

"Maybe you should just settle for money and power," Scotty quipped, an irksome remark.

"Man, you guys are weird," Rich said. "None of you mention other people. Like, you're the only ones in your lives. Progress means helping the human race, if it means anything. You make me think nothing at all has changed."

"What are your plans then, Rich?" Scotty asked.

"I plan on a happy life. I'll succeed better than any of you."

"What about graduate school?" I asked.

"Might as well use my veterans' benefits for something. I'll study Fuck-off-ology. Maybe get a doctorate in it and teach it at Podunk U. You'll be there, too, so we maybe can have lunch together at the Faculty Club."

Such sarcasm got my goat. I jumped up to bolt for home, but in light of the dreariness awaiting me there, I sat back down. "We're playing Euchre," I announced, ripping the cellophane off Dickinson's new deck.

"Never heard of it," Scotty said.

"Then you had a deprived upbringing." I succinctly explained the four-player, trick-taking game. Partners sat opposite each other. Twenty-four cards, nines through aces. The jack of trump and the jack of the same color, called the Right and Left Bowers, were the two highest in rank, followed by the ace, king, queen, ten, and nine of trump. The goal each deal was for the declarers to win at least three of five possible tricks, thereby scoring a point. Two points, if they took all of them. The defenders themselves scored two points, if they won at least three of the tricks, known as "setting" or "euchring" the declarers. Everybody caught on fast except for Will, who preferred to keep on reading, which was fine with me since only four could play Euchre at a time.

I taught Tom nothing new, it being *the* card game of Wisconsin, which he had been playing since junior high. I asked whether he minded using the Double Euchre rule, by which a player going alone, i.e. without his partner, scored four points by taking all five tricks. Though if that individual got euchred, that is, failed to win at least three tricks, the defenders received those four points.

Tom said this variation unknown to Hoyle was the only way he had ever played.

"The four undealt cards each hand make it more a game of luck than skill," Dickinson muttered. "Let's play Bridge instead."

"The skill is in stretching your luck," I snapped. "In the long run the better players win no matter how the deals happen."

Scotty yielded to my glare with an easy grin. He and Bakken agreed to pair off against Hoffman and me. After I demonstrated several hands face up to teach strategy, Rich and I won the first game to ten in six quick hands, my making all five tricks going alone twice scoring eight of those. The second game they out-pointed us ten to nine on mediocre hands all around, winning their last three orders on minimal trump, while Rich and I sat by helplessly.

"The skill is in stretching your luck," Dickinson teased. I wasn't amused.

Scott and Tom took the first point of the rubber game, but Hoffman and I came back for the next seven, as twice I got lucky that Rich was good for two of the three necessary tricks. Like all good Euchre players, I was sometimes making orders on near garbage. In a very rare display of temper, Tommy snapped at Scotty, "You don't always need a Bower to order, even without the deal. We can't score if we don't order, so take more chances."

"Not true," Scotty told him. "You score points twice as fast by euchring the other guys. So you can win on defense." To prove his point, he euchred our next two questionable bids, and they pulled close to us at seven to five. Everybody passed on Dickinson's next deal.

After doling out the requisite twenty cards, Rich flipped over the Queen of Spades. Three passes later he turned it down. Three further passes and Hoffman named Diamonds trump. I dropped the King of diamonds on Tom's lead Ace of hearts. Giggling, Scott outtrumped me with the Ace and threw down the two Bowers for another easy Euchre to tie the score. I flung my cards on the table. "Four damned trump between us and we couldn't make the point?" I grumbled.

"I had the three highest trump," Scotty said with that infuriating giggle.

"We know, asshole," I replied.

Two more deals without anybody willing to bid. Then Scotty turned up the Ace of Diamonds, and we all passed. And Rich and Tom did a second time. Holding both black Bowers and the Ace, King, and Queen of Hearts, I chose to go alone in Spades, eager to end it all with this hand. Tom cleverly led the nine of Trump, which I was obliged to take with the jack of Clubs. When I played my slough ace, Scotty followed suit, but Tommy trumped it with the ten. Bakken came back with the queen of trumps, which I had to take with the Right Bower. Tom thereupon trumped my king, too, and walked his Ace of Clubs for their third trick and a Double Euchre, giving them four points, the game, and the match.

"Outfuckingstanding!" Scotty squealed.

I glared at him.

"The skill is in stretching your luck," Scotty taunted one too many times.

I clenched my fists. "Mellow out, Zielsdorf," Rich told me. "You don't have to win at absolutely everything."

At my favorite game I do. The bastards only won because I was too reckless in going without a partner. To hell with any more card playing.

Feb. 5, 1970

To hell with the treads, too. I won't yield another inch. I've compromised my ideals far enough. I refuse to keep swallowing all the crap they dish out. Look what happened to that sorry trainee from St. Louis in Basic Combat Training the night before graduation. One punch sufficed to knock the bastard on his butt. The candy-striper was insisting I pitch in a quarter to buy our puke CO a bottle of Scotch as a farewell present. Contributing to a gift for a prime tormenter? Hell no! I won't live long enough to forgive that bastard lieutenant for breaking his walking stick on my helmet or kicking my thighs to force more pushups out of me. My hand felt broken for days after that right cross, but that was a small price to pay.

Losing sleep in Madison to finish term papers never got to me like this. That was my choice then, and, above all, it served a good purpose—I did get all A's, I did win scholarships, I did build toward a future. But what am I accomplishing now? I'm greasing an unspeakably evil war machine. I'm compromising my every ideal. I'm betraying my very being to the treads' immoral goals.

Feb. 9, 1970

I met her. Finally.

I feel like I'm doing backwards somersaults at my kitchen table. I haven't felt this dizzily happy since my very first romance back in high school. There's too much to say to record only as fast as I can write, but I'll try. First of all, I want to thank the universe that my life has unfolded this gloriously.

Her name is Katja Wendt. Kah-tya. Vent. By birth Katharina Wendt. What a beautiful name! She grew up in West Berlin, where she attended the venerable Freie Universität. After dropping out and working a few years as a research assistant in Stuttgart, she's back in school at the Braunschweig Teachers College to become a *Gymnasium* instructor like Karl-Heinz.

We're a perfect match. I can hardly believe my fantastic luck in meeting her. All because I took up Karl-Heinz's offer to visit his old haunts in Braunschweig. Last Friday night he picked me up, and we drove on down in his old diesel Mercedes and began our pub crawl along the Old City's cobblestone Altmarktplatz. The funky student bars were all lively, but Karl saved the best for last, Zum Grünen Kakadu—At the Sign of the Green Cockatoo.

He led me to a thick, unpainted wooden door I wouldn't have noticed strolling past. It opened with a creak, and we pushed our way through coarse, musty woolen blankets, hanging overlapped to keep out the cold. The scene inside startled me. Instead of another dim, smoky room crammed with students in denims, cords, turtlenecks, and ratty jackets, everybody was dressed in *Fasching*, i.e. Mardi Gras, garb—clowns, chimney sweeps, firemen, sailors, doctors, nurses, princes, princesses, knights, serfs, angels, and witches. I grabbed Karl by the shoulder. "Let's go someplace else. We're not in costume."

"Nonsense," he replied. "I'll make us fit in." We hustled back to his car, where he scrounged up two masks from the trunk and slipped a freezing rubber one on me in the darkness. A bit tipsy from the beer already downed, I trusted Karl-Heinz's judgment that it would do. Did it ever.

Guffaws and shouts greeted us upon our return. I had to laugh myself, when I saw that Karl was the Devil. But who was I? Whoever I was, people welcomed me raucously.

We wound our way among the tiny flat-topped stone tables furnished with wooden-barrel chairs. We had just halted for Little Red Riding Hood and her Wolf's dart game, when an alto voice behind us purred, "Karlchen."

I faced a blonde fairy princess dressed all in white, holding a magic wand in one hand and a glass of golden wine in the other. An iridescent silver mask concealed her brows, nose and cheekbones, but not a finely chiseled jaw and delectable mouth. Beside her sat a green-skinned witch, all in black with a long, crooked nose and dark caps on two front teeth.

"Karlchen, don't you recognize us?" the fairy princess asked in German.

"Katja!" Karl-Heinz squealed. "Uschi!" he added with even more enthusiasm. He ducked under the dart trajectory, gave each a limp handshake, and motioned me over. "This is my American friend, President Richard Nixon," he said, at last revealing my costume to me. Katja laughed like tinkling bells. I shook their hands, Uschi's warm and moist, Katja's cool and dry.

"It's an honor to meet a princess and a witch," I said in my best High German.

Both women giggled. "Actually, we're both witches," Katja told me with a flirtatious tilt of her head. "But who are you really?" My eyes zeroed in on her exquisitely chiseled mouth, the lower lip sensuously full, the thinner upper lip rising to a bee-stung dip in the middle. Her gray-blue, yellow-flecked eyes sparkled under the harsh, overhead light.

"Pay-tuh Tseelss-dorrf," Karl-Heinz carefully enunciated my name. "He lives in Knittelstedt. Didn't I tell you about him?"

Slyly grinning, Katja scrutinized me. Tickling me under my rubber chin, she teased, "Would you kindly remove your mask a moment?" Her addressing me with the familiar *du* felt like a caress.

"If you remove yours, too," I said, and her grin widened. I pulled mine off, and she looked pleased by what she saw. "Your turn."

She carefully doffed her silver mask, and I found myself face to face with the prettiest woman I've ever met. I was sorry to see her disguise slip back on.

Karl plopped down on the wooden barrel next to Uschi, so I shyly took the one beside Katja. He ordered us two Becks and asked about their costumes. Katja explained she was Glinda, the Good Witch of the North, and Uschi the Wicked Witch of the West. Karl-Heinz didn't recognize the characters, so Katja told him about *The Wizard of Oz*, amazing me with her knowledge of the American film. She explained how the three of them knew each other from classes together at the Teachers College and had kept in touch since Karl had passed the state exam and begun to teach.

While he and Katja chatted about her courses, Ursula spoke with me in the Oxford English that most Germans learn as the world standard, though her "th's" were mostly "z's." She asked what part of Germany I was from.

"He's a native American," Katja said with a cackle. I still couldn't place her German accent.

The bad witch, Uschi, looked perplexed. "But you appear like one of us," she said in awkward English.

"In a way I am," I told her. "Since I'm German-American." I explained that my grandparents in Wisconsin never did learn proper English, and my mother still prefers German. Until World War Two, that language got you farther in my little hometown than English. My generation was the first among relatives to truly become American, though all of us still speak at least a little German.

"You do not seem very American," Katja said, as fascinated by my mouth as I was by hers.

"Living anyplace else I'd feel in exile," I replied.

"You're not like the other *Amis* over here anyway," she said. "The soldiers, I mean." Her pink, moist lips mesmerized me.

I refrained from mentioning I was a GI, too, and she didn't ask. If she had, I was prepared to lead her astray to protect Det Q's special, highly classified mission. She felt no such reluctance in asking about my family, and no matter how much I told her she was eager to hear more. I said it was just my mother and me now, implying my father was dead and not mentioning how modestly we had lived. A brother had died at two, but we never talked about him, so I didn't now, instead claiming I was an only child. I added that my aunts and uncles and their children were no longer in contact with us outside of weddings and funerals. They had all settled much farther north in Wisconsin, around Rhinelander, and I hadn't even met all of my first cousins. Every detail seemed to fascinate her.

My studies interested Katja even more. I told her about the University of Wisconsin in Madison and the languages I'd learned. She asked me to say something in Russian, so I said, "*Ty samaya bol'shaya krasavetsa vo vsei Germanii.*"

Acting touched, she asked me to translate.

"You are the greatest beauty in all of Germany."

"*Selbstverständlich*—of course," she said with a cheeky smirk.

Slurping beer through my rubber mask's mouth slit wasn't easy, but I kept at it while Karl entertained us with hilarious anecdotes about his *Gymnasium* colleagues and pupils in

Knittelstedt. Katja's furtive glances my way made me yearn to grab her on the spot.

Upon Karl's suggestion, we left Zum grünen Kakadu for some fresh air. At minus four degrees Celsius—twenty-five Fahrenheit—the air was a mite too fresh even for this Wisconsin boy. Karl kept chattering nonsense to distract the women from the chill. Katja and I lagged behind, jostling elbows and shoulders. In low, private tones she told me more about her five semesters at the Freie Universität in West Berlin, where she had studied English and German literature. She had dropped out of school before her state exam to follow Hans, a man she had known for years and wanted to marry, when he landed a research position at a Stuttgart institute. At first they got along great, until their bourgeois lifestyle gradually began to annoy her. Sexy though he might be, Hans was still a classic patriarch, striving to bring her under his thumb. He even wanted her to forget about a career and do nothing but stay home and raise kids. Could I see her as a *Hausfrau*?

Well, no.

After they split, she went back to school with new resolve to qualify for teaching at a *Gymnasium*. She wanted to do at least a little good on a small scale somewhere, even if she couldn't make the gigantic difference she had once dreamed of. How about me?

I shrugged, scarcely believing my astounding good fortune in meeting so intriguing a woman.

Karl and Ursula climbed into the front of his Mercedes, while Katja and I slid into the rear. The old vehicle was slow to heat up, so Katja snuggled her legs flush with mine, saying, "May I please warm myself against you?"

"*Selbstverständlich,*" I replied and pulled her closer. I took off my mask, and she removed hers, revealing a stunning silhouette in the dim light. I dared to touch her chin with my fingertips and gently nudge it toward me. Slowly her delicate mouth, flashing in and out of the darkness with the oncoming cars' headlights, faced mine. I inhaled her sweet, piney aroma and kissed her exquisitely soft lips, while we bounced and lurched down the Old City's narrow, twisting cobblestone streets. I slipped a hand under her sweater, where it found warm, hard-tipped flesh. "*Trägst du keinen BH*?"

"I don't need a bra," she said without embarrassment and opened her lips to meet my tongue for the most beautiful kiss of my life. Her teeth nipped my chin and cheek and neck and ear, and I ached to devour her headfirst.

The side windows fogged up, as Karl-Heinz sped toward the outskirts of Braunschweig. At a stoplight Katja's angular facial bones appeared almost Slavic. I asked where her family was from, and she told me about peasant Sorb ancestors in Mecklenburg, now part of East Germany. The Sorbs were a tiny ethnic group within Prussia related to the Poles, their enclave long since fully assimilated, leaving only traces of their Slavism in the names of families and towns. Her relatives had moved to Berlin last century, when Wilhelm the First was Kaiser to join the "urban proletariat." I chuckled at her Marxist jargon, so beloved by West German students, whatever their politics.

"I could tell right off you were a Prussian, too," she whispered between kisses.

"How?"

"Your look, your manner." I felt flattered.

Karl steered onto a soft road in total darkness and announced we were in the suburb of Riddagshausen's nature conservation area. We parked on a stretch of causeway hidden among a stand of firs. Karl took Uschi for a stroll along the dike, while Katja and I lingered in the back seat. I gently tugged her down alongside me, and we entwined our legs and squeezed our bodies close. I already knew then that she had to become my wife. From inches away I stared at her gorgeous face, scarcely believing my eyes.

"It's me," she whispered. "It's Katja." Kah-tya. She chewed on my lips and tongue, and I fondled her breasts. But when I reached under the hem of her dress, she bolted upright and suggested we go for a walk. I slammed the door.

We headed fifty feet up the dike away from Karl-Heinz and Uschi, both of us coatless in the freezing air, clinging to each other wherever we could grab hold. We stepped between two prickly evergreens, and she kissed me again with her entire mouth and unzipped my pants. Her hot tongue and frigid fingers sought me out and stirred a thirst a mighty river couldn't slake.

"Come on! Uschi has to get back!" Karl-Heinz shouted from the car a few deft strokes too soon.

"Later, Peterchen," Katja promised. I zipped myself back up, gnashing my teeth.

While Uschi snuggled close, Karl-Heinz took his time cruising back into town, and Katja and I spread out again in the back seat. At the touch of my lips the tip of her tongue met mine. If any moment of my life were to last forever, this was a prime candidate.

"How do you like to spend your free time?" she whispered, unzipping me again and grabbing hold. Not being able to take her on the spot was torture.

I told her about my doctoral reading program, which fascinated her. Propping her elbows against my chest, she asked about my favorite authors. Some of Kleist, I answered, all of Büchner, and most of Goethe. And, oh yes, Schnitzler.

"Goethe is boring," she replied matter-of-factly. I chuckled at her cheekiness. The Shakespeare of German literature boring? "Büchner is an obvious choice for any progressive," she went on, "but Kleist I wouldn't have predicted. Despite his irrationality, he's still one of Germany's best. Forget about Schnitzler. He's a shallow psychologizer."

"*Penthesilea* is my favorite Kleist play," I said, enjoying her unusual, original assessments.

Her stare locked on mine in the moonlight, and her nostrils flared. "Who do you like that's more modern?"

"Martin Walser, Hermann Kant, and Günter Grass. And Heinrich Böll."

"Kant?" she asked in disbelief. In the glare of a passing car I detected a hint of laugh lines. So what if she's a little older than me?

She insisted Kant was playing it both ways, still living in East Germany, but not truly loyal. Walser wasn't bad, but she had little time for Grass or Böll. Grass's style was unique, but he kept repeating himself. She much preferred Bertolt Brecht and Brechtianer dramatists like Heiner Müller and Peter Hacks. For her, literature had to be "civic," as the Russians put it, that is, esthetically pleasing and socially useful. Brecht excelled at this.

"Who's more repetitive than dear Brecht?" I countered and kissed her nose. Brecht I had never liked or found profound. He wrote as if he knew all the answers, which meant he was either ignorant or stupid.

Suddenly Karl-Heinz hit the brakes so hard we almost rolled onto the floor. Hammering the horn, he cursed the other driver, honking just as loudly.

"What do you want out of life, Peterchen?" Katja asked, crawling back into my embrace.

"To prove myself."

"Prove what?"

"My worth."

She guffawed. "But you are an adult. Don't you realize that yet? Look within and ask if what you see is worthwhile. What do you contribute to human progress? To the lives of others? Follow your conscience, and it will force you to be worthy. Your problem is that you don't accept yourself for what you already are. It's okay to be Peter Zielsdorf."

That remark struck where it hurt. Adrenaline spurted, and I sat up. "Where would I be today if I had just accepted myself as I was when I graduated from tiny Chute Noire High School? I've *never* accepted myself for what I am. And look where it's gotten me? Here I am talking to you."

She laughed again. "Calm down, Peterchen. I'm on your side. But your ambition is misguided. You truly are okay now."

"Ha! I've hardly begun. If I had just accepted myself as I was back then, I wouldn't have gone to college at all, much less gotten a master's. I wouldn't have learned Russian in Monterey.

In fact, my butt would be in Vietnam right now, and I couldn't even consider becoming a professor."

"And you wouldn't be stationed over here," Katja said, leaning close and caressing my cheek. Between kisses, she told me about growing up in Berlin, claiming there was little in her life worth mentioning till she got her *Abitur* at nineteen and became a "wild leftist" at the Freie Universität. We both had to laugh at that. More recently, she said she has gotten more spiritual in approaching life's problems. "Perhaps I am maturing."

Karl brought his diesel Mercedes to a stop and walked Uschi to her door, while Katja and I lay in the back seat. "To relax, I love listening to serious music such as Bach," she said, "especially while reading good fiction. Lately, Zola."

Though I vehemently disapproved, I calmly explained my preference for reading in total silence, so that nothing interfered with the music of the prose or the images it alone evoked. Adding Bach made it mixed media, another genre entirely separate from literature, one without tradition or depth.

"Pay-dahnt," she called me, the German pronunciation of *Pedant*, and tweaked my nose. All of a sudden I lost control and pulled back her coat and slipped her dress off her shoulders and exposed dark nipples that I sucked on till she moaned. I yanked her dress up to her waist, tugged off her panties, lowered my slacks, and was about to roll onto her, when Uschi's front door opened and Karl-Heinz emerged.

We tore our clothes back on, while I cursed in English and German. "What should I do with this?" I asked, holding up her panties. She stuffed it into her jacket pocket.

"Do you ever regret not finishing your studies in Berlin?" I was saying as Karl hopped back in.

"No, because I didn't like where I was headed," she replied, her tone turning earnest. "It felt right to leave, so I went with the feeling. One feels trapped there, you know. It's like an island."

What about her lover Hans, the patriarch? Had she already forgotten telling me about him? It was odd that a student bright enough for the Freie Universität in Berlin would now settle for the Teachers College in Braunschweig. Not that I minded whatsoever. No, indeed, not when what I really wanted was to sink my teeth into her thighs. I made do with her lips and tongue. She nipped back, as I reveled in holding not only the most attractive woman I had ever met, but the brightest and most fascinating as well. From an inch away, I pored over her beautiful face and shuddered at the unreality of it all. "It's me, Katja," she whispered and kissed me gently.

Karl careered across the Old City and screeched to a halt beside an old gray VW Bug, Katja's car.

She and I got out, and I pressed her hard against the driverside door. "When can I see you again?"

She slipped her gloveless hands inside my parka and hugged me close. "Soon."

"How about next weekend?"

"*Nein*, Peter. I must finish my seminar paper."

That cool response took me aback. "When then?"

"I'll write you. Your Knittelstedt address is Bismarckstrasse 33, correct?"

"*Ja*," I said, though I didn't recall mentioning that detail. I made her promise not to tell Karl that we're seeing each other. Because no one else in Knittelstedt must ever learn she even exists.

Katja reacted with an oddly distracted smile and a trace of unease. Because as much was at stake for her as for me, I surmised.

After a parting embrace so tender I teared up, she climbed into her car. "What about your address?" I shouted, but she was already driving off.

Karl-Heinz hustled us to the room rented by his sister's boyfriend, Bernd, visiting Knittelstedt for the weekend to see Dagmar. There I curled up on a throw rug next to a black pot belly wood stove, for once unable to sleep because I was too elated. With every breath I inhaled Katja's piney scent, her smiling face dancing before my closed eyes, her tinkling-bell laughter echoing into the silence of the night. What if Karl and I had skipped Zum grünen Kakadu? What if Katja had left before we arrived? Then our paths would never have crossed, and my life would have taken an entirely different course. A sense of humble gratitude overwhelms me and without reasoning why I fold my hands and stretch them toward the sky and express my most heartfelt thanks.

Feb. 12, 1970

I sit at the site, shuffling papers, but only see, hear, and smell Katja everywhere. This humdrum reality pales beside the blazing glory of recent memories. I can't wait to be discharged so I can resume my civilian life with her at my side. She'll make me the perfect partner no matter what I do or where I end up.

This all really happened! I swear it! I never expected to find anyone with Katja's good looks, joie de vivre, and natural earthiness—so different from how I was raised. But I've done it. She's bright and cheery and idealistic, even more so than Rich. And that silky, alto voice, that gorgeous face, and that slender figure—I would be satisfied with so much less.

I'd love to have the other Monks meet her, but of course don't dare. Because of Det Q's rule that no GI is allowed a close relationship with a foreign national.

It's amazing how little Whitman and the other treads now annoy me. For days Sergeant Witless has been storming around the site demanding more production and ranting about Nixon's so-called Vietnamization. "The ARVN can never win the war on their own!" he bellows. "It's all a ploy to hide the betrayal of our South Vietnamese allies. We're leaving them at the mercy of the communists." So what? Pukes like him can't touch me anymore. They could pile duty rosters of shit as high as our antenna tower, and I'd cheerfully shovel a convoy of deuces-and-a-half full of the crap.

How could I care about politics after meeting Katja? Besides, worrying about it in the past has only made me miserable. Whatever else I do from now on—and of course it'll be with Katja—I am determined to concentrate on my best skills, namely foreign languages, especially *Deutsch*. I could teach German ably and perhaps add a couple of insights to the potpourri of aperçus that the cognoscenti call the History of German Literature. Why couldn't I dig up some forgotten third-rate writer from a sexy era like the Weimar Republic and tout him to other second-rate literary bureaucrats and so establish myself as a Fellow Scholar? There are less noble paths toward a share of the glory out there, even if I don't contribute much—or even anything—toward mankind's progress. Hey, I knew full well that literary criticism exercises the intellect as a hand does one's manhood, in the hopes that when the time comes for real work it'll be up to the task, but so what? What isn't a grand idea with Katja at my side?

I was fortunate to be gone from the site last weekend. A private from an East German motorized rifle regiment defected by slipping through a gap in the Iron Curtain. Interrogation revealed his unit was moving out, and it wasn't on exercise. To be safe Whitman telexed SACEUR and the Pentagon, and all of NATO ended up on alert for forty-eight hours. Finally, Captain Slater had the guts to admit the private was bullshitting us to make himself sound important, and everybody relaxed. Wouldn't it have been easy for leaders on either side to have misread the other and attacked in self-defense, bringing down Armageddon?

I know Katja won't write this week, but I bet she will the next, so I'll see her in about ten days. It'll be a long wait, but I'll grin my way through it.

Feb. 13, 1970

Was I nice enough to her? I don't think I impressed enough upon her how much she means to me. Next time it'll just be her and me, no Karl-Heinz, no Ursula. Every night joyful dreams sweeten my sleep, and I lay awake reliving our every kiss and caress, dozing off and on to memories of her touch and taste and smell.

Will asked at trick change today whether I had undergone a religious conversion. He doesn't recognize me anymore. My upbeat mood changes my whole face.

I shrugged, suppressing laughter.

Lately, Tommy is smiling slyly at me, too, and Rich greets me with a conspiratorial grin. Of course I can't tell a Monk or anybody else one word about Katja, so I'll just have to keep writing everything down here.

Tomorrow I'm going to the Valentine's Day party at Club 69.

Feb. 15, 1970

My head is swollen double and my eyes burn, but I'm laughing to myself in this tiny, cold apartment. Katja and I will go on trips together. We'll hike in the Harz and picnic on the Lüneburger Heath, visit Thomas and Heinrich Mann's homes and haunts in Lübeck, and swim in the Baltic Sea. And every evening go to bed early—and barely sleep.

Last night's Club 69 party was the best one yet. Since all five of us Monks had the evening off for a change, we went out to dinner together first at the local Ratskeller. We were just finishing, when Rich piped up, assuming Gospodin Markov's voice and accent, "Before we move on to party, let me give honors for the great achievements at DLI. New Russian verbs have been coined from your names. You will join the Hooker and the Crapper as undying words in major living language. Gospodin Burke, in your honor we have created new Russian verb, *Burkovat'*. It means to prefer fucking own mind to flesh and blood women."

We all laughed, Will as heartily as any of us. "Second meaning of verb," Rich went on, "is to have seventy-year-old mind in twenty-four-year-old body." This time Burke wasn't so gleeful.

"Gospodin Bakken, in your honor, we now have new verb *Bakkenovat'*. It means to sit motionless, watching the world pass by, and to take notes. Gospodin Bakken, you have achieved impossible. You have defied Heisenberg's Uncertainty Principle, major tenet of the modern science. You can observe universe and not disturb it, neither for better or worse."

Everyone roared even harder than over *Burkovat'*, including Tommy, though the remark obviously stung.

"Gospodin Dickinson, in your honor, we have *Dikinsonovat'*. It means to shout radical slogans on way from frat house to golf course." Will squealed like a stuck pig. Dickinson's grin was pained.

"Gospodin Zielsdorf, for you we have *Zijlzdorfovat'*, which means to study incessantly. There is no perfective aspect because action is never completed." I howled as much as anybody, since the would-be jibe was in fact a compliment.

"Related verb, *Preuzijlzdorfovat'*, means to transcribe five-hundred-word Russian dictation and afterwards comment, 'I think my only misspelling was an 'a' for an unstressed 'o.'" I bent double with laughter. More flattery. Man, what was Hoffman on?

At Club 69, a smalltime British rock group on a tour of American bases was doing a set of Rolling Stones tunes. After a few beers, all of us—excluding of course Tommy—danced with Dagmar, Gitty, and Bärbel. The three Fräulein, along with Karl-Heinz and Bernd, joined us at our table, where Bakken had switched to drinking whiskey straight. And out of a beer mug at that.

In German, Karl-Heinz asked whether I had heard from "her." Tommy's ears perked up. None of the other Monks understood the language well enough.

"Are you kidding, Karl?" I replied *auf Deutsch*. "Things didn't go anywhere with what's-her-name. I'm still on the prowl."

Karl screwed up his eyes. I followed him into the john, locked the door, and said I wouldn't look up Katja again, because GIs at Det Q weren't allowed close relationships with German women. I begged him never to mention my meeting her that once to anyone, not even Dagmar. And if Frau Hecht or Bernd ever asked about Katja, he should say she had been his guest, and not mine.

Karl-Heinz good-naturedly agreed and asked whether I might get him some cheap Marlboros and Jim Beam again from our PX. It's illegal as hell, but I agreed.

Before I finished my business, Scotty lurched into the john, jostling Karl on his way out. "Why so long-faced?" I asked Dickinson. He had hardly said six words all night.

"Bad news from Beth," he muttered, referring to the Ohio State coed he had met while home on leave after Monterey. We knew Scotty had been counting on her visiting here this summer, but her last letter said she wouldn't be coming. Apparently, she thought it best to break things off now before they got more deeply involved. Because they were too different, no matter how attracted to each other.

The royal kiss-off, in other words. I felt bad for my buddy. I could never stand such a rejection from Katja.

I asked to hear more about Beth, so Scotty obliged. She's a native of Worthington, Ohio, just north of his hometown, Columbus. He adores everything about her, from her cute wire-rims and waist-length black hair to her quick wit and ready smile. They even share the same favorite books—*The Lord of the Rings* and *The Once and Future King*.

"So how are you two incompatible?"

"She can't see herself as a professor's wife. Now don't laugh, but she wants to live out in the country and raise goats and chickens and grow vegetables. And never again live even near any big city."

I couldn't help laughing out loud. Here I was a small-town boy and farmer's son, busting my butt to leave the land behind my ancestors had tilled for half of forever, while the Stanford grad and Columbus, Ohio native Scotty was being pushed back to it. "Keep writing to Beth," I teased. "If you won't, I will."

Back in the bar, Tommy, drunker than I had ever seen and still not the least bit cheered, was hugging a warehouse column to hold himself up. He staggered over and slurred, "Being a good student never made anybody a good teacher or scholar, did it? Because the skills are unrelated. So I'm forgetting about becoming a professor."

"Don't be ridiculous," I said. "You'll be one of the great ones, Tommy, much better than me. You've got genuine perseverance. I'm just stubborn." I had to grin to see Dickinson dancing with Dagmar. Karl's sister was pretty as ever, but still no Katja.

“Cut the flattery,” Tommy told me.

“I’m not flattering. You underestimate yourself.” To prove it, I rattled off a list of Russian authors he knew better than I did. That finally brought back his innocent Norskie grin. I ordered myself another beer and him coffee, but before they arrived, Bakken stumbled onto the dance floor and cut in on Scotty with Dagmar. I’m not kidding. His dorky jerking around was really a stitch.

Will gave up on hustling Gitty and joined me. I asked about the clear, syrupy liquid in his glass.

“Slow, sweet death, my good man. Pray tell, have you finally seen the light?”

“Which light is that?”

“Saul’s on the road to Damascus. I’m serious. You have definitely changed.”

What could I say? I was hell-bent on hiding Katja’s existence, no matter how well the Monks had proved they could be trusted. Too much was at stake, and besides they didn’t need to know. “I’m sleeping better,” I simply said. Which was true.

Will confided that he had met a girl named Charlotte from a village north of Knittelstedt in the Lüneburger Heath. Only eighteen, but very mature for her age. Though anyone Dagmar’s age is too young for Burke.

His smirk so annoyed me I took a toilet break I didn’t need to escape and inside found Rich leaning against a wall and hanging his head. His widely dilated pupils were having trouble focusing.

“Too much firewater?” I asked.

“Hey, man, you know me. I haven’t had a drop. All the pukes at this party are just bumming me out. The whole military is such bullshit. Fucking treads everywhere. I’m not just cooperating with the enemy, I *am* the enemy. And I want out now.”

“We’ll get out soon enough.” But since meeting Katja I was in no hurry to leave the Army anymore, was I? Because Knittelstedt had become an ideal place for me. Only Braunschweig would be better.

I led Rich to the bar and bought him a double bourbon and water. I considered making it a quad, or double double, a common serving at Club 69, but none of his Boston chums or family drank, so he wasn't used to it. Though for a short-hitter, he did fine. The second one was no problem either.

"You need a woman in your life," I said. "That'll cheer you up just like"—I didn't finish the sentence.

"Like what? Who is she, man? Why are you so secretive with *us*? Do you think we'd tell the treads? Why, we don't even talk to those assholes."

I nodded. No way was I going to let him know about Katja. I may have to say I'm hitting the bordellos every break, a vice the treads tolerate because no close relationships form.

Gradually, the Early Times and the undulations of Dagmar, Bärbel and Gitty distracted Rich, and his smile came back. I offered to show him around Braunschweig. And quickly changed the destination to Hamburg.

He wasn't interested.

"Getting assigned here was very lucky," I said. "When our country's in a hot war in Vietnam. Tens of thousands of Americans have already perished over there."

"And we're still waiting to hear one good reason why."

Rich ordered himself another single shot of bourbon, risking the proverbial one drink too many. Though this ferocious mood tolerated alcohol better than his mellow normal self, he overshot his capacity, so I walked him home. I got him safely to his apartment on Südstrasse and tucked him into bed, where he went out fast as a SPETSNAZ radio signal. On the way down the darkened Bismarckstrasse toward my rental, I couldn't help whistling for joy. It's not just working out over here for now, but for the whole rest of my life.

Feb. 17, 1970

This weather sucks. Give me Wisconsin's cold, dry winter anytime instead, and I don't care how much it snows. Of late it's been 30s and 40s and rain and even sleet, but barely any sunshine.

I should hear from Katja any day now.

Feb. 18, 1970

This evening I ate supper with Rich at the site and made fun of his threat to join MacIntosh in Stockholm. "Sweden's boring," I said. "A paradise only on paper. Too controlled, too homogeneous, too cold, too uptight. Sure, it's efficient, but it's just not you."

Feb. 20, 1970

She still hasn't written.

The constant rain is depressing. And I'm catching another cold.

Feb. 25, 1970

I'm considering asking Karl-Heinz to see what happened to Katja, but I can't let him know I care. So I'll have to go look myself. It's hard not to panic. What's going on? I didn't completely misread her, did I?

March 4, 1970

She wrote! I have an address in Braunschweig!

I walked to the post office and mailed my reply within an hour of receiving her note. I said I'd arrive on the 7th and asked where I could meet her. I gave the number of the nearest public phone booth here and told her to call on the sixth at twenty-one-hundred hours.

I'm worried she won't receive my letter in time. I can't call her, because like many Germans she has no phone. Do I dare just show up at her apartment?

March 5, 1970

Even if she doesn't reply I'm going to Braunschweig.

March 6, 1970

A telegram arrived today that consisted of two words: Domplatz and *Mittag*—Cathedral Square and noon. Tonight I waited in the phone booth an hour in vain for her call.

March 11, 1970

Katja, Katja, Katja. Thank you, Lord, for sending me here.

High fifties yesterday, more spring than late winter, so she and I took a walk along the causeways of Riddagshausen east of Braunschweig, where we had gone our very first night. She was wearing denims and a cashmere sweater without a jacket and leather boots laced to her knees. She looked a bit fuller in the face than before, and healthier and even more gorgeous.

The first hour we strolled across the narrow strips of earth separating the shallow pools, stopping often to embrace and kiss. She carried a thirty-millimeter camera on a strap across a shoulder and took pictures of me against scenic backdrops. I insisted on photographing her, too, so she posed with clown faces so outlandish she was unrecognizable. I suggested we stop at a small clearing in the beech forest.

The sod was still wet from the winter thaw, so I spread out my field jacket. The ungirlish roundedness of her buttocks strained her pants, as they did mine. She lay back on it and basked in the sunshine with closed eyes. "I want to say hello to the sun," she told me and blithely pulled off her sweater to expose the shapely little, hard-tipped breasts I had been kneading. With no sense of nakedness or striptease, she proceeded to take off her boots, jeans, and *Höschen* as well and stretched out stark naked.

"You need sunshine also," she muttered nonchalantly. "You're much too pale. If there's any god we should worship, it's the sun, the source of all earthly life."

I felt self-conscious, getting undressed, even though she didn't watch. Propped on my side only inches from her and shivering in the fresh air, I was peculiarly hesitant to touch her unclothed body. Finally, I slipped an arm beneath her shoulders, nestled close, and reached between her thighs.

She calmly removed my hand. "Our task is simple," she said. "Keep moving forward. You and I don't matter much in the grand scheme of things, but we still must do our part for human progress. If enough of us succeed, eventually all mankind will be able to lead lives worthy of our natural dignity. And we shall build an earthly paradise that will last millennia."

"Or until humans make the earth unlivable," I replied. "Everything else is interim."

"Peter, sarcasm is the lowest form of humor, and cynics are the leeches of history. You call millennia an interim? Maybe from the viewpoint of the galaxy Andromeda, but not from any human one. To us, thousands of years *are* forever. You have so little faith, so little hope. What do you believe in?"

"I believe in Katharina Wendt."

"That's the stupidest remark I've ever heard," she said, rolling away. I tried to snuggle close, but she held me at bay with a firm arm, claiming she wasn't in the mood. "Wait until the sun goes under a cloud and sends a chill. I'm still too warm." Warm in March? It was clear overhead, but welcome dark clouds were approaching from the west. With arms stretched behind her head and legs slightly spread, she dozed off.

Lying beside her, ogling her body, inhaling her aroma—it was more than any man should have to bear. I rolled onto her, shoving my thighs between her knees, and glued my mouth onto hers. Her tongue met mine, and we clawed at each other, till she whispered, "Peterchen, not here."

Not here? No, precisely here. My pulse thumping in my throat, I lifted her completely off the jacket onto me and spread her legs by raising my thighs and arching my back and entered her—finally!—by pulling her down deep around me. She wound her legs around mine and dug her heels into my calves. With a tight grip on her shoulders, I rocked her taut body against mine until she came. When she reached orgasm a second time, I joined in the shuddering, groaning ecstasy.

Afterwards, she lay limply atop my torso, not disconnecting, and I relished bearing her weight. Then slowly she began squirming until her rhythmic grinds turned into regular thrusts, and we came together again, this time my back spasming with the rapture. I proceeded to kiss her beautifully curved lips a hundred times, thanking my lucky stars that our bodies fit together as perfectly as our personalities. Sexually, intellectually, emotionally, Katja is as good as it gets.

I drove her VW back to the Old City, where we took in the movie made from Thomas Mann's novella, *Death in Venice*. Afterwards, we discussed it over mulled wine in a restaurant. Katja's critique, delivered in a dry, precise German, reminded me of my Madison professors: "Its insistent melancholiness is posturing, a sure sign of shallow art. Leave sadness to those who are honestly grieving. Books and movies should transcend life and never wallow in its meanness. Such negativism only discourages progress."

I admire her idealism still all of a piece, while my own beliefs remain so shattered. I want to worship progress as much as she does, but I'm naturally too skeptical. "What exactly do you mean by progress?" I asked.

"Better lives for everybody," she replied with a note of impatience. "For all, enough to eat, a place to live, free education and health care, full employment, culture generously supported by the public. Lives closer to what we humans are worthy of. It's a simple concept."

So she was talking about social progress, but not scientific, spiritual or metaphysical. Madison's New Left, not unlike West Germany's so-called Extraparliamentary Opposition, espoused similar ideas. Of course, everyone of good will wants such progress, but compared to solving the the mystery of our existence it seemed rather paltry. So what? Next to her, I feel like a mercenary. I asked if, like Karl, she was a Social Democrat, the most leftist of the major West German parties, though all three are quite socialist compared to even more liberal American Democrats.

"Actually, I'm not that political. The truth is like a forest. The more paths you take, the more trees you see."

Katja not political? Her ideas are vague, almost intentionally so, as if to broaden their appeal, but she is painfully political.

She agreed the film was a pale shadow of Mann's superb fiction, but still a noble attempt in an unsuitable medium at capturing the symbolic complexity of the purported literary masterpiece. She preferred Heinrich Mann to his younger brother, Thomas. Since the former's critical realism is socially useful, unlike Thomas' calligraphy for the elite. His writing only sounds like serious discourse, while actually closer to word music. Some of his characters are interesting though.

"Preferring Heinrich is bizarre. Thomas is so much the greater writer."

"He has never impressed me. I would much rather read rough-hewn substance than a polished hollow shell."

"By substance you mean progressive politics?"

"That and more."

"Heinrich isn't all that good, if you don't agree with his politics."

"How could you not agree, Peter? Are you secretly fascist?"

I bridled at that absurd suggestion, but otherwise controlled my pique. I had gained new respect for her intellect and the masculine edge to her rhetoric, though this debate was annoying me, too. Then I noticed the flush in her cheeks, betraying an irritation she was only half-voicing. But we kept at it anyway until we were both close to rage. "You had better take me to the train station now," I said. "Tomorrow morning I begin a string of days." The most grueling of our rotating shifts because of all the treads present, and I wanted to start off well rested.

"Okay," she agreed too hastily.

She squealed her VW into the Main Train Station. I hesitated to climb out. In the twilight her gray-blue eyes appeared green.

I reached over to caress her breasts through the soft cashmere sweater and kiss her one last time. "It seems like I haven't touched you in six months," I whispered.

Her nostrils flared, her gaze narrowed, and our lips met again. Still embracing me, she said, "There is so much yearning in your voice it makes my stomach sink."

"I ache to make love to you again, Katja."

She held my hug without speaking a long time before gently pushing me back into my seat and turning the ignition. "Stay in my apartment tonight, Peter. And catch the first train back to Knittelstedt early tomorrow."

All that night I held her close and slept with my face nestled in her hair. Twice I roused her from sound slumber to make love yet again, and each time the pleasure-pain was more intense. A hundred precious details linger in my mind—the curl of her ear, the swell of her lips, the taste of her tongue, the hardening of her nipples, the softness of her inner thighs, her yielding flesh, her trembling thrusts. And afterwards the soft rustling of her breathing in my ear. How much can you stand to hear about a visit to paradise? It was barely a half night's rest, and I almost missed the 5:57 a.m. train.

The world is more delightful than all its books can begin to describe. It has been so ever since Katja and I first met. She is very well read in all the European classics, and, like me, loves foreign languages. Her English is American accented. She has a good Midwestern pronunciation, but she can't say or understand very much, so we always speak German. She is *gebildet*, as her countrymen would say, meaning both cultured and educated. At her side, I'm both relaxed and excited, more truly myself, finally able to say everything I've been wanting to convey and express it better than ever before. Even *auf Deutsch*. Nobody has ever brought this much good out of me.

I seem to be as great for her. She adores my company. We talk effortlessly about every subject, and we touch as if we have always been intimate. A lover who's a peer? Isn't she exactly what

I seek in a wife? Who in their right mind wouldn't? Now I don't care where I live as long as it's with her. Why not in Germany? Seriously, why not?

She might be slightly older than I am, but I hesitate to ask. But she's mentioned too many things she's done since getting her *Abitur* at nineteen for being only my age. So what if she's in her late twenties? That would only make her at most three or four years older than me. In energy, she's still as youthful as a teenager. I've never wanted to yield to any force more or felt better about the surrender. Our next rendezvous I want to take her so many times that my hunger for her will be stilled—for at least an entire day.

Today at the site Sergeant Whitman eyed me gravely and asked if I was sick. "Take better care of yourself, son," he growled. Tommy stopped by my desk, wondering whether I'd suffered from insomnia again. I claimed I had stayed up late reading Heinrich Mann.

"I thought Thomas Mann was more your speed."

"I need to know *all* the German authors," I told him with a chuckle. That night I went to bed right after supper and slept like a cadaver.

The third day into the trick, Rich cornered me at the site and flashed his toothiest grin. "So did ya score?"

I froze at first. "Not since Madison. How about you?"

"No, not that way, man. Come on, you scored. I know you did. Don't bullshit me. It's written all over your face. I don't know whether you getting laid or this zombie act you're pulling now impresses me more. But whatever you do, and however you do it, are okay by me. We're buddies, remember, so act like it."

"There's nothing to tell."

Hoffman scowled. I felt bad that I didn't dare confide in him, but I couldn't. Not Rich nor Tommy nor Scotty nor Will. I've never been closer to anybody than these guys, but I can't mention Katja, not yet. I have way too much to lose.

March 14, 1970

I should return to my doctoral list, but right now I could no more read Kleist or the Manns than cuneiform tablets. About all I do manage are the Schultzes' family magazines, the German equivalents of *Life* and *Look*, with fluffier articles and more graphic photos. Scotty lends me his *Newsweeks*, but the news in them is too depressing. Besides, politics don't matter.

I know I'm being irrational, but I fear losing Katja. I should have been more careful about seeing her and not mentioned Braunschweig to a soul. From now on, if anyone sees me at the local train station, I'll say I'm headed to Hanover or Hamburg. It's just too suspicious always to be visiting Braunschweig, a much less interesting city than others. Eventually I hope I can maybe trust Rich, but not yet. He's not one hundred percent sure I scored, but he'll give you odds I did. Tommy would never tell anyone, but I can't let him know either.

Is it my imagination that Katja is holding something back, even while giving me everything physically? It's like she's carrying deep secrets she doesn't dare so much as hint at.

I will risk writing her a letter. I'll address the envelope in an angular German script, so no one suspects she has an American friend.

March 18, 1970

Her reply could arrive as early as tomorrow.

So I had to write again first? So I like her more than she does me?

She's more Prussian than I am in concealing feelings. Though quite temperamental, often flooded with emotions, she remains outwardly calm, never ruffled, too stubborn to be anything but what she has to be.

Why do I fear I might never see her again? Because she's too good to be true. She acts strangely serious whenever I mention being a GI, probably because that status sounds absurd. Or does she realize just how difficult an ongoing relationship between us will be?

None of these reasons hold any water. I won't even consider breaking this off. She and I can handle the risk. We have to. We'll be extremely careful.

Some days I'll tell a Monk I'm going to Helmstedt and really head there, only to catch a connection from Berlin to Braunschweig. It's a roundabout way to reach Katja without anyone else knowing, but the misdirection hides my actual destination. Nobody must know that is always Braunschweig, except Katja herself. The Schultzes, Karl-Heinz, everybody else can be led astray, if each time I tell a consistent lie. Or Katja can meet me in cities other than Braunschweig. I'm not giving her up no matter what.

March 20, 1970

This break I entertained myself around Knittelstedt and avoided my room except to sleep. Alone, I couldn't bear not seeing Katja, but among buddies I felt okay. Sort of, anyway. On Sunday, Umlaut, as we all call Dave Mueller—or Müller as he somehow got his fatigue nametag spelled, hence the nickname—needed help with his hobby of "spotting game." He's a guy everybody likes right off because of his humor and good cheer. Despite a hangover, I agreed.

He crept his Volkswagen down double ruts across farmers' fields to sneak up on roe deer, while I manned his portable camera from the passenger seat. But no matter how quietly we moved, we never got close. We couldn't figure out why the creatures were so wary, since hunting them has been banned in Germany for decades.

We were heading home in frustration through a beech forest, when Umlaut braked hard. A red-eyed wild boar stood right in our path, threatening to charge. "Film away," Umlaut whispered. Which I did, till the woodland hog finally retreated. Twenty minutes later, we were sipping Jim Beam and branch at

Club 69 and teasing people about the squat, short-legged doe we had seen. Are the wild pigs what's scaring the deer?

Tommy wasn't around, but Scotty and Will were. Rich showed up later, too, for a repeat screening of *Barbarella* by popular demand. "This is Fonda's finest film," Will said. "I'm interested in seeing a lot more of her now. Free Jane Fonda."

"She isn't imprisoned," Rich muttered.

"She ought to be, Hoffman."

"You fascist asshole, Burke."

"With all due respect, my good man, smile when you say that."

"Haven't I always given you all the respect you deserve? And would you please cut out that my-good-man crap? It makes you sound like a British twit." Will flashed Rich his best German-shepherd grin.

Later that night at the site, new duty rosters struck Rich as absurdly funny. The stupider the assignments or the bigger the personal plans they ruined, the more hilarious it was to him. His eyes looked suspiciously droopy.

The next morning when the CO showed up for a surprise building inspection, a falsetto voice greeted from every speaker, "Chicken Man-n-n-n." We all roared with laughter till Slater blew up. Looking like he couldn't decide whether to have a stroke or rip himself in two, he stormed around in a futile search for the culprit. Hey, this time it wasn't me.

At oh-eight-hundred hours the next morning we started paying for the insult. The CO lined up everybody, except for a skeleton crew manning the site, outside the barbed wire for a personal inspection and handed out a shitload of cleanup details for long hair, including one to yours truly. Slater's ranting only amuses me because as long as we don't break ranks—and we'll never break ranks—this is the worst he can do to us.

Of course we really resent our convict haircuts, living among all these shaggy young Germans, but what choice do we have? Shorter hair hurts me more than the other guys, because I otherwise can easily pass for a German. So I guess I'll always be flirting with a gig, because I'll be damned if I'll keep my hair that well trimmed.

March 24, 1970

Katja wrote.

She's fine, studying hard and relieved she has only one more year until graduation. Unfortunately, she said she won't be able to see me for a while. She claims we were moving too fast and letting lust consume everything else. Our attraction was threatening to burn out before anything lasting developed between us. She'll contact me in a month or so, and in the meantime I must make no attempt to contact her.

I'm devastated. I will see her later, I will see her later, I keep telling myself. No matter what I have to do.

March 25, 1970

A SPETSNAZ radioman bragged that his company killed "a puppet," and a buddy laughed at the news with merry spite. Two other ops mentioned "drop points" and "rendezvous sites" in perfect High German. East German troops must be on a joint exercise with our Soviet targets.

March 26, 1970

A SPETSNAZ company on drill scared the crap out of us today. Their radio signals were hardly up, before they went back down. A couple messages were about butchering swine. Suddenly the Soviet ops are deadly serious and have stopped joking on the air. Did they get a new strack CO?

March 28, 1970

There are twinges of pain in my temples after a dissipated evening at Club 69. Kentucky's best sour mash and Scotty's conversation entertained me into the wee hours. In Beth's last letter she agreed to marry him, so he was buying rounds. She's confident they'll find a compromise that makes them both happy. Where there are wills, there are ways. Hear, hear.

I probed Scotty's feelings about Beth. He loves her more tenderly than I had believed him capable. Because he grew up privileged doesn't make him an asshole, so I was selling him short. I sincerely wish them well. The hardest part, finding himself a good woman, is behind him.

March 31, 1970

What is going on inside Katja's mind? I'm sure as hell not going to forget about her. I must get out of the Army so I can see Katja openly. So I can marry her. Why should she want to play secretive games to see me? But even with an early discharge I'm still committed to military service until at least a year from this fall. An ETS that soon will only happen if Nixon keeps his promise to cut military manpower.

April 3, 1970

I can't help but resent her failure to write. How could she turn her feelings off like this? I'm hoping when I lay hands on her again, I can fan her smoldering passion full-flame. Because we're so fantastic together. Because we make each other so much better than we are separately.

April 4, 1970

Next break, Monday and Tuesday, I *must* see Katja. I'd gladly give up years off the end of my life to spend another night in her arms. But what if she doesn't want to see me?

I'll get back to my reading schedule. I must do something different to stop obsessing about her. And cut back on drinking.

I've been struggling to read Theodor Fontane's *Schach von Wuthenow*, an alleged masterpiece by the 19th-century German realist, but it's just not grabbing me. I've tried to force concentration by reading the novel aloud, but I can't keep my mind off Katja. So last night I hit Club 69 yet again.

Will was at the bar nursing a Johnny Walker Black on the rocks, and for a change I honestly enjoyed his company. Of course I couldn't mention what was lying heavy on my heart, but his eloquence about everything from medieval theology to chess grandmasters distracted me. Umlaut joined us a few drinks later for a three-way argument about the best American sport. Burke and I both drunkenly championed baseball for perhaps our first agreement on anything, and ridiculed Umlaut's preference for football.

April 5, 1970

I decided against a trip anywhere this coming break. I'll spend it here and make progress on my reading list. One night I'll maybe get together with a Monk not working at the site.

April 13, 1970

I completely wasted my last break at Club 69 again and don't have any plans for my time off tomorrow or the next day except to read. But what? Nothing holds my attention. I won't attempt another German novel. The plays are even worse. But hanging out at the NCO club so often could ruin a guy's health.

I wrote Katja a single sentence: "I must see you." No need to sign it.

April 18, 1970

My birthday came and went without a fuss, though Mom sent a card. I was proud of myself for not getting drunk again for the occasion. I've been reading Karl-Heinz's old issues of *Der Spiegel*. If the left-leaning newsweekly isn't on my reading list, at least it's in German. Three East German spies were arrested in Bonn, one the chief secretary in the West German Ministry of the Interior, and the other two her couriers. The woman made copies of classified documents she handled daily and passed them on to East Berlin. Her position was sensitive, but at least she wasn't in Chancellor Brandt's office. Could the Warsaw Pact ever get an agent that highly placed?

The pacifism I idealized in Madison seems stupidly quixotic over here. The Soviets exercise their tactical nuclear missile forces just across the border, and the British Army of the Rhine to our rear roars its tanks. We GIs at Det Q aren't worth even a pawn in this chess game, because if all hell breaks loose, we'll be instantly blown off the board.

These constantly rotating shifts are making me half-sick again. Without a regular daily schedule, I just can't sleep decently.

April 25, 1970

Unbelievable.

I woke up at 1:00 p.m. yesterday after three hours sleep and was about to write in this diary, when there was a loud knock. I hid these pages beneath my bed, slipped on a shirt, and opened the door. Katja! She handed me a bouquet of lilies-of-the-valley and barged in without a word of greeting. I put the roadside wildflowers in a water glass, since I don't own a vase, and pulled her red cotton sweater off over her head. No bra on this time either. The boots and denims took a tad longer. The next ten hours I held onto her for dear life until it was time to don my fatigues for work. All we talked about was literature, and we didn't say much. I was too tired to accomplish anything that mid, try as I might, but Tommy covered for me while I napped in the privacy of the Green Room and eventually translated a Russian memo before dawn.

To hold and kiss and caress Katja was more beautiful than words can express. I relished every instant with her, hoarding it even while it was happening, knowing the next famine was only an *Auf Wiedersehen* away.

The more I think of Katja, and every week the hours do increase, the more ridiculous monks, hermits, and ascetics strike me. No matter how many their virtues, I laugh at them into my fists, because they never drink from the only river of divinity there is—or even wet their lips. For what earthly reason are they denying themselves the most beautiful human experience, namely, making love to a cherished person? One good night of that can make a month. And the intense joy lingering afterwards can suffuse weeks of dreary routine with a grinning afterglow.

May it not have to linger too long. She said the next time would be soon. As long as I know that "soon" will come, I can wait.

May 5, 1970

Today I rode along as interpreter with Slater and Whitman and a British major and sergeant major to the Iron Curtain north of Wolfsburg. Last night three East German teenagers from Magdeburg tried to sneak out of the German Democratic Republic, but only two made it. The kids negotiated the mine fields fine, but then one hit a trip wire, flares flashed, and *Vopo* guards opened fire. The West German border guard—the *Bundesgrenzschutz*—shot back with automatic weapons to cover the youngsters' escape, not really trying to hit anything, while the two boys scrambled over the last fence to safety. But the eighteen-year-old girl got tangled on the barbed wire, and the brave defenders of socialism riddled her with bullets. They let her hang there for hours before daring to remove her body. The *Vopos* weren't about to trust their lives to BGS orders not to kill. This morning East Germany released a statement declaring her "an enemy agent." What bullshit.

It's clear I am no friend of socialism in any of its forms. I fear the problem inheres in the philosophy and economics. It never works, no matter how idealistic the theory.

The distraught youngsters, one the dead girl's brother and the other her boyfriend, didn't have much to tell us. They had always avoided the Russians in Magdeburg, as everybody there does. Young East German women are terrified of them and don't go outside alone after dark. So the Soviets aren't living among the natives, not at all like us *Amis* in Knittelstedt.

Rich has gone nuts since President Nixon bombed and invaded Cambodia, after claiming he was winding down the war.

And now the National Guard has shot three students protesting at Kent State. What the hell's going on over there? Rich asked if I knew where to buy some cyanide to put in the treads' coffee machine. "They're the only ones who use it," he said with a crooked grin. I'm not certain he wasn't serious.

Captain Slater asked me not to disclose to anyone at Det Q or anywhere else what I knew about that "border incident." When our official report comes out, I'll get a cleared version I can use for allaying suspicions. Military intelligence is such a tangle of distortions and lies.

Though I will tell Katja our next rendezvous. She has always sounded naively sympathetic to East Germany, like almost all West German students. That artificial country is a puppet of the Soviet Union. Its socialism prospers only because Germans work hard no matter what hardships they must endure.

May 15, 1970

Since Katja's surprise visit, I've been plowing through the novels of Wilhelm Raabe, starting with his acclaimed first-person Braunschweig trilogy. I can't wait to make love to her again.

May 23, 1970

I got a note from Katja. Just one sentence: "See you the second week of June." I have to wait two more weeks?! I'm back to reading less and hanging out at Club 69 more. Because sitting alone in my room here gives me such crazy thoughts.

June 6, 1970

Another note from her today. Until it arrived, I was truly worried she was ready to drop me. All she wrote was: "*Ich rufe Dich an um 2100 6.6.*" So tonight I was waiting in the nearby public phone booth as directed. It rang on the dot at 9:00 p.m. I picked up the receiver. "Katja?" I whispered.

"Peterchen," she implored like a prayer. Of course I agreed to go with her to the Baltic Sea over Pentecost, a German national holiday. For her I'd even walk across water. I'd do anything to see her, anything at all.

June 8, 1970

It took us three stops to make it to the Worpswede artist colony just outside Bremen. Once we even had a bite to eat. The first evening we never left our room. The next day we toured a local art gallery and small museum before driving to the fishing village of Dangast with a fine North Sea beach. The water was too cold for her and a dozen other scattered sunbathers, but not for a Northerner like me. When I staggered out thirty minutes later, my ankles and toes ached from the chill. Katja was still stretched out on a beach towel, her untied red bikini top resting freely over her breasts. When I dripped on her, she jerked upright, tossing the flimsy cloth to the sand and exposing hard, dark pink nipples.

"Can we go back to the guesthouse already?" I whispered.

"*Ja.*"

On the next day's drive home through the flat scrublands of the Lüneburger Heath, she broke a lengthy silence. "Why are you being so quiet?"

"It seems like I haven't made love to you in months."

She put a hand on my knee. "Let's stop, Peterchen."

I veered onto the next side road and spun down a pair of sandy ruts. For an hour, pine needles prickled my back and neck, but Katja never felt a one. By the time I trudged back to my Knittelstedt room it was almost midnight, but my heart was chirping like a robin at dawn.

She satisfies me as salt water does thirst. I know she loves me almost as much as I do her, though she won't admit it. She says picking love apart is like killing an animal to dissect it. If it's no longer alive, what does it matter what it's made of? She's right. If a force bonded us for life upon first sight, who cares what it is?

When I'm lying in her arms, the whole world seems created anew, and I feel reborn. When she kisses passionately, her soft, moist lips caressing mine from corner to corner, I know without having to hear reasons why that all is well, and I want to thrive on this earth as much as everything else alive. Of course everything will work out. I accept that it isn't all good in the world without conceding there is no higher meaning. Though I can't explain any of these insights rationally, I don't feel I have to. *Selbstverständlich.* Just accept what is. The feast has been spread, so dig in. *Guten Appetit*! When it's over, say goodbye, die, and decay. Nothing else lasts forever, not even a mountain or monument, so how dare we expect anything better for our mortal shells? To memories of Katja's warm breath and earthy scent, I could gladly drift off into eternal sleep. Who cares why we're here? It feels like blasphemy even to ask.

June 15, 1970

Before today's train to Braunschweig had screeched to a halt, I bounded onto the concrete platform and hit full stride, the crimson roses in my hand bobbing with every step. But Katja wasn't among the crowd as planned. One curious stranger acted as if he recognized me before glancing away. I marched into the vast hall of the Main Train Station, memories of Katja's many faces floating like luminous shadows over the station's drab concrete. Joy, passion, impatience, irritation, devotion, adoration—her features kept metamorphosing in my mind, not unlike the colors of her chameleon-like eyes. And her two types of laughter echoed in my ears, the tinkling giggle and that uproarious guffaw. I adore every one of her mercurial moods, no matter how swiftly they ebb and flow—just as I love every instant of grasping her lithe body and hearing every syllable pronounced precisely with those delicate lips.

When she wasn't in the waiting hall either, I doubled back to the platform. No better luck there. So I stepped outside and found Katja dawdling at the station's fast food stand, as if that's where she had said she would meet me. "Aren't you hungry, Peterchen?" she asked blithely.

"No," I snapped, yanked her out of the queue, pulled her behind the kiosk out of other customers' sight, and with one arm hugged her off the ground and kissed her hard, my loins quickening at the touch of her tongue.

"*Danke,* Peterchen," she cooed in accepting the flowers.

We jostled hips in walking to her car. There I nuzzled the smooth skin of her thin neck and with a cracking voice declared, "*Ich liebe dich,* Katja."

"I love you, too," she replied with a chuckle.

I started undoing her blouse, but she grabbed my wrists. "Let's go to my place."

"No, let's drive out in the country. To a place where we can picnic."

So we bought oranges, tomatoes, cheese, sourdough rye bread, and a liter of apple juice and headed north. Twenty kilometers outside of the city, Katja directed me onto a gravel road, and then down two sandy ruts that strained the engine for a quarter mile before we parked.

Katja jumped out and raced me up a knoll. From atop it, she pointed down at a pond like an exuberant child and whispered, "Listen."

All I could think of was, who had she been here with before? No matter, the bullfrogs' absurdly bass belches soon brought a smile to my face, too. From behind I clasped Katja's waist and squeezed her tight, and she playfully pushed her head up against my chin. In the cool sunlight, we watched a bird of prey effortlessly wheel overhead, silhouetted against the pale azure northern sky, its colors hidden in shadow. I reached for her zipper, but Katja suggested that we drink something first. The fruit extract swiftly quenched our thirst, but it took all afternoon to still our hunger.

I was dozing on top of her, when her squirming awakened me. She was silently weeping. "What's wrong?" I asked, licking away the tears.

"A dear friend was killed last week," she muttered. "A man I grew up with and always felt close to. Even though we had been in poor contact lately."

"How did it happen?"

"A car accident. In Berlin."

"East or West Berlin?"

She glared at me a full minute. "What makes you think I have friends in East Germany? In West Berlin *selbstverständlich*."

"I'm sorry." I let her roll out from under me. "How about a massage?"

Katharina stretched both arms back and spread her legs. Gently rocking to my touch, she told me, "Your hands feel so magical. Such long, delicate fingers should sooner grace a piano than a rifle."

I kept caressing her hot skin, arousing us both, till I found my hands encircling her neck and squeezing. When she coughed, I let go, reached under her back, and kneaded her shoulders till her nipples were pointing straight at me. "Katja, will you marry me?" I whispered.

She giggled. "But you can't let people know I even exist."

"I meant later, after I'm out of the Army. Because I want you forever."

"You've already got me. What more do you want, chains?"

"Katharina," I pleaded and kissed her. Her tongue came out to meet mine, and her fingers snaked inside my clothes, and my question quickly seemed irrelevant. Afterwards, we lay nose to nose and lightheartedly argued about who loved the other more, till it grew so dark we could hardly find our way to her VW.

June 17, 1970

I won't bother to record my every erotic adventure with Katja. No one needs to know all the details, just the highlights. Suffice it to say, I have never felt more blessed, more at peace with the universe than since we met. Katja and I are quickly becoming as good friends as we have long been ardent lovers. I have decided irrevocably that she must be my wife, since I could never find a better match. How could I get this lucky twice? Wasn't all this already in the cards the first evening when we met at Zum grünen Kakadu? If I could only live with her now already.

It's gotten easy to ignore the pukes' military emergencies, as I now sit aloof from the treadiness surrounding me at the site. Let Slater and Whitman have a stroke if that's what they're into. Pondering Katja's multiple delights makes me feel like I'm floating downstream on a perfect summer afternoon, just as I did as a kid south of my home town in the Noire River, knowing the rapids and waterfalls wouldn't come for miles and miles.

I don't just feel born again—I *have* been born again. Thank you, God, for sending me to Det Q. Military Intelligence duty in northern Germany is an ideal assignment, far from the barracks and mess halls other Americans endure in Berlin or farther south. And far, far from the brutal war in Vietnam.

June 22, 1970

After working a swing shift, I got up early, took a train to Braunschweig, and met Katja for a couple hours at the *Schwimmhalle*, the municipal swimming pool. An hour in transit each way is always worth any rendezvous, no matter how brief. My hands kept clawing underwater at her tiny, fire-truck red bikini till she snapped, "Let me swim my laps!" To save energy for later, I floated on my back. When that got boring, I took a deep breath, kicked my way to the concrete floor, and ogled the red patch of her swimsuit bottom. I couldn't help lunging for it, grasping a thigh, and yanking her under.

I had already surfaced, when she popped up sputtering and cursing, "*Du Arschloch, verdammt noch mal*!" Laughing at the vulgar outburst, I hugged her slippery skin, apologized, and begged for the chance to make amends between a pair of cool, dry sheets. We sped to her apartment across town and made love twice and then, after a brief rest, once again, before I hurried off to catch my train. Was I ever tired that shift. That night back in my own bed I couldn't roll over without strain.

Katja is fascinated by my foreskin—"just like a European's." She had heard all American men were circumcised, but is curiously pleased that I'm an exception. She is more natural about the human body and sex than any American I have ever known. Absolutely nothing embarrasses her. To her making love is both totally serious and delightful.

Every rendezvous Katja is teaching me to take less of the outdoors for granted. As a student in Marburg two years ago, I didn't notice a single horse chestnut, but so common a German tree had to have been growing there in abundance. Knittelstedt's streets are lined with them. Last month, I waved at their large, erect white blossoms every time I walked down the Bahnhofstrasse to take yet another train to Braunschweig.

June 28, 1970

I just spent my days off with Katja in Hamburg, where I slept with her eight times. On the train ride back home I dozed cadaverously against the window and almost missed my stop. Only the jolting squeal of the brakes kept me from heading straight into East Germany.

What I want now and forever after is to lie in Katja's arms. Everything else is meaningless. I know enjoying the flesh by itself can neither damn nor save, but her intimate embraces have made my whole life worthwhile. Even if I accomplish nothing else.

June 30, 1970

Last night the Forty-Second SPETSNAZ Sabotage Group of the Two Hundred Ninety-Fifth Independent Reconnaissance Battalion practiced a low-level parachute drop near Magdeburg. A Junior Sergeant broke a leg, so a Senior Lieutenant "shot" him, because they couldn't take him along or let him be captured. The drop zone was a model for a meadow two clicks north of Det Q. My blood chilled when their CO ordered his men to capture us

Americans alive, once they sever our communications. And to interrogate us brutally—"until the GIs sing like nightingales"—and only then slit our throats. If everything went according to plan, they wouldn't need to fire a single shot. Once their troops operating behind NATO lines have blinded the Army of the Rhine, they expect their tanks to reach Amsterdam in forty-eight hours.

July 2, 1970

Sgt. Whitman congratulated me at the site today for my "exceptionally conscientious performance," as he phrased it. The tread is not uneducated. I have indeed been working extra hard. He said a writeup of my recent intercepts made it all the way to NATO headquarters.

Our scribes don't call me a gunner for nothing. I record more minutes of radio traffic per shift on average than any other Russkie lingie, of course including broadcasts of dubious value. Every word of which they must type up on their Cyrillic keyboards. My entire life I've striven for thoroughness whatever the endeavor. Though now my motive is to accrue leniency in case the treads ever find about Katja and me.

July 7, 1970

Guess what I did for the Fourth? I shouldn't have skipped Det Q's big holiday bash, which the other Monks attended along with almost everybody else except for the mini-crew on duty out at the site. But I couldn't wait to experience yet again the shadow crossing Katja's face, that dimming of her cockiness, whenever I enter her and plunge to the hilt. What are softball and beer and brats and buddies compared to that? I will never get enough of her, but I'll be damned if I won't try.

I arrived in Braunschweig, feeling oddly out of sorts. Katja was in a peculiar mood herself. She refused to head straight for her apartment and wouldn't explain why. Instead we went to a hotel room in the Old City near the State Theater. Within minutes

I once more reveled in ecstasy. It gets more beautiful every time we make love. Once above me, once back to front, once head to toe.

Since she had a busy day scheduled at the *Hochschule*, she went home well before dawn, leaving me in the hotel alone. I planned on buying myself two or three pair of German corduroys, before catching the Knittelstedt train. At 9:00 a.m. I finally awoke after sleeping through my travel alarm and hurried out into the hall barefoot in only my trousers to use the toilet. I returned and brushed my teeth in the sink. Suddenly a naked woman jerked upright from under my bedcovers, a woman who looked exactly like Katja, her pinkened lips maniacally grinning. But that was impossible. For a long moment I truly feared I had gone stark raving mad. I charged across the room to touch her and confirm my sanity. Thank God, I grasped Katja in the flesh.

"You left the door unlocked," she teased, provocatively nipping her lower lip. "You deserve a scare for such carelessness." My pulse didn't slow till two orgasms later.

Downstairs, we ate crisp breakfast rolls, a wedge of soft cheese, and a hard-boiled egg balanced on a tiny plastic stand. Afterwards she helped me shop for slacks and talked me into buying German colors I wouldn't have considered—plum, cherry, and turquoise—all to make me look less like a GI.

On the train back to Det Q, I stared out the window at the countryside racing past and did my best to ignore a middle-aged business man on my right in a charcoal-gray suit with tiny lapels and a cinched waist. All Germans stare without embarrassment, but this stranger's brazenness unnerved me. His position controlling the compartment's sliding door made it hard not to squirm. In self-defense I glared back—till he took refuge behind a newspaper.

When the trains' iron wheels screeched to a halt in Knittelstedt, I excused myself in my crispest High German and sidled past his knees. A minute later I was striding down the Bahnhofstrasse toward my room after yet another marvelous rendezvous. May they occur more often.

Did the dude in the train notice something unmistakably American about me? If he did, I need to eliminate it.

July 10, 1970

At trick change today, we five Monks met coming and going at the gate. Scotty voiced his pique that I had skipped the Fourth of July party. Umlaut was ticked, too, after all the trouble organizing the celebration. Even Bakken looked annoyed.

"Don't you want to see your friends?" Rich chided.

"If any of you gentlemen are ever as fortunate as young Zielsdorf, you will understand," Will piped up in my defense. "When are we going to meet her, my good man?"

Burke's good guess disconcerted me, but I didn't confirm or deny a thing. But what was there to do otherwise in Braunschweig or elsewhere that couldn't be postponed?

"We'd all like to meet her," Scotty said. "Bring her up to Knittelstedt."

"There is nobody to bring," I replied lamely. "I've just gotten fond of the Bruchstrasse, where I always get exactly what I pay for. I'm really into sex. What more can I say?"

They let me have it my way, but it was clear none of them believed my lie.

July 26, 1970

Katja and I just spent the warmest night of the year at a *Pension* in Siebeneichen, a village in the northern Lüneburger Heath. During the day, we hiked for miles near the Elbe River, especially enjoying the storks' nests atop chimneys of farmers' thatch-roofed homes. After a languorous supper, we opened our screenless French windows and for once fell asleep without first making love.

Around 3:00 a.m., I awoke to Katja's moist kisses. "Listen," she whispered. Outside, a nightingale was singing in a burry warble. She rolled on top of me, and I pulled her down deep around me. "*Mein Gott*, Peter," she gasped. Have I ever heard anything more beautiful?

I'm not as potent as I once was. The first time I'm always strong, but afterwards I lose it for a while. After the second time the same night, I sometimes have worse trouble. After the third orgasm, I'm definitely finished till morning, most days anyway. The problem is that Katja sometimes doesn't come until the third time, though she never complains. Whatever I do, she stays with me until I'm finished, and we doze off in a tight embrace.

Aug. 1, 1970

Every day the past week somebody at the site shit on the CO. It started Monday on his regular morning walks through Ops, when that same falsetto voice jeered over the intercom, "Chicken Man." Slater tore around the building but couldn't locate its source. The next three days his arrival inspired the same mockery, so on Friday Sergeants Whitman and Wilhelm positioned themselves in corners with good overviews just before Slater showed up. The voice only twanged, "Chicken," this time, before the three treads stomped around desks, again in vain. Whitman was suppressing a grin.

Aug. 11, 1970

Tommy stopped me just inside the gate at trick change to tell me about the Sterling Hall bombing in Madison. Young urban guerrillas were trying to force my alma mater to end all collaboration with the military-industrial complex. They weren't trying to kill that unfortunate researcher, because they didn't expect anyone in the building so late at night. This and the Ohio National Guard's shooting of the Kent State students have chilled the protests. It's still lurching along faster than it can step, but it's just inertia pushing it forward now till it stumbles to a halt. I'm afraid the movement ain't gonna make it.

Aug. 18, 1970

Half the site was just gone six days on Exercise Forester. The treads simulated a Soviet Third Shock Army invasion north of Helmstedt, and during the tank battle we lingies interrogated captured "Russian" troops played by GIs from a Munich unit. Whitman and Wilhelm were barely faking the torture it comes so naturally to them.

I shared a tent with Tommy and didn't mind that he wasn't much help setting it up. After long days in the field, we chatted about literature, but even he now prefers politics. It's as if the times have gotten too serious for fiction. Bakken is still so agreeably noncommittal that it irks me. Still, I always enjoy his company. It's as if he's so intent on studying the world a leaf at a time that he overlooks not only the forest but also the trees. Why doesn't he crave the big picture like me? And why do I intimidate him?

The maneuvers proved Det Q wouldn't survive an attack, but that wasn't news. All along, Soviet artillery units have been training by zeroing in on the site. So I guess it's smart on the treads' part to keep our M-16s locked up in a shed out of harm's way. We wouldn't want to hurt ourselves before we get killed.

It drives me nuts that the treads are obsessed with the *how* of waging war but never give a second's thought to the *why*. I don't see how come the two sides can't coexist without either seeking advantage. Is that so impossible? Of course there is more right on our side than theirs. I know that now, but still. I'll never forget the interrogation of that East German teenager whose girlfriend died on the barbed wire in an escape attempt.

It's suicidal that the East and West confront each other in Germany, guns poised at point-blank range, both refusing to lower their weapons first for fear the other side will get the drop. Where will this confrontation end? If in total holocaust, this one won't be the Germans' fault, and it'll be a thousand times worse than World War Two.

Aug. 23, 1970

Once I'm out of the military I can see Katja as much as I want or maybe even marry her. I mean, of course I'll marry her. And get a degree to teach English at a German university. If my great-grandparents could leave their native Prussia to seek a better fortune in Wisconsin, why can't I return to pursue mine?

I've been translating an education article from a British journal into German for Karl-Heinz. It was the least I could do after the gigantic favor he did for me by introducing Katja, even if he doesn't realize it. "Dagmar heard from an *Ami* that you're seeing a woman in Braunschweig," he told me yesterday. "Could it be Katja?"

"Only if she's working on the Bruchstrasse."

He guffawed at my fib. And bought it.

Sept. 2, 1970

Two days ago a SPETSNAZ op radioed, "The war will start tomorrow." We immediately informed SACEUR, the Supreme Allied Commander of Europe, and the Pentagon, again by secure teletype, and NATO went on alert. Fortunately, it was just another Soviet exercise. The Third Shock Army pretended to overrun the British Army of the Rhine, rolling right through Det Q on its way to Hanover, before reeling south to attack the rear of the strong West German and American forces plugging the Fulda gap. It's a clever plan.

The incident so excited Spec 6 Boudreau he briefly chattered away. Normally our Green Room supervisor and smartest local tread barely speaks.

Sept. 15, 1970

This last break I got up early, took a bath in the Schultzes' *Badezimmer*, dressed head-to-toe in German clothing, and caught a *Personenzug* to Braunschweig. The slow three-car train without compartments departed exactly on time like always. I sat back with a *Spiegel*, expecting an uneventful ride. But at the first stop twenty British infantrymen clambered aboard, lugging rifles, submachine guns, and full ammunition belts. A sergeant plopped down beside me and clumsily bumped my thigh hard with his Sten gun.

"Sorry, mate," he said in English and squirmed, thinking I hadn't understood him. I kept my gaze glued to the newsweekly, ignoring the sharp pain in my leg.

The ruddy-faced NCO glanced at my periodical and clothes. And asked with a Scottish burr, "You aren't a Yank perchance?"

A ring-necked pheasant, spooked out of the tall grass along the tracks, flapped away from our speeding engine like a crashing helicopter. What had he noticed? My hair? But that was long enough for a gig. "I am very sorry, but I do not speak English," I said in my best High German.

"Never mind," he mumbled, his voice trailing off. He turned away and left me alone until his squad scrambled off in Celle.

When I met Katja as arranged at the *Mensa*, her Teachers College cafeteria, a man in a maroon sweater and blue jeans was taking leave of her. She stood up, shook my hand limply, and introduced Jürgen as a fellow student. When she begged him to stay, he reluctantly agreed. So the two of us sat there scrutinizing each other, neither much liking what he saw. Mid-twenties, six feet, medium build, rat-brown hair, eyes dark blue like mine, a broad smile that exposes too much gum and, worse, buck teeth. Bright and charming in a reserved way, yet deadly serious. Majoring in American Studies. Except for occasional non-native syntax, he speaks a decent Midwestern US English. Even his "t's" in "better" and "water" were soft "d's," like mine. I strove to respect Katja's judgment of him as a friend, but it was an effort.

Jürgen asked what I was doing in Germany.

"Serving in the US military," I said. He nodded like he knew all about it.

Katja begged us both to speak German so she could better understand. So he switched into a rapid, snotty Berlin dialect, and his personality opened up. In his native language, he could joke and tease, no longer shackled by imperfect diction. I might have enjoyed him more if he hadn't made me so jealous. He and Katja addressed each other with the familiar *du* like all German students, but I still hated hearing it. Except for the buck teeth, Jürgen actually resembles a few of my cousins.

Sept. 30, 1970

Guess what Katja and I did the last two breaks? It's just a question of where we go to make love. We're running out of new places, but, hey, what's wrong with repeating ourselves? She's enjoying our sex as much as ever, but she's gotten so earnest. Saying goodbye in her car yesterday, she only tolerated my kisses and suddenly burst into tears. I fear Jürgen has something to do with this new moroseness.

Oct. 7, 1970

Last week Katja wrote a long, romantic letter that quoted Goethe from both his youth and old age. In my reply, I accepted her rendezvous plan as usual, even though I had to make duty by midnight that evening, and playfully quoted a Pushkin line in Cyrillic script from "The Gypsies," showing off my Russian, even if she couldn't comprehend it.

We met not far from the Braunschweig train station in the Leonardstrasse cemetery and wandered among the old graves. I yearned to tell her that Jürgen had been poisoning many an hour of mine since meeting him, but face to face it was hard to bring up.

She asked what was wrong.

I decided against telling her for fear it would only aggravate my annoyance.

We came upon the weathered tombstone of Gotthold Ephraim Lessing. The "1781" was barely legible, the year the greatest eighteenth-century German dramatist paid an ill-fated visit to this city, fell gravely sick, died, and ended up buried far from home. "Who the hell is Jürgen really?" I suddenly blurted. "He's not just a fellow student."

Her troubled gaze studied mine long and hard. She said she'd explain everything in due time. For now, I should rest assured he was just a comrade and not fret over him. She asked how good my Russian was.

"I'm fluent within a restricted vocabulary," I replied. "I love Russian. It's more emotional and expressive than your native language. High German can sound like chopping up a side of beef. As if afterwards you could count all the discrete slices and stack them up. But Russian oozes along bonelessly, filling every crack."

"*Konechno,*" she said, Russian for "*selbstverständlich.*"

"*Ty govorish' po-russki*?" I snapped. Do you speak Russian?

With a perfect Muscovite accent she said she had learned it in school, like all of her classmates. At first, I was too stunned to let the import of those words sink all the way in. Instead I leapt into a Russian interrogation we Monks had drilled in California. We both laughed over her effortless answers. She knows every word, almost as if she has two native languages.

Switching back to German, she asked where I had learned Russian so well. "In Madison, too?"

I briefly described the Monterey language school and its émigré teachers.

"I bet you were the best student."

"Yes, but only because I out-psyched my roommate. He's a great linguist, but couldn't compete with me emotionally. Tommy's a super nice guy, but the Norwegian King of Dorks. It's no wonder he's only had one girlfriend in his entire life, and she sounds dorkier than he is."

"I don't understand 'dork.'"

"It's untranslatable American slang. Where did you learn Russian? In a Berlin *Gymnasium*?"

"Right," she said flatly and asked to hear further details about Tommy.

"Like me, Tom Bakken is from Wisconsin."

Her gaze locked on my mouth. "Tell me more," she said.

“He’s an expert at watching life go by and my only true friend”—I started lying—“but we don’t talk all that much anymore.” I clammed up and demanded that she not ask me further about him. Because I wasn’t supposed to talk about “buddies”—I used the English word—to anybody, especially not a German.

“But you are just as German as I am. I cannot believe you when you say you are not one. Just because you were born in Wisconsin? *Und was sind ‘Buddies’?*”

I let the first remark go as flattery. “Buddies are like friends but in ways even closer. Soldiers get thrown together into the same boat and help each other survive. Tommy and I will always be close, whether we ever see each other again after our discharges.”

“Is he stationed in Knittelstedt then?”

“Yes, but we really must drop this subject. Why are you so curious?”

“Peter, you talk of marriage, and I cannot meet your friends?”

“*Nein*, you can’t meet them for military reasons. Besides, I’m not actually that close to Thomas. Buddies often don’t have much in common. And I’m not at all close to anybody else either.” It felt terrible to be misleading the woman I adored, but I saw no other choice.

We wound around the graveyard till we found a soft, grassy spot between two large tombstones. There we made short, sharp love without undressing, while keeping alert for approaching footfalls against the background rumble and honk of traffic. Afterwards as we lay languorously nose to nose, she asked how Russian had been taught to me. I described the DLI classroom techniques in detail.

Next she wanted to know how well I knew the idioms. The slang? Which jargon? The Red Army terminology?

I answered truthfully until the last question, fearing where that might lead.

“Do you know the swear words also?”

"Quite well." Then in Russian I said, "*Yop tvoyu mat'*," or, "I fucked your mother," a common Soviet curse, not nearly so vulgar to their ears as it strikes us.

She grinned without embarrassment.

"We have a glossary of Russian vulgarity where I work," I foolishly said.

"Interesting. I never learned those words. Our teachers were too properly Prussian to bring them up. But those terms are real Russian too, aren't they?"

"Katja, you should teach at a university. You're much too bright only to be a *Gymnasium* teacher."

"I can take care of my own life, *danke schön*."

"I'm just being a good friend. I'm giving you sound advice."

"Do you realize what you are saying? That would mean I'd have to transfer to a better university in a different city."

"*Nein*!"

"Don't forget you're not my boss." Then, her voice oddly breaking, she said, "Could you get me a copy of those Russian swear words?"

"I'll try." The special dictionary was stamped "Secret," but I could see no reason for that or any other security classification. These were common Russian words, and if they didn't appear in most dictionaries, that hardly made them secrets. Many a defector or radio op can't speak without cursing, and of course we want to understand everything they utter.

That day's goodbye kiss was especially tender.

Oct. 10, 1970

I didn't really know Katja until today. I fear I've gotten myself into big trouble. I don't recall my first mistake, but I just committed the single worst. It was easy enough to sneak a copy of the vulgar word list home from the site inside my lunch bag and deliver it to Katja this morning.

She whispered a soft, "*Danke*," and slipped the pamphlet into her purse, looking both pleased and strangely troubled. No, nothing was wrong, she insisted. We enjoyed a beautiful, sensuous day under the bright sun on a blanket outside of Braunschweig in a beech forest, its leaves fast turning amber.

On the drive to the train station that evening, she stopped at her student union, while I waited in the car. When she returned fifteen minutes later, she said, "Here's your original back. I just made myself this photocopy. Why would anyone want to keep such colorful vulgarity secret?"

A photocopy?

Squirming, I put the original back in my plastic shopping bag. All of a sudden I snatched the duplicate pages off her lap and tore them to shreds. She shrugged. "Do you seriously think I only made one copy? I left another with Jürgen inside. Say, are there many of you Russian linguists in Knittelstedt?"

I glared at her until she lowered her eyes and slumped in her seat. She dropped me off at the *Hauptbahnhof* without saying goodbye. Last night I had to drag my carcass through work, and back here in this room now I can't sleep.

She gave Jürgen a copy of the glossary? That feels like a gun aimed at my head. I kept telling myself it's just dumb Russkie swearing, maybe funny to adolescents, but just more necessary vocabulary to a serious student of the language. How could they be a secret to anybody? But that wasn't the right question.

Oct. 14, 1970

Katja and I met in Braunschweig as planned. She insisted on driving to the Hanover opera, because it was not "*feministisch*" to let me drive so much. Ten minutes into the trip she handed me a squarish, German-style envelope.

"What's this?" I asked.

"A small payment for the glossary. Fifteen hundred marks." Close to a month's salary for me.

I tossed the cash back into her lap. "I did it for you, not for some damned money."

Fifty kilometers later, she broke the tense silence. "A SPETS—I mean—a *special* Soviet defector must have helped you compile that little dictionary."

"What?"

"It's not simply vulgarity in it. There's also special slang. At least according to a colleague."

"What are you talking about?"

Refusing to elaborate, she accelerated past the speed limit, as if deliberately risking a traffic ticket. This despite knowing full well what sticklers the German highway patrol was about enforcing the law.

As we raced along, I contemplated what she had just told me. Didn't she start to say the Russian word "SPETSNAZ" before switching to the German word for "special"? Especially since the latter "*spezial*" begins with a "shp" sound and not the plain "sp" of Russian that she had in fact pronounced. Hadn't she given that initial syllable the short, squeezed "e" vowel of Russian instead of the long, open "a" of its German equivalent? Or had she simply stammered and I was imagining things? Since it made zero sense for her to know *anything* whatsoever about the Soviet SPETSNAZ.

We drove on forty more kilometers without talking. "I had better transfer to Munich," she finally piped up.

"Munich? But you could hardly be farther away and still be in Germany."

"Peter, let's just say I am taking your advice to heart and switching to a more challenging university. Maybe I'll like living in the Bavarian Beer Heaven."

I was speechless. Munich was much too far for even weekend visits. Day trips would be out of the question. I'd barely ever see her anymore. "But why?" I asked.

"I do need to graduate from a better university. A mere teacher's college will not 'cut it,' as you say in English."

"But it does cut it for a *Gymnasium* teacher," I replied, rage surging inside me. She was willing to move away from me just like that?

Tension in her features hinted at both guile and guilt. Then she dropped an even bigger bombshell. "Whether I go or not, we must stop seeing each other. For a long while at least. Believe me, it'll be the best for us both." No matter how hard I pressed her, she wouldn't explain further.

I wanted to trust her judgment, but not at this horrendous price. I want to marry her, for God's sake. I'll live here, or in America, wherever she wants. Even in East-fucking-Germany.

We took our seats inside the Staatsoper Hanover and *Tosca* began, but instead of concentrating on the Puccini tragedy, I studied the German audience in their ill-fitting black suits and silver ties and dowdy dresses and gowns, every last one of them paying rapt attention to the performance. During the intermission, they stuffed themselves with beer and sausage and walked abreast in peculiar, tight circles around the lobby, as if marching in lockstep. Katja was going to abandon me just like that?

"What about us?" I asked, at the wheel myself on the way back.

"If we don't stop, we'll get caught, Peter. You'll regret ever having met me. You know you're not supposed to be this close to any German. Why, you even passed me a classified document. You'll pay a horrible price."

It was then at long last that I finally admitted to myself who Katja Wendt worked for and so who she really was. For a few seconds, I felt like I was going to detonate. But I contained myself for fear of losing everything. I had to be positive I wasn't mistaken, but how could I be?

"I'll be more careful," I said. "We'll both be more careful. But please, please stay here up north. What about transferring to Hanover or Hamburg or Kiel? Those are good universities, too." And, above all, within day-trip distance.

"Peter, I said we must stop seeing each other. Believe me, we must. Does anybody at Det Q know about me yet?"

"Not a soul. But even if you do move to Munich, we can still see each other at least once in a while. And then after I'm discharged next year, all of the time."

"*Nein,* Peter. Find somebody else. I will."

"I'll wait for you."

"I won't wait for you."

I tried to tell myself I wouldn't want to force her to see me. Like hell I wouldn't. "But things have been going so well."

"No, they haven't."

"What are you talking about? My superiors will never find out about you. Never. Trust me."

"You think it's just up to you?"

"If you really cared about me, you'd find a way to stay."

"Peter," she said in a silky voice while caressing my cheek. "It's because I really care about you that we must stop seeing each other. Trust me, it's better this way."

"Better for you?"

"Better for all of us."

"Who does this 'all of us' include? Jürgen? Who the hell is he anyway?"

She laughed mirthlessly. "Peterchen, you're jealous. He's just a comrade."

"*Selbstverständlich,*" I snapped and pressed down on the accelerator.

Katja ridiculed my "bourgeois" notions of fidelity, saying it would be stupid of me not to find another girlfriend. "What does jealousy mean after all? We don't own each other. You feel jealous because of an infringement upon your perceived property rights. If you truly love me, whatever makes me happy should make you happy, including seeing other men. Of course I can't promise to be true. If I want to, I will, and if I don't, I won't. What if another man really needs me?"

"Women make good money on the Bruchstrasse because men need them."

She raised her hand to slap me, but stopped mid-air. Though my last remark did succeed in shutting her up. She took leave at the train station with a curt "*Auf Wiedersehen.*"

“When can I see you again?” I asked, stunned that it might be over between us.

“Soon. I’ll contact you.”

I slammed the car door and marched off toward the platforms.

Oct. 20, 1970

The past few days I’ve convinced myself that I only imagined Katja starting to say, “SPETSNAZ,” during our Hanover excursion. And I’ve vowed to quit looking back at old diary entries because that only makes me more miserable.

Oct. 25, 1970

During slack hours at the site lately I’ve skimmed that glossary of Russian vulgarity twice and failed to find any instance of special slang. But then do I know Russian well enough to recognize it?

Oct. 30, 1970

This week Katja drove us for a nippy picnic in the moors of the Lüneburger Heath. She turned east off Highway 4 onto a narrower road and parked a half mile down it. My goal this rendezvous was to persuade her to stay in Braunschweig no matter how.

Our food had to wait. I spread the blanket over curling hawthorn leaves and minutes later was deep inside her. The tingling was just beginning, when she whispered, “Stop!” but it was too late. The explosion in my loins was already shuddering its way into her, when I heard the clicking. My head jerked up—there stood a man not twenty feet away, photographing us. Fortyish, blonder than Katja, graying temples, balding, jowly, short salt-and-pepper beard, a bit paunchy. She and I jumped to our feet, turned away from the stranger, and got dressed.

We grabbed our wine and food and rushed to the nearest village, hardly more than a crossroads. I registered us in a country inn as “Peter Wendt and wife” and paid cash in advance—fifteen marks, about four dollars. My signature wasn’t questioned. In a much happier mood a couple of hours later, I came downstairs for two Becks to take upstairs and chatted with Herr Zahn, the portly innkeeper.

"Are you from Berlin, mein Herr?" he asked with an ingratiating grin.

"*Jawohl,* how could you tell?" I replied.

"*Ach ja,* many Berliners stay here."

Pleading my wife's impatience, I graciously excused myself. Before falling asleep, I made love to Katja again, terrified we were running out of tomorrows.

The next day we visited northern West Germany's salient of territory jutting into East Germany, where the Elbe forms the border. East German *Vopo* patrol boats slowly chugged up and down the river to intercept fleeing fellow citizens, who had somehow gotten past their formidable fences and mines. We hiked along the sand embankment to the ruins of a railroad abutment, sat down, and dangled our feet over the jagged concrete. On the opposite bank stood a matching structure in even worse disrepair, these two ends all that remained of a bridge bombed out during World War Two, never to be rebuilt in our lifetimes. Near it lay a sleepy village of stucco buildings and steep red roofs, just like the one on our side.

"When do you think we'll see a unified Germany?" Katja asked wistfully. The settlement just across the water was so inaccessible it might as well have been on the moon.

"After World War Three. The victor will claim the unified wasteland as his spoils." Had she set me up to be photographed, I couldn't help but wonder? Or had a perverse hiker simply chanced upon us?

She snorted. "Why so defeatist? History is progressive. Can't you see the human race moving forward over the centuries? Even the superstitions of Christianity would be better than your pessimism. We humans must look ahead to something better or we lose the will to go on. Do you any faith in anything?"

"I believe knowledge is the path, wisdom the goal."

"But *whose* path, Peter? Which side are you on?"

"How many sides are there?"

"Two big ones."

"I'm on the side of knowledge. I refuse to get mixed up in politics."

"As if we had a choice. Staying aloof from politics is itself a very political act, one that always helps the wrong side win. If you would only see the light. In your heart I know you're not so apolitical as you sound."

"True, but I don't let my heart overrule my intellect."

"I laugh myself sick. You're with me right now, aren't you? You don't really know yourself and what you're capable of."

That evening we ordered a Cordon bleu special at the Lüchow *Ratskeller* and picked at our meal in pensive silence.

"Which two big sides did you mean today?" I said.

Her troubled gaze showed she meant what I feared, and she knew I knew. She did set me up in the woods with that cameraman, didn't she? For minutes we stared deeply into each other's eyes, searching for the perfect partner no longer present. NATO versus the Warsaw Pact. The Free World versus Communism. Good versus Evil. How could Katja be on the wrong side?

"Anything else?" the waiter asked.

I ordered another beer, and Katja, looking stricken, asked for mulled wine. I reached across the table for her hand, but she refused.

"So this is it?" I said.

"Almost. After tomorrow you will never see me again. There'll be no *Auf Wiedersehen*. I've made up my mind once and for all what must be done."

I paid the waiter at our table and followed Katja to her VW parked halfway on the sidewalk. She let me drive us to her apartment in Braunschweig, where we went straight to bed without so much as a goodnight kiss.

The next morning we slept late, and at noon she drove me to the *Hauptbahnhof* and, unusually for her, accompanied me to my platform. "I don't want to have to say adieu instead of *Auf*

Wiedersehen," she said, "but I must. Don't ask me to explain why and never tell any comrades anything about me. I swear that I am leaving you for your own good. Trust me now, even though you know I have lied to you before. Be aware I have also had to lie to my superiors about you. Now I have to persuade them that you are hopeless material as a secret agent. And that you are no longer in love with me and are only seeing me for sex, which you can just as easily get someplace else. They will believe me because they haven't caught me in a lie yet. But I had better not press my luck. I took your soul. Now I give it back. *Tschüss*." That last tearful word German for adieu—or go with God.

"We'll see each other again," I told her.

She shook her head.

"I'll find you."

"Don't try. If you do," she said, her voice cracking, "I will tell your Commanding Officer Slater that you passed me a classified document and everything about you and me. Forget that I ever mentioned the word Munich or you will face court martial as a traitor. Find somebody else."

I pored over her features, stopping at her moist, bloodshot eyes. She kissed me again chastely, turned around, and walked down the platform with slow, even steps, leaving me forever without once looking back.

Feb. 1, 1971

My rage against Katja is going nova. My pulse pounds to schemes of revenge, all unworthy of me and too embarrassing to record here. I just tore up three months of pissing and moaning. Did anything eventful happen in the interim? What follows at least.

Following a swing shift before Christmas, I changed from fatigues to dress greens, and an MP drove me to Helmstedt to meet the 2:00 a.m. duty train from Berlin to Frankfurt am Main. Rocking in my bunk to the rhythmic clatter of iron wheels on rails, I debated what I should have done with Katja to keep her in Braunschweig, till I dozed off. And again suffered a nightmare that the clear light of day and sober reason could scarcely dispel. In this wretched dream I was hiking outside Chute Noire in the Wisconsin State Park with the sandstone buttes. They're an odd geologic relic hundreds of millions years older than the surrounding woodlands, ground flat by Ice Age glaciers. Ignoring the clammy swelter, I skittered like a lizard up a ridge till I was overlooking a sea of jack pine. I had no sooner caught my breath than my sweating turned to shivering. To my horror, the broad mound beneath me had shrunk to a tiny pinnacle, itself fast disappearing under surging waters. Within seconds, numbing waves lapped at my ankles, and I faced imminent death.

I showed up before the promotion board in Giessen, bleary-eyed and muddleheaded. Three grim lifers—a first lieutenant and two sergeants—grilled me about current events, military duties, and etiquette. I ably explained the conflict on the Indian subcontinent and Nixon's rationale for his Laotian incursion, but garbled commands for dismounted drill and the charge for company CQ.

Afterwards, the officer and master sergeant acted placated, but the sergeant first class kept glaring at my hair that I hadn't given more than a minor trim. They wouldn't tell me whether I had made the promotion to Spec Five, but said I'd be notified soon. Of course I only wanted it for the extra pay.

A letter from Mom waiting on my pillow back in Knittelstedt jerked me out of my holiday doldrums. Her poor health had taken a marked turn for the worse. Her blood pressure was now two hundred over one forty, and she suffered daily headaches and chest pains. Doctor Frenzel claimed she could go tomorrow or last a year, only God knew which. Her only prayer was that His will be done as it always has been, and she wouldn't ask for a longer life, if that wasn't His plan. Besides, I didn't need her anymore now that I was a grown man, and she was looking forward to joining her parents in a better world.

I read it again and then a third time and broke down bawling. Her letters always touched me no matter how good or bad their news, but this one after losing Katja was unbearable. I longed to see my mother immediately, but decided to wait until her illness got even more serious, because I couldn't keep flying back and forth to the States.

I told myself I should envy my mother's happier life. After all, her simple, yet profound, Christian faith has held her above every hardship and answered her every question. Never once has she known the slightest doubt about what she is, where, or why. Her biggest disappointment, long since accepted, has been my unwillingness to use my God-given talent to become a Lutheran minister, like my cousin Paul Zielsdorf, a rural pastor. As if I could preach a credo, I didn't myself believe.

Feb. 2, 1971

Let me mention New Year's Eve. Unlike last year I had both the 31st and 1st off, but didn't do anything special to celebrate other than sit quietly among the rowdy crowd at Club 69, sipping bourbon and grooving on the Moody Blues, Jimmy Hendrix, Gordon Lightfoot, and Rolling Stones, playing on a stereo.

I hesitate to write down more crap that happened at the site, but why stop now, especially since nobody but me will ever see on these pages? Anyway, after Halloween—so not a holiday in *Deutschland*—the SPETSNAZ unit we regularly monitor went oddly silent and stayed down a whole month, leaving us Monks and other Russkie lingies with nada to do at the site. At first alarmed and then furious, Whitman and Wilhelm vented their frustration by assigning us obnoxious cleanup details. It got so bad even Tommy complained.

Eventually the SPETSNAZ radios came back up, and my Green Room crew resumed eavesdropping and recording like before. Within a week, Spec 6 Boudreau claimed this Soviet Special Forces traffic had fundamentally changed. Though not so far as our ops could tell, these Russkies again yacking away on their frequency-hopping, synched radios.

Feb. 4, 1971

Since Katja left me last autumn, it seems about all I've done is wait in vain to hear from her and write letters to my mother. I've tried to keep busy when not at the site, but most days I've had too little energy left after work for reading, inviting Tom or another Monk over or joining them at Club 69.

Deep down I know it is all over between Katja and me, but I refuse to admit it. Every ounce of good sense tells me to rejoice in our breakup, because she easily could have ruined my life. What if Whitman or Slater had found out about us? I couldn't have kept our relationship secret indefinitely. But didn't meeting her also save my life? What would have happened to me last year, if I hadn't accompanied Karl-Heinz to Braunschweig—or if we hadn't run into Katja at Zum grünen Kakadu? The prospect is frightening.

Bakken was the first to notice I no longer spent breaks on trips. Over a sack lunch together at the site, I claimed the reason was a New Year's resolution to save more money each month for graduate school. The sweet Norwegian looked skeptical, but didn't press the issue.

How can I describe Katja's departure from my life this calmly? Because it has so devastated me I'm too depressed to be upset. That's really why I interrupted this diary. And let me confess a simple secret—every day after work I returned to this room and poured myself a stiff shot of bourbon.

The first couple of months without her not even alcohol could quiet the raging in my soul, but now I'm slowly reconciling myself to returning to graduate school. And to losing Katja forever. Every day I remind myself to forget her. But I simply can't.

Last summer, not long after meeting Katja, I was considering re-upping for two more years on condition I remain assigned to Det Q just to stay near her. That would have meant giving up my plans for a doctorate, but that seemed like a small sacrifice. But now I'll be leaving Germany as soon as possible. I've already jeopardized my glorious academic future enough. No one has found out about her, thank goodness, so I should leave well enough alone.

Feb. 5, 1971

That Katja is an enemy agent still seems totally absurd. Isn't she more a flower-child lover of beauty and nature? Sure, she believes in a human progress that eventually will mean a decent life for all, but that's a vague ideal shared by everyone of good will, even American right-wingers.

Feb. 6, 1971

Okay, I do admit something is definitely different about SPETSNAZ traffic since their month-long hiatus. Now their ops often sound bored and no longer ever tease or curse—almost like they're reading from scripts. Worse, they no longer say anything Boudreau or other analysts find of intelligence value. Sure, they still discuss staffing, supply shortages, and the like, but that's not important. What happened?

Feb. 9, 1971

It's been a long, lonely, wretched winter without Katja, so two days ago I tried to cheer myself up by going on an excursion. Hamburg was my first choice, but it seemed too far away. Hanover has a fine opera house, but no way was I going back there alone. So I made it old, familiar Braunschweig.

On today's one-year anniversary of meeting Katharina Wendt, I walked past Bernd's apartment and sauntered around the *Pädagogische Hochschule*, clenching my teeth at times to fight back the tears. I strolled through the freezing drizzle to Zum grünen Kakadu and forced myself to enter. The same mix of German students as on the night Katja and I met was at the bar, but this time in denims and turtlenecks instead of costumes. Two women at a stone table kept ogling me, but I wasn't up to accosting them, so I abandoned the nearly full stein of beer I had ordered and bolted.

I marched over to the Domplatz past the city's symbol—a medieval statue of a lion—and wandered smack dab into a group of German students dressed up as Uncle Sam in red, white and blue and Vietnamese peasants in black pajamas, performing a haranguing piece of Street Theater. A stringy-haired joker in a US Army field jacket jolted me out of my reverie by thrusting a beret under my nose and begging for money to buy the Vietcong bicycles. I adamantly refused. No way was I going to contribute to the deaths of buddies, no matter what I might think about my government's foreign policy.

"Does the money really mean that much to you?" the dude said, jostling me. "As easy as you have it just being a student? The Viet Cong are fighting this war on your behalf, too, you know."

I shoved the jerk so hard he stumbled into another student. Sure, I hate the war and want it stopped, but his hat full of marks meant American deaths. I thought of those flares over Fort Ord visible from the DLI barracks and all the young infantry trainees there, who no more deserved to end up cannon fodder in Vietnam than I did.

I turned my back on the asshole to keep from punching his ugly face in and wound my way to the Bruchstrasse, where an eight-foot brick wall narrows to a shoulder-width entrance. Behind it stretched a block of street-level windows, each with its own little red light. Avoiding eye contact, I traipsed past the row of women, leaning against the glass in garish makeup and brief lingerie. Until at the end, a skinny, haggard blonde caught my gaze and snapped, "*Komm mal her*!" Come here!

I made a return pass, pausing before a fetching whore, who looked barely the minimum age of twenty-one. Long, tousled, ash-blonde hair. Lush body spilling out of a diaphanous bra and panties. Black garter belt flattering strong thighs. "Only fifty marks," she said by way of introduction and curled her lips into an enticing pout.

I asked where she was from, addressing her formally as *Sie*.

"From the Heath," she said. "What's it to you?" She used the informal *du*.

"It seems like I should get to know you a bit first. How did you ever end up here?"

"I'm Christa. I cost fifty marks. That's all there is to know. Do I please you?" She cocked her right hip.

"Very much. But I don't think I can do this to you." I cringed to envision the rough circumstances that had resulted in this wretched life for her.

"Why not? I work here."

"Not of your own free will."

"Don't tell me what I'm doing, asshole! If you can't afford me, get the hell out of here, you cheap bastard!"

"I don't want to exploit you is all."

"Don't give me this shit. I make good money. Better than you do, I bet. I'm a bargain at fifty marks."

"Okay, you please me."

She was cheap at that price. I paid fifty more. The young Heath whore with the quick pelvic thrusts made me forget Katja—until the next morning. I skipped the hotel breakfast and caught the first train back to Knittelstedt.

Feb. 10, 1971

Today Sergeant Whitman told me to drop everything I was doing and report ASAP to the CO. Two minutes later, I was trembling outside Slater's office.

I rapped twice. Somebody grunted inside, so I sidled in, gently closing the door behind me. The Captain was digging in a cabinet, while Lieutenant Colonel Van Dyke, Slater's own CO from Giessen, was glowering at a personnel file from behind a desk. Namely, mine.

So this is it, I thought, panicking—they've found me out. I braced myself for the worst, while neither of them said a word. I debated whether to confess part of what I had done to win leniency or to deny it all. If I'd had a relationship with Katja, that didn't necessarily mean I knew she was an East German. But what about the glossary? I locked my knees to stop their shaking, wishing I'd been assigned to Vietnam after all.

Slater slammed the cabinet drawer shut and jerked around. "Is this any way to report to your Commanding Officer?"

"No, Sir!" I said and snapped off a sharp salute. "Specialist Fourth Class Peter Zielsdorf reporting as ordered, Sir!"

Slater reciprocated with a perfunctory salute and stepped closer. Van Dyke didn't even look up. If I sprinted out the door, could I make it past the gate before the CO alerted the MPs? But how far could I actually run in fatigues and combat boots? "Zielsdorf," Slater said, "Lieutenant Colonel Van Dyke would personally like to put on your new insignia. You made Spec Five, soldier. Congratulations."

I squelched a giggle. The bald, wrinkled old man reeking of Old Spice pinned the new tin chevrons into my lapels and snapped on the stays. He thanked me for the fine job I was doing at Det Q and said our country would never acknowledge good men like me, because they'd never learn about our classified work. But Sergeant Whitman had told him about my diligence, and he wanted to express his gratitude on behalf of the whole nation.

"Thank you, Sir," I said, saluted again, and exited. Outside, I could have done flips. I had made Spec Five, and nobody knew about Katja!

I've decided that the smartest thing for me will be to get discharged over here and travel around Europe a while, before diving into my doctoral program back home. I can't wait for Umlaut's ETS party this coming break.

Feb. 14, 1971

I should have waited. But I had to do something other than sit here brooding about Katja in Munich. Approaching Club 69 on foot, I could hear Jimi Hendrix's anguished guitar a block away. I swung open the iron door, and the crowd inside roared, "Zielsdorf! Come on in, Troop! Get with the program! Hit the deck and give me ten, Greasy!" Fifty guys were there already, and more than a few tipsy.

"Barkeep!" Umlaut shouted, his shit-eating grin beaming good cheer. "A double Chivas Regal for Det Q's gentleman scholar, Herr Zielsdorf! Say, Petie, you speak pretty good Amurrican for a Kraut." Scotch wasn't my first choice, but I acted delighted. Pink-eyed Umlaut was still in fatigues, having come straight from a shift at the site.

I drank deeply of the liquor on the rocks, ignoring the smoky taste. "Bet you wish you were short as me, huh, Petie?" he asked.

"Yeah," I said without conviction, doubting I could ever just give up on Katja. But was finding her even remotely possible?

"Shit, buddy, you like it over here or something?" Umlaut said with a cackle. "Man, I can't wait to get back to the World. This place is Timbuktu."

"Germany is also part of the world," I muttered. "And I like living here."

"You're weird, Zielsdorf. But I guess that's why the treads brought you here. You seriously mean you're going to stay in Krautland one minute longer than you have to? And do what?" He screwed up his face, as if contemplating the mysteries of the universe.

"Eventually I'll go to grad school at UW-Madison. But before then, I want to get a European discharge and travel around."

"I thought you already had a Master's?"

"I do. Now I want a Ph.D."

"Ph.D.? No shit. Dr. Zielsdorf. Doctor of what?"

"German most likely."

"Hell, Petie, you'll tear 'em up. Nobody speaks Kraut better than you. 'Cept maybe the Herms themselves." Umlaut guffawed again. "I can't believe it. Old Lardass Whitman telling a future professor when to shit and when to blow his nose."

"I try not to let it bother me." Another lie.

"What choice do you have? It'd be stupid to let it bother you. Want another drink? I sure do."

"Not yet."

Local Germans began arriving in US Army field jackets and denims, a delightful combination strictly forbidden to us GIs when off duty. I slid down the bar and greeted guys, not a one a stranger, no matter what their military specialty. Umlaut handed me another Chivas Regal, before joining the rest of his trick. I took a stool and scrutinized photos from last summer's Fourth of July party, tacked up on tagboard above the shelf of fifths. One showed a heavy-lidded Umlaut, proudly holding a scrawled certificate that declared him, "Det Q Derelict of the Year." I squirmed at another of the Monks minus me, seated around a card table, playing cards. I had skipped those festivities to see Katja.

A glance across the room at Whitman, Wilhelm, and Slater made me cringe. What a conniption fit these treads would throw if they ever heard about Katja and me. I damned her to hell and back for what she'd done. Making me believe we were going to be together forever, while playing me like a puppet. What crap to claim her transfer to Munich was for my own good.

I gulped my drink like Kool-Aid and walked over to Burke, together with a cute brunette. He introduced "Sharr-low-tuh" in a game attempt at her name in German—Charlotte. The kid was sincere and sweet and, above all else, naive. Everything Will isn't. She deserves better.

Bakken popped over, slung an arm around Charlotte's shoulder, and flashed that dorky grin. Loaded again. And not just a little bit, if he was laying hands on a woman. Tom invited us all to join him and Scotty and Rich in a back corner, so we did. There Umlaut came by with a tray of punch, and we graciously accepted a cup each to imbibe along with our highballs, beer, and wine.

"Purple haze before my eyes," Jimi Hendrix wailed, as Umlaut sidled his way to the dance floor and undulated to the beat like a bread-dough puppet.

When Tommy invited Charlotte to dance, Will leaned his pudgy face into mine. "I presume you can keep a secret, Zielsdorf."

I nodded.

"Charlotte thinks she's pregnant."

"Where are you going for the abortion?" I said, feeling far more sympathy for Charlotte's plight than Will's.

"Abortion is murder," Will slurred. "The Church could not be more unequivocal."

This was a larger dose of morality than I could bear, so I shifted next to Rich. "I can't stomach working for these pukes anymore," he told me. "Next break I'll be in Stockholm for sure."

"Come on, Rich," I said. "How many times do I have to tell you? You'd hate a country that tight-assed."

"But I'll be free. And no longer working for the fascists."

"My good man, what do you mean by 'fascist'?" Will butted in. "The term is frightfully vague."

"Vague, my ass!" Rich snapped. "That's like asking, 'What is air?' Fascism is, like—everywhere. I mean, the military is practically by definition fascist, and the site is Fascist City. Humans shouldn't ever have to do the things soldiers always do, and I don't mean just not to others. Not to themselves either. Fascism is having the pigs and treads in control. It's uniforms and short hair and weapons and power. It's threatening people you have no quarrel with. It's the opposite of hippie. And I'm getting myself the hell as far away from it as possible."

"Young Hoffman, I advise you to exercise forbearance until your discharge next year."

"Do you compromise that easy?" Rich's voice was shrill. Will wisely chose not to reply. Hoffman helped himself to my punch.

As the scotch kicked in hard, I ogled Pam Cook's jiggling curves out on the dance floor. One of only eleven wives at Det Q, she soaked up all the flirting and attention a hundred lonely single GIs could muster. Not that I knew she was having affairs, but if any wife was stepping out she was. Rumor had it she was a head, too—or at least had been back home. Not that her husband dared to be here. Bill Cook was the orderly room clerk and the CO's batman, a sincere St. Louis boy, if not overly bright. Pam was studying German at home from a grammar and audiotapes and improving fast, while all Bill could manage was *Ja*, *Nein*, and *Max nix*.

Tommy plopped into the chair beside me with a goofy grin. "*Kak ty pozhivayesh*?" he asked with a decent Muscovite accent. How's it going?

"Could be worse," I replied in Russian.

"By now," Tommy said, switching to English, "you must have read all the works of German literature twice over."

"No, I haven't made much progress lately. I can't concentrate."

He half-shouted at me, "Maybe Russian Lit would be better for you then! For one thing, there's a lot less to read! The Russkies barely got their literature going before Pushkin! As for me, I've finally settled on a grad school major!"

"Comp Lit, right? Then tenure at one of the better colleges."

"You silly boy, Peter. Fat chance I'd ever end up at a place like that." His eyelids were drooping and his shoulders sagging. "I've decided on getting a Master's in Teaching English as a Second Language."

"Come on, Tommy. You're too smart for that. Your Karen will get tenure somewhere prestigious, so you'd better, too. Go for a doctorate in Comp Lit."

"No, no, no," he slurred, staring down at his little paunch. "I don't have what it takes. I'm not brilliant. I'm not even smart. Sure, I work hard, but I'm still second-rate. Especially compared to you."

"Nonsense, Bakken. You focus way better than I do. You're steadier. Me, I can't even decide on what I want a doctorate in."

"What bullshit, Peter." Bakken's rare use of vulgarity was proof of serious inebriation. "It's got to be German. You're as good at that as anything."

"Politics interest me more than lit lately. Literature doesn't explain why the world's divided into two armed camps ready to blast each other to kingdom come." Every time I ogled Pam again, Katja's labored panting echoed in my ears.

"Politics don't matter, Peter. People will still be reading Pushkin when the terms 'USA' and 'USSR' will have to be explained in footnotes."

"But I live in 1971, and now these terms mean everything."

"What are you talking about? Since when?"

I couldn't say, "Since getting screwed over by Katja." Instead I got Tommy talking about his Karen Tollefson. He had been planning on marrying her, he told me, until they discovered that the less they wrote, the less they bored each other. Besides, how could he write an interesting letter about life in Knittelstedt, if he wasn't allowed to mention the site? She made graduate school sound bleaker than Basic Combat Training.

Tom excused himself to "bleed the lizard." Before he could return, I got up and joined Scotty alongside the dance floor, checking out the action. "See anything you like?" he said, locking his gaze on Pam Cook, doing the Monkey to the raunchy beat of the Stones' "I Can't Get No Satisfaction." With Bakken no less. Was his dancing ever pathetic.

"We're worried about you," Scotty told me. "You were so happy there for a while."

I shrugged and turned my back on sexy Pam. "How are you and Beth doing?"

"Still in love, I guess, though lately I'm having reservations. Beth's a hippie, you know, counterculture, so I don't think she'd make much of a college professor's wife. Though sometimes instead of teaching history, I long to live in a style at least as nice as my father's, and that means earning bigger bucks than a prof ever could. For Beth, that'd even be worse. I'm even considering becoming a corporate lawyer."

All of a sudden I missed Katja so intensely my eyes teared over. "The cigarette smoke's getting to me," I said, blinking.

"Not that we've ever been incompatible in bed," Scott went on. "And Beth is especially sweet and kind. And a knockout in an original way."

"If I were you, I'd go with your gut feeling. And do whatever it takes to reel her in." So why was I ignoring my own advice?

"Maybe you're right. Man, I can hardly wait till my own discharge. That lucky bastard Umlaut. If Beth and I could only be together, I bet our differences would clear up just like that."

"Where there's a will, there's a way," I muttered. In that moment I resolved that once I was a civilian, I would find Katja and make everything work out for us. But what if she was no longer available?

On the dance floor, Umlaut's loosey-goosey watusi had degenerated into wild flailing, like a whirling dervish on speed, as though expecting to become airborne if he only flapped hard enough. "Short! Short! Short!" he kept hollering.

Sergeant Wilhelm made him sit down, not pulling rank, but just protecting the poor son of a bitch from himself. His gross drunkenness was technically a security violation, but like whoring wasn't enforced at Det Q.

It was high time all of us switched to Pepsi, but one glance at Pam Cook's tight slacks and I made my refill a Jim Beam straight up. I was edging closer to dancing myself, when a firm hand gripped my shoulder. I gulped to face Sergeant Wilhelm. "Zielsdorf," he said with a deep growl, "I'd like to thank you personally for your conscientious work at the site. You set a fine example for the Newks."

Embarrassed by the kind words, I dutifully shook the Sarge's beefy hand. Like the other treads, he didn't have a clue why I worked so hard. Not out of any belief in our mission, but to cover my ass, however little, if I ever got hauled in over my affair with Katja. The more valuable I was to them, the more lenient they might be—unless they found out she was working for the Warsaw Pact, that is. Then I'd be better off dead.

Umlaut was bringing out the best in everybody, that is, everyone except me. All the alcohol in my blood only fueled my rage against Katja. Why the hell wasn't I looking for a new girlfriend?

I joined the gang in singing Umlaut "For He's A Jolly Good Fellow," the short-timer basking in our affection. With a thudding beat, more felt than heard, Jimi Hendrix's freaked-out dissonance again blared. Whopper was hoisted atop a pair of shoulders. From there he grabbed a bare girder buttressing the warehouse ceiling and, gripping that with both hands, swung among the beams like a monkey to the music's spacey anguish. The whole barroom crowd huddled beneath the spectacle. Finally, to shrill hooting Whopper dropped safely into their grasp.

Wild Bill Johnston was lifted aloft next, and he clambered around the ceiling with vice-like hands to screams of "Short! Short! Short!" When he finally let go, Henry Smith and Umlaut elevated Bakken, but all Tommy could manage was to grasp a girder with all fours and pull himself flush with the ceiling. "Short! Short! Short!" the crowd chanted, until Tommy lost his grip and hurtled down onto Smith and Johnston, all three collapsing on the floor in laughter. Whereupon CO Slater put an end to the ape antics.

The heavy iron door to the street swung open, and in walked Karl-Heinz, Bärbel, Gitty and, last but certainly not least, Dagmar. Her boyfriend Bernd nowhere in sight. Braless in a tight turtleneck, Karl's sister was no Katja, but then who was? I welcomed them all *auf Deutsch* and hustled them cups of punch.

Karl-Heinz told me about the threatened teachers strike at his *Gymnasium*, a rare lapse of discipline for a German union. By the way, had I heard anything from Katja?

A beat too slow, I replied, "I haven't had any contact with her since that weekend with you in Braunschweig."

With a wink Karl-Heinz said in English, "Once is not enough."

"GIs here aren't allowed intimate relationships with German women."

Karl-Heinz winked once more. "Okay, you never saw her again. How tragic. Say, did I ever tell you how Katja got interested in you? Last winter I met her for lunch in Braunschweig, and she asked about Knittelstedt. I mentioned the Americans stationed here and said you really brought some life into this sleepy burg. Even if you riled the parents of a few nubile daughters."

I didn't laugh.

"A friend was with her," Karl went on. "An older guy she seemed to know pretty well."

I glared at Karl-Heinz, but didn't dare ask about him. "I told her about Will Burke and Scotty Dickinson, but her ears didn't perk up till I said there was one American fluent in both German and Russian. Katja insisted she meet you somehow, so I arranged it."

I lurched away from Karl livid enough to rip the club's steel door off its hinges. If a man had done to me what Katja had, I'd have crushed him like a bug. She set out to entrap me from the very start? Lucky for her she was out of reach in Munich. Things we had done together raced through my mind, our trips, hikes, and shared beds. It didn't seem possible she hadn't loved me, too. But of course she did. Perhaps not as much as I loved her, but she wasn't acting in my arms. And I still believed her when she said she left Braunschweig for my own good. Though she owed me a better explanation.

Why did I persist in obsessing about Katja? As if I was determined to poison the present with the past. Why couldn't I dwell on the sweet things in my life? Such as resting my gaze on Dagmar Schneider's pretty face at that moment. Recalling Pam Cook's interest in a tutor, I told Karl-Heinz about a sexy American in Knittelstedt, eager to learn German. He could have a lot of fun teaching her.

"Really? What's she doing in Germany?"

"Her husband is stationed here."

Karl-Heinz guffawed. "Why not? Are you sure she's willing?"

"*Selbstverständlich.* She knows who you are, and she said she's attracted to you." Pure hogwash.

I excused myself to tell Pam that a local German acquaintance was willing to tutor her for nothing. "You might be able to score through him, too," I said, implying a drug deal, another pure fabrication. "But don't mention it first. He'll want to get to know you before he'll bring it up."

Positive he'd never bring it up, I fetched Karl and made the introductions. The two of them hit it off. And just like that, Dagmar was freed of her brother's protection. If she wasn't Katja, she was still Dagmarchen.

She and her girlfriends were talking to Shotgun of all people. John Jenkins actually, a dim-bulb electrician from Dubuque, Iowa. My speaking fluent German with the Fräulein made him so uncomfortable he sauntered off.

Dagmar said that after Easter she was switching to the Freie Universität in West Berlin to major in *Englisch* and minor in *Deutsch*. Her new plans were to teach German for a couple of years at an American high school. How about teaching there forever, I wondered, but didn't express.

"What do you *Amis* do at your 'site' anyway?" she asked. "You're all so secretive."

I shrugged.

"That big a secret, huh?" Her smile was inviting. At nineteen she was maturing nicely indeed.

"How about another drink?" I said. What could I get her? A vodka tonic? Perfect. Gitty and Bärbel were "going for a ride" with Whopper and Shotgun, but I talked Dagmar into staying by promising to practice English with her.

I made her drink a double and mine a seven-up. In slow, precise English, I asked, "How is Bernd doing in Braunschweig?" She had already implied the answer, but I needed to know for sure.

"Very well, I hear."

From up close her skin looked divinely smooth. "So you two split up?"

"Last summer. He did not want me to go to Berlin. I did not want to stay in Braunschweig."

"Why not?"

"How can Braunschweig compare to Berlin? I prefer the political activity at the FU." A drunken GI stumbled into me from behind, making me lurch into Dagmar's soft chest. When I sincerely apologized, she blushed.

Eventually, I had to leave her alone long enough to use the john and on the way ran into Jim Fry. I asked our most lenient trick chief about switching Hoffman to his Delta trick, claiming there was a horrible personality clash between Rich and Sergeant Hill on Able trick. Besides, Rich would be far more productive under someone like him. Nice guy Fry promised to bring it up with Whitman.

When I got back, Dagmar was gone. Across the room, Umlaut was leaning against a wall with lowered head and closed eyes, asleep on his feet. Over the Stones' "Let It Bleed" someone screamed "Short!" in a hoarse imitation of Umlaut. I pushed my way through the crowd and found Dagmar dancing with the Norwegian King of Dorks, Bakken. The staggering Prince Charming's jerky frug was painful to watch. When the music switched to Crosby, Stills and Nash, I cut in on Tom, and he stumbled off to the bar.

Nestling close, Dagmar purred, "Tommy is very nice. But I guess that is an American national trait." She and I waltzed—more or less—the whole album, and then I got us more drinks, double vodka and tonic for her, ice water for me.

We hadn't half-finished these, when one good look at her droopy ice-blue eyes made me feel ashamed. Katja was the only woman I'd ever want, not this child-woman. I could only feel protective toward young Dagmar. So I walked her home and helped her with the house key. For my kindness, she gave me a cousinly kiss goodnight and stumbled inside.

Dagmar hardly seems ready for big-city Berlin. I felt guilty for getting her drunk, but also high-minded for not doing anything about it. Still, I was sick of acting like a monk. After seemingly getting my life on track, here it had again derailed. But what could I do about it? What else? But how was I going to find Katja? If I went to the University of Munich, perhaps I could track her down.

It was at least worth a try. Or was the wiser course to leave well enough alone?

Since I wasn't at all sleepy, I marched back to Club 69. Rich, Scotty, Will, Tommy, and Karl-Heinz had long since left, but a few bitter-enders still lingered, including Umlaut. He handed me a cup of punch and begged for a toast.

I uttered the first thing that popped into my head: "May we all be dealt a hundred laydown loners for every time we get double euchred." Umlaut gladly drank to that, whatever the hell it meant.

Whitman strolled over to our table, for a rare exception out of uniform in ill-fitting cords and a checkered shirt. Leaning his broken veins close, he said, "Son, take some of that leave you've got coming and enjoy yourself someplace for a couple weeks. I'll definitely approve your request. The work has been getting to you. I can see the difference in you from across the room. Go to Hamburg or Amsterdam, but use condoms, for God's sake. I'll swear you're a damned liar if you repeat this, but, Zielsdorf, you may be the only man at the site who works too hard."

I thanked the sergeant for his concern and agreed to follow his advice. But not where he suggested. Marburg would be a better stop, the historic university town, where I did graduate work almost three years ago. Several professors of mine and a few student acquaintances should still be there. Actually, a trip was a great idea to help me forget about Katja.

A hard shoulder nearly bowled me over. "Specialist," Captain Slater slurred, "report to my office at oh-eight-hundred hours Tuesday morning with a regulation military haircut. And trimmed sideburns. This is still the United States Army, and not some hippie happening. Get in uniform, soldier."

"But I'm going on leave first thing after midnight early Tuesday."

"Report to me Tuesday at eight hundred hours. Do I make myself clear? *Before* you sign out on leave."

"Yes, Sir." Shorter hair on leave? So I couldn't pass for a German?

Having had enough fun for one night, I found Umlaut close to falling off a bar stool. We shook hands firmly in saying goodbye. "I'll see ya stateside, buddy," he told me. "We ought to have a reunion down the road."

By the time I got home, I was really dejected. It was a damned shame Dagmar was who she was, but the sooner I irrevocably accepted that piece of reality the better. I slept straight through for six hours and awoke even more upset about Katja. How could she have simply walked out of my life? To save me? What bullshit. If she had only been willing, we could have disappeared somewhere together. If not in Europe, then in the States or Canada. It couldn't possibly have been only Karl's chance remark that brought Katja and me together. Because it was destiny that she and I should meet. So what if she learned about me before I did her? Of course she sought me out first in that case.

The idea that Katja and I still could find a workable accommodation refuses to quit nagging me. As if there really might be some middle ground that pleases her superiors without disclosing anything important. It might violate the treads' sense of integrity, but not a reasonable person's. Not in any genuine sense.

More bullshit. Get real, Zielsdorf.

If I met a Katja once, why couldn't I meet someone like her again? A woman like Dagmar, but five years older?

A minute after midnight early Tuesday, I'll sign out on leave and by 8:00 a.m. be hundreds of miles south of Captain Slater. I'm betting he won't remember that haircut inspection. Even if he does, I can't find myself a new girlfriend looking like a GI.

March 4, 1971

By Tuesday noon, I was pacing the castle walls high above Marburg and praying I had given two pursuers the shake. Man, were the pests relentless. A young couple disguised as students had climbed aboard my train in Hanover and just happened to take the compartment behind mine—or so they acted. As we chugged south, their suspicious strolls up and down the corridor past my door kept me on edge. When they got off with me in Marburg, I went on full alert. Sloshing with adrenaline, I tore out of the *Bahnhof* with my little suitcase and lost them in the Old City's steep, narrow streets.

I had to take my hat off to their disguise. Jeans, backpacks, sky-blue eyes, and corn-silk hair made them dead ringers for young Nordics on vacation. The vowel-rich, softly enunciated language they spoke sounded vaguely Swedish, only with falling instead of lilting tones. Questions about who they were and what they wanted buzzed inside my brain.

Marburg's damp air reeked of auto exhaust and coal smoke. Down below, the fog lifting from the murky Lahn River revealed piney ridges holding the meandering stream within its banks. For centuries, whenever enemies appeared, all the townspeople had fled to this hilltop fortress. Here Luther and Zwingli had met a half millennium ago to reconcile their renegade Protestant faiths and miserably failed. Three years ago, I was a student in the German Institute of this town's venerable university. After a rough start, I adjusted so well to foreign ways that I suffered culture shock upon my return to the states.

But now I was in no mood to look up anyone from the *Universität*. The last thing I wanted was to talk about German literature or my academic future, especially when I was being tailed. Instead of checking into a *Pension*, I sneaked back to the train station and met the *D-Zug* to Frankfurt. To satisfy myself that my shadows weren't also boarding I lingered on the platform till the stationmaster blew his whistle, and only then hopped on and bought a ticket from the conductor.

Darkness had already fallen when I arrived, famished and shivering, at the Frankfurt *Hauptbahnhof*. At the first bratwurst stand I came upon, I wolfed down two sausages with French fries, while keeping an eye out for anybody who gave me a second glance. Two fiftyish men in greasy, tattered suits loitered nearby, throwing back shots of Schnaps. Suddenly one of the drunks reeled right into me and slurred, "I was with Paulus at Stalingrad.

Field Marshal Paulus! I spent seven years in a Siberian prison camp. Seven years!"

Nodding emphatically, his jowly buddy shouted, "I was on the Azov Sea!"

"*Ach ja, das Azovskoye Morye,*" the first man said, mixing Russian into his German.

"*Jawohl, das Azovskoye Morye!*" the other completely agreed.

I booked a room at a *Pension* six blocks from the Main Train Station. After a supper of *Weisswurst* and *Spätzle*, I cleaned up and strolled the Kaiserstrasse, where I managed to forget Katja for an hour inside a tiny room with a red lamp in the window. The young woman was a Hessian from Bad Arolsen, a spa town west of Kassel as well as the former seat of a duchy, back when Germany was part of the loose hodgepodge known as the Holy Roman Empire. Her hair was darker and longer than Katja's, her lips glossier, her body fuller. We had nothing to say, and it wasn't ecstasy, but for sixty marks it met a need.

The next day I loafed in my Frankfurt hotel room and read—until between the pages of Thomas Mann's *Confessions of a Swindler* I found a long blonde hair. Katja's. From when I had lent her the novel.

I spent sixty more marks. It didn't help.

Twelve more days of leave to find Katja.

I arrived in Munich late the following afternoon and found a cheap hotel north of the train station on the Dachauerstrasse—once the road to the infamous concentration camp, but now merely to a mundane suburb. Beneath my second-story window, electric streetcars crackled past, throwing off sparks.

For supper I ate *Schlachte Platte* alone in a beer cellar with my back to the wall. Nobody gave me a second glance—till two American matrons sheepishly approached and, mangling German from a phrase book, asked directions to the Hofbräuhaus. Pleading ignorance of English, I drew them a map on a napkin. They departed, praising the locals' friendliness.

That night I slept hard, awakened before dawn, reached over for Katja, but felt only cold bedding. After breakfast, I took the Ludwigstrasse trolley to the Geschwister-Scholl-Platz in the middle of the university Katja claimed she would attend. Twenty thousand students were scattered about this large academic quarter of sturdy Victorian stucco called Schwabing.

My first complete day in Munich, I hung around the student union without turning up a trace. Reasoning that Katja had more than likely kept the same major, the second day I tried the Pedagogical Institute, which like most German office buildings greeted visitors with a forbidding hall of closed doors. I chose one at random. Inside, a Frau Hermand directed me to the next floor, where I inquired from a Frau Grüber whether Katharina Wendt was enrolled at this *Institut*. Two phone calls later she reported no record of any such person.

She could be using another name. Most likely Katharina and Wendt were themselves pseudonyms. Under overcast, gloomy skies, I roamed Schwabing until late into the evening and overtook a woman who from behind looked like her and ended up startling a stranger. I apologized in my best High German.

Would Katja have told me Munich if she wasn't actually coming here? Why even mention it, unless she wanted me to find her?

The next day, I methodically combed every street in the student quarter, silently rehearsing how I would persuade her to emigrate with me to the US. That evening I checked out local restaurants and bars, till waiters and maitre d's grew alarmed by my nosiness and asked me to leave.

By the sixth day, I felt close to panicky. Maybe Katja wasn't here. But if not, she could be anywhere. Or maybe she was indeed in this city, but just not at the university. So the next three days, I spent downtown around Stachus, Marienplatz, and the Sendlinger Gate. Evenings, I hit the the beer halls and eateries. No better luck anywhere.

The following morning, I was waiting at a streetcar stop, when I felt a tap on a shoulder. I jerked around. There stood the same young blond couple who had plagued me in Marburg. "Do you speak English?" the guy asked with an Oxford accent.

"*Nein,*" I snapped and turned away so fast I plowed into an elderly man, who cursed, "Careful, you Sow-Prussian."

"*Govorite po-russki*?" the woman asked. Do you speak Russian? Her Muscovite accent sounded near native.

I angrily shook my head and backed into a cantankerous Bavarian, while the two youngsters chattered away in their weird language with falling tones.

When the *Strassenbahn* finally came, I stepped onto its rear entrance ahead of the couple, shoved my way past standing passengers to the front, and hopped off just as the pair climbed aboard behind me. And so the street car left with them but without me, thus getting the two pests off my back, at least for the time being. What in the devil did they want from me anyway? The entire subway ride back to Schwabing, I fretted over having stupidly signed the guesthouse register under my real name.

The tenth day I spent around the Pedagogical Institute, once even beseeching God in prayer for assistance. I was loitering in the hall by a bulletin board, when I heard a tinkling-bell laugh strikingly like Katja's. I spun around so abruptly I terrified a brunette my age. I rushed outside without apologizing, marched straight into the English Garden, and plopped down on the first bench I came to.

There it dawned on me—the couple I kept running into had to be Finns. Their native language sounded so peculiar because Finnish is a tongue of Asian origin brought to northern Europe by wandering tribes. It made sense that Finns would be helping the Warsaw Pact, because their official neutrality in the Cold War tilts toward the Soviets. But how did they know I was coming here? Or was this all one gigantic coincidence?

The next afternoon I staked out the *Pädagogisches Institut* from a pastry shop across the street while lingering over a cup of strong coffee and a newspaper. I read and re-read an article about another border incident in which East German *Vopos* had shot a truck driver to foil his escape. I was standing up to pay, when I froze—and sat back down with trembling knees. Katja herself in the flesh. No doubt about it. Exiting the Institute. Hair shorter than before, wearing a new suede coat, and a leather mini-skirt that really flattered her long, lithe legs. She looked absolutely stunning. Had I truly made love to a woman this gorgeous—and so many times? Oh, did I ache to take her again. Accompanying her was a man ten years or so her senior in a well-trimmed Van Dyke and professorial woolen jacket who vaguely resembled that photographer in the forest. He couldn't possibly be Jürgen.

I hurried after them on foot along the Leopoldstrasse and down an alley, and almost missed seeing them slip into a bar. I waited outside five minutes, before I entered myself. Inside, hats adorned every wall ceiling to floor. Derbies, fezzes, bonnets, mitres, sombreros, bowlers, cockades, Stetsons among many others. The clientele looked typically Schwabing—pasty-faced, long-haired students in jeans, turtlenecks, and shabby coats.

Katja and the bearded fellow stood in a corner, talking to a young fellow in a cowboy hat, doing his darnedest to grow a moustache and failing. When the boy turned his head, I spotted white walls and sideburns cut to mid-ear—a GI! He stood like an American, too, leaning against the wall with both hands in his front pockets, legs crossed at the ankles, and his weight over one foot.

The *Ami* was listening carefully. The unnatural twisting of Katja's lips meant she was speaking English. The soldier kept nodding and smiling forlornly. I bet they were blackmailing this poor schmuck, too.

I found myself an empty bar stool near the women's room—to keep an eye on the threesome and to check out the rest of the crowd. All Germans except for a French couple, several Asians, and a few Africans.

Katja got up and headed my way, walking with that familiar, deliberate gait. At her approach, my pulse quickened. I glanced away from her tight black turtleneck hugging high, braless breasts as she strolled past into the john without giving me so much as a glance.

I slipped out of the professor's view behind a group of *Studenten* and faced the restroom. The seconds slowly ticked by while memories of all our nights together raced past like a train heading in the opposite direction. When she finally emerged, I stepped into her path, and we collided. "We meet again," I greeted in German.

Katja gasped and slapped a hand over her mouth. Just jostling her excited me. She had never looked sexier. After making sure her colleague wasn't watching, she hugged me with all of her might. Between dizzying kisses, she cooed in the alto voice that had always struck my ears like a caress, "Peter, I will come for you in Knittelstedt, but it won't be soon. Now disappear fast. And don't use the front door." She turned and strode on with studied nonchalance.

But there was only the one exit.

Could I hide inside the bar until they left? But what if they lingered until closing, and we were forced to leave together? Lowering my head, I sidled along the far wall and barreled hard into a broad-shouldered man with thinning hair. The professor! "Excuse me," he grunted and shoved past without paying me any heed. Once out on the sidewalk, I ran to the Odeonsplatz, where I took the subway back to my guesthouse. And ate supper in its dingy restaurant to avoid showing my face again on the streets. Early the next morning, I paid up, took an express train north, and spent the final two days of vacation in Knittelstedt inside my room, reading between half-delirious bouts of sleep.

I found her finally! And she'll come for me! That much she promised. And her buddy didn't recognize me. Probably because he had no reason to expect me there. It was highly reckless on my part to seek Katja out, but I couldn't just forget about her. Now if I can only keep her attached to me until my discharge, afterwards we can do whatever we want. Right?

March 10, 1971

Did she truly persuade her superiors I would never turn them in no matter what the price to me personally? A better lie on her part might have been that I had a low-level position at the site without access to anything important. Or do they already know that's false from somebody else at Det Q? What an upsetting thought. I wish I had a way to contact her and tell her not to come.

Lies and rationalizations. I hope Katja doesn't wait long before returning. The possibility of losing her forever terrifies me.

March 15, 1971

When was the last time the SPETSNAZ unit we monitor went on maneuvers? Not at all recently. In fact, it was before their November hiatus. Maybe they've been taking a winter break. Which makes no sense because they are Russians after all and trained to operate no matter how inclement the weather.

Showing Katja the glossary gives me an nagging sense of guilt, but was it truly so terrible, even if technically a security violation? Especially since it did zero damage to our mission. Hardly worse than abusive drinking then, another venial sin. Actually, that's just a vice, isn't it? Because without God there is no sin, and right and wrong are only what we humans choose to declare as such.

Man, what bullshit.

March 30, 1971

I just returned from emergency leave in Wisconsin. Two weeks ago the Red Cross contacted me at the site to report that my mother had suffered a coronary and I should fly home immediately. The next morning, I took off from Rhine-Main Air Force Base, seated sideways on canvas straps in the unobstructed, unfurnished hold of a C-130 transport among its jeep cargo. I arrived too late. Once Mom's heart went into fibrillation at home, the lack of oxygen irrevocably damaged her brain. She died a week after I got there without ever recognizing me.

At least she knew I loved her. Her last years after the divorce from my father were the happiest of her life. Though she lived alone, she was in daily contact with loving friends and neighbors. Her Christian faith never once wavering, she lived every day ready to die, at peace with herself, the world, and her God.

My estranged father showed up for the funeral, as did aunts and uncles and cousins. He and I shook hands and muttered condolences but didn't have any more to say to each other than ever. "Take care," Dad told me in German and sauntered off. I doubt I'll see him again before his funeral.

My first cousin Willy greeted me with open contempt. He has taken over my great-grandfather's homestead and expanded it by buying up neighboring farms. How come I wasn't more like him, or another cousin, Paul, the pastor, I could tell relatives were thinking.

In staying aloof from you, I'm not being arrogant, I longed to tell them. We're just so different that we can't even communicate. But then as now I am in no mood to justify my existence to anyone, be they treads or kin.

April 9, 1971

Last night I joined the whole detachment at Club 69, except of course for a skeleton crew manning the site, for Henry Smith's ETS party. I was reluctant to go, but hoped it might distract me from the crazy thoughts I've been getting lately alone in my room. At first, I just sipped Pilsner Urquell and observed the scene. Scotty and Will danced a lot with Bärbel and Gitty, while Rich didn't even show up. Tommy, looking unpleasantly thin and acting quieter than usual, moping by himself in a corner.

About two beers after midnight, I was staring at Gitty's jiggling behind, when it suddenly struck me—what if Katja had tricked me in Munich? What if she had been willing to say anything to get rid of me and save her mission with that young GI? It didn't take long to convince myself the bitch had no intention of ever seeing me again. My revenge started on the spot. I got Bakken alone upstairs in the Det Q library. "Please keep to yourself what I am about to reveal," I began.

Tom nodded with a furrowed brow.

"I met a German woman last year and fell in love with her," I said. "I saw her many times, and we became lovers. For a while I wanted to marry her. But we eventually broke up." I paused. "It still tears me up to think I'll never see her again."

"I won't tell anyone," Tommy replied, looking oddly stricken.

Immediately I regretted opening my mouth. I made sure I left him with the impression that my worst offense was "an ongoing, intimate relationship with a West German National," as the treads' charges would read. By no means a small offense, and if caught, I wouldn't get off lightly, but a trifle compared to the truth.

"It sounds pretty minor." He sat scrunched up like he'd been poisoned.

"Thanks, Thomas. That's how I feel, too. No harm, no foul." I gave him a one-armed embrace across the shoulders, which he tolerated. "Anything the matter?"

"I've had it over here. I can't wait for our discharge."

"That's not it. Come on."

Bakken shook his head sadly.

"You don't actually mind that I had a relationship with a German woman?"

He shrugged. And then nodded.

But what earthly difference might Katja make to him? He should be happy for me. I wouldn't begrudge him anything with Karen—or another woman—not that there ever would be another woman. My partial confession turned out to be a mistake, because it not only failed to lighten my burden, but worsened Tommy's funk. The two of us trudged back downstairs.

Dagmar and Karl-Heinz were just arriving from a family celebration at the Schneiders. Where they had imbibed a little wine, which was nothing compared to what we *Amis* were consuming at Smitty's party. I bought Dagmar a vodka tonic, slyly making it a double, and Karl a beer. Two drinks later, I talked Dagmar into going upstairs to check out our little library, where I switched off the light, clasped my hands behind the small of her narrow back, and planted a kiss on her beautiful lips.

"Are you crazy?" she said, laughing and pushing me away.

"No, just drunk," I replied, half-lying, pulled her squirming body close again, and played kissy-face until somebody flipped on the lights.

"My turn," Dickinson said with a smirk. But Dagmar slipped his grasp, bounced downstairs, and headed out the door with Bärbel and Gitty.

Cold rain drenched me on my walk home.

How long before Katja shows up?

May 10, 1971

The treads learned from a trusted East German that the SPETSNAZ unit across the border went on maneuvers last week without mentioning a word about it over their radios that we monitor. Whitman and Wilhelm are understandably having a conniption. It's not that the Soviet ops have quit transmitting. They just don't mention anything of intelligence interest.

Boudreau came up with a wild explanation. "What if our SPETSNAZ guys switched to double radio networks?" he surmised. "One to punk us and another to conduct real business. And we've been listening to the wrong one." Nobody took his theory seriously, least of all Whitman or Wilhelm, especially in the absence of hard evidence.

Talk about one strange dude, our Green Room supervisor Spec Six Boudreau. Nobody says fewer words or makes those count for more.

May 17, 1971

By "special slang" might Katja have meant "SPETSNAZ slang"? Or is that even crazier than Boudreau's guess?

May 19, 1971

I combed through every page of the glossary yet again and still couldn't find anything except Russian cursing. Though I suppose some terms might be both vulgarity and special slang. Only a native who served in SPETSNAZ could determine that.

June 8, 1971

I am so sick of waiting for her. Yesterday one of the gate guards found boot prints in the mud outside our barbed-wire fences. It couldn't have been locals, because they know better than to hike anywhere near Det Q.

The Pentagon is cutting back on manpower, so I am to be discharged six months early this September and should get an European out approved. That way I can travel as a civilian for a while over here and fly back to America on a military plane for free, whenever I'm ready. Graduate school can wait no matter what I do. Maybe I'll let it wait forever.

My first choice will be to make it work out here in Germany with Katja, but I must be realistic. If that plan fails, I'll go home. To Wisconsin, not Chute Noire.

The longer I go without hearing from Katja, the more I fear I'll never see her again despite her promise. I certainly couldn't flush her out by turning her associates in, because she'd be arrested, too. And woe betide me.

The longer she stays away, the likelier it is she really did play me for a fool in Munich. But I'm still keeping the faith. Because we make such a great couple. Because nothing ever went wrong between us without outside interference. So what if she kept things from me? I kept things from her, too.

June 9, 1971

I simply cannot accept Katja's rejection. If I could just see her one more time, she'd realize we were meant for each other. But what if I never get the chance?

Recently I tackled *Effi Briest*, a classic Bourgeois Realism novel, but Fontane's obsession with the Prussian ideals of honor and duty left me so cold I quit.

If I am ever to excel in graduate school and earn tenure, I must regain my old resolve. But becoming another literary scholar knowing everything about a specialty so narrow it's almost nothing seems stupid. If I'm not making progress with my doctoral reading list, maybe I should try something else. Like *Spiegel*, *Konkret*, and the *Frankfurter Rundschau*—standard periodical fare for West German student radicals. And skim old *Newsweeks* to keep in touch with what's happening in the States.

Katja *has* to return. She promised she would. If she doesn't, I'll go find her again and this time not leave her side no matter what.

June 28, 1971

I heard from her! A postcard picturing the Geschwister-Scholl-Platz in Munich arrived in yesterday's mail. When I flipped it over, my heart leapt at the sight of Katja's familiar crabbed handwriting. The brief, unsigned message read: "*Am 10. 7. 1971. Ich denke an Dich.*" On July 10th, 1971. I'm thinking of you. A caption explained that the Scholl siblings were Munich University students, who together with a friend printed and distributed leaflets, signed "The White Rose," criticizing the Nazi regime, when none of their countrymen dared. The Gestapo eventually hunted the trio down and beheaded them.

I'll see her in two weeks! But at the Braunschweig train station or here? I wish she had spelled that out.

July 1, 1971

What a nutty mid Dickinson and I just had. Immediately upon my return to this room, I scribbled down every word that I could recall from the strangest SPETSNAZ transmission, hoping that black on white it might make sense, because it certainly hadn't while listening live. I ended up tearing that page out of this diary and shredding it. Better safe than sorry.

July 3, 1971

I'm still shaken by what happened two mids ago and the measures it forced me to take. For minutes on end the Russkie Special Forces sounded just like they used to before their hiatus last November.

Yesterday I made Scotty swear to secrecy about the weird SPETSNAZ transmission only he and I heard. And shut him up fast when he joked about the audiotape I had sneaked home. "Now you see it, now you don't," he teased, followed by that irksome giggle. For the time being the recording is hidden behind my book shelf. Burning it would be ideal, but where to accomplish that discreetly? Cutting it up into tiny slices with scissors and flushing those down the toilet may have to suffice.

July 7, 1971

I won't bother to describe our Det Q Fourth of July beer blowout. I more observed than participated anyway. That missing page—or the incident it described, to be precise—was bumming me out too much to celebrate. Somehow I am really regretting this gap in my diary, here when last February I tore up three months' worth of entries with impunity.

"Regret" isn't the right word, is it?

July 9, 1971

Is Katja really going to show up tomorrow as promised?

July 12, 1971

On the Tenth I opted for waiting in my room all day. Instead of the usual cool to balmy German summer, the temperature had climbed to an eightyish American-style steam bath, murderous swelter to the locals. I sat at my table and read Dostoevsky's *House of the Dead* in Russian, using Constance Garnett's English translation as a trot.

At 8:00 p.m. there was a sharp, masculine knock on my door. Herr Schultz or Karl-Heinz I guessed. But when I opened it, Katja jumped into my arms. We fell onto my bed laughing and kissed a hundred times before either of us said a word. I nuzzled her shorter hair and thinner cheeks that make her look like the younger sister of the woman I had known in Braunschweig. But the soft lips and clutching embrace were the same. The instant I got her in my grasp, all my resentment evaporated. The first time our lovemaking was painfully urgent. The next two tender and unhurried.

We lay close for hours without feeling much need for conversation. I didn't ask what she had been doing in Munich, and she didn't bring it up. She didn't care what I had been up to either while we conversed with kisses and caresses.

I awoke from a short nap to find her eyeing me like a stranger, her troubled gaze reflecting a danger she didn't dare mention. I didn't have to voice my own misgivings. She knew we were hopelessly stranded on opposite shores of the Cold War, and it would never again be the same between us. Because deep down I realized I never could fully forgive her for tricking me into betraying my country, and she could never abandon her cause to live with me. Not that I condemn her for remaining the better patriot. Her cold scrutiny—like a painter studying a subject—gave me chills. As if her love all along had been a role she plays like a master thespian.

When I brought her apple juice from my tiny fridge, she was sitting up and holding photos in her slender fingers. I recognized the two of us stretched out naked in the woods. The so-called photographer's handiwork.

"Peter, let me finally express what must be said," she began. "The photographer, who is also the professor, and in fact neither, is my superior. He is demanding that you make a commitment now to the cause you support deep down. He only allowed me to come back here because I promised I could get a pledge from you to help us. So it's time to stop leading us on, so we can work together for peace and deflect history toward the more humane path all progressives seek."

"I get it, Katharina," I said, balling my fists. "Either I go along or you guys will screw me over royally. At best, you'll leave me to the mercy of our merciless Uniform Code of Military Justice. At worst, you'll"—I had to squelch a mad impulse to smash in her gorgeous face.

"Peter, you've already decided in your heart, so just act on that decision. Trust your instincts. Cold reason isn't enough in the face of the world's suffering. Think of what's going on in Vietnam. And Bangladesh. And Biafra."

"Don't forget about Poland and Czechoslovakia."

"It's just a police matter in Poland," Katja snapped. "Unruly elements got out of control, but the situation is calming down. Mistakes were made with the food pricing policy, but it's not like Vietnam. We cannot tolerate anarchy and selfishness, because they leech the heart's blood from socialism. Czechoslovakia was truly on the verge of counterrevolution due to outside agitation. You can't deny Western complicity in trying to subvert our progressive system there."

"There's no point in arguing, Katja. I'm not going to join you. Whatever my faults, I'm not a traitor. The American dream changed the course of my family's history. Since recorded time all my ancestors had been German peasants—till they emigrated to the United States."

"Don't be blind," she said, shuffling through the photos till she came to one of her naked atop me.

"Turn me in then to my Commanding Officer. If you do, I'll be sure to mention you guys."

Her smile was pained. "It's foolish to threaten us. You're hurt, so anger controls your tongue. But I know you'll change your mind. There isn't much time. My superiors are impatient."

Her gray-blue eyes were darting, as if she were the cornered rat instead of me. The more she talked, the more she sounded like a dangerous stranger I would have been so much better off never knowing. For an instant I wondered how far I could go to save my own life. "Why can't we both leave the security organizations we now serve and lead normal lives together someplace in a neutral country under pseudonyms? Where neither side will ever find us."

"What are normal lives?"

"Earning a living, raising a family."

She snorted. "That's letting the world go to hell in a basket. It's giving up."

"Or is it preserving a little piece of sanity on the piece of the earth we happen to inhabit? You can't change the whole world."

"Not alone we can't. And maybe it won't occur in our lifetimes. And maybe I personally will only make a small contribution to the good cause. But we already have changed the world, and we are continuing to do more. Just look around."

"I don't want to look around. What about us? Let's set up our own tiny world and make that perfect."

"You are making it very difficult for yourself. Take these photographs and think it over for a week. Do not underestimate the unpleasantness of military prisons. And that would just be the beginning. You wouldn't just suffer a ruined career."

"How could I enjoy any career as a traitor?"

"But you'll get away with it! Besides, you'll only be a traitor to them. To us, you'll be a hero. You will be named at least a colonel and receive commensurate pay. In this way, we will guarantee you success. Just don't do anything dumb. We would never tell anyone of your dealings with us as long as you cooperate."

That last threat went too far. I backed across the room to keep from hurting her.

"Peter, listen," she said, edging closer. "Our new life can be more glorious than anything you ever imagined. And if you can't stand working for us as Peter Zielsdorf, you could assume another identity. We can give you a legend to live by and whatever else you need and, above all, important work for the good of mankind. You and I can live together, Peter. I can be your wife. Think of it. We could have children. We could bring them up to become even greater heroes for the cause of progress than you and I personally ever could. We could groom them from birth to serve high in the American government."

My whole body trembled with rage.

"Peter, you always said you wanted to marry me. Finally I'm answering yes."

"Katja, you had better leave now. I refuse to cooperate. Rest assured, I won't reveal anything about you either as long as you leave me alone."

How could I have ever loved anyone capable of telling me such awful things? But didn't I still? Haven't I adored her ever since the very first night we met? Yet standing there I had to stuff my fists in my pockets to keep from battering her senseless.

"You could help choose your own legend, Peter. Who do you want to be? You could become the ideal Peter Zielsdorf you always strove to be."

Listening to her preach and pontificate like this was a waking nightmare.

"But if you don't cooperate," Katja went on, "you'd be better off dead. My superiors won't just let your bosses punish you, not after you've led us on and learned so much. Please be rational, Peter. Take my word for it that you will be serving a greater cause than you have ever dreamed of in America. Agree to work with us, and everything will turn out not only better for us both, but the whole human race. You've been miserable as a cynic, so join us and find the higher purpose in life you crave. You have no idea how much more beautiful your whole life could become if devoted to a movement that will eventually prevail."

"Your Marxist cant about progress makes me want to puke."

Katja stood up in a huff and quickly dressed, cursing under her breath. "You know I am a moral person," she told me. "You've had to do things for your country you didn't want to, as I have for mine. Why can't you understand that to achieve progress, to save everybody else, a few of us have had to sell the devil our souls? But we are forgiven our misdeeds, because whatever moves history forward is right."

"Do you honestly think it's been moving forward lately? Or is it grinding us up to grease its gears?"

"What is more morally rotten than your cynicism, Peter? It has undermined all your naturally noble motives. You don't believe anything is worth fighting for."

"Does 'cynicism' mean I see better than you?"

"Witticisms are not logical arguments, Peter. Of course your vision is worse."

"I'm sick to death of hearing about history and its so-called progress."

"I must go, Peter. Please think hard about what we have discussed and come to your senses. Choose me, choose us—that is the only reasonable choice. Cooperate and you can play a role greater and nobler than you ever dreamed of."

She kissed my cheek and left.

July 16, 1971

I keep trying to figure out how things could work out for us together without betraying my country. Where there's a will, there's got to be a way. I still detect the Katja I fell in love with lurking behind those cold, scrutinizing eyes. So maybe it's not too late. We are indeed soulmates—or could become so again. I've never wanted anything or anyone in my life more than her, and I'd rather die than give her up. So my only real choice is somehow to change her mind.

July 17, 1971

At 11:00 last night, shortly before another mid began, I was awakened by a sharp knock. Katja again already? Excited by the prospect, I opened the door for her, but instead in barged Katja's colleague, the erstwhile photographer and Munich professor, this time disguised as a businessman in a gray suit. Close up, he looked even older.

"Good evening, Herr Zielsdorf," he said in hypercorrect High German. "Please excuse my intrusion, but the matter is pressing. Fräulein Wendt tells me you are having trouble, deciding to cooperate."

"That is not exactly accurate," I muttered. Katja I didn't fear, but this man might be violent. I eyed the paring knife drying in my sink.

"Go on."

"I could never betray my country. But I have decided not to betray you and Fräulein Wendt either. Just forget about me, and I will forget about you."

His laugh was malevolent. "You have decided? How precious. As if you might report us to your superiors—or the West German authorities—and live. Don't you dare ever threaten us again. Don't you realize who you're dealing with? We're not all pussycats like Fräulein Wendt. No, the rest of us can do whatever must be done. And we're not like a capitalist business. If you don't want to buy from us, we won't just go away and try to sell someplace else. If you don't cooperate with the Soviets, they will crush you like a potato bug."

"Don't you mean *Stasi*? Or is the East German Security Service just a puppet of the Russians?"

"How do you Americans become so insolent?" he said with a sneer. "You all act like spoiled children."

"We're taught to love freedom."

"*Ach, ja*, freedom, a tricky concept. But we have no time now for dialectics. Herr Zielsdorf, you have hopelessly compromised yourself, so from now on we decide the terms, not you. So listen carefully. Either you cooperate with us or you will die."

"Give me time to think," I said, turning sideways, as taught in Basic Combat Training, poised to parry a martial arts kick.

"You were already given close to a week."

"Don't be so eager. I say no to the hard sell no matter how great the deal."

"You are not buying, we are not selling," he said, switching to Oxford-accented English. "You capitalists have business on the brain. Rather I am just explaining how to save your life."

"You know our language well."

"Come now, Herr Zielsdorf. Your time is running out. Next week Fräulein Wendt will contact you and explain the first step in cooperating. Please do not make us resort to 'wet affairs.' *Auf Wiedersehen.*"

In less than two months, I will receive my European discharge and then have more options. But if they aren't giving me a week, do I have that choice? Whatever I do, I won't let myself go to jail or be killed. Or let harm come to Katja. Could I sneak an M-16 out of the site?

July 19, 1971

There's no way to get a rifle out of that padlocked shed. So after finishing another mid this morning, I walked downtown and bought myself the biggest steak knife I could find and hid it under my bed. It's not designed for mayhem, but it's still plenty deadly.

My easiest recourse would be indeed to cooperate with Katja and her handlers, but of course only on my terms. Unfortunately, that's not a choice. Could I somehow pretend to go along, but only hand over garbage.

July 20, 1971

I managed to nap a little this afternoon, but that was it for the day. I've changed my mind again about helping Katja. To hell with her and her comrades. My decision is irrevocable. I won't even pretend to work for them no matter what. Why can't they believe I won't turn them in? I haven't done it yet. If I did, I'd have too much to lose myself.

But too much is at stake for them to trust me, isn't it?

Once I'm discharged, I can disappear and hide, that is, if I last that long. Could they find me in Sweden? Sure.

July 21, 1971

When I finally got up after dark to work another mid, I put all the loose-leaf pages of this diary, excluding tonight's entry, in a manila envelope and sealed it with tape. Between sporadic naps, I had thought about who best to entrust them to and finally decided. That person must be willing to make the diary public, if something happens to me—to salvage at least some of my reputation. Hoffman I rejected because he would never help the treads, even if I begged him to. Burke I feared would immediately open the package, read the contents, and discard it. Dickinson would probably do the right thing by me, but Tommy I'm positive would. And I feel the closest to him, so Bakken it is.

I found Tommy in his apartment on Salzstrasse reading a copy of *The Uniform Code of Military Justice*. Huh? Decked out as usual in mismatched shirt and slacks, the sweet dork invited me into the library foxhole he calls home over here. All four walls are now hidden behind stuffed board-and-brick shelves that dwarf his meager furniture—a tiny desk, a wooden chair, and a cot. He has collected books so much faster than he can ever hope to read a person can barely turn around.

I told him the package was an odd insurance policy to be opened only if harm befell me. "Otherwise just give it back, when we're both stateside. Above all, never mention it exists to another soul. To get past customs, say it's thesis notes, and in all likelihood nobody will ask to look. If they do, I bet they won't actually read the text. You be sure you don't either. Then please reseal it."

Later at the site it bothered me that Tommy hadn't asked a single question. His emotions are like subterranean currents, flowing far beneath the surface.

July 27, 1971

Two days ago I received the first letter from Katja I truly dreaded. Yesterday we met in the Braunschweig *Hauptbahnhof* at noon as planned. In greeting she kissed me with her entire mouth—tongue, teeth, and lips—and again in her car, but neither kiss was heartfelt. She feels less womanly at this thinner weight, but her face is even more striking. Braless under a thin cotton top, she wore a mini-skirt so short she could barely walk without flashing her *Höschen*. As if making an extra effort to turn me on.

Insisting upon driving, I headed west on Highway One and found us a private clearing inside a beech forest. There we made love on a prickly army blanket till we had drenched ourselves in sweat. Afterwards, I lay still cooling off while she knelt, fondling me with her mouth. She whispered that before my discharge I must be sure to get her copies of all the site's manuals.

"I can't give you any of those. Unlike the glossary, they're not harmless."

Katja gave me a puzzled look. "But this is what you must do," she continued. "This is what cooperation means."

"Count me out. My answer is no."

"That is impossible, Peter. Today is the deadline. And no means losing me. Don't be foolish."

"The decision has already been made."

"That's what I have been saying all along. Only you don't seem to recognize what your real decision is."

"Don't put words in my mouth, Katja."

The feigned smile vanished from her face. She quickly dressed and drove me back to the train station. Neither of us said *Auf Wiedersehen*.

Aug. 17, 1971

What are they waiting for? They're like a firing squad taking a month to load.

Sept. 3, 1971

I'm still here.

Every day the past three weeks I expected to be my last on earth. I doubted the "professor" would off me himself, but I still kept an eye out on the way to and from my pick-up point to the site. Each time I ran into an unfamiliar German I braced for impact, especially if they paid me any attention, and unlike us Americans, they do stare.

But an obvious murder would mean an investigation, and that could expose them all. So they'd be smart to make it look like an accident—or a suicide. Somehow I feel a lot safer now that Bakken has my diary, even if he has no idea what he's got.

Dickinson asked which day would be best for my ETS party.

"Don't bother," I said. "I won't be going anywhere after discharge. Everybody will still see me here." Though in fact I'll bolt the instant I'm again a civilian. Too bad I can't risk letting anybody, not even another Monk, in on my plans.

Sept. 7, 1971

Whenever I sleep, day or night, I barricade my door with a chair, and twice stayed in Tommy's apartment, while he was working a mid. It's strange that he lets me without asking why.

Sept. 13, 1971

The Army movers didn't need to come the day I went ROD—Relieved of Duty—because I had already given away most of the little that I own. Herr Schultz was thrilled to receive my American shirts, slacks, and sweaters, even if they fit him poorly. Bakken wanted my books so badly he borrowed Dickinson's VW to come pick them up. I've left myself only one small suitcase, containing items all purchased in Germany—four changes each of pants, shirts, underwear, and socks, the few recent diary pages I haven't yet given Tommy, my birth certificate, passport, driver's license, diplomas, and photos of relatives back home and of buddies at Monterey and Det Q. I always keep it packed in case I have to escape at a moment's notice.

I finished ETS-ing in Giessen last week by turning in my equipment and debriefing at G-2. There a lantern-jawed Spec Four with a Kentucky drawl made me swear never to reveal anything about my military specialty and the site's missions or to visit any communist country. Next he had me sign a form and pronounced the memorable words, "Okay, that's it, buddy. You're discharged. Get out of here, you lucky bastard."

Outside, I just stood there, disoriented by my new status, a civilian again as free as any other American to go where and when I wanted. Entertaining countless options after more than three years of mindlessly obeying orders was bewildering. I considered at least checking out Sweden, but since I knew I couldn't hide there indefinitely, why bother? Meanwhile, till I thought of something better, I returned to Knittelstedt, where Katja could at least find me. So I haven't given up yet on the two us disappearing somewhere together.

Sept. 16, 1971

Last night, Scotty cooked me a farewell dinner and invited the other Monks. The five of us split a fifth of Jack Daniels and a bottle of Mosel and ate coq au vin, pasta, and tossed salad. Will pronounced it superb and I suppose he wasn't mistaken. My thoughts were everywhere but on the cuisine. Should I fly back to Wisconsin immediately? But why couldn't they hunt me down just as easily in Madison? What are they waiting for? What am I waiting for?

Katja.

I told the guys I would travel a bit in Europe, on and off stopping in Knittelstedt, and then fly home for graduate school in Madison, maybe already this January. "Is your German girlfriend going to accompany you?" Will asked.

"I'm not taking a Braunschweig whore anyplace," I replied with a poker face.

They all laughed, except Tommy, who was oddly blushing.

Ever the good host, Scotty changed the subject and brought taciturn Rich into the conversation. "How about some new Russian verbs, Hoffman?"

Flashing a sly, sweet smile, Rich agreed. "*Burkovat'*," he began. "To boff German piglets." It was funny, but nobody so much as chuckled.

"*Zeelzdorfovat*'," he went on. "To get laid more than anybody at Det Q, including the married guys, and not tell a damned soul." Again, no one was amused, though I feigned a smile. Why was Tom so preoccupied?

"Come on, Zielsdorf. Tell us about her," Rich teased. "Not the gory details, but at least her name. Do you realize what your shit-eating grins have been like while we're eating our horny hearts out? Hey, if we Monks can't trust one other, who can we trust?"

He was right. I could trust these guys with anything, including Katja. None of them would turn me in—at least if I didn't reveal she was a spy. Striving to be a better friend, I said, "Yes, I was seeing a German woman, but it's been over now for some time. I guess that means it wasn't ever very serious."

"Where's she from?" Will asked.

"Hanover," I replied, lying. "But she attended the Freie Universität in Berlin."

"Where does she live now?" Will continued.

"Frankfurt. Or is it Stuttgart?" More facile lies. I couldn't stop fidgeting.

"You don't have her address?"

"Didn't I just say it was over between us?" I snapped. "Which of course means I won't see her ever again."

"Why did you say 'of course'?" Burke asked, irking me with his persistence. Let him stick to his piglets and leave me alone.

"You still haven't mentioned her name," Scotty said. "Why so secretive, Peter?"

"This conversation has degenerated into an interrogation. I can't tell you her name for reasons you don't need to know." Three pairs of eyes glared at me, while Tommy's studied the floor. "Okay, I was more involved with the woman than I just let on. In fact, I wanted to marry her. In fact, I still do. But so long as she doesn't want to marry me, it's hopeless."

"Just be sure she's worth it, my good man," Will said. "I should think you might spend your time here more profitably, touring by yourself. Who knows when you will return to Europe, especially with this much time at your disposal? Certainly not until after your dissertation."

I balled my fists under the table.

Rich piped up that as soon as he ETS-ed at Fort Dix he planned to visit his folks in Boston and travel out West till he got tired of bumming around. He didn't have a clue where he might end up. Scotty and Will were flying to Dix within two weeks for their own discharges. Dickinson would arrive a bit late for the fall semester at Stanford, so he would take a lighter load to make it easier to catch up. By next year, he hoped to be back on track for a doctorate in Tudor-Stuart English history. Will would be a week tardy at the University of Washington, but was still enrolling for all his planned courses, figuring that since most work in graduate school came due at semester's end, he wouldn't lag behind by much.

Subdued Tommy had been oddly monosyllabic all evening. "My ETS isn't till December thirty-first," he finally admitted. "I'll pass up most of the Early Out to earn more money for graduate school. I figure I can save at least eighty percent of what I make here, if I stop buying books. The three extra months will be sort of like this year's summer job. I've had worse. Boxing batteries in Madison, for example."

Rich rolled his eyes. "How can you stand one extra day around these fucking treads?"

"I don't mind it that much," Thomas said. "Besides, grad school will cost more than I expected, because my grades weren't good enough to win a fellowship. To be honest, I'm wavering about even going, but I can't think of anything better to do."

For dessert, Scotty brought out chocolate mousse he had made himself. Sweets are never wasted on my uncultivated palate, and I marveled at the range of Dickinson's culinary skills. Next came after-dinner liqueurs, Rich preferring apple juice. Will tried to get each of us in turn to bet against Bobby Fischer in next summer's world chess championship, but none of us were fools. Three triple secs finally loosened Bakken's tongue enough to reveal, "Karen and I will probably get married in a couple of years."

"You should live together first," Scotty told him. "That's what Beth and I intend to do."

"Karen would never approve," Tom muttered, as if concurring.

"I wish we could meet her," Scotty said, trying to sound conciliatory. Though it was clear he wasn't impressed by Karen, no matter how brilliant her intellect.

"Peter," Tom went on, "you and I will probably run into each other at UW, since we'll be in the same building. The German Department is on the eighth floor of Van Hise, Comp Lit the eleventh. And I'll be taking some German Lit courses."

"It sounds like we will," I said lamely. The prospect horrifies me I'm sorry to write, Tommy. I had envisioned myself together with Katja in Madison far from anybody I knew at Det Q.

Tommy remained so troubled no matter how much he imbibed, I began to fear he had opened my package. But Bakken would never betray my trust. Still, something was bugging him.

Sept. 27, 1971

I'm getting sick of hanging around Knittelstedt like a sitting duck. I never fail to barricade my door and practice snatching the knife from under my bed if the need arises. Scotty and Will are back in the states for good, and Rich will leave this week. But I keep staying here for Katja's sake. It was dumb not to give her a Stockholm address.

Sept. 28, 1971

Returning from the grocery this afternoon, I found a telegram Frau Schultz had left on my table. "*Ich rufe dich an um 2000 am 30. 9,*" it read. I will call you at 8:00 p.m. on September 30th. Unsigned, but then there was no need.

Oct. 1, 1971

Last evening I was waiting in the public phone booth two blocks from the Schultzes as directed. It rang at eight on the dot. "*Ja*?" I said breathlessly.

"Peterchen," Katja purred. "I miss you so much."

Just hearing her soft, silky voice turned me on. "Katja, where are you?"

"Munich." Three hundred miles away. At the opposite end of Germany. "Peter, let's get together, but not in Knittelstedt. And go on a picnic."

"Selbstverständlich," I replied, my voice breaking. Our conversation sounded weirdly normal, like one of many before all her demands and threats. So we were going on a picnic just like old times? And ignoring who she worked for and what she was? Recalling the feel of her body against mine, I ached to take her yet again.

"When can you meet me in Braunschweig?" she asked.

"Tomorrow?"

She chuckled nervously. "Make it the day after tomorrow. In the Main Train Station at noon. How about a picnic in the Harz, Peterchen?"

"Okay," I said, my heart in my throat. Those picturesque mountains lay half in the West and half in the East, split by the Iron Curtain.

Oct. 4, 1971

What happened yesterday in the Harz? Did Katja save me or did she almost get me killed? I arrived at the Braunschweig train station on time, Katja nowhere in sight unlike our agreement. I paced the hall for a good ten minutes before charging outside. Her gray Beetle was nowhere in sight. In my paranoid state, I imagined all manner of awful things that might have befallen her—till I spotted her behind the wheel of a boxy green Audi sedan with unfamiliar license plates. Closer up, I noticed she was studying a map. Without a word of greeting, her eyes darting fearfully above a pained smile, she slid over to let me drive. Quite an inauspicious reception.

"My VW is in the shop," she explained tersely. Whatever. My goal was to win her over to my thinking, but until I succeeded I was willing to play the game any way I had to. If necessary, I would even go along with her superiors far enough to please them, so long as I didn't have to betray anything that mattered. Meanwhile, I'd keep working on persuading her to join me someplace far from East and West. Once she agreed, the two of us would simply vanish.

The ninety-minute trip to Goslar on the northern edge of the Harz passed in tense silence. Upon arrival contrary to our plans to hike she perversely demanded a visit first to the city's medieval castle, the eleventh-century Kaiserpfalz, where we joined a tour. A sixtyish tourist's sneaky glances at us so distracted me I barely heard the guide's canned speech.

Again instead of heading into the park's beautiful scenery, Katja insisted we first eat lunch in the *Ratskeller*, where she chose a table in a corner away from other customers. And there she brooded in sullen silence. Something highly unusual was up, but what? I had seldom experienced her this troubled.

"Let's say I did return with you to America on your terms," she finally said. "Wouldn't we always have to hide? That way you couldn't be a professor."

"Why not? We could find an obscure German Department somewhere filled with people sharing our love of your language and culture." Was she finally coming around? With Katja as my lover and spouse, a marvelous life beckoned.

"It's insane enough to think my bosses would just forget about you, but it's even crazier to imagine they would forget me. We could never hide well enough. If they ever found us, my colleagues would kill us—"

"—like a potato bug."

"Exactly."

"Does it warm your heart to be serving such a virtuous organization?" I shuddered to recall one SPETSNAZ Captain's cold-blooded orders to cut our American throats during a practice assault on Det Q.

"Peter, why can't you get it through your thick skull that we must accept smaller evils now for the greater good to come. What makes everything worthwhile for you?"

"You. I do so want to marry you. But then never hear another word about politics so long as we both shall live."

"That's not only impossible, but immoral."

"Okay," I said, switching tactics, "if I can't have you, I still don't understand why I have to hide. Your colleagues know full well I won't turn them in, just as they know they don't have anything that serious on me for blackmailing."

She opened her mouth, as if to correct me, but then didn't.

"I'm just going to do what I've decided," I went on. "Which is to earn a doctorate and teach at an American university."

"What nonsense. Peter, make it easier on yourself and me and everybody else by cooperating. You'll get me and so much, much more. As long as you don't let us down. My control and I really caught holy hell when you refused to bring us the other manuals from the site. Why settle for being a professor? You're versatile. What about the Foreign Service? With your energy and discipline and gift for languages, you could go far. Who knows, maybe even close to the top of the State Department."

I chuckled bitterly. "So that's why you picked me out from all the other GIs. Your people could use an agent that highly placed. So are you working for *Stasi*? Or is it the KGB?"

"Tweedledum and Tweedledee, as the great Lewis Carroll put it. It makes no difference except for the official language of our reports. The two agencies work closely to fight for peace and defend socialism." She curled her lips in bitter irony while she spoke, as if such slogans were as empty to her as me.

"Katja, I was foolish to give you the benefit of the doubt for so long, not questioning whether you were a West German student, but also freelancing for another country because you believed in their cause. I'm not sure what I believe in, but the peace and justice you work for are meaningless inside barbed wire and mine fields and machine guns and guard towers. Your citizens want to escape. So your side can't possibly be right, even if mine is wrong."

"Radio Free Europe propaganda. We have not yet achieved true socialism, but we will. For us there is a better future ahead, while your capitalism only becomes more decadent by the day."

"Katja, as a great book puts it, beware of false prophets—ye shall know them by their fruits. You can see something terribly out of whack with your ideology by taking one hard look at all the attempts to put it into practice."

"There has not yet been one single fully socialist country anywhere on earth. Socialism has never had a real chance. You cannot condemn what has never been. But we are slowly making progress toward true communism."

"Slowly as a glacier."

"Peter, you make such a cult out of standing alone, beholden to no one. You should feel a duty to the whole human race."

Didn't she realize if there was any duty I felt it was to turn her and the professor in? As well as myself. The urge to face the treads and get it over with no matter what the consequences felt overwhelming. But that seemed tantamount to suicide, and I'd be damned if I'd do anything that cowardly.

"You would hate prison," she coldly went on. "Your superiors won't ignore what you've done. Your career is ruined unless you work for us. We will make you greater than you ever would have been on your own. Just do what I say, and you and I can live together in the States. Don't worry about the terms. If you can't make up your own mind in this matter, just trust my moral judgment. Don't I always strive to do the right thing? Why can't you see the light? You already believe in most of what we do."

I chose not to respond.

At last we drove on to our planned destination. Traveling just this side of the border with East Germany toward Braunlage and the Brocken, the range's highest peak, I found it odd to label the Harz mountains, since they were more large, forested hills. Still, strikingly scenic.

"*Nicht so schnell doch,*" Katja begged. I slowed down.

"Turn left here," she directed, pointing at two ruts twisting into an evergreen grove. Three hundred yards later, a sign warned, "*Einfahrt verboten*"—entry forbidden. I was keen to obey, but Katja insisted we continue.

I swung around a loop off a bumpy stretch and stopped. "Let's backtrack," I said. "This is too close to East German territory for comfort."

I reached over and caressed her cheek. This was as good a place to make love as anywhere. I lowered my seat, expecting her to do the same, but she instead jumped out of the car and bounded off into the woods. I quickly caught up, wrestled her to the ground, and unzipped her slacks.

"Not yet," she said, pushing my hand away. "I know a special place."

"You were here before?"

"Yes, back when I was a student."

"That's what you are now, Katja, remember?"

For that snide remark she bit my biceps hard enough to leave a bruise. A twig cracked up ahead. I held my breath, but only heard her panting. As we walked on, something rustled among the thick Scotch pines. Most likely a small mammal. The shadow of a bird of prey soaring overhead flitted across our path.

"A goshawk," Katja whispered, as though frightened.

I grabbed her bottom, but she grasped my hand and twisted it away. Relenting, I let her lead me through sharp-needled boughs up rising terrain. Before long we emerged onto an overlook with a good view of the Harz's highest peak as well as a picture-postcard pond nearer to us. Katja tugged me onward. "After coming this far, we have to climb at least part way up the Brocken."

"No, that's too far east," I said, resisting. "Their, I mean, your fences often lie well within the actual boundary."

"Peter, I am very aware we are near the border, but we'll be careful. There'll be signs."

Now it was my turn to I tear a hand free. "Just what in the hell are you doing, Katja? You're dragging me straight into East Germany!"

She mirrored my glare until her gaze gradually softened. "Okay," she muttered, "let's just go down to the pond." With that she again took off sprinting, and I pursued. With a final burst I beat her to the water's spongy edge and pulled up so close I stepped in with a foot. Katja grabbed my hand and yanked me out. I deliberately lurched into her and pulled her onto the ground alongside me. She rolled out of my grasp and jumped up, not in the slightest amused. My whole right side was sopping wet as was my shoe.

Katja gently squeezed the water out of my shirt, till the wringing turned to fondling. Yet try as I might I was unable to coax her into making love. "Not now, not here," she insisted, and her eyes teared over. "I'm so sorry, Peterchen," she whispered.

"For what?"

No response to that question. For minutes on end she stared inwardly until she set her jaw, as if with an unspecified new resolve. She grabbed my hand, and thus attached we strolled along the pond's pebbly bank. "Can you throw as well as I'm told most American men can?" she asked with a dreamy smile.

"I was a decent small-town high school pitcher," I said, but she didn't understand the word "pitcher," and I was in no mood to explain.

The first rock, one robin-egg size, landed silently on the other bank. "*Nein, nein*, make it splash." She handed me a stone big as a softball, which I flung like a forward pass. It hit the water with a kerplunk, startling an animal in the bushes on the opposite side.

“Farther,” she teased. I grabbed an even larger chunk and heaved it like a shot. It landed with an explosive splash, and she clapped her hands in delight.

Suddenly, two soldiers came running out of nowhere, shouted, “Halt! Halt!” and leveled rifles at us. Katja and I raised our hands. They wore unfamiliar fatigues grayer than GI green and were wielding semi-automatic weapons larger than an M-16, but shorter than an M-14. East German *Vopos*, I thought, feeling panic. In crisp German the taller one reported via his walkie-talkie, “Two intruders. We are detaining.”

Moments later a jeep came bouncing down the trail behind us and braked hard, the passenger jumping out. “*Was machen Sie hier*?” he screamed. What are you doing here?

In deliberate English, I said, “I am very sorry, but I do not speak German.” This burly guy was obviously in charge. And no doubt an officer.

“*Die zwei sprechen kein Deutsch*,” the radioman relayed. They don’t speak German. Then I noticed their insignia—BGS, i.e. *Bundesgrenzschutz*. The West German Border Guard. Thank God.

“Are you an American?” the officer asked next in English, butchering the “r’s.”

“Yes,” I told him. “I am a soldier on a weekend pass, visiting the Harz. This is my girlfriend, visiting from America.”

“How did you hear of the Harz?” the officer snapped.

“Aren’t they famous? Like the Alps?”

He asked Katja where she was from.

“Chicago,” she told him.

“Al Capone’s town, right?” the BGS officer said.

“That is correct,” Katja responded with a fair-to-middling American accent.

“And from where do you come?” he asked me.

“Wisconsin. It’s one of the fifty states.”

Sneering at us two supposed dumb *Amis*, he demanded to see identity cards. I showed him my Wisconsin driver’s license, claiming I had forgotten my military ID, which I had actually been obliged to turn in upon my discharge. Next, Katja showed him her own Wisconsin driver's license! So she had switched cars in case she needed to back up this new ID.

"Chicago is not in Wisconsin," he said, eyeing her cautiously. "Chicago is in Illinois," pronouncing the final "s."

"I was born in Chicago," Katja replied, again in English and with complete aplomb. "Now I live in Wisconsin."

He asked if we had seen the sign forbidding access to this road. We both answered no. "You entered East German territory," he said gravely, pointing toward the Brocken. "The *Vopos* had every right to arrest you, and once you were in their custody, your government would not easily have gotten you back. You Americans act so carefree. Hasn't anything ever gone wrong in your lives?"

I explained that we were simply touring the beautiful Harz and planned to visit nearby Braunlage next. He touched his right index finger to his forehead and translated for the radioman, who duly reported that two foolish *Ami* tourists had almost touched off a border incident.

Katja's trembling hand took mine, and we marched between two soldiers to her parked Audi. With a thumping pulse, I took the wheel and followed the BGS jeep out of the hilly woods to the highway, where to my tremendous relief we parted ways. In Braunlage, Katja picked out a *Pension* for the night. I registered under my real name and Katja's new fake one, Kathy Zielsdorf. So her superiors already had us married. I loved the sound of it.

We lingered over dinner at a Yugoslav restaurant, sharing a platter of spicy sarma, krvavice and cevapcici, and, before falling asleep, made love yet again. I awoke not long after dozing off and lay there, listening to her breathe and struggling to figure out what in the hell had just happened. The *Bundesgrenzschutz* had rescued me, but from what? What good would I be to the East Germans or Soviets in their countries? Were they planning to brainwash me into doing their bidding? One thing for certain, whatever their scheme, it had nearly succeeded.

It was clear Katja and I would only be safe living in the American underground, and so she was right that if I wanted to be a professor it had to be on their terms. There was no doubt I couldn't abide a state like East Germany, run by a committee of unelected party leaders obedient to Moscow, even as Katja's husband. That country enjoys the highest standard of living in the Warsaw Pact only because no economic system good or bad can make Germans lazy. But its way of life is too repressive and austere, no matter how allegedly just or egalitarian.

The next morning we ate a late breakfast, and she drove me to the Braunschweig train station. In saying goodbye, we savored kisses and caresses like a last meal before execution. When I tried to push her away, Katja held on tightly, warm tears rolling down her cheeks. "I've come up with a new plan," she whispered. "But for it to work, you must do exactly what I say. You will hear from me soon. *Auf Wiedersehen*, Peterchen." I took a deep breath and climbed out.

How could I even consider forgetting about her and pursuing some stupid doctorate? But then how can I continue to let Katja's comrades operate freely? If I got Katja out of Germany with me and us safely hidden in the States, I could turn the others in, whether she agreed to it or not. Maybe I wouldn't even ask her to agree. I'd just do it. But for now I have no choice but to go along with her new stratagem, whatever it might be.

Oct. 5, 1971

I'm renting Hoffman's place on Südstrasse now that he's been discharged and gone back to the States. I'm keeping my face off the streets until well after dark and only then sneaking over to the Schultzes to see whether Katja has written. Bakken's still here in Knittelstedt, but I don't dare visit him. I pay my new landlady extra to buy me groceries.

Two days ago, I was sitting in my old room, daydreaming over a *Spiegel*, when a sharp knock jerked me to my feet. I bowled over a chair in my haste to let Katja in. But it was Karl-Heinz and Dagmar, both looking drawn and sallow, she the worst I had ever seen her.

"*Wie geht's*?" I greeted.

"Terrible," Karl-Heinz said. "Yesterday East German and Soviet officers interrogated Dagmar on the train from West Berlin about you *Amis* in Knittelstedt. An East German captain barged into her compartment and took her to another car, where a Soviet major was waiting. The whole trip to Helmstedt the senior officer posed questions in Russian, and the East German translated."

"I claimed to know nothing about you Americans," Dagmar added, her voice raspy and unsteady. "I said you aren't allowed to fraternize with Germans. They told me I was lying, and as proof showed photos of me dancing with Tom Bakken at Club 69. 'So I went to a party once,'" I replied. "That doesn't mean I know anything about them." No matter how hard they pressed me, I wouldn't give in. Just before we reached the border, they finally let me return to my seat. Last night I didn't sleep a wink."

"What are you Americans doing here that interests the Soviets so damned much?" Karl snapped.

"Sorry, but I'm not allowed to answer that question. Dagmar, please accept my apologies that this happened. From now on keep your distance from the Americans here."

"What in the hell are you people doing at your precious 'site'?" Karl asked.

"I already said I can't tell you. But rest assured our work benefits West Germany as much as the US. Believe me, you're better off not knowing. Dagmar, did you report this incident to the *Bundesgrenzschutz* or the police?"

"*Nein.*"

"Good. Because that would only make everything worse."

"Kiss my ass!" Karl-Heinz yelled. "Worse for whom? Just look at her! And it's all you damned Americans' fault. We Germans are at the complete mercy of all the foreign troops on *our* soil! Would the United States like hundreds of thousands of soldiers occupying it for decades and stockpiling nuclear weapons? And threatening to turn our country into a battlefield without even consulting us! Just what do you assholes think you are doing in Germany?"

"Defending it."

"But that's what the Russians say! How can two enemies defend the same country? When you're at each other's throats!"

Actually, I couldn't agree more. "The Americans you know are mostly gone from Det Q," I said. "From now on don't meet any new ones and stop going to Club 69. I'm leaving Knittelstedt for good soon myself."

They shook my hand limply in saying goodbye. Karl lingered in the doorway for a wistful final wave. Although I couldn't thank him, I am still grateful that he introduced me to Katja, despite all the trouble that has entailed.

My photos from Umlaut's ETS party were indeed missing, so they were the ones used in the interrogation. Katja must have filched them. My stomach sank at the thought of Dagmar's ordeal, all of it my fault as much as Katja's.

I greatly regret that Tom, Rich, Scotty and Will know *anything* about Katja, though I have also greatly mislead them. Bakken could learn it all if he opens the sealed diary. Did anybody really notice Katja and me in all those hotels and restaurants? Nobody paid us any attention, except for Katja's colleagues. I doubt any German outside Knittelstedt recognized me as an American, despite tiny mistakes of pronunciation or word choice early on I've long since corrected. Now Katja's and my only hope is to vanish together in the States without a trace. If not to Wisconsin, then someplace else where we can lead the rural, Zielsdorfian life of my ancestors.

Oct. 8, 1971

Timmendorfer Strand.

I'll write as fast as I can, Tommy. Please safeguard these new diary pages like the ones you already have. If anything happens to me, publish them immediately. Make people aware. Whatever you do, don't turn them over to the treads, because they'll bury the story and leave the graves unmarked.

On the six-hour train trip to the Baltic coast this morning, I didn't bother trying to read. Riding backwards, rocking with the rhythmic clacking, I sat like a ticking time bomb, staring at the landscape receding into the distance and brooding over my terrible choices. A stout, felt-helmeted German matron blocking the compartment door with her huge frame really tested my patience. I ached for her to take her tabloid with the double-slaying headline and waddle off. In Hamburg, thank God, she finally did.

I long to do the right thing, but what the hell is that? Turn us all in? No way. I won't make Katja suffer or myself. End it all alone? No way. Whatever I do, it must include Katja. If we could only figure out a way for both of us to escape.

At 12:37 p.m., exactly on schedule, the train screeched to a halt in Lübeck. I hopped off with the black suitcase, containing everything I still owned, and marched down the platform toward the main hall, scanning every face I met. To my relief, everybody ignored me. I bought a *Frankfurter Allgemeine* at the kiosk beside the streetcar stop out front and pretended to read the newspaper, while keeping an eye out for Katja. What the devil was keeping her?

I jaywalked across the Lindenplatz, joined a crowd waiting for a bus, and debated whether to return to the *Bahnhof.* "I'm right behind you, Peter," Katja muttered, startling me. "Don't turn around. Just walk across the Stadtgraben and turn right at the park. I'll meet you there."

I did precisely as told and ten minutes later was strolling along the murky Trave River's banks and kicking at the gravel. What was holding her up? I was about to double back, when suddenly there she stood, her hair darker than in the Harz, barely blonde at all anymore, her face so thin it looked almost peaked.

A spark of rage flashed inside me over Dagmar's harsh interrogation, but failed to ignite. Because I still loved Katja. Because she has only been doing her duty. I reached for the woman I couldn't live without. She fell into my arms, and we passionately kissed.

"This is our last rendezvous, Peter," she said, softening German's harsh gutturals and sibilants. "Prepare for the worst. It isn't possible that we flee to America together, but you yourself can escape, if you do exactly what I tell you."

"I won't leave Germany without you."

"Please accept what must be. You must leave this country or you will be killed. Once in the United States you must never contact anybody you've known up till now. Never. Is that understood, Peter?"

"Why can't we hide in Europe? Say, in Spain. We could get there without being spotted."

"Wrong."

"Can we at least go off somewhere together for a little while first?"

"Be serious, Peter. This is the end."

"Not even one last time? For a proper goodbye? After all we've meant to each other?" My hope was that in some romantic setting I could weaken her resolve.

"There is no time for that now, Peter." She pulled a dark blue West German passport out of her purse. "You are Reinhold Schmitt, a *Gymnasium* teacher from Braunschweig. Use this fake ID for your escape to the United States. As Schmitt, you have studied exactly what I did. I trust you have listened to me enough, and I have shown you Braunschweig and its university. You can convince people."

My stomach sank at these words. Yes, I could persuade them, but how could I leave her behind?

"Get accustomed to using it the rest of this weekend. It should save your life."

"Why have you decided to save me now?" I said, struggling to fathom her plan. "After trying to get me kidnapped by the East Germans in the Harz?"

"Peter, you don't understand what happened there."

I didn't contradict her. She kissed me hard again, as I grabbed her buttocks, pulled her up onto her tiptoes, and nipped her tongue. She glanced around and, spotting no one but an elderly couple a hundred meters down the path strolling away from us, unzipped me and grasped tight.

"You did try to get me kidnapped in the Harz," I said.

"*Nein, nicht kidnappen*. Yes, we wanted to capture you and force you to cooperate. I shouldn't tell you this, but it doesn't matter anymore now. The old plan was to make you remain in East Germany forever."

"Why? To work as a linguist? But what country on earth has more people who speak both German and Russian than yours?"

"You should have accepted the better offer. Now at best you will have to hide for the rest of your life. You will find it was much easier to win top grades than to survive as a fugitive. At worst"—her voice trailed off.

If she had already accepted the unspeakable for herself and was refusing to disappear with me, why then I'd have to either vanish on my own or—chills went up and down my spine over the alternative. All I knew for certain is that I wouldn't cause her any harm. Maybe right there I flushed away all semblance of morality and now was just considering tactics. But what kind of morality would ask me to hurt my loved ones? The biblical story of Abraham and Isaac always infuriated me for preaching mindless obedience to a whimsical, openly immoral God. In my shoes, my mother would have prayed. But then she would never have found herself in my shoes. If the greatest man who ever lived couldn't escape His fate, how could a mere mortal like me expect a better destiny?

While I kept caressing her and she fondled away, my thoughts returned to the Harz. So the *Bundesgrenzschutz* had saved my butt, and Katja had been willing to let the East Germans capture me. The more I thought about that, the angrier I felt.

Noticing my loss of ardor, she let go. "You must leave Germany tomorrow and fly to the United States and hide. After you're safely gone, I'll face my comrades. But at least we can enjoy today at a beach, and then in the morning say goodbye forever. Are you listening, Peter? What I'm telling you is your only hope."

She drove her trusty VW Bug with the familiar plates the thirty kilometers north from the Hanseatic city of Lübeck to this Baltic Sea resort. The weather is *Nachsommer*—balmy Indian summer. Still too cool for most Americans to swim, but not for Germans. Well past its high season, Timmendorfer Strand, a small town of half-timbered restaurants and guesthouses catering to tourists, was half-deserted. We chose a *Pension* down a dead-end street five hundred meters from the water, where I registered us as "Jost and Katharina Schottenstein," the surname of a Wisconsin classmate. Again, staff mistook me for a German. Katja was right—it is easy for me to fool people.

After we dropped the luggage off in our room, Katja drove us past the municipal beaches and continued farther north up the coast. "Where are we going?" I asked, recalling the Harz fiasco only too well.

"You'll see." Her smile was vacant.

She parked her VW alongside the road a few miles outside Timmendorfer Strand, and we headed on foot toward the nearby sea across a narrow dune of soft, pebbly sand, keeping clear of its eroding sides, till we reached a steep drop-off, overlooking the water. From our elevated perch, the calm sea looked gorgeous. Without warning, Katja grabbed my hand and jumped, jerking me after her. We tumbled together down the crumbling embankment, riding a small avalanche, sharp little rocks nipping at me through my clothes. We came to a giggling halt ten yards below on a tiny beach hidden between two ridges, out of sight to anyone not standing directly above us. "This is as far from East and West as we're going to get," Katja quipped.

Neither of us laughed.

She changed into her red bikini and I my blue trunks, and we waded in. It was so cold she hopped right back out, spread the beach towel, removed her top, and lay down to catch a little sunshine. Meanwhile, I crawled fifty meters out full speed and swam back even faster the water was so bone-chilling.

I dried myself and tried to nestle against her, but she shoved me away, claiming I felt cold as an iceberg. I glared at her dull gray-green cat's eyes without a trace of their former luster. "Peter, it's time I confess something so you don't misunderstand later. When you were home on emergency leave and I had no idea where you were or whether you would ever come back, I drove to Knittelstedt and called upon a comrade of yours."

Adrenaline spurted inside me. "Which one?"

"That is not important."

"Which one?" She knocked my hands from around her throat and sprang to her feet.

"I'm sorry," I muttered. "But I must know which one."

"It doesn't matter, Peterchen. Nothing important happened."

"If it was anything at all, it was too much! Especially with one of them! Who in the hell was it? My God, I'd better get out of here before I kill somebody!"

"Peter, don't be stupid. It was meaningless. I was just looking for you."

"Or were you recruiting a replacement for me just in case I didn't come back?"

Regret passed across her face like a cloud's shadow. She reached for me, but this time I did the shoving. When she tried again, I pinned her onto the sand, braced my legs inside her knees, and spread her thighs. "Who are the professor and Jürgen to you?"

"Comrades, colleagues. What else?"

"You mean you never slept with either?"

"Why do you care who I slept with? I am not your property. You have no right to tell me who I should see and who I shouldn't. There are things that I've had to do."

"Sometimes I wonder if I know you at all." I tugged at her bikini bottom, but she held it on. Still grasping her wrists, I tried to kiss her, but she nipped my lower lip. With a strong thigh, she rolled me off and I landed in the sea, sputtering salty water. She scrambled halfway up the bank, before I bear-hugged her from behind and twist us both back down into the freezing waves. I yanked her out, flung her onto the sand face-first, pulled off her bikini bottom, and fell on top of her. "We can escape together and set up new lives," I said.

"It's too late," she mumbled, squirming under me.

I pressed her flat until she quit resisting, and I also went limp. We both sat up, and she faced me teary-eyed. "Yes, I tricked you into being photographed with me and smuggling out the glossary, but I also lied to my superiors more than once for your sake. I convinced them that you couldn't be blackmailed into helping us and deliberately betraying your country no matter what the threats. And that you would never turn us in, because you were sympathetic to our ideals, if not our methods, so there was no need to eliminate you. At first they believed me, until they decided the risk was too great to take the slightest chance. So I told them about your headaches and insomnia, claiming you were close to a nervous breakdown. Now my assignment is to push you over the edge."

My body trembled from the emotions weltering inside me. In this last assignment of hers she was succeeding. "You threatened to turn me in to my CO!"

"*Selbstverständlich.* We couldn't have you mention us to anyone. For a time it seemed that you would, so I had to say whatever it took to shut you up. I didn't entrap you in the Harz. I saved you. Because I was the one who got the *Bundesgrenzschutz* to come. Didn't I ask you to throw stones into that pond? If the BGS soldiers couldn't see us, they could certainly hear the splashes."

"That was only at the end! You started off entrapping me!"

That she didn't deny.

"Why did you leave me alone in Knittelstedt for such a very long time?"

"Because I had no choice. Because I claimed you would rather turn yourself in than cooperate, that you were hopeless."

"Then why did you come back? And what was the hike in the Harz really about? If I didn't have to be eliminated before, what changed your people's minds? Katja, you're not telling me the entire truth."

"You're too clever, Peter. They aren't going to risk liquidating you now. Not when they're certain you're going to do it to yourself."

Were they right? "Have you done this to other GIs?" I asked. Her refusal to answer meant she indeed had. "You still haven't told me why you came back, if I was such a hopeless prospect?"

"Peter, don't you know me by now? I love you." This time I didn't doubt she was telling the truth, but the pain in her gaze meant there was much more to reveal. "I could never have become an American anyway," she muttered wistfully.

"Yes, you could. I'd make it easy for you."

Katja's chuckle was sour. "Who do you think you are dealing with? They would never simply let us escape. You act so naive sometimes, Peter. If we flee, they will hunt us down no matter where we go."

"Why are you asking me to join such cutthroats?"

"Because it's my side, and I won't betray it. Now stop arguing." She paused. "*Ich bin keine Ostdeutsche*—I am not an East German. What I have done to you is very logical, considering my true identity." Switching to perfect Russian, she went on, "I am a Soviet citizen. My ancestors, all farmers, accepted Catherine the Great's invitation and emigrated from Prussia to the lower Volga in the eighteenth century. Yes, Stalin punished us severely for being German during the Great Fatherland War, but you Americans interned your Japanese, too. And it's true that, though I am a loyal Soviet citizen, I am still German to the core. Exactly like you."

Her confession terrified me.

"Peter, you are no less German than I am. It's disgraceful that we have both been so disloyal to our true fatherland."

"Why are you telling me this?"

"Keeping secrets doesn't matter anymore. Since I am doomed, I am free to entrust you with everything. My superiors have become aware of all my lies to protect you. Believe me, they don't ever forgive. As a Soviet citizen, of course, I am not in the East German *Stasi*. Nor in the KGB. I'm in Soviet Military Intelligence, the GRU, where I'm a captain. Recruiting you to our cause would have gotten me a promotion to major. Obviously, a US Army unit in the field like yours is targeted by the GRU, not the KGB. As for the *Stasi*, they help us however ordered. You Americans must get to know your enemy better, if you hope to have a chance against us."

For once I believed her every word. This total openness on her part proved this was indeed the end. I did know the GRU well. Det Q had to encipher its communications, because the GRU's Sixth Directorate eavesdropped on us electronically. As a Captain in Military Intelligence, Katja of course should know about the SPETSNAZ forces in East Germany that our stolen radio enabled us to overhear. They're Soviet MI, too, in the Third Department of an Intelligence Directorate. Her cool beauty was never more chilling.

I kissed her softly, and her tongue sought mine. Our gentle caresses soon turned rough, and we made love with an urgent edge. Then we just lay there, tightly embracing, till the cold, rising tide was lapping at our necks. The drive back to Timmendorfer Strand passed in anxious silence.

After a seafood supper of *Dorsch*, a delicate Baltic codfish, I rested in Katja's arms inside our *Pension* room, recalling my mother's equanimity in the face of death. But then she felt saved for all of eternity. Out the window the twilight darkened to twinkling blackness, and I nestled closer to my beloved, thus awakening her. I rolled on top of her and entered her. Lying there like a limp corpse, she let me make love to her yet again.

Afterwards, she whispered, "That was the very last time." We lay entwined, the only sounds her slow breathing and the occasional rumble outside of a passing car. My body ached to fall asleep, but my pulse wouldn't stop pounding. Katja's musky aroma, redolent of overripe mayflowers made me desire her again, but she pleaded fatigue. So I just hugged her tightly and waited for her to doze off. When she did, I carefully slid my arm out from under her, dressed, and slipped out the door.

I wandered the moon-lit beach, weighing my options one final time and finding no good way out. I walked over to the *Bahnhofsrestaurant* and there wrote out this entry as fast as I could. All the stale cigarette smoke gave me a headache, but I kept scribbling away to make sure everything got said.

3:45 a.m.

My apologies that the following entry is even less legible than the previous pages, but it's written in even greater haste. It was 3:00 a.m. by the time I sneaked back into our room. I shut the door as carefully as I could, but it still made a distinct click. "Where'd you go?" Katja asked, sitting up in bed.

"To use the toilet." Like most German guesthouses, the john was down the hall. "Go back to sleep."

"It seems like you were gone so long."

I climbed under the comforter, and she snuggled close. "You're freezing!"

"Then warm me up."

That she soon did and then asked me to get us some water. I drew a glass from the sink in our room. When I turned around, Katja sat propped against the headboard, naked to the waist, two white capsules resting in the palm of her right hand.

"You must take yours first," she told me. "I don't trust you otherwise."

I shook my head.

She reiterated the hopelessness of our situation. "I don't want to end it all with a pill," I said, "not in this cooped-up room. I'd rather head out to sea and there slip under forever. I'm told if you inhale the water, you pass out so fast the pain is brief. I'll leave my suitcase and clothes with my wallet and wristwatch on the beach to let people know what I've done. There are far worse ways to die."

Her eyes teared up. "Your friends will mourn you."

"I don't have any close friends," I said, lying. "I'm not in touch with any relatives either, so nobody will miss me."

She smiled weakly, as if pleased, and I reciprocated her adoring gaze. After one final kiss, I walked out the door without glancing back.

So, Thomas, I hereby conclude this document. Make of me what you will, at least you know the truth. You know how Katja and I died and why, whatever the official reports. I realize you cannot tell my tale without revealing hers, but that doesn't matter anymore. You decide whether to make public my side of the story. Whichever does my reputation the least harm. I don't want people who knew me to think mine was a pointless, cowardly suicide. But I would also rather be forgotten than not remembered fondly and well.

I'm embarrassed to be showing fear like this in front of you, Thomas. None of us should be that afraid of dying. In the end, we all share the same fate, each of us born only to perish, some in due time, some prematurely. But no one in his right mind should want it to come soon, since the rest of eternity is such a very long time to be dead. I can't comfortably accept a world where there's no better reason I should suffer this fate than bad luck and dumb decisions, but what choice do I have? Of course I got where I am by my own free will. Though where was the freedom in decisions made without any inkling of their full consequences?

So another favorite gets knocked out of the tournament early. It happens every season. My biggest regret is that I've been too busy making myself into somebody I wasn't, too guarded about what I was and soon no longer would be, to afford the luxury of being this sincere. Just think if I had been as honest my whole life as I'm being with you right now. Why then my reputation would simply have been the real me. But of course that was never good enough, not when I was capable of so much more. Didn't I prove that again and again?

So it's a final farewell, Tommy. I'm sure you would have wished me a bon voyage, if given the chance. Anyway, I wish you a good one, five or six decades hence. Or sooner if you're ready. The note I left in the *Pension* doesn't explain much, just that I couldn't take the pressure anymore. You fill in the details. I'm sure Katja has swallowed her pill by now. No way is she going to hang around long enough for her so-called comrades to do their dirty work. I can't let her body be found before I hit the beach, so I'm off to get this in the mail to you and then go under myself.

Adieu.

Part Three
REUNION

Chapter Six

What indeed must it feel like to drown?

I just read Peter's diary again and have been staring out a window of this northern Minnesota cabin at the nearby lake. It won't be long before the water freezes over and the ice thickens daily, making the eventual challenge of penetrating it that much greater. Wherever I gaze, shadowy images of young Peter and Katja float before my eyes like flash-photo afterimages. After the passage of a decade and a half, agonizing memories from their ill-starred romance ought to have faded, yet they still cut to the quick.

If only he hadn't gone barhopping with Karl-Heinz in Braunschweig. If only they had skipped Zum grünen Kakadu. If only he hadn't fallen head over heels in love with Katja. If only he had refused to sneak her a copy of the glossary of Russian vulgarity out of the site. If only he hadn't decided to look her up in Munich after their break-up. If only he hadn't accompanied her to Timmendorfer Strand. On and on the fateful decisions stretch till death at last severs the string for good.

Then there is my personal culpability, starting with the disastrous failure to publish Peter's diary immediately upon his disappearance—and not just to help the Timmendorfer Strand police solve two baffling murders. To make amends as best I can this late, I shall continue my account of relevant events below in order of their occurrence till the truth stands revealed in its unvarnished entirety.

* * *

After rejecting the Army's early discharge offer unlike the other Monks, I remained in uniform the fall of 1971, pulling regular shifts out at the site, only no longer inside the Green Room, since our SPETSNAZ intercept mission had gone defunct. The *Braunschweiger Zeitung* published the following on October 12th. Translated into English, it reads:

DOUBLE MURDER AT RESORT PENSION

> Katharina Marie Wendt, 29, current Munich resident and former student at the Braunschweig Teachers College, and Wilhelm Breitenbach, 40, a self-employed Hamburg businessman, were found deceased inside a Timmendorfer Strand Pension According to the coroner's report, Fräulein Wendt died from strangulation and Herr Breitenbach blunt-force trauma. The Special Commission of the Criminal Police speculates that Breitenbach, a guest on the same floor, heard Wendt struggling with the assailant, rushed to her aid, and was himself overpowered.
>
> The *Polizei* are seeking Jost Schottenstein, around 30 years of age, 185 centimeters in height, medium build, light brown hair, and blue eyes. Schottenstein and Wendt registered as husband and wife at the guesthouse and were seen together the entire weekend. Clothes matching those worn by the suspect were found on a nearby beach, but without a wallet or ID. Footprints in the sand led to the water's edge, so authorities are combing the seashore for Schottenstein's body, while *Interpol* continues to hunt for him across Europe.

The piece left obvious questions. For instance, what happened not only to Peter's wallet and ID, but also his suicide note, suitcase, and watch? These couldn't have been found, if the police never discovered it was Zielsdorf who drowned. And what about all the cash, easily many thousands of dollars, that he had been carrying?

At the time I saw no reason to doubt the GRU had killed Katja and Breitenbach, an apparent good Samaritan, who suffered the horrible misfortune of stumbling upon the Soviets' bloody work in progress. Of course the diary's final pages didn't mention him because he showed up after Peter had mailed those to me before hitting the beach and drowning himself.

After the first mention of the Timmendorfer Strand double murder, I checked the *Braunschweiger Zeitung* daily for updates. On October 18th, it reported that Katja's body had been cremated and fellow students had gathered in the Andreaskirche for a memorial service. In early November, it wrote that authorities had suspended their search for Jost Schottenstein. The November 22nd edition stated that the name Jost Schottenstein was an alias, so the case had been re-opened. Apparently to no avail, since no further news ensued.

I personally saw Peter return that glossary of Russian vulgarity to the site. I was already at my desk in the Green Room when he came in, slipped a booklet from his lunch sack into his Out basket, and chatted briefly before knuckling down to work. Later when he got up to use the latrine, I glanced at its title page and recognized our special lexicon. So he was expanding his vocabulary with the real Russian our DLI teacher Markov insisted we must also learn if we were to master the language. What was the harm in taking it home, I reasoned, even if technically a violation of security regulations, so I said nothing.

Why is it more painful to envision the corpse of a lovely woman? The first time I laid eyes on Katja, I was browsing through the periodicals on the kiosk racks outside the Braunschweig *Hauptbahnhof*, after taking a train from Knittelstedt to shop in the bigger city for classical records. Was I taken aback when not fifty feet away Peter exited the passenger seat of a gray Volkswagen. I hid behind a corner and watched him remove a suitcase from the trunk in front of the vehicle as the tall, blonde driver climbed out.

He gave her a lingering embrace before rushing off toward his platform. Long-legged, slender, fine-boned—even at my distance, she was striking.

The past fifteen years, I never saw another word in print about these people or talked to anybody who had known them. Meanwhile, my guilt for failing to help the West German police solve the Timmendorfer Strand murders only grew more acute, since all along I could have revealed Jost Schottenstein and Katja Wendt's true identities. Not that I didn't concoct many a rationalization to assuage my troubled conscience. Such as—why should I care any more about the Cold War than I did who held office here or there? Or—I had never been political and wasn't about to begin. Over the years, I learned to suppress concerns about the Soviets similarly recruiting other GIs to undermine NATO defenses. Still, despite my pathetic excuses, deep down I couldn't deny that the treads deserved to know about Katja and Peter and it was my duty to tell them, no matter what the personal cost to me. Yet, I didn't lift a finger.

Gradually, I lost interest in my academic research and hence career, not that I spent the hours saved on anything else constructive. Then out of sheer self-disgust this past New Year's I resolved to publish a new scholarly article and chose the Soviet reception of Nietzsche's philosophy as its topic. I got off to a decent start till chronic insomnia struck and soon I had to drag myself through workdays. Finally, I admitted I could never get decent rest or know peace of mind unless I came forward and revealed what I had been concealing about Peter. But to do that I needed moral support and didn't have a clue from whom.

Then this past June I got a life-changing phone call. When I picked up, a familiar voice said, "Hey, troop, wanna party?"

"I beg your pardon?"

"Bakken, this is Dave Mueller! Your old Army buddy over in *Deutschland!* You know, Umlaut! Remember?"

How could I forget? Umlaut told me he was organizing a Det Q reunion at the Chicago Beacon Hotel over the upcoming

Labor Day weekend. Everybody stationed over there between 1968 and 1973 would be welcome. "We won't get *too* drunk!" he said with a chortle. "I was wondering if you could help me make a few arrangements."

I asked how he had gotten my address.

"From your mother," he said, laughing.

I pleaded a lack of free time.

"How about at least contacting Scott Dickinson? Since you guys live so close."

We did? It turned out Scotty had moved back to his home town of Columbus, Ohio, after working several years in New York City. Umlaut couldn't remember what Scotty was doing for a living, but the dude wasn't hurting for money. "Why're you asking me?" he teased. "You knew him better than I did, troop. Anyway, I'd sure appreciate it if you could call a few guys for me. As a personal favor to an old Army buddy."

I truly was busy, I insisted. But did I truly want to write that Nietzsche article? How could contacting old Army buddies not be more important than dissecting the scribblings of a long-dead German philosopher? It wouldn't to my chairman, of course, but then the only place he had ever experienced friendship was in novels. Of course I wanted to see those guys again. Especially when for years I'd been meeting people I had a lot in common with, yet never connecting. But back then just being thrown into the same boat sufficed to make us buddies, but middle age, alas, for me was boatless. And of all the buddies I had, I felt closest to the Monks. You bet, I knew Scotty better than Umlaut did. Sure, I'd make those calls.

"Outstanding!" Umlaut said and gave me Dickinson's phone number and address. "I'll have to get back to you on Hoffman and Burke. Somebody must know how to get messages to them. You're on your own with locating Peter Zielsdorf. Nobody seems to know where that dude's at."

"I certainly don't," I blurted.

"Do you think he's someplace back in Wisconsin?"

"I haven't heard that he isn't."

"Or maybe he married that Fräulein he was dating and settled down in Germany."

"You never know." I hated lying. His marriage to Katja should have been the epitome of conjugal bliss. A woman like her—so unlike Karen—would have made me happy, too. I only laid eyes on Katja twice, but that was enough to know she was as every bit as remarkable as Peter insisted.

Umlaut didn't get back to me until mid-July. This time he asked me not only to get the other Monks to come but to persuade them to help him organize as well. "If I don't find some more assistants, my old lady's moving out. See as many of our buddies as you can in person. Because you can really count on a person's word when they give it to you face to face."

I seized the opportunity. Because I wouldn't just look up the Monks, I'd show them Peter's diary and together we would decide how to deal with its devastating revelations. Dickinson I could see on the drive to my parents in Madison, Wisconsin the next month, Columbus being on the way.

I thought about phoning Scotty, but it was easier to send a note. He wrote right back: "Thomas, stop by anytime and stay as long as you like. Scott."

Two weeks later, I still hadn't responded. The prospect of betraying Peter, even to another Monk, so unnerved me I kept putting it off. Three days before my departure, I finally forced myself to call. A soft female voice purred, "Scotty's right here," and a man came on the line. It was Dickinson all right, his voice lower-pitched, less excited, more controlled than I recalled, but the whinnying giggle was the same. I agreed to arrive in time for lunch on Saturday, August 2nd, though that meant moving my departure back a day.

The next day a note arrived from Will Burke, postmarked Austin, Texas, saying he would be in Milwaukee the following weekend. If convenient, I should drive over from Madison, and we could have dinner together. So Umlaut had gotten in touch with him, too. I made another photocopy of Peter's diary for Burke.

It annoyed me that my yard badly "needed mowed," as the locals phrased it, but did a lawn honestly require a fresh military buzz cut? In unshaded patches the grass had even gone to seed, but I didn't see the harm in having it thicker in spots next year. I wasn't going to worry about the weeds either, since many of them were in fact wildflowers. What was the point of beheading blooming dandelions for no better reason than to prove I was the boss and not the plants? There was earth and water and sunshine to spare for whatever wanted to flourish. As for my cluttered rain gutters, the leaves, twigs, and black walnuts would just have to sit and rot a while longer.

I packed light and dropped my tubby, orange tabby tom, Nebuchadnezzar, off at Mrs. Gardiner's, a widowed neighbor with five felines of her own. Finally, I set out for the fresher, nippier air of the North, happy to escape the stifling heat and humidity of southern Ohio my body had never adjusted to. In Columbus I veered off Highway 33 into a neighborhood of mansions surrounded by perfect putting greens, as though the owners couldn't get in enough strokes at the country clubs. The fiercely trimmed lawns were a dismal display of nature controlled and tamed, like teary-eyed elephants compelled to perform circus tricks.

This was Upper Kensington, the other Ohio, the one still prospering during the 1980s. Unlike the southeastern mining towns, already depressed now for decades, or the more recently impoverished smokestack belt in the state's northeast corner. I quickly got lost in this strange suburb without sidewalks, as if people were helpless to get around without vehicles. By sheer dumb luck, I chanced upon Walnut Creek Crescent, where house numbers led me to a white brick palace with rounded upstairs windows cut into a high, steep roof. The Dickinson mansion.

I couldn't deny its grandeur, but it still looked as out of place in the Midwest I knew as a diamond tiara on a dairy farmer.

Four or five of my parents' ticky-tacky tract Cape Cods near the Oscar Mayer plant in Madison would have easily fit inside this palace, which probably cost ten or twenty times as much. And we hadn't been poor, living at least on the lower fringes of the middle class. Compared to Peter's hardscrabble family, we had been downright affluent.

I parked my Toyota in the spacious driveway between a boxy, black BMW and a sportier, burgundy two-seater Porsche. I supposed I would have taken either in trade for my Corolla, but only if they were as maintenance-free. All I ever asked of a car was that it got me where I needed to be with the least possible fuss. It didn't matter what it looked like, and the cheaper the better.

The polished brass doorbell chimed, and a puffy-faced man with thinning hair, a deep tan, and estuaries of wrinkles fanning out from both eyes emerged. His jaw dropped, as if in happy recognition, and he burst forward and gave me a muscular hug. "Hey, Bakken!" he greeted. This old geezer was Dickinson? I wouldn't have recognized him in a crowd. Contact lenses now instead of wire rims, and hair so uniformly blond it had to be dyed. A canary yellow polo shirt with a green reptile sown above its pocket and sleeves pinching biceps bigger than they had been in Monterey. There was no visible membership tag on his immaculate white slacks. But why the lurid splotch on his left cheek?

"Get your stuff, Bakken. No, hell, I'll carry it for you." I beat Scotty to the backpack with the diary photocopies, leaving him the suitcase. What in the devil had happened to his face?

On second glance, his body was slim as ever or even slimmer, so the puffy cheeks were deceptive. His smile was still wide and bright, but his eyes no longer joined in the mirth. And why were they so bloodshot? The minty, medicinal smell he exuded hinted at an explanation.

I followed him into a kitchen so wall-to-wall white I had to squint. A pretty brunette, standing over the sink, said, "Hi, Tommy," as if we already were acquainted. Five-seven. About thirty-five, or if older, well-preserved. Long, thin, angular features.

Skin too fair to tan—like mine. Jet-black hair pulled back into a bun and the rest hanging airily to her waist like Spanish moss. No makeup that I could detect. Nervous eyes.

Scott introduced his wife, Elizabeth Brown Dickinson, with ironic formality. In a husky voice, she asked me to call her "Beth."

"Give me your rucksack, too, Tommy," Scott said. "I'll carry everything up to your bedroom."

"No-no," I stammered, "I need that close-by."

"Whatever." He zipped off with my suitcase.

"I've heard a lot about you, Tommy," Beth droned, as if reading from a script.

I scanned the kitchen for a safe place to put the backpack down. Finding none, I slung it around a shoulder.

"Scott said you weren't a talker, but this is ridiculous," Beth muttered.

Dickinson popped back in. "So what have you been up to, Thomas?"

I didn't want to bring the diary up in front of Beth. The only other thing I could think of were the Soviet misinterpretations of Nietzsche I had been scouring and synthesizing, but I was too polite to mention those. So I said, "Not much."

Scotty chuckled nervously and picked up an opaque blue tumbler from the counter. "Beth has already begun lunch," he announced with forced good cheer. "You can set another place, right, honey?"

She glared darts at him.

"Thomas, let me give you a tour of my humble abode, while Liz finishes up. Could I get you a G and T?"

Before lunch? I made it a coke.

Scotty snatched the backpack out of my grasp. "Let me at least put this in the hallway closet. You can get your pills or whatever you need from it any time." I carefully watched him hang it on a hook and close the door. Beth grimly thrust a frosted tumbler into my hand, and I pursued Dickinson into a monstrous living room. I slowly turned full circle to take in the Persian rug, American colonial furniture, and an indoor jungle of exotic ferns and vines. Mirror-lined walls reflected the two of us like a kaleidoscope, our image shrinking inside of images till the two of us disappeared into a point. By no means was this room small, but its enormity was an optical illusion.

"It has class, doesn't it?" Scotty said, beaming with pride.

I nodded, though that depended on which class you meant. The freezing soft drink hit my queasy stomach exactly wrong. Dickinson pointed out objets d'art scattered oh-so meaningfully about the house, but my mind kept drifting back to what was hanging in his closet. Did I ever long to hand him the copy of the diary and scram.

"So what are the other Monks up to?" Scott said, patting his reddened cheek.

"I have no idea. I'll be seeing Will next weekend, when he visits Milwaukee for a chess tournament. Rich I'll contact as soon as Umlaut gets his address. He lives someplace without a phone."

"Not having one sounds about Rich's speed."

I grimaced to hear Scott slurring his "s's."

"Oh, I like Hoffman all right," he went on, "but we never really got over a tiff in Knittelstedt when he called me 'a bourgeois asshole.' So he was at least half-right. Seriously, I'm not that bourgeois compared to everyone else here in UK. But I can't abide people proud of being hippie-dippy either."

He led me upstairs to his study overlooking an immense backyard. I recognized a television, two VCRs, and a stereo system with speakers the Rolling Stones could have used at Altamont, all the equipment more overwhelming than impressive. Perhaps because I never could cozy up to any man-made object with moving parts or electrical wiring, as much as I depended on some of them.

We stomped downstairs and headed out back, where I stepped gingerly across the putt-perfect lawn. "How are your parents doing?" he asked, a sweet question.

"Just fine for their age," I said, glancing away from his discolored cheek.

New, cooler air blowing in from the west began to condense the stifling humidity into a fine mist. Ignoring the precipitation, Scott and I circled the house. "Remember how I used to whip everyone's ass running?" he said. "Hell, I was even faster than Zielsdorf. But now I'm too pokey for slow-pitch softball. Without legs, my tennis is a joke. And you know the latest? No matter how skinny I get I can't flatten my stomach."

I said nothing, debating the best way to bring up Peter's diary.

"Don't you hate getting old, Thomas? I mean, aging's a bitch. My back hurts a lot these days. Not that I can't manage the pain with exercise and pills. The tea helps of course, too." He hoisted his tumbler, wrinkling his facial splotch with a grin. "The other day I glanced down, and it looked like I was riding a chicken."

Maybe he should eat more and worry less, I thought but didn't voice. Had he somehow hit his cheek falling?

"Now don't get me wrong," he went on, guiding me back into the living room. "I love Beth and the house and the kids. I love being a family man. But little things are driving me crazy. Like Beth's refusal to cut her damned hair. I mean, I don't really care, but her billowing tresses make her look like an adolescent getting wrinkles. She'll turn forty in October, for Christ's sake. And why won't she gain some weight? That way her curves would come back."

I didn't respond. It wasn't exactly accurate that she had no curves, not from behind anyway, though I tried not to notice. Scott fidgeted with his empty tumbler. "It bugs me how I always play things safe now. I'm a coward compared to the old days, when everything didn't depend on the bottom line. I used to accept people for whatever they had to offer personally no matter who they were or what they earned, but that's not how UK works."

A lump formed in my throat. I missed Company D, Det Q, and, above all, Peter.

"Not that I want a different job," he added, "or to move somewhere else. You can't go backwards in lifestyle and ever be happy. But I wish I wasn't such a clone. Ring the doorbell of any house around here and somebody like me will answer. Sure, I liked settling down, but I never expected it to be a life sentence. Right now I can tell you exactly how I'm going to spend the next twenty-five years, and that scares the crap out of me. So I'm a nice professional with a nice house and a nice wife and nice kids in a nice suburb. What's missing? Everything. I'm winning a game I don't even want to play."

"You seem really good at it though," I said.

"For that, I have to thank my father. He showed me the ropes. And to beat the tax man, he's been giving me some of my inheritance in advance every year. Which has made a big difference. But where is all this heading? It can't be just so the next generation can do more of the same, can it?"

"Why are we here?"

"Exactly. Where's Zielsdorf when we really need him? He could really contribute to this discussion." Scotty tried to take a swig from his empty glass. "But then maybe we're not supposed to ask the questions Peter always did. It struck me one day that my cat can live without knowing why, so why can't I? Since I'm supposed to be superior to the dumb animal. So now when negative thoughts arise, I drive them out by dwelling on positive things like sexy broads. That black despair just below the surface with Peter was such a waste of energy. What was bugging him so much anyway? Remember how he acted in Germany? He was in such bad shape when I flew home to ETS I felt guilty leaving the poor bastard behind."

This was the perfect time to fetch the diary and fork it over. Still, I just sat there.

Scotty swirled the sliver of ice left in his tumbler. "Where'd you say Peter was living?"

"I didn't." A hot flush suffused my face. "I mean, I don't know."

"You haven't heard from Peter? Good grief, I'm surprised. You guys were really close. Wasn't he a character though? I bet he's got tenure at some place like Yale."

"I don't think he's a professor."

"Come on. Who would be, if Peter isn't? No, I'd bet my house he's teaching at an outstanding university. Why makes you say he isn't?"

"I don't think anyone knows what happened to him. Umlaut thinks he might be in Germany, since nobody he's called knows anything about him. That theory is plausible." Yet obviously false. Why was I lying? Because if I had said Peter was dead, I would have to explain how I knew it, and that would open the floodgates to everything I was holding back and wasn't ready to confess. Not yet. But I had to very soon. Before I left, in fact. Why not right now? I felt close to bawling.

"Hey, you don't know much, huh, Tommy," Scotty said with a smarmy chuckle. "I miss old Zielsdorf. Wasn't he a great linguist? Don't laugh, but when I arrived in Monterey, I expected to be the best student. I had been pretty good at Stanford, you realize. The best thing about Peter is that he refused to accept himself as he was. He just never stopped growing."

"No!" I snapped. "Not accepting himself was his worst fault! At some point enough should have been enough! He didn't have to keep on proving himself over and over!"

Too late, I regretted my vehemence. "But he always managed to pull it off," Scotty rebutted, staring at me with alarm. "I think we should all be more like Zielsdorf. Tom, the way you talk about him makes it sound—"

"—I fear he's dead." There I had said it.

Dickinson's jaw dropped.

"I mean, why else wouldn't anybody have heard from him? He would never have settled in Germany."

I was on the brink of revealing it all, yet face to face with Scotty I still held back. Had I waited too long to come forward? Once the story got out, the FBI couldn't help but suspect complicity on my part. But I couldn't bottle this story up forever either. Still, wouldn't it be better to wait until breakfast the next day just before departing? Dickinson was in no condition now for what I had to say anyway.

“So what do you do to pay the bills?” Scotty asked, again rubbing his cheek.

“I’m a professor at a little college down in Brownsville.”

He looked dumbfounded. “But of course. Got tenure?”

“Yup.” Not that I would ever advance to full professor.

“Hey, congratulations, Bakken. I knew you could do it.” He didn’t sound convinced. “So what do you teach?”

“Comp Lit. Russian. German. Linguistics. Whatever they want me to do.”

“Do you publish?”

“I revised my dissertation and published that. I get a book review in print every year. And thus far a grand total of three journal articles.”

Scotty insisted I tell him everything that had happened since Det Q, so I obliged, keeping it brief. I had earned a doctorate in Comp Lit at UW-Madison in 1979, passing prelims without distinction after four years of course work, and then researched and wrote my thesis for three more. I compared Wilhelm Raabe to Joseph Conrad and proved the German hadn’t influenced the Anglicized Pole, despite similarities. At best it was journeyman research, and my career reflects its mediocrity. My achievements, modest though they were, I owed to a good memory, because I wasn’t that smart. I just keep plugging away.

“Who the hell is Wilhelm Raabe?”

“A nineteenth-century German Realist. Fairly well-known within Germany, unknown outside of it.”

Scott nodded vacantly. “Do you still buy books faster than you can read?”

“My walls are double shelved.”

He guffawed. “My, you ended up off the beaten track! How in the world did you choose Brownsville, Ohio?”

“It chose me. I sent out fifty résumés and got exactly one interview. I took that job at at Northern Appalachian State, and I’m grateful for it. Thousands of better scholars than I am don’t have tenure and never will. Some of my colleagues see NAU as a life sentence, but I don't. I haven't even bothered to apply anyplace else. Brownsville is an island of the Sixties in the wash of the Eighties. The quaint, laid-back college town was laid out among thickly wooded hills long before the invention of the automobile and so has many narrow, brick-paved streets. I can't complain."

"Outstanding," he said with a frown. "And you're married to Karen, right?"

I shrugged, my temples tightening.

"How come you didn't bring the little woman along?"

"Karen lives in Grand Forks, North Dakota, where she's been teaching linguistics for three years. We got a dissolution last year. "

Scott eyed me with grave sympathy.

"I'm still adjusting to being divorced."

"Well, at least you're no longer getting screwed on taxes, Bakken. That damned marriage penalty."

"I don't give a shit about money."

That unexpected bile startled us both. I tried to explain what had gone wrong between my undergraduate sweetheart and me, but it was obvious I didn't really know. It seemed Karen's and my emotions were too similar, too Norwegian, for us to get along. We both had abandoned the marriage years before we separated, after while becoming mere roommates, always in each other's way. And she had become a more serious scholar, but then she had more aptitude. It was a relief for us both when she took the assistant professorship at UND. Our split was just a legal technicality, recognizing what had long since occurred.

"My God, Brownsville, Ohio and Grand Forks, North Dakota," Scotty said like they were Timbuktu and Machu Picchu. Probably because they were.

"Karen won't be stuck there long. At the rate she's publishing she'll land a job at some major university."

"You know," Scotty told me, "Beth and I are heading apart, too. Right before you got here, I almost punched the bitch out. Would you be dumb enough to slug somebody bigger than you?

Well, she is. I was so dumbfounded by her punch that I didn't hit her back. It's kind of funny actually."

About as funny as a hit-and-run accident.

He quickly freshened his "ice tea" and returned. "I want more of everything and Beth wants less. I want to speed up. She wants to slow down. Hell, the way I figure it, after we're dead we'll have all of eternity for mellowing out, but for now I resent the day's measly twenty-four hours. In fact, I hate to relax. The only time I try is when I'm asleep." He paused, swirling the ice in his glass. "Maybe we'll stick it out though for the kids' sake. You didn't mention any kids of yours. Got two myself."

"None for me. Just as well in light of how things turned out." What if I just handed him the diary copy and left?

"You wanted some, right?"

"Yup. Still do."

"It's not too late. Find yourself a younger wife. Or one who already has children. So do you date?"

I shook my head.

Scotty giggled at that preposterous notion and began chewing on a chunk of ice. "Hey, you really are still a secular monk. So what do you do for sex?"

I said nothing, my forehead prickling with chagrin. Noticing my discomfort, he kindly launched into a practiced spiel about his work. Investments in commercial real estate earned him the real money, but he spent most of his time handling dissolutions, divorces, and pre-nuptial agreements, for which he was a local legend. "For really big bucks I ought to move into tort law, but, believe you me, Bakken, there still are some things I won't do for money. So I use the law to protect my clients' wealth? Excuse me! That's what lawyers do."

No doubt. Maybe he'd sober up after lunch, and then I'd give him what Peter had written. No way could I stand to wait till tomorrow.

"Graduate school was my biggest mistake. I got my Master's at Stanford in English history and worked two semesters toward a doctorate before calling time out. My father took me aside and advised a more practical tack. A couple of phone calls from him got me into the Ohio State University Law School, and here I am practicing in my home town. Sure, I feel sheepish living where I was born and bred, but I am good at what I do. Still, I wonder whether I should have stayed in New York. I was good enough to make it there, but really miserable, and so was Beth. Hell, she thinks Columbus is too urban."

"Do you keep up on English history?"

"Hell, no. I have trouble keeping up on the Buckeyes. Though while in New York I did read a slew of history articles and monographs in my spare time."

Whether he was drunk or not, I simply couldn't wait. I walked over to the hallway closet and grabbed the photocopy from the backpack.

Scotty chortled drunkenly.

No, I decided, he was too far gone. Right after lunch would be better. I put the diary back and handed him Umlaut's list of names to call for the Chicago reunion.

"Outstanding," he said, skimming the sheet. "This reunion really sounds like fun. You know, it's weird, Thomas, but I can't talk to anybody I know in town the way I can to you. My UK friends here are like clothes in a closet. Every so often new ones get added, worn out, and replaced. The turnover is so slow you don't even notice there's almost nobody left you were seeing five years ago. I always used to think friendship was easy, but it sure hasn't been. But we Monks were different. So you want me to phone these guys?"

"Exactly."

Chapter Seven

To my relief, lunch was ready at last. Beth had spread the table with a rainbow of ceramic ware, each piece a single color and none of them matching. I could have sworn they were the same style as my mother's during my youth on the wrong side of Madison, but how could that be? For the rare occasion of my visit, Scotty opened a bottle of genuine Champagne from the actual French province. So to a CD of *Don Giovanni*, I finally experienced the real thing, not that I noticed any difference.

My small glass of bubbly lasted the whole meal, while Scott and Beth quaffed the rest. I didn't catch what they called the little rolls of raw fish and rice wrapped in weird vegetation, but it sounded Russian. If you could get past the consistency and texture, which to me had always been the most salient features of any dish, it did have an interesting taste. If one was "into" interesting tastes. To me, analyzing food has always seemed like rating brothels, a gross abuse of intellect in pursuit of sensuality.

Scotty babbled on about their delightfully remote cottage beside a tiny Minnesota lake with the deepest, cleanest water. From the pier you could watch muskies lurking in the weeds and perhaps even witness the sudden vanishing of an unlucky duckling. Ha ha. I did my best to listen, but my thoughts kept drifting back to the Baltic Sea.

Though once a favorite piece—before classical music began to aggravate my depression—this Mozart opera now struck me as sheer torture. Such poignant sublimity made me feel like Peter's waterlogged corpse had been hauled ashore and left dripping at my feet.

Beth made it till the chocolate mousse dessert before she began slurring her words. "Lasht" year she had persuaded Scott to let Jennifer and Jason be exposed to Christianity. So Saturdays the kids took special classes at the local Congregational church and Sundays attended the actual services. Later they'd move on to the Episcopalians, so the kids could be exposed to "a range" of religious beliefs.

Scotty glowered at her.

"So you belong to a church?" I asked. I personally didn't.

"Beth does," Scotty said with a sneer. The mark on his cheek had almost faded.

"I only went there twice," she rebutted.

"We don't mention it around here, Thomas. It's one of those off-the-wall outfits that crawled out of the woodwork in the Seventies."

Beth's eyes flashed pique. "It's the New Age Church."

"Never heard of it," I replied. "Is it Protestant?"

"Protestant? Shit, it isn't even Christian. Sure, you went only twice, honey, but you really wanted us to join, remember? Thomas, it's a bunch of hippies finally dressing like normal people and worshipping only God knows what."

Since when had Dickinson ever cared about religion?

"The members work on getting in touch with Light-Fire, the Godhead principle of the Cosmos," Beth explained. "And learn to beam that energy toward benevolent ends."

Scotty tossed back his head. "Needless to say, it's not in Upper Kensington."

"It's near Yellow Springs, this side of Dayton," Beth added, hopping up to fetch a carafe of white wine. In her absence, Scott whispered that it was good for business occasionally to attend the Congregational services downtown, and he was considering becoming a Mason for the same reason. Besides, it was hard to make their Jennifer go, if they never set an example, not that he wanted his children to believe in any mumbo-jumbo.

Upon her return, Beth asked about my own denomination.

"Like most of us Norwegian-Americans, I was brought up Lutheran," I said. "But I haven't gone since—well, since meeting

Zielsdorf." I cleared my throat. "Brownsville has untraditional churches, too."

"Untraditional?" Scotty blurted. "You mean hippie-dippy?"

"Counterculture they prefer to call it. If I were a joiner, I'd join, too."

"Whatever," Scotty said. "It must be tough for aging longhairs to build an entire life out of not accepting responsibility."

"Actually, it's easy. And you miss the whole idea. They absolutely refuse to accept responsibility for the wrong turn America has taken since Jimmy Carter, and they try to point a better way with their own lives." To my dismay, lunch wasn't sobering Dickinson whatsoever.

The phone rang, and Scott excused himself to answer it.

After an awkward silence, I asked Beth, "Where was it that you grew up?"

"Worthington, just north of UK. Did you drive through Lower Kensington getting here?"

"I must have." I glanced away from the goose bumps plainly visible on her chest.

She chortled bitterly. "There is no Lower Kensington. There is no Kensington. There is only *Upper* Kensington." I contemplated that long and hard, but it still made no sense.

Beth leaned forward, tears oozing from her eyes. "You know what bugs me the most? I do want children and I do want to be a mother, but I also want to live out in the country and be self-sufficient. Not live like this. Who's impressed by all the crap we own? If anybody is, I don't want them around. UK is a terrible place for kids because the families are all so isolated. It's enough to make a person puke."

What could I say? Scotty stumbled back into the room, and I started worrying about their staying on their feet till sundown. Was he ever going to sober up?

"Who was it?" Beth asked.

"The FBI."

I flinched. For fifteen years I had dreaded nothing so much as their knock.

"You mean Robert?" Beth said.

"Yeah, Bob Blair. His wife screwed up royally by accepting a second bid on their house. So he's going to pick me up and we'll straighten things out. Sorry, Tommy, but it shouldn't take long."

The meal resumed in sullen silence. A creature rubbed on my shins. I glanced down at a jet-black, golden-eyed tomcat, whining at me like a child. Beth bent toward me to offer the kitty a morsel of raw tuna, cooing, "Here, Henry." Before I could look away, I had glimpsed her entire exposed breasts.

Henry meowed approval as I said, "Holy moly," under my breath. I scratched the backs of his ears and stemmed the shove of the muscular beastie's head. I longed for Nebuchadnezzar's gentler touch. Or even better, getting the hell out of there.

Beth's gleeful grin showed she was fully aware of what she had done and its effect on me. I noticed makeup wasn't the reason her cheeks looked sunken. They were genuinely hollow. Other fine bones on her head also stuck out, rendering her otherwise pretty face a virtual skull with skin on it. Add a little dust and dirt and she could have gotten work as a Holocaust film extra.

A cup of espresso got Beth chattering about her jogging, and Scott's mood turned edgy. Most Saturdays she "carbed up" before the week's biggest run Sunday mornings, but today she needed protein because it would slow the absorption of alcohol during the party.

"What party?" I blurted.

"Just a little summer soirée," Scott explained. "We've been planning it for two months. My birthday's next Tuesday, but we're celebrating it tonight. The big four-oh. You'll love it."

I nodded gravely. The thought of two dozen Prince Charmings drunk as Dickinson within four walls was alarming. And we still hadn't discussed Zielsdorf's diary.

"Are the spouses coming to this reunion, too?" droopy-lidded Beth asked.

"They're certainly welcome," I muttered. "As are kids."

"No way am I leaving you here alone, Liz!" Dickinson snapped. "Forget about taking the rug rats." At that, Beth jumped up and stalked off.

My stomach churned at the prospect of consuming even one more spoonful of mousse.

"Give up on it, Bakken," Dickinson muttered.

Grateful words indeed. I excused myself to use the john. The bathroom door was ajar, so I nudged it open and immediately yanked it back shut. What had I just seen? Beth kneeling over the toilet bowl and retching. Could she be that drunk?

"You forgot to knock," she teased, when she emerged. She looked embarrassed.

Once I rejoined them at the table, Beth stuck the tip of a little finger provocatively into the corner of her mouth and winked. "So how's the single life in Brownsville, Tommy?"

Dickinson glared at her. "Don't ask."

"Don't answer for him, Scott," she snapped.

"I didn't answer for him, *dear*."

I ducked the question by describing instead the uneasy truce between town and gown and the whole gamut of American lifestyles living elbow to elbow. The fundamentalist natives didn't exactly hanker to outsiders, but all of us got along reasonably well. Everybody was somebody, everybody worth an hello.

Bob Blair's arrival rescued me from this interrogation. The square-jawed six-footer, five years my junior, was wearing a navy blue suit and had a ROTC haircut. Beth's long, welcoming hug wiped the scowl off his face, especially when she rubbed her pert chest against his arm.

Scotty slipped on a camel's hair blazer, and the two men departed. Unfortunately, that left me alone with Beth. "Why did Scott say Bob was an FBI agent?" I asked her.

"Because he is. Last month Bobby nailed some schmuck at Wright-Paterson Air Force Base for selling the Soviets photocopied blueprints of a new airplane prototype. A co-worker caught the guy sneaking them back to work and called the Bureau. For this, Robert's getting a promotion and a transfer to DC."

My first impulse was to sprint for the closet, snatch the backpack, and flee. But I controlled myself and despite throbbing temples politely sauntered after Beth into the living room, where we sat down together on the couch. For the next hour I endured the Dickinson photo albums, beginning with a page from Scotty's Army days, taken at Umlaut's ETS party. In one, young, robust, handsome Zielsdorf sat exactly how I remembered him. Another showed Peter in profile with Karl-Heinz, obviously speaking German, his jaw, lips and posture so altered he no longer looked like the same person. It tore me up inside to contemplate my best buddy's wretched demise.

The next page was worse. In one picture I was drunkenly hugging a column at Club 69. Another captured me dancing with Dagmar. I flipped ahead, but mischievous Beth turned right back to the shots of me. "This one of you dancing is my favorite," she said. "The others make you look like some sort of bewildered tourist."

I blushed, feeling stripped naked.

"Why are you guys so fond of Peter? He sounds selfish. Cute though."

"Too bad you never met him. He didn't—I mean, doesn't—come across as selfish. He likes most people, and they liked him."

Beth put a cassette in the tape deck and sat back down so close I retreated flush against the sofa arm. To Bob Dylan's adenoidal twang, we paged through her college-era photos of pickets and policemen blocking High Street and flower children hanging out on the Ohio State campus.

The next volume documented their son and daughter's growth from infancy a season at a time to their current ages of seven and thirteen. Both blond like Scott, Jason had his father's sky-blue eyes, while Jennifer's were chestnut like her mother's. Beth assured me she truly loved them both, even Jenny. What in the devil was holding Dickinson up, I wondered.

Next came pages of Beth and Scott in sportswear over the years. Dickinson had indeed regressed from the imposing mini-brute of Monterey to a well-biceped scarecrow. "This is Wolfgang," Beth said, fondly fingering the photo of a beefy, bronzed athlete in tennis whites, standing close behind her to guide her serve. "He's the secret to my ground strokes. And the best instructor in Columbus. Scott hates his guts. He's a teetotaler and a vegetarian. So what if he doesn't earn that much? Wolfie's a real man."

The next section consisted of a too trim Beth in various revealing swimsuits. She needed to gain at least twenty pounds. "It isn't hard for me to keep my weight down," she said, flipping forward to a buxom blonde in a low-cut knit top. "Take a gander at Linda. Would you leave me for a slut like her?"

I shrugged. Come on, Dickinson, hurry up.

"What does Scott see in such a whore? Sure, she's a looker if you're into sleaze, but dumb as tits. All that money of his and he's still got zero taste. The bastard truly disgusts me sometimes. And he's getting blitzed today again, but what else is new?"

"What about his kindness, charm, and good cheer?" I said, feeling obliged to defend a fellow Monk.

"Constant buzz you mean. Would you want to live with a drunken comedian? Sure, he's a terrific host and guest, but one shitty husband. If I had only a fraction of his dough, I would have moved out ages ago. But I can't live alone without money. Not with two kids. But I'm sick of talking about myself. How come you and Karen split?"

I sat there with my mouth agape. Discussing Karen threatened almost as much pain as would talking about Peter. I could have betrayed my ex by confessing that if she hadn't learned about sex from books and movies, it would never have occurred to her, since she had no instinct for it, her every desire actually a should. But we had not parted bitterly and were still friends, even if we had lost contact, and so I kept her secrets. Just as I always had Peter's.

"You're lucky you don't have kids," Beth told me. "My Jenny's a budding fascist. Openly racist and elitist and doesn't feel there's anything wrong with it. She knows product labels better than a retailer. UK to the core."

A car door slammed outside, and two slim, blond youngsters scampered into the house and gave their mother a perfunctory embrace. Scotty soon followed, looking upset.

Jason lugged a colorful book over from an end table and asked in a high-pitched, angelic voice, "Will you please read to me, Uncle Tommy?"

"The babysitter will read to you tonight," Scotty told him an octave lower.

Jason stood at our knees, examining us each in turn. His flawless skin and perfect hair made our adulthood look like physical corruption.

"I'd be happy to read to him," I muttered.

"We wouldn't hear of it!" Scotty snapped.

"Calm down, asshole," Beth said.

"I'd enjoy doing it," I insisted. "Really."

"Read me 'Rumpelstilzchen,' Uncle Tommy. Please, please."

"Stop pestering company, Jason. And go to your room," Scott said.

Jennifer grabbed her brother's wrist and told him, "You should be able to read fairy tales yourself at your age, Dummy." Chuckling triumphantly, she tugged the boy toward the stairwell.

"Leave me alone," he cried, struggling to twist free.

"Sit on it," she jeered, tugging him along.

"Stop it, you two!" Scotty yelled. "Don't go anywhere, son. You can't run away from your problems."

"But you told him to go his room!" Beth shouted.

"Shut up, Liz. Jennifer, why can't you two behave in front of company? You guys could have done a lot worse job of choosing your parents, so show some appreciation."

"Give me a break, Dad," Jennifer whined.

"Let the boy go to his room!" Beth screamed.

"Daddy," Jason pleaded, wiping his eyes.

"Jenny, what's the matter with you two?" Beth snapped.

"I've got a nerd for a brother. You can't expect me to get along with *him*."

"My God, Jenny," Beth said, "he's only seven years old! We're taking you kids to Dorothy's right now—for the night. We don't want to carry you both home asleep again."

"Good excuse," Jennifer said, setting her jaw. "Maybe I should carry you to bed, Mom. I weigh more. And I won't be drunk."

"Jennifer Dickinson!" Beth shouted. "Go to your room! Both of you. Go on, Jason. Change clothes this instant."

Smirking Jennifer stalked off, her head held proudly erect, while hangdog Jason whimpered after her. Minutes later, they returned in new outfits, carrying little overnight bags, and tolerated a hug from each parent. "Can we stay there overnight tomorrow, too, Mom?" Jennifer asked. "I can't stand the stink of our house the day after your parties. You'd ground me for a month if my room looked as filthy as our living room will."

"I'll ground you for the rest of your life if you don't watch your tongue."

"Come on, Mom, you're not that out of it. My room is perfect, while yours is a pigsty, and I still get all the criticism around here."

"That's because," Scotty said, butting in, "you're the kids and we're the parents. Guess who makes the rules?"

"It's not fair," Jennifer said.

"Whoever said life is fair?" Scotty snapped.

Letting her father have the last word, she led her brother out the door. Such a hellish exchange left my body shaking.

"How about we all take a nap before the party?" Beth asked.

"Excellent idea," I agreed, figuring the Dickinsons couldn't drink while they slept.

"I hope you brought a tie and jacket," Scotty said.

"Sure. For attending church with my mother in Madison."

"I thought you said you quit going?"

"I did. I only go when I'm home to make her happy. Otherwise she worries about my immortal soul. As do I."

"Whatever gets you off. Anyway, people dress up for parties here in UK."

While they napped, I lay in my canopy bed and struggled further with the Constance Garnett translation of *The Possessed*. Tolstoy's clear, Frenchified prose I always read in the original, but not Dostoevsky's more genuine, idiomatic Russian. Twenty pages later I dozed off with my glasses on. Before long a dreamy voice gently commanded in my slumber, "Rise and shine, Tommy." It was Peter, somehow still alive and well. I opened my eyes, and there he stood in our DLI barracks room, dressed in a preppy pink shirt, navy blue blazer, and red tie with little indigo polka dots, and grinning just like Scott Dickinson. No, wait, it really was Scotty, and I was in Upper Kensington—and Peter had been dead fifteen years.

"Thirty minutes till blast off," Scotty announced. "All systems go. Name your poison, and I'll fix it for you, buddy. To help you get totally geared to party hearty by the time the door bell rings." He was slurring his words worse than ever, and his flushed skin nearly matched the pink of his shirt.

"A gin and tonic," I said. How I was ever going to endure this soirée?

"Excellent summer choice, Specialist Bakken. Get dressed ASAP and I'll bring you the cocktail. How about a cup of coffee, too, for an extra boost? Tonight I'll be sure to introduce you to some foxy chicks."

I cringed.

"Now to hustle, Bakken, you have to be totally on. Like a standup comedian finally getting his big chance on the Johnny Carson show. I've discovered the surefire way to impress. In the Sixties, people called it good vibes, but it's really pheromones, which people smell subconsciously. So flood yourself with these miraculous biochemicals by lusting. That'll be easy with tonight's crowd. Thomas, if I may be so bold, you did well to divorce Karen, because you need an earthier woman. Some gal like Linda Atkins."

Somehow I didn't groan.

"Hey, get fired up, troop. Parties make the world go around. If I see an attractive woman, I'm always attracted to her. And I never apologize for it. Often as not they enjoy my attention, even if we're only friends. And we are only friends—mostly." He chortled. "If anyone disapproves of my flirting, I tell them my parents blew it, when bringing me up, and I ended up heterosexual."

"But aren't you married? Is this why Beth hit you?"

Bitter anger I never saw in the Army flashed across his eyes. "Yeah, I'm married, but so what? I wear this gold band around my finger, not my penis. There's nothing wrong with flirting. Beth flirts, too, as I think you've noticed. It's just a way of saying I think you're attractive, and I hope you think I am, too."

Was I ever regretting this stop in Upper Kensington.

Scotty took a deep drink from his opaque glass and pranced out of the room like an adolescent following his very first kiss.

I got dressed and moped my way downstairs. Beth, stunning in thick makeup and a short, diaphanous aquamarine dress, her waist-length hair now pinned atop her head, was anxiously rearranging objets d'art.

"Liz," Scott said, "give Wolfgang a call. It'd be a shame to let the jerk pass up a chance at mooching. Maybe he can take you upstairs and show you a few new strokes."

"Sure, darling. We'll try not to walk in on you and Linda."

"Bob Blair's coming, too," Scott told me. "You'll enjoy meeting him. His work reminds me of our old days at Det Q."

"Great," I said, suppressing panic.

The telephone's abrupt jangle startled me. Scotty picked it up, listened a moment, mumbled something, laughed, and murmured some more before motioning me over. My mother no doubt, since nobody else knew I was here.

"Hello, Mom," I said into the receiver. The response was a sharp click. "They hung up," I added.

"You'll never guess who it was," Dickinson said, his grin closer to a grimace. "It was Peter, Tommy! Peter Zielsdorf! I swear it! He was affecting an odd drawl, but I'm positive it was him. I don't forget voices."

Suddenly I felt so unsteady on my feet I plopped down on the nearest chair.

"The guy claimed to be an old Army buddy of Thomas Bakken's," Scott went on, "eager to get back in touch. He said years ago he had given you a manuscript for safekeeping. Now he wanted it back and thought I could maybe help find you. I said, 'Is this Peter?' Instead of answering, the guy asked for your address, so I told him, 'Why don't you just talk to Tom right now?' And handed you the phone."

Why was Dickinson playing such a mean prank on me? My pulse thumped in my ears.

"I sure hope he calls back," Scotty slurred.

God help me if Scotty wasn't joking.

"Not used to the demon rum, huh, Bakken? Or were you always a short hitter? I forget."

Could it really have been Peter who called? Dickinson had no reason to deceive me. But if it truly had been Zielsdorf, then he had played me for a pathetic fool all these years. But why? If he hadn't drowned himself in the Baltic, like the diary claimed, it made me question how Katja and Breitenbach had really died? Could the lying bastard have killed them both himself and not the GRU? Might he have thrown in his lot with the Soviets after all? Which would make him not only a cold-blooded murderer, but also a traitor? And me guilty of aiding and abetting espionage.

"Man, I miss old Zielsdorf," Scott said. "We'll get that guy to the reunion yet, and it'll be the time of our lives. What else with every Monk present along with so many other guys? Peter must have gotten my phone number from a Det Q buddy, and that person knows where he's living. Probably Umlaut. Out-fucking-standing, Bakken!" Giggling with boozy effervescence he slapped me on the back and glugged more gin into his glass. "By the way, what's this manuscript Peter was asking about?"

"Some weird confession. It's hard to know what to make of it." Peter alive? If true, what in the world could I say when we met again? I felt like such an idiot that my body trembled. Zielsdorf couldn't have possibly deceived me worse than this.

"Elizabeth, you brought out the wrong dishes," Scotty said. "Fiestaware's too dorky for this crowd."

"What else? Your mother's fucking china?"

"Exactly."

The second G and T Scotty handed me reeked of juniper berries it contained so little tonic mix. I handed the drink back and muttered that no matter how much they might be offended I couldn't possibly stay. The divorce was getting to me, I said, lying, and so wasn't up to a party.

Scowling, he opened the cupboard and began reshelving Beth's cherished dinnerware. "Don't be silly, Thomas."

"Stop it, you asshole!" Beth screamed.

"You and your beloved Fiestaware. You practically have orgasms over the damned things."

"At least they stay hard."

At that, Scott stretched his arms high overhead, threatening to fling the ceramic collectibles onto the floor.

"I dare you," Beth taunted.

With a jump, Dickinson heaved his handful of dishes against the kitchen tiles, smashing them to bits.

She flailed her puny fists against his chest, and he didn't resist, while protecting his face with open hands. I squeezed my way between them, her weak punches hammering my shoulder and aching head, before she collapsed onto the broken pieces in a sobbing heap.

"Don't cut yourself," he snapped and added more softly, "I'm sorry, Elizabeth. I'll replace them all." Close to tears himself, he bent over to caress her neck, and she didn't object.

"I'm splitting," I announced.

Morose Scott didn't argue with me. He moped his way upstairs to fetch my suitcase, while I retrieved my backpack from the closet, its potent contents still intact. “See you at the reunion” were his parting words.

I headed west on I-70 toward Indiana in a daze, the sights and sounds of what had just transpired playing over and over in my mind. The farther I drove, the more I convinced myself that in his drunkenness Scotty had imagined the impossible about long dead Peter. That guy calling him had never claimed to be Zielsdorf and never in my experience had he affected a drawl. Instead it had to have been another Det Q buddy, playing a lame practical joke.

Chapter Eight

That night I only made it as far as Indianapolis and went to bed so upset I didn't doze off till dawn and then slept in till a surly motel maid roused me shortly before noon checkout. When my Toyota refused to start, it took me hours to find a repair shop willing to fix the balky beast immediately. Thus I pulled into Madison far later than promised. The clicking of the front door latch woke up my mother, dozing on the living room couch. Mom greeted me with an awkward hug and a kiss on the cheek. Delicately cradling her slender, brittle frame, I told her not to bother rousing Dad, and we also postponed our own conversation till the morning.

Stretched out in the single bed of my sheltered youth, a thin wall away from my well-meaning parents, I slept soundly till a nightmare interrupted. I dreamt I was playing Euchre with a trio of middle-aged strangers, when the door flew open and in stomped a lanky soldier wearing dripping fatigues, combat boots, and a steel helmet. Zielsdorf I recognized to my horror, looking not a day older than when we parted ways at Det Q. I bolted upright, choking on a stifled scream. Afterwards, I lay there fully alert, worrying that drunken Dickinson had not been wrong after all when he claimed Peter had called him.

When I moped my way downstairs mid-morning, Mom was frying bacon and French toast, just as she had every school day till I left home for college. I had never felt less deserving of her devotion. We chatted about aunts, uncles, and cousins, while she cooked, her Wisconsin accent striking me as even broader than Zielsdorf's at his most drunken.

She coaxed me into the front room to greet my plump, bald father, buried in *The Wisconsin State Journal,* Madison's early newspaper, just as later that day he would await supper by reading virtually the same news in *The Capital Times*. I cleared my throat. Dad read onward. I coughed.

"Congratulations on getting tenure," he at last muttered, rustling the paper down into his lap.

But the promotion had occurred ages ago. I excused myself to help Mom in the kitchen.

"Your father despises retirement," she whispered. Dad didn't want to hunt or fish any more now than ever and loathed the very idea of recreation. All he had ever wanted was to keep on teaching and leave reading for his spare time, not build the whole rest of his life upon what, after all, was at best a pastime.

After breakfast, I gave *The Possessed* another go in my old room, but I couldn't cease obsessing about that phone call at Dickinson's enough to concentrate. No way could it have really been Zielsdorf, right? But if not, why did the caller ask about a manuscript he had given me for safekeeping? Since only Peter and I knew of the diary's existence. Memorized passages of Peter's diary about Katja echoed in my mind.

"Dinner, Tommy!" Mom shouted from the landing, meaning lunch. In my honor, she had fixed lutefisk, a dubious Norwegian delicacy. As always, I ate her entire generous serving and requested seconds, even though I had to force down every bite of the slimy boiled cod. The lefse and fattigmann—unleavened potato bread and deep-fried, knot-shaped cookies—simple fare that Dickinson would have disdained, I found more of a treat. Zielsdorf would have relished the whole meal.

"So how are things down in Brownsville?" Dad asked.

"I teach, do research. That's about it."

Dad nodded, my terse reply sufficing.

Mom asked about Karen.

"About the same." She got the picture.

That afternoon I spent meandering around the University of Wisconsin campus and then up State Street to the Square. I didn't like what I saw and sensed in Madison now, as fond as obviously I still was of the place. Oddly grim people everywhere as if in mourning. The town's spirit was no longer thriving, not like it once had. It might still think of itself as a last bastion of the Sixties, but in reality it had become a Nordic Yuppie Heaven, a mini-Minneapolis, dominated by a megaversity, state government, and large insurance companies. Up close, Wisconsin's paradise on paper was too cold for comfort. The city that once had demanded from every enterprise a pledge to public service and questioned the very profit motive had abandoned such idealism to join the Everybody-For-Himself-Get-Rich Eighties. And together with that surrender, the city seemed to have slipped into a collective identity crisis and depression.

My fourth afternoon in Madison, Will called from New York, saying he would be at the Badger Inn in West Allis the 7th through the 10th for the annual Wisconsin Chess Open. He suggested I drive over Thursday evening before the tournament began. His voice was the same tenor, though now oddly pinched, and I detected a wheezing. I hoped he was still in good health, since like me he was only forty, not exactly old.

I was more awkward on the phone with Will than I had been with Scotty, but so was he with me, so much so in fact that I sought an excuse not to go. But Mom insisted I visit my Army buddy, and as usual Dad didn't object—or offer an opinion.

On the drive over, I did my utmost to shove thoughts about the tragedy at Timmendorfer Strand out of mind, but the possibility that Peter might not have perished after all kept resurfacing. If he wasn't dead, everything had changed—and for the worse. My guts felt tied in knots. I zipped along I-90 past County Stadium, zoomed up a viaduct within sight of Lake Michigan, and looped south past Milwaukee's industrial basin before realizing I had made a wrong turn.

It took twenty minutes to backtrack to the Badger Inn. Clutching the diary photocopy I hadn't managed to give Dickinson, I pushed my way through a glass door, bar-handled like a drugstore entrance, into a lobby, where a fleshy desk clerk was studying a glossy gynecological magazine commonly sold at newsstands. "Sorry, all booked up," he said with a nasal whine. "Another convention."

"I'm looking for a guest named William Burke," I told him.

The guy's dull pig-eyes lingered on one particularly garish specimen before scanning the ledger. "Room three thirteen. The elevator's past the bubbler on the left." I took the stairs.

A good half dozen knocks later, an obese, middle-aged man answered the door. "Excuse me," I told him. "I'm looking for William Burke."

"You found him." Unfortunately, he was right. Now jowly and wrinkled, Will had lost all trace of his once boyish handsomeness. A faded paisley shirt, washed-out cords, droopy socks, and filthy sneakers gave Burke the air of an impoverished college student. Both haggard and fleshy, my Army buddy looked at least fifty. Whatever he was doing for a living, he was paying too steep a price.

A chess game was set up on the night table, and a magazine lay open on the unmade bed. *Sahovski informator* I correctly guessed, *the* chess journal, published in Yugoslavia. "I've nearly finished the last of two Karpov-Kasparov duels," he told me, plopping down hard into a chair. "No doubt you've heard about the ongoing fiasco in the Soviet Union, my good man."

"Which one?" I replied with a sinking sensation. I had heard more than enough lectures on the evils of Soviet communism from Burke as a GI. I untied my manila envelope and pulled out the copy of Peter's diary.

"Morally I'm offended, but esthetically I'm pleased that they continue to play. Now Garri Kasparov will have to beat Karpov three matches in a row before the Soviet chess establishment names him world champion. Five games out of twenty-four into the third match, they're dead even and still feeling each other out, but it's clear who will emerge triumphant. As Black, wily Garri keeps answering pawn to Queen Four with the Gruenfeld, a defense neither used once in their previous seventy-two games. Kasparov has some excellent new ideas."

Had Will always been this oblivious?

"Though Karpov's cautiousness is tedious," he droned on, "he plays a superb positional style, working for the slightest advantage, which he then methodically exploits and thus often as not wins. Kasparov is more like Bobby Fischer, both romantic and tactical, daring to make bold sacrifices to set up brilliant attacks that smash his opponents. The two are polar opposites in strategy. Anybody with any esthetic sense for the game has to prefer Kasparov, the commando versus the sniper."

Burke ridiculed Karpov for salvaging the first match by feigning ill health. The twerp even pretended to collapse at the playing board on the verge of losing a huge early lead. This, after Garri had brilliantly out-Karpoved him with deliberate draws. What a ham.

Will resumed the match my arrival had interrupted, snapping pawns and pieces around the magnetic board. "So do you play chess, my good man?" he asked. "I don't recall."

In junior high, my father had indeed taught me the rules, but I could never learn to enjoy a game so similar to taking yet another exam. Where was the fun in struggling to prove one more time that I had as much intelligence as my opponent, especially when often as not I failed? "Euchre's more my speed," I muttered.

Waving off that ridiculous response, Will predicted this Milwaukee tournament was finally the one that he would win. Since he'd really been cramming openings as Black, his opponents wouldn't dare begin with pawn to King Four more than once after they saw his new line of the Sicilian. Pawn to Queen Four he planned to defend by fianchettoing king's side. As White himself, he would play the Queen's Gambit until someone refuted his new idea and then switch to the perennially acute Ruy Lopez, Fischer's old standby.

I glanced down at Peter's antsy scrawl, resting on my lap.

After finishing the game, Will restored the pawns and pieces to their opening positions and launched into a diatribe against the new Soviet leader, Mikhail Gorbachev. The only aim of this so-called reformer's phony hostility to Star Wars was to retard our research long enough for the Russians to catch up.

"President Reagan says SDI is a purely defensive weapon," I said, meaning of course the Strategic Defense Initiative.

"Honestly, Bakken. So what have you been doing, my good man? I presume you went to graduate school."

Again, I summed up my past fifteen years, repeating almost verbatim the potted reply I had given Scotty the weekend before, the copy of Peter's diary wrinkling in my sweaty grip.

"Northern Appalachian State? It sounds dreadful."

"Actually, it's an oasis of 1960s idealism in the middle of this 1980s spiritual desert." My pulse was pounding over his gratuitous insult.

Will took a pawn en passant. "Sixties idealism indeed. You surely don't mean all that self-righteous indignation and woolly-minded protesting. That decade's only lasting legacy has been a general loss of moral fiber. Now too many people think that if something feels good, then do it."

"Right on," I said sarcastically.

"Remember the movie *Who's Afraid of Virginia Woolf*? In 1965 its vulgarity burst the limits of what could be shown and said in commercial American cinema, but it's tame compared to today's flicks. Is that progress? Or did America split at the seams after President Kennedy was killed, and all the crazies and freaks oozed out from between the cracks?"

"The freaks freed the human spirit!" I said, infuriated by Burke's condescension.

"Free to do what?" He flashed his best screw-you grin, satisfied I had been refuted, especially since in his view losing my cool by itself had lost me enough debater's points to forfeit the contest. "Then Nixon came along," he continued, lowering his tenor voice. "Now I voted for Tricky Dick the second time, but—"

"—Nixon excelled at foreign policy."

"No, that was his major failing, my good man. He made overtures to China and sought detente with the USSR."

"Exactly." My entire head was burning with indignation. "Those were his greatest triumphs. He was a good man that an impoverished childhood left scarred. Wouldn't you rather have him as President now instead of this dumbbell actor?"

Will rolled his eyes and chuckled at his forensics victory, even if it had come too easily. So Burke had indeed improved over the years, upgrading himself from a fourteen-carat asshole to eighteen. But I had never let his assholedom interfere with our friendship before, so why start now? Besides, I sorely needed his help. I was itching to toss the diary into his lap, but refrained. His sense of sympathy seemed so underdeveloped. Yet, Burke was still a Monk and a buddy, and I felt closer to him than to anyone I had met in Ohio.

I brought up Umlaut's planned Det Q reunion over Labor Day weekend in Chicago. To further rapping of pieces and pawns against the chess board, Will switched the subject to graduate school. He had never completed his doctorate in Soviet history, despite being only a thesis shy. He had begun a dissertation on Soviet espionage within the United States, but there was so much material he never finished taking notes.

Okay, so Peter wasn't really alive. Okay, Scott had made an honest mistake. That changed nothing about the unsolved murders of Timmendorfer Strand. Or Soviet efforts to penetrate our top-secret missions then as now. No matter how much revealing what I knew might hurt my deceased friend's reputation—or, for that matter, me. Above all, it changed nothing about my burning desire to share the diary with a trusted friend and the two of us deciding how to proceed.

Then I finally did it. "By the way," I said, my voice quavering, "would you please read this?" I thrust the photocopy between Burke and his chessboard.

"Read what?" he said, shoving the pages aside.

"A diary that Peter Zielsdorf kept at Det Q."

"For Christ's sake, do you honestly think I would read *anybody*'s diary?"

"You must. I desperately need your help."

"It'd be worse than sniffing the bloke's underwear. Would you want someone to read your diary?"

I clasped the incendiary document against my chest.

Peter's Russian is wonderfully fluent," Will commented matter-of-factly.

Debating what tack to attempt next, I slipped the pages back into the envelope. "He was certainly a great linguist," I muttered.

"Not 'was,' my good man. 'Is.' When he and I played each other in New York last month—"

"—Who in the hell did you play?"

"When Peter and I played against each other at a New York tournament last month, I asked him something in Russian, and his reply sounded native. Let's face it—Zielsdorf's an ace at foreign languages. Have you seen him lately?"

"Not in fifteen years," I rasped. My heart was thumping in my chest like it wanted to escape. Perspiration trickled down my ribs.

"He didn't look you up either?" Will said with a smirk. "I guess the good man has been too busy with his superb career in Cambridge. Married now with a child. My, I am surprised you haven't seen him, Bakken. You two always seemed so close. Didn't you share a barracks room with him in Monterey?"

I nodded in total bewilderment.

"I must say it was truly a pleasure running into Peter again," Burke continued. "His profile caught my eye instantly in the hotel lobby, but at first I couldn't place the face. Later I skimmed the registration list and was delighted to spot his familiar name. I accosted him, and he was pleased to see me, too. He hasn't changed that much, less than I have, I'm afraid. Tommy, I'm honestly shocked you two haven't keep in touch."

"Me, too. What's he doing in England?" My mouth felt so parched I grabbed Will's glass of water and chugged it.

"No, Cambridge, Massachusetts. Zielsdorf teaches computer science at MIT. I learned he was working out East somewhere years ago, when FBI agents looked me up in a background check for a Defense Department contract. Of course I was careful not to reveal anything that might jeopardize his prospects, but then his German girlfriend at Det Q was too trivial to mention. Who didn't have a Fräulein or two over there?" Will giggled. "Peter and his wife own a condo in Boston, and he travels a lot. In fact, he's registered for this Wisconsin Open. He's doing some consulting at the Army Math Research Center at UW-Madison and hopes to finish in time to drive over tonight. I told him you might stop by, too." Burke moved a knight. "Check. No, checkmate. Anyway, when I saw him, Peter refused to talk about Monterey or Knittelstedt and made some remark I didn't get about national security. Did something happen between you two?"

What could I say? That I hadn't seen Zielsdorf because I was convinced beyond any doubt that he was deceased?

"His German is fluent as ever. But then didn't he grow up speaking the language? Remember how his Russian blew us all out of the water in Monterey? Not you so much, Tom, but I sure got blasted ashore."

So Scotty had been right about that phone call? And Zielsdorf was coming to this very chess tournament? My limbs trembled. Did Peter honestly expect me to hand back the diary, say, "No hard feelings, pal," and simply forget about his deceit all these years?

Will announced that dinner would be at an adjacent German restaurant and that "Dawn and Andrew" would be joining us, whoever the hell they might be. I followed him in a walking stupor to an unpretentious family joint, reeking of beer and vinegar. Burke ordered a Wiener Schnitzel, French fries, and red cabbage. Too flustered to read the menu, I made mine the same.

While we waited, Will sipped a glass of mineral water and prattled on about his greatest chess victories. I pretended to listen, but my mind was everywhere but in this eatery. What would Peter look like after fifteen years? Wrinkled and jowly like Burke? Scrawny, yet paunchy, like Dickinson? Or about the same like me? How in the devil could the guy still be alive?

“Don’t laugh,” Will said, “but after my discharge I considered working for the CIA. Knowing Russian, more or less”—he waggled his hand— “and having studied KGB and GRU history was an ideal background. But I just couldn’t see myself as a professional spook. Then my father died, I received my inheritance, and I decided to devote my life to art.”

“Art? What kind of art?”

“The art of chess, my good man.”

With a deep sigh, apparently having attained the limit of his self-restraint, Will hauled out his pocket chess set and resumed clicking iron pawns and pieces on the magnetic board. Food was served. I ate mine in silence while stewing over Zielsdorf’s appalling betrayal of me. If Peter was going to show up here any moment, hadn’t I better skedaddle immediately? Or was it better to wait and confront the bastard? Will ordered another Perrier and leaned close. “Do you promise never to tell another soul what I am about to reveal, so help you God?”

That I swore, bracing myself for even worse news about Zielsdorf. But this time I caught a break. In a low, controlled voice, Burke delineated his weaknesses at chess, as if confessing grave sins. I supposed there was nothing more vulnerable about himself he could have revealed, but next to what I ached to hear it was drivel. So what if he couldn’t really play numerous lines of the Sicilian?

I was about to bolt for my car, when to my amazement a young Asian girl no taller than five feet slid into the empty chair beside Will, nestled close, and stared at the board. Of Chinese or Japanese ethnicity, I guessed. Not Vietnamese or Thai anyway. Straight, black hair down to her shoulders. In a glossy, scarlet jump suit. She hardly looked nineteen or twenty. More like an adolescent disguised as an adult.

Who is this person, I wanted to shriek. Far better question, how in holy hell could Peter still be alive? Sitting here like this, waiting for him, after what I had just learned was insane. Without a word of explanation, she reached across the portable chess board and moved the Black King's Knight into danger.

"Black goes down two pawns in the exchange!" Will snapped, moving the piece back.

"It's a sacrifice, William," she softly rebutted.

"Two pawns?"

"In five moves Black gets a passed pawn, controlled by his free bishop," she calmly explained in an unfamiliar English accent, "so it's worth the loss. White will be bottled up the rest of the game, blocking its advance."

"The move isn't sound."

"Play it out, William."

Will snapped the pieces against the board in testing the variation. Five minutes later, he was mumbling to himself, shaking his head, and copying her suggestion down.

She stretched her hand across the table. "I'm Dawn," she said, as if that explained everything. It was a small, feminine hand, and her smile was as open and broad as any American's. How could Peter dare to face me after lying so outrageously?

"Dawn is my wife," Will told me.

His wife? I would have sooner believed foster child.

"We married a year ago-la," she said with a toothy grin. The peculiar "la" she tacked on sounded like a Southern German diminutive, but she was speaking English. When she peered downward, her face acquired a foreign, Asian cast, but when she gazed straight ahead, she looked native American. Visions of Peter, seated on the floor outside the orderly room in Monterey, reading Hesse's *Der Steppenwolf novel* the day I met him, danced before my eyes.

"She's my unofficial second," Will said.

"Your English is impeccable, Dawn," I blurted, meaning her diction more than her pronunciation. "Where are you from?"

"Guess."

"Hong Kong?"

"Not bad." In fact, she was from Jakarta, Indonesia, and of Chinese ancestry, but now of course as American as any of us. She wolfed down most of Will's heaping plate of knackwurst, French fries and red cabbage, while he kept clicking away.

Burke had literally sat across a chessboard from Peter just last month? As if everything in his diary were a wild fabrication. If Zielsdorf was alive, then I had been the dumbest of dupes. I braced myself for Peter's appearance, like a condemned man awaiting a firing squad's fusillade. Or was Will putting me on? But that had never been his shtick. Or could another Det Q buddy be playing an elaborate hoax? Two things for sure, Will was positive the man he had played chess against was Peter Zielsdorf, just like Scotty was about his caller's identity, even if the person spoke with a drawl. My legs trembled beneath the table.

A bald, swarthy, sixtyish man joined us without a word or glance in my direction. He couldn't be Dawn's father, because he was Caucasian, and Will's I knew was deceased. Dawn introduced me to "Andrew," again twice throwing in meaningless "la's." His fractured English had a heavy Slavic flavor. The geezer whispered something into Will's ear that brought a gray-toothed grin to Burke's face and left.

Will bickered with Dawn over whether to play a variant of the King's Indian his first chance as Black.

"The idea is not that profound," she insisted. "Peter was lucky it worked against you. You overlooked the proper countermove." So Will wanted to borrow Zielsdorf's strategy? My stomach kept turning ever more queasy.

"Wrong," Will insisted.

Dawn laid a tiny hand in his. "William, why don't you think about something else for a while. You've prepared enough." She gave me a beatific smile. "Perhaps you might be up for a friendly game, Thomas?"

"No, thanks. I don't find chess relaxing."

"Whoever said it was relaxing?" Will snapped. "That's the most ignorant remark I've heard in a month. No game is more demanding. Intellectually, emotionally, and physically."

"Why?" I was so anxious I couldn't stop fidgeting.

"To win, idiot."

"Why do you have to win?"

"Why do we have to breathe? We don't *have* to."

"Arguing by analogy begs the question, Will. I don't accept your comparison. Who's this Andrew anyway?"

"Andrew is Andrew."

"His name is Anton, actually," Dawn explained. "Anton Pavlovich Shirokin."

"Shut up, my dear," Will told her, flashing a German-shepherd grin.

None us said anything as Will explored another opening. I was poorly controlling my panic at the prospect of Zielsdorf showing up any minute. Why stay if Burke refused to read the diary? Or didn't that matter anymore if Zielsdorf was actually alive? "So you know Peter, too?" I asked Dawn breathlessly.

"Of course," she replied.

"What was your impression?" My shirt was soaked in sweat despite the restaurant's strong air-conditioning.

"To be honest, he is too distant to suit my tastes. And so cold-blooded it gives me the creeps."

"Dawn, don't exaggerate," Will said. "Peter was concentrating on chess. On test days in Monterey he acted the same."

I had seen Peter acting aloof, but never cold-blooded or creepy. Timmendorfer Strand must have really changed him. Or might those particular diary entries be a cruel hoax at my expense? But what about the Braunschweig newspaper clipping, reporting Katja's death? That much at least had truly occurred.

"At some point after his discharge he was in a serious car accident," Will went on. "He suffered a concussion that impaired his memory of younger days, though not otherwise, thank God. It also left him with a permanently wired jaw and conspicuous dental implants. Surgery managed to fuse the broken bones and erase the scars, but left his face with little play in it. And he walks with a pronounced limp."

"He always has a frog in his throat, too," Dawn added with a laugh, taking a foreigner's delight in the odd English idiom. Chills ran up and down my spine.

"You'd recognize him at a glance, Thomas," Will said. "He's not that different. Just older and more mature and responsible. All in all, the crash could have been much worse. It didn't so much as scratch his brilliant intellect."

I was speechless.

"He's calmer now, too," Will continued. "Remember how high-strung he was in Monterey? And even worse at Det Q."

What could I say? All along I had thought Peter had only confided in me, but here Burke knew far more about him than I did. It felt asinine even to consider showing Will the diary. In my state of paranoid confusion, I couldn't help but wonder whether Peter might have gotten hurt beating Breitenbach to death?

"Peter is a genuine American success story," Will told me. "Hats off to our old buddy, I say. I used to think he was a great linguist and a dilettante at everything else, but, boy, I was wrong. Why should anyone be surprised that he's excelling at computer science? At what couldn't he excel? One odd quirk, he still wears that chintzy watch he won in Monterey like a badge of honor."

Try as I might I couldn't envision Peter without a military haircut or out of Army uniform.

"The most uncanny difference is the improvement in his chess," Will said.

"In New York he whipped Williams's posterior," Dawn commented blithely.

Burke scowled, but didn't disagree. "Somehow I don't feel embarrassed losing to him. He's gotten that good. It's amazing what a new sense of direction has done for the bloke."

This barrage of shocking news made my head spin. I wanted Peter dead again, how he used to be, as awful as that had always been. I was all poised to split, when I remembered my promise to Umlaut. "Will, do you think you could help with organizing the reunion?" I asked, hardly knowing what I was saying.

The request took Burke aback. "Frankly, Bakken, it all sounds like a splendid idea, but I'm seeing you now and I've seen Zielsdorf recently and will see him again tonight. Dickinson and Hoffman I can look up when I play chess near where they live. Besides, Labor Day weekend I already have plans for a chess tournament in Dallas. So why should I bother with a reunion?"

So we can crucify Peter together, I wanted to scream. "So you still don't give a crap about anybody but yourself, eh, Burke? Too bad your buddies aren't pawns and rooks, because then maybe you'd pay them more attention."

That insult really struck home. "My goodness, Thomas," he muttered, meeting my glare and lowering his gaze. "All right, if you and Umlaut insist, I'll come. Just tell me who I should call."

"Hey, guys!" Dawn squealed. "Peter Zielsdorf just stuck his head in the doorway. I'll go fetch him."

"Splendid!" Will said. "Andrew whispered a bit ago that he had arrived. Here's your chance to renew an old friendship, Bakken."

Dawn tried to rise, but I clutched her forearm and held her down. "Wait!" I pleaded, my pulse pounding in my ears.

"What's wrong, Thomas?" she said. "You look ill."

"Excuse me a moment," I said, stumbling to my feet. I dropped a twenty on the table, staggered to the men's room, and moments later sneaked past the dining room and out the front door. I'd write Will later, apologize for my rude departure, and send him Umlaut's list of contacts.

During the drive back to Madison, I feverishly imagined what really happened at Timmendorfer Strand, if the diary account was so inaccurate. If Peter's suicide was a big fat lie, how much else in it was false?

Instead of pulling into my parents' 1940s Cape Cod, I sped right past and instead paid a visit to a neighborhood bar. A double brandy on the rocks delivered the expected punch and gave me at least a semblance of a good night's rest.

I reluctantly stayed the three further days I had promised my parents, the whole while dreading a call from Peter, which never came, thank God. I managed to get off a special delivery letter to Will, apologizing for my rude departure. And visited the Vilas Zoo and the Olbrich Botanical Gardens, their many attractions passing in a distracted haze.

Sunday as promised, I donned suit jacket and tie and attended church with my mother, Dad staying home to finish the thick weekend newspaper edition before the Brewers' game came on. Reverend Berg's sermon topic, "Blessed are they that have not seen and yet have believed," consoled my mother, but it devastated me. Hadn't believing without seeing been precisely my blunder with Peter?

After fifteen years at the bottom of the Baltic Sea, Peter was again walking the earth? But how, since no man, but perhaps one has ever come back from the dead. But what evidence did I have of Zielsdorf's actual suicide? Just the intentions expressed in the diary. It was strange how miserable I felt knowing my best friend was alive after all. Because if he had betrayed me this badly, how could we have ever been close?

The entire six hundred miles to Brownsville, Ohio, I drove in a daze, struggling to fathom Peter's duplicity. I knew I should have stayed and confronted him in Milwaukee, but I simply wasn't up to it.

What did I know for certain at this point? That Peter had at least pretended to drown, abandoning his clothes and shoes on the Timmendorfer beach. If he hadn't in fact killed himself, that could still have been his intent up until the very last moment when, staring imminent death in the face, he had changed his mind. Then once he suffered that head injury, he might very well have forgotten about this passing desire to perish, his torrid affair with Katja, the diary, and even his close friendship with me. What else but amnesia could explain the audacity of his very public career at MIT under his real name? Though how badly could the brain damage have been if he still became an accomplished academic? I was dying to discuss all of this with a sympathetic ear, but who might that be?

I pulled into my gravel driveway in southern Ohio and lugged my suitcase and backpack onto the front porch. Among the junk in my mailbox was a personal letter, postmarked Charlotte, North Carolina, addressed in penciled capitals to "T. Bakken." But I didn't know a soul in that state. I was still puzzling over the childish scrawl when I noticed the front door was unlocked. But hadn't I checked it twice before departing? Maybe not. My spaciness of late was getting downright dangerous.

Inside, nothing appeared disturbed. I dug into the stack of papers concealing the original copy of Peter's diary. Every page still where I had left them, hidden in plain sight. So I indeed must have forgotten to lock up. Or had Zielsdorf come hunting, broken in, and failed to find it?

I stopped by Mrs. Gardiner's to pick up Nebuchadnezzar, the adorable kitty purring at the sight of me. Once back home, I hid the three diary photocopies around the bungalow and for the time being slipped the manuscript itself inside my pillow, my head crinkling against the loose-leaf sheets off and on all night.

The next morning I secured one copy in my Brownsville safety deposit box, and circled around town till I convinced myself I wasn't being tailed before proceeding to Chillicothe, Ohio's original state capital. There I opened another bank account for safeguarding a second copy. The last one I hid under the front seat of my car, intending it for Rich, wherever the dude lived. I was counting on him being the Monk I could share everything I now knew with, if Scotty and Will hadn't been.

Once back home I tried to resume work on my article on the Soviet reception of Nietzsche, but the whole project had never seemed pointless. Who cared if the Russians had perfectly understood the German philosopher or totally misconstrued him—or even adapted his writings into a Bolshevik musical?

On a whim I telephoned information at MIT in Cambridge, Massachusetts, and a spacy employee gave me Peter Zielsdorf's number. I dialed it and got five rings before a recorded woman's voice said with a slight foreign accent, "Thank you for calling. Pete and I are unavailable, but if you leave your name and number, we will call you back." Followed by a hum, a pause, and a beep. I cleared my throat to speak, but instead hung up.

I was positive Mrs. Zielsdorf's alto voice couldn't possibly be Katja's, though her "r's" did sound German. I tried to envision Peter lecturing on programming and systems analysis in Cambridge, but couldn't imagine the Zielsdorf I knew teaching anything but literature and foreign languages. My God, my once dearest buddy was still alive!

Was he ever fortunate I had kept my trap shut all these years, after leaving it to my discretion whether to publish the diary and explain to people why he had taken his own life at Timmendorfer Strand. No, not lucky—he had tricked me into that silence. But if all along he wanted a very public academic career, why mail me the diary and pretend to drown? No matter how I pondered this question, no interpretation made sense. In my bewilderment I shuffled my Nietzsche note cards like a euchre deck, put those aside, and switched to browsing in the philosopher's masterpiece, *Beyond Good and Evil*, anything to postpone writing more of the detested article. Though to be sure eloquent, the philosopher's aphorisms too often struck me like random dots, few of which connected.

A wasted half hour of dillydallying later, I set the research materials aside and composed a letter in my best German to the Timmendorfer Strand *Kriminalpolizei*, but then couldn't bring myself to mail it. Not before I had spoken with Peter in person. Until I heard him fail to explain his baffling behavior to my face, I felt duty-bound to give him the benefit of the doubt.

The oddly addressed envelope in the mailbox upon my return popped back into my head. What had I done with the blasted thing? I combed my apartment high and low till I located the crumpled letter with the childish penciling in the clothes hamper. I tore it open and flipped to the closing, which read, "Hope to see you soon. Rich." Hoffman had written!

The manually typed note inside said Umlaut had informed him of the Det Q reunion, which he planned to attend unless "unpredictable commitments intervened." Meanwhile, I was welcome anytime at his place and could stay as long as I desired. He gave directions to a spot near the North Carolina-Tennessee border, a long day's drive from Brownsville. All terrific news.

Still, something about the letter bothered me. Its diction was too formal for Rich, and only the signature was handwritten. Its huge, looping "R" looked authentic, as best I could recall it from DLI homework and test papers. I feared getting lured into a trap. Still, I felt I had to incur the risk.

The next morning I packed for a short visit and left the original diary hidden where it had been, knowing two copies were secure in separate safety deposit boxes, and I was carrying a third. This time I made sure the front door was secured, though I wouldn't have minded if a burglar broke in and stole every last one of my Nietzsche notes or, even better, the draft scholarly article.

Chapter Nine

I set off toward the South for the first time in my life, my eyes wide open for whatever might arise after Will's shocking revelations. I swerved around squashed opossums and ground hogs and passed ramshackle houses and yards strewn with cars and pickups on blocks and rusting refrigerators and stoves. Boys still in grade school drove whining dirt bikes up and down hillsides, cutting paths into unsightly gashes. Yellow letters on black barn sides declared, "Chew Mail Pouch Tobacco," and the locals obeyed. Natural-gas pump jacks cranked in fallow fields like gigantic metal mosquitoes that never tired of sucking. Turkey vultures soared on upswept wings, patiently awaiting lonely deaths in the woods below. No taint of soulless affluence here. Would Beth like it any better than Upper Kensington? I sincerely doubted it.

I crossed the Ohio River at Gallipolis and steered toward West Virginia's state capital, Charleston. Before long I was traversing twisting lanes at the bottom of a ravine slashed through mountains, water oozing from exposed coal seams. Dark-green plumes of alien cedars sprouted among lighter, fuller native hardwoods and pines. Freshly fallen chunks of slate in the road twice made me slam on the brakes. Up the hollows, abandoned coal conveyors rusted in place. Again and again I passed a trio of bare crosses, a golden one always flanked by two silver companions, the sight never failing to bring a lump to my throat.

After the lengthy Big Walker Mountain Tunnel, I drove into rolling hills with pastures and dairy cows that reminded me of Wisconsin and made me choke up worse. All the hours on the road were taking their toll, but I was in no mood to pause for a rest. After Fancy Gap, Virginia, I encountered sand piles along the shoulders for stopping runaway trucks. I crossed the famous

Blue Ridge, an ancient offshoot of the Appalachians rounded over the passing millennia, and then finally took the welcome break. The diner waitress asked in a pure drawl instead of the more familiar West Virginia lilt if I wanted my coffee "regular." I told her yes, but she didn't bring it black. So I had entered the American South.

Around six that evening I turned onto an unpaved road as Hoffman's letter directed and drove for miles through a dense forest of gorgeous sycamores, sweetgums, locusts, hickories, and oaks till I came upon a fork that Rich hadn't mentioned. I parked the car under a huge sycamore shedding bark in curls colored camouflage tan, brown, and green and climbed out. It was so much hotter and sultrier here than it had been in Ohio that I quickly was drenched in sweat. High overhead, cicadas hidden in the foliage rasped their buzz-saw love songs.

A young chap with a scraggly beard and gnarled hair dangling to his shoulders came strolling down a lane overgrown with multiflora rosa. In a T-shirt tie-dyed red and blue, dirty jeans worn through at the knees, and toes sticking out of shabby sneakers, he acted as at home as a boy on a small-town Main Street. "Man, did you lose the Interstate," he said and let out a high-pitched giggle. He looked pale for late summer and had dark circles beneath sky-blue eyes.

"I'm looking for Rich Hoffman," I told him.

"Rich who?"

"Hoffman. H-o-f-f-m-a-n."

"There's a Rich Huff who lives in these parts," the guy drawled, breaking into a toothy grin. "That's Huff, H-o-u-g-h."

"Hoffman and I are old Army buddies," I said. This gentle, almost effeminate, man reminded me of the kitschy portrait of Christ my parents had hanging on their bedroom wall, though with a sparser beard and dirty hair. In the hot, humid air I could smell him from three feet away. Not the foul stench of white collar stress, but an honest, unwashed scent.

"The Rich I know never talked about no army."

But I was positive that I had followed the directions. "I'm Tom Bakken," I said, awkwardly offering him my hand. He took it straight on and rotated his wrist, but I fumbled the unfamiliar maneuver.

"Toboggan, huh? That's a weirder name than Hoffman. You part Indian? You don't look it." There was mockery in his grin as he eyed my red hair and ivory, freckled skin, but no ill intent. He had heard me right, but I spelled out my first and last names anyway, and asked him who he was.

"Dwayne Crabtree." It was no Wisconsin name.

He might have been thirty—or maybe just dissipated for his early twenties. I asked him to take me to this Rich Hough.

"Sure, man, why not? Though if Rich ain't the right dude, you can stay with us just the same." A flabbergasting invitation.

He climbed in beside me and guided me another two miles down the left fork over weeds taking back ruts that Dwayne called a road. He was amused by my brightly lit "instrument panel," as he called the Corolla's dashboard. I explained what each component indicated.

He had me pull up behind a rusty old Ford pickup and asked me to ride the rest of the way with him. I debated whether to take the diary photocopy along and decided to lock it in my trunk.

The truck's engine strained up a bumpy hollow road. Dwayne nonchalantly wound over a hilltop crest, scraping low branches, and bounced down into a valley, like we were traversing a deserted interstate. He braked hard, pulled up under another towering sycamore, and jumped out like we had arrived. Then I spotted it, half-hidden behind hemlocks growing flush with a clapboard exterior—an unpainted, two-story frame house.

He skipped down a dirt path past an overgrown vegetable garden, hopped onto the covered porch, and barged right in. Following close behind, I entered a simple but functional kitchen furnished with a pair of matching homemade butcher blocks hewn nearly level, a cast-iron wood stove, a bare wood floor, and throw rugs woven from random rags.

A tall, thin woman in a loose denim shift moseyed in from the next room and greeted Dwayne. Her voice was incongruously high-pitched for her age, which I estimated close to mine. She faced me expectantly. "Sarah, this is Tom," Dwayne said and winked knowingly. Long, wavy hair, jet-black except for a few white strands, dangled to her shoulder blades, setting off sharp cheekbones and glistening hazel eyes.

"I like your energy," she said with childlike openness. "But then I guess I always like Rich's friends."

"Do you know Rich well?" I asked.

"Pretty well. We've been together the past fourteen years. Married for seven."

Dwayne giggled. As out of it as I was in this setting, I still felt more at home than I had in Upper Kensington or West Allis. Still, I was at a loss for words.

"Cat got your tongue?" Dwayne teased. "No need to be guarded around here. Mellow out and stay with us as long as you like. When you think about it, there's nothing worth getting uptight about."

"Who's this 'us'?" I said.

"The family," Dwayne told me. A puzzling reply, since his features didn't remotely resemble Sarah's or Rich's.

A hunched-over, emaciated man with a short, gray beard and long, salt-and-pepper hair strolled in through the back door. At the sight of me the stranger bridled ironically and gave me a big, lingering hug. I felt protruding ribs.

"Professor Bakken," he greeted with Rich's voice. I stared hard, imagining the smooth, unbearded face of Monterey and Knittelstedt instead of these lines, pouches, and graying hair. It was Hoffman all right. But his smile was different, no longer so broad, his top lip now always concealing his upper teeth. Though the close-mouthed smirk was the same.

We embraced again, and Sarah guffawed, her laugh hearty for a woman. "Come here, Nathan!" Rich called out. I expected another aging hippie, but instead a gawky boy appeared. Sarah introduced their twelve-year-old son. Too shy to look me in the eye, Nathan fidgeted with his thick glasses and stared curiously at my watch. Was something about to happen?

Dwayne insisted I take a gander at their livestock, so he and Nathan led me to an outbuilding, reeking of rotting hay. There Rich's two daughters, aged thirteen and seven, were petting a goat.

I asked the kids their names, and the older girl said, "I'm Annie, she's Melanie, and he's Beeper."

"The goat has a name, too?"

"Of course," Melanie replied in a tiny voice like I was stupid.

"Look, he's wearing a watch." Annie said, pointing at my wrist, and the three children cackled. Melanie had me pet Beeper, till he kicked up his heels, and Annie gently slapped him. She was only thirteen months older than Nathan, but six inches taller.

"Why are you dressed so funny?" she asked. I blushed over my khaki slacks and pastel button-down shirt. These same clothes did indeed look ridiculously formal here, just as they had been too informal in Upper Kensington.

Nathan led me around the corner to a nanny goat lying on straw at the feet of an adolescing kid. Annie explained without embarrassment, in language as natural as the event, so that even Melanie understood, how the baby had been conceived, carried by its mother, and born. Nathan smirked while she spoke, but Melanie listened intently, staring wide-eyed at the miracle.

We returned to the house in single file past three beat-up, rusted-out cars stored in sod-roofed dugout garages that I hadn't noticed walking out. No doubt the vehicles all ran.

Once back inside, Nathan asked, "Dad, can we go visit Buddy's tree house?"

"I'm not sure he's there," Rich told him.

"Where else would he be, Dad?" Annie piped up.

"It'd be better if he came here," Sarah said. "Of course you'll be eating with us tonight, Tommy."

I thanked her kindly and asked where their restroom was. Sarah pointed out a dusty window at a small outbuilding fifty yards away. I trudged off through a swelter so close it almost seemed like wading in lukewarm water. By no means had I forgotten the reason why I had come to Rich's, but I felt so welcome and comfortable here I was in no hurry to bring up the painful topic of Zielsdorf. On my way back inside, I admired its homemade, unpainted wooden furnishings.

Rich suggested a tour of his property before dusk. Grabbing the chance to talk with him alone, I accepted. We headed up the shadier side of the hollow and crossed the ridge at its lowest point. I was curious to learn the source of Rich's apparent self-sufficiency, but wasn't about to pry. It certainly couldn't be their scruffy little vegetable garden. Soon vines dangling from hardwoods were clawing at my clothes, gnats whining in my ears, and hidden ovenbirds taunting, "Teacher-teacher-teacher."

Thick brambles forced us to backtrack and hunt for an easier course. "What happened to the path?" I rasped, panting from the exertion. This southern woods was like a jungle compared to the sparser forests of Wisconsin.

"There is none," Rich said. "We let the old one grow over. We don't want anybody coming in we haven't invited, so each time we take a different route. Otherwise we'll end up with a trail any pig can spot."

I wheezed to ascend yet another hill and was grateful when Rich stopped to point out a tiny clearing overgrown with long-stalked weeds, their heavy, dark-green buds towering over our heads. "Hill tobacco," he said with a wink. I pondered a moment what that might mean. Recalling the sweet, pungent smoke at a few Northfield college parties I had promptly abandoned, I understood with a gasp. So this explained the mystery of Rich's livelihood. The harvest of the lovingly nurtured plants didn't look all that far off, but what did I know about cultivating cannabis?

Once I had regained my wind, we trudged on. Suddenly Rich spread his arms and dropped into a crouch, so I hunkered down as well, feeling rather woozy from the heady reek all around. In a meadow twenty yards up ahead more pot plants grew half-hidden among tall weeds. Behind them towered a stand of hardwoods dominated by a gigantic red maple. Rich stuck two fingers into the corners of his mouth and shrieked three times. "It's the call of the rough-legged hawk," he whispered.

I picked off the burrs needling my shins and to my dismay discovered a sizable tear in my khakis. "What in the devil are we waiting for?" I snapped.

"We don't want to get shot," Rich whispered.

Shot? For doing what? Because this was a different "family's" patch? Flies sucked the backs of my hands, gnats buzzed my ears, and sweat glued my shirt to my ribs. Were we awaiting a countersign? "I thought this was all your property," I muttered.

"It is," he said softly. "But Buddy's vision is pisspoor, especially through the leaves in this light. He's only had to kill whistle pigs so far, but he'll plug any two-legged varmints he thinks are going after our crops."

"Whistle pigs?"

"Ground hogs. Woodchucks. You know, whistle pigs. The fat beasties whistle. And destroy our money-making plants."

Rich slowly rose to his feet, raised his hands high, and edged out into the clearing. "We'll catch you later, Buddy!" he shouted. "An old Army friend, Tom Bakken, is visiting, and I thought you might like to meet him. If you want, I'll send relief so you can join us for dinner." I stared hard into the thick foliage but couldn't make out anything other than branches and twigs. "I guess Buddy's not feeling sociable today," Rich told me.

A quarter mile along the walk back, Rich once again allowed himself to speak at normal volume. "I can't even remember how many summers Buddy's been perched in that tower. To pass the time he reads used paperbacks Sarah buys him, while keeping his ears alert like browsing deer." One peculiar dude, but then who was I to talk? I was in no hurry to meet the guy whoever he might be.

It was high time I brought up the real purpose of my visit, especially since Hoffman was my last hope. Yet no matter how much I ached to share my burden, I hesitated. We crossed two ruts I recognized as the road Dwayne had driven us in on. I asked about my car.

"It's perfectly safe," Hoffman told me. "There'll be a few more miles on the odometer when you get it back, but no sweat. The little extra wear and tear will do us more good than you can imagine. Consider it a deposit in your karma bank."

"Happy to oblige," I replied, half-lying. And then I simply said it, "Rich, have you heard anything from Zielsdorf?"

"Daddy!" Nathan squealed, running to meet us, Melanie and Annie close upon his heels. Rich hoisted his cherished son off the ground and spun him around. Okay, I'd try again later.

In the meantime, I mellowed out on the front porch with Sarah and Dwayne, while Rich hiked the hollow and invited neighbors over. Lounging between these totally accepting virtual strangers, I managed to relax for the first time in years. Before that evening I had truly never watched nighttime fall, but now I joyfully studied the leaves' lime-green slowly fade to chartreuse and then brown in patches that widened and darkened until the woods had turned pitch black. At last, at long, long last—after fifteen years—all felt well. No matter how everything worked out in the end. Whether I confessed or not. Whether justice was served. There was no need to worry. About anything. No matter what. If everything still up in the air came down wrong, so what? Who cares what we are, or where, or why? Isn't just having been alive for a little while glorious enough? Over this simple, profound truth I belly-laughed till my stomach hurt, my diaphragm clapping applause. Yes, I partook so much of the Hoffmans' hospitality that my frenetic thoughts came to a serene halt. For once—for once!—I couldn't care less what Peter had or hadn't done and how much I had abetted his wrongdoing. I took a dip in ignorant bliss and what a blessed swim it was.

My memory of what happened next is spotty. I do know we enjoyed a tasty banquet of cold rice, green onions, raw carrots, and another root sharper than radish, washed down by hard spring water served in fruit jars. I stuffed myself.

Eventually, I wound up on a ratty couch alongside Dwayne, watching the other guests like television. In the smoky haze, thickening around their shaggy heads, they made for a motley, mesmerizing bunch. Sarah chatted with a pleasant-faced, fair-skinned woman about "puttin' up" and "barn raisin'" and "goats" and "co-ops" and "French intensive gardening." Belinda openly nursed a beautiful infant, whose fiddlehead ears and goofy expressions made Dwayne and me roar. She handed the boy to a gangly man in a straw hat, who fixed his piercing brown eyes on me and waved exactly like Dave MacIntosh had before vanishing for good down that DLI stairwell. I waved back, and the dude snapped to attention and saluted. Belinda plopped down between us, soft thigh brushing mine and remaining flush. "Have you found your clothes yet, Dwayne?" she asked.

"Nah, but no sweat. I guess whoever's got 'em needs them more than I do. It all evens out in the end."

"Do you have any left?"

"Sure, what I got on. No problem."

Dwayne suggested we mellow out further, and I didn't resist. More flooding sensations and impressions slaked my parched soul, and sounds resonated until they buzzed, and outlines of dark forms undulated in the night. I feasted my eyes on the gorgeousness of the humanity I was immersed in, their gauntness luxuriating in its own wan palette. All was well—with me, with them, and with the entire world. Tomorrow would be plenty soon enough to haul the diary out. And if tomorrow never came, who honestly cared?

Nature's call finally forced me to rise, and I had trouble negotiating the floor heaving beneath my feet. I stumbled off the porch and landed on all fours upon soft, friendly dirt. I inhaled the sweetly rotten night air more aromatic than fresh baked bread. A swooping bat made me duck, and I laughed at myself for bothering. Why doubt that the fellow creature's sonar would safely guide it? The next time it dive-bombed I stood my ground without flinching and waved at my agile little friend flitting by.

When I returned from the outhouse, I found my place on the couch occupied by a bald, silver-bearded geezer. The guy tilted his head in checking me over, the thick wire-rims he had on reflecting the lanterns' flicker. Thin, sunken lips, partly hidden in facial hair, made him seem a mite old to be Rich's friend.

Hoffman asked him how it was going, and the dude just blinked. "You don't have to stay up in the tower so much, man," Rich said. "Dwayne can relieve you."

Crabtree grimaced ironically before agreeing with a giggle. Facing me with an oddly tight grin, Rich introduced his right-hand man, Buddy McCracken, who gave me a strong handshake without standing up. His strained smile revealed bare gums. The dead, utterly expressionless features under the gnarled beard unnerved me, though he wasn't dampening anyone else's high spirits. His scuffed combat boots looked hellishly hot in this swelter. Puzzling over how he and Hoffman might have met, I sensed bad karma.

Rich announced that I had gotten so mellow I was uptight, so he fetched me the only beer in the house, left by a guest two parties ago. Of course without electricity the Pabst was warm and gave off a funky odor. No big deal. I relished the bitter nectar.

Buddy's persistent glances my direction gave me the willies after while, so I moseyed into the kitchen, where Belinda and two guys were drawing runes. She held open a leather pouch of irregular stones incised with the angular alphabet of ancient Germanic tribes, and a small-headed fellow reached deep into the sack and drew the symbol for "Loki." Belinda chortled.

Sarah lifted a six-year-old boy onto the butcher block beside me and pressed her hands against his temples and mumbled a healing chant. The little tyke was one of a dozen kids present, all of whom belonged at this party as much as we adults. How delightfully natural. Infants clung to swollen, bared breasts, thigh-high toddlers played tag among parents, and two boys, aged nine or ten, crawled across a rafter high above our heads, no one the least concerned about their safety. To a boom-box tape of Blind Faith, Dwayne danced all jerky arms and rubbery legs with Nathan, Annie, and Melanie. The effortless grace of Rich's three beautiful kids turned my mood melancholy, so I strolled out onto the porch.

After the album ended, a beaming Dwayne joined me on a smelly couch that had been rained on too many times. "Do you blend in with the locals?" I asked. I never had in Brownsville. Nor with its university crowd for that matter.

"I am a local," Dwayne said with a chuckle. "So is Belinda. And Rich practically is by now, too."

"Then why'd he change his name?"

"He'd always be an stranger with a weird name like Hoffman. Locals resent outsiders for coming in and exploiting the land and sending the money out of state."

"I thought you weren't sure Hough and Hoffman were the same person?"

"I brought you here, didn't I? First, I had to check you out on the way. If you'd been a narc, I would have led you straight to the main patch and sent you on ahead. With an M-16 on automatic, not even half-blind Buddy could have missed you." We both guffawed.

"Who is Buddy really?"

"The guy who guards our crop. A mountaineer from up north of here a state or two, the poor bastard experienced bloody hell in Korea or Vietnam, I forget which. Buddy's a good ole boy. We trust him with our lives."

I yearned for more, but that was it. "So what do you do?"

"Ain't you figured that out yet? I raise hill tobacco. I've always been a farmer, only now I'm finally getting paid what I'm worth. My poor folks were never shy of work and always went to bed tired. Compared to them, I'm loaded."

Dwayne sauntered off with a crazy giggle, and Rich took his seat. My old Army buddy passed me a fruit jar of fresh spring water so cold it made my teeth hurt. "Remember Umlaut's ETS party?" he said. Scenes from that rowdy affair years ago flashed across my mind—Scotty dancing with Pam Cook, Rich chatting with Uschi, and Tom Bakken—hey, that's me!—dancing with Dagmar Schneider. I had always found it nearly impossible to toe the fine line between drunk enough to dance and too drunk to stand up, but that night I had walked it like a tightrope artist.

"Didn't you take Dagmar home that night?" he teased.

"Who knows?" I answered, and we both chuckled. Till I recalled what Peter had written in his diary about walking Dagmar home. I suspected he had also lied about how far he had gone with her. "Scotty's the hustler now," I said. I cringed to recall how close I had come to running into Peter in Milwaukee.

"Dickinson a hustler? Come on. Are you sure he's even heterosexual?"

I told Rich about my recent visit to Scotty's place in Upper Kensington and suggested he do likewise.

Rich shook his head. "Dickinson and I never did get along. A personality clash, I guess. He's too uptight, I'm too laid-back. He's bourgeois, I'm a freak. He's an asshole, I'm a nice guy."

"Bullshit. You guys are both still Monks. As different as you and I are, we're still friends, so why can't you and Scotty be?"

His high spirits fast deflating, Rich said, "Dicko and I had a falling out at Det Q over clothes of all stupid things. Remember how you used to praise my clothes for being so functional? Well, dickhead called them mediocre. Said I had no style. What a bourgeois, asshole thing to say."

"Maybe Scott always was a bit of an asshole. So was Will. So what? You can't let stuff like that stand in the way of friendship. If you saw where he grew up, you would expect nothing less."

"You should see where I grew up near Boston. A good look at my family would convince you on the spot of reincarnation. My soul must have been born already formed, because there is no way my family could have shaped it. My brother's a doctor in internal medicine, and my sister's a management consultant with a Harvard MBA. I have nothing in common with either. And now Sarah's saying she's had more than enough of the so-called good life out here in the sticks. She's sick of doing without and doesn't know what we're proving anymore by it. She claims she's feeling dumber by the day. In other words, she *wants* to be bourgeois. Hey, maybe I am wasting myself here. In more ways than one."

"But don't you miss Boston? It's not exactly Boston here."

Rich let out a loony giggle—just like the old days. "I do miss the Red Sox and the Italian restaurants, but that's about it. Boston invented Yuppiedom, and this is about as close as I ever want to live to Yuppies. I am going to get out of this business as soon as I can afford it. A couple of more good harvests should do the trick."

While he excused himself to use the outhouse, I lingered in the sweltering night alone with my thoughts, pondering where I belonged and deciding nowhere. Or how about here? Some guy inside began singing the Beatles' "Norwegian Wood" to an acoustic guitar in a voice eerily similar to John Lennon's. Might it be Crabtree? I had to admit I should have married a woman like Sarah and had children and just forgotten about graduate school. With a good family, nothing else would have mattered.

I stood up, circled the house, stumbled on a wood pile, and scraped my shins. I thought I heard Rich humming out in the woods, so I called out his name, but the only reply was a chorus of crickets. I detected another noise, a rhythmic scraping, like an off-key cicada. I headed toward it.

"Wanna swing?" Rich said, flicking a flashlight beam onto my face. "If you want, I'll push ya." He sounded upset.

"No, thanks. What's the matter, Rich? Why aren't you at your own party?"

"I am at my own party," he said, still swinging. "It's cool to sit out here if I feel like it. Besides, I can't stand Beatles music. They're the group that had to make fun of everything and spoil the positive stuff Dylan, Baez, and others had gotten going."

The fog was lifting fast inside my head, and we were alone, so it was high time to bring up Peter. "So do you think you'll move back home?" I began.

"And abandon all these people? Like Dwayne? Buddy? When they depend on me."

"They can take care of themselves."

"Take a closer look. Buddy on his own? Dwayne? Come on. What else would I do anyway?"

"Go back to school. Get some practical degree."

"No way."

"Why couldn't Buddy, say, go back home?"

"This is his home."

"Where did you meet that guy anyway?"

"Oh, here in the hills. Same as Dwayne. Crabtree showed us how to make a good living off this land, and I used my contacts out east to market what we grew. Buddy's always done more than his share of the work and doesn't mind being a guard. Actually, he gets off on it."

"He scares me."

"He should. Cross him and you're dead. Or cross me and if he finds out about it, you're dead, too."

"You don't seem happy, Rich."

Hoffman didn't reply right away. "I'm happy enough. I fit in here in my own unique way. The men hereabouts are handymen, jacks of all trades, able to fix anything, stubbornly self-reliant, but they're no good at organizing. So I make the contacts and contracts, and they do everything else. Hillbillies—I use the term affectionately—don't like hippies much, but the two groups have a lot more in common than you might think. Neither is much interested in the mainstream American way of life, especially not success at any price. And they believe in the message of the Good Book, and they know who they can count on. Well, my family doesn't believe in any scripture, but we sure know who we can depend on, too. And we respect other peoples' religion."

"So what is your faith?" Sincerely hoping he had a good answer, and not just for his own sake.

"Live and let live."

I sighed. That shallow a belief had already failed me. I took a deep breath and braced myself for what I no longer could postpone. "Have you kept in touch with Zielsdorf?"

"Nah."

"Did you ever meet Katja?"

"I doubt it," he replied. "Did she hang out at Club 69?"

"She was Peter's girlfriend on the sly over in Germany."

"Really? Oh, now I remember. She lived in Braunschweig, right? He told me about her once. I understand he was really in love with her, even hoping to get married."

"Do you know why he stopped loving her?" I asked.

"He got discharged and came home. Many a GI has left many a Fräulein behind. It's an old story. Why? Do you know what became of her?"

"Yes, I know exactly. In the fall of 1971 she was strangled at a Baltic Sea resort." There I had confided that gruesome fact to somebody—finally. It felt like a huge boulder had been lifted from my shoulders.

"Does Peter know this?" Rich's voice suddenly sounding oddly tense.

"He ought to since I fear he's the person who killed her. He told me another story that I swallowed for years, but not anymore. There's way too much his version doesn't explain. So the next time I see him again, I won't be able to just let bygones be bygones and act thrilled to be reunited."

"Come on, man. Stop feeding me crap."

I proceeded to tell Rich all about the diary that Zielsdorf had entrusted to me fifteen years ago with a request to make it public, if in my judgment people should know exactly what he had done and why. In what amounted to a long suicide note, it described how he fell head over heels in love with a Soviet agent named Katja, who pretended to be a West German, and hopelessly compromised himself. I used to believe Russian handlers had killed her for betraying their cause to protect Peter, and he had drowned himself in despair, since his life was totally ruined. I had decided all these years to preserve his reputation by keeping the existence of the diary secret and so suppressing the truth, since the parties involved were dead. Not that I ever slept easy with this decision. Until recently, when I learned he had tricked me by faking his suicide and instead had established himself as a computer science prof.

Rich gave me a double take. "Prof? You mean, like, professor?"

"Peter teaches computer science at MIT."

"Zielsdorf? No way."

"What's so difficult to believe about that? His intellect was incredibly versatile. Burke claims Peter wised up and switched to a more practical major. Maybe I should have been so smart myself. Maybe you should be now, too."

"What complete bullshit, Bakken."

"Believe me, Rich, there was a Katja. I saw her twice. And she was a Soviet agent. And she was strangled at a Baltic Sea inn, where another guest was beaten to death. And Peter pretended to drown himself, only to end up an academic success at MIT. I swear all of this is true."

"Thomas, where did you get all this crap?"

"From Will Burke. He's played Zielsdorf at chess tournaments and was about to play him again in Milwaukee when I bolted. Also, Peter called Scotty while I was visiting Upper Kensington. Later I phoned his home in Massachusetts and got his wife's recorded message, which mentioned both of them by name."

Rich cradled his head in his hands.

"I've got a photocopy of the diary for you in my car. Read it. I hear Peter is coming to the reunion, so you be sure to come, too."

Rocking back and forth, Hoffman was acting like my news was killing him.

"Rich!" Sarah's voice called out from the house, her slender frame silhouetted in the doorway. "Come join us!"

"Don't leave, man, till we can discuss this more," Rich said. "And by all means show me this fricking diary."

"A *copy* of the diary," I corrected. "The original's back inside my Ohio bungalow."

Once back inside, we did our best to soar back above the clouds, but it was too late for another takeoff. So I made do with stretching out fully dressed on a living room throw rug and quickly crashed for the night.

After dawn a deafening EEEE-AAAA-UUUU startled me awake, a plane having just buzzed the house. I rolled off my stomach, scraping a cheek on a floorboard splinter, and inhaled a deep whiff of dusty pine and stale smoke. "Raid! Raid! Raid!" Dwayne screamed from the front porch.

"Women and children leave in the cars!" Rich hollered. "The rest of you hustle up the hill to the main patch! Nobody take the same path! If the fuzz get on your tail, do your damnedest to escape! If they catch you, admit nothing, and sit tight till we bail you out! Now move it! Dwayne, you get Tom to his car!"

"This way!" Crabtree shouted. I stumbled to my feet, my mind still foggy from the party, and froze. What kind of buddy would abandon Rich during an emergency?

"You idiot, Bakken!" Hoffman yelled. "Go with Dwayne, man! He'll show you a back road out! We'll be okay! Move it, troop!" He flashed that crazy grin I first witnessed after Captain Toddhunter's introductory tirade way back in Monterey.

I ran close behind Dwayne up and over a ridge, my heart pounding and lungs heaving from the strain. Once we rounded the crest, we slowed to a panting rapid walk and sidled through a prickly stand of hawthorn, and the sharp stitches in my sides eased. I tripped on a stump, fell, and banged my forehead against a bough. Ignoring the pain, I sprang back up and soldiered on. "We'll head for Gubb Creek and escape up one of its branches," Dwayne said. "It's longer that way, but dogs can't smell our tracks in water."

Dogs?

A twig cracked up the hill behind us and then another. "Deer," Dwayne whispered. "I hope."

A unfamiliar male voice cried out from on high, "There're down there! I heard 'em." The accent sounded Texan.

"Over here!" another man yelled with a Chicago nasal twang. I flattened myself against the ground alongside Dwayne.

"Keep an eye out for that Corolla with the Ohio plates!" the Texan bellowed. "That sucker's gotta be parked someplace here. When we find the driver, we'll cook that Yankee doper's ass but good."

Yankee doper?

I low-crawled as fast as I could along the hollow bottom after Dwayne. A thorn nicked my right eyebrow, and soon blood mixed with sweat was blurring my vision. My right forearm got slashed and my pants ripped, but I kept up.

"What's keeping those damned dogs?" the Chicagoan yelled. "The bastards are down there, I tell ya!"

Dwayne raised his head just high enough to peer uphill, his cheek now bleeding as well. I made out the baying of bloodhounds down the ridge and fast approaching. So I was about to get busted during my one and only visit to this old Army buddy. Talk about atrocious luck. "We'd better surrender," I whispered, fearing gunplay.

Dwayne slapped a forefinger across his lips and angrily shook his head. Lying flat against crushed Queen Anne's lace tickling my nose, I held my breath and fought not to sneeze. The barking was almost upon us, when shots rang out from an M-16 on automatic. From up on the ridge, where the tree house stood. A brief pause and another clip was emptied.

"Jesus Christ!" the Texan shouted. "Get the hell over there! Everybody! Give 'em some help!"

More shots were fired before it fell eerily silent except for gnats whining in my ears. My clothes stuck to my clammy skin, my eyebrow stung, warm wetness trickled into a sneaker, and a kneecap throbbed. But this was no time to worry about any discomfort. We forgot about the Gubb Creek detour and scurried like salamanders the rest of the way directly over the hill. Once out of sight, we stood up and ran.

We came to the dirt road we had driven the day before. Ten minutes later, Dwayne had me behind the wheel of my Toyota. I handed him a copy of Peter's diary to give Rich. "Mellow out, man," Dwayne teased in farewell, his gory cheeks stretched into a wide grin. "You've made it. But to be safe, head down to Charleston and up the coast, and swing around through Pennsylvania back to Ohio."

So I sped off straight toward the Atlantic, images of what all I had just experienced, swirling through my mind like cyclone debris. Good thing I always kept a first-aid kit, clean towel, and bottled water inside the trunk. Halfway to the ocean, I stopped at a gas station to clean up, bandage my nicks and cuts, and change into a fresh shirt and pair of pants. That first night I spent in a northern Virginia motel outside DC, and only two days later made it to the Ohio-Pennsylvania border, where I hesitated. Till I reasoned that if the authorities had my license plate number I was a goner anyway, so I might as well return to Brownsville and face the music.

I found my bungalow door again unlocked, definitely not how I had left it. I held the knob a long time before daring to tiptoe inside. Nothing in the living room appeared disturbed. But my study was a horror. Papers, lecture notes, research cards—everything was flung pell-mell. It'd take a week to collate it all. If I even bothered. I dropped to my tender knees and gathered the papers into random piles, checking for sheets not in my own handwriting.

I didn't find a one. So the diary manuscript was gone. The intruder had discovered its hiding place inside the stack of lecture notes.

I longed for safer shelter, but was too exhausted to drive farther. I made do with both locking and barricading the front and back doors and did my best to get some rest, which unfortunately wasn't much. Who else but Peter would want the original diary? Hoffman and Burke now also knew of its existence, but Rich should already have his own copy and Will had shown no interest.

Did I ever long to leave Brownsville for good.

Chapter Ten

Who else could the burglar have been but Peter, keen to recover the diary Will had told him I still had? The night before leaving for the reunion I was so upset about the break-in I slept only in fits and starts between horrific dreams. In one, I enlisted for infantry combat duty in Vietnam with Captain Toddhunter's sarcastic approval. In another, I blasted Bob Blair's head off with an M-16 on automatic. In a third, I dragged Peter's waterlogged corpse ashore at Timmendorfer Strand. In the worst of all, I stood by paralyzed to intervene, watching Peter strangle Katja and bash in Breitenbach's skull.

Was he capable of such violence? I couldn't rule it out, not after experiencing his ferocious temper at the DLI and Det Q. More and more I felt it was my duty to turn him in, but what about my own legal jeopardy if I did? Wouldn't my silence all these years earn me at least a criminal charge of aiding and abetting? The more I pondered this, the more I dreaded the reunion, especially the inevitable confrontation with Zielsdorf there, yet I still felt obligated to attend.

Despite my exhaustion, I gave up on getting more slumber and just lay there, clutching Nebuchadnezzar. I rose before the alarm and packed everything I owned worth keeping into my Toyota and had to slam the trunk to shut it. I slipped my Nietzsche notes and article in draft inside manila folders to take along, too, reconsidered, and tossed them in the trash. I dropped my kitty off at Mrs. Gardiner's along with a sizeable supply of cat food. I emptied my bank account and stuffed the wad of twenties and fifties into my dop kit beside the toothbrush, toothpaste, shaving cream, and razor. I was never coming back. Never mind my commitment to teach that upcoming semester.

An hour's drive west to Chillicothe, I closed my second bank account and retrieved the sole remaining copy of Peter's diary from that safety deposit box. Finally, I set off for Chicago. Exiting the wooded hills of southern Ohio, I entered the Midwestern plains, extending across Indiana and beyond. As I drove, I pondered the baffling behavior of my one-time best friend. An acrid industrial stench jolted me back to reality outside Gary. Just because Peter hadn't gone ahead with drowning himself didn't make him a a murderer. Nor did his never having contacted me in the interim. Though those two facts didn't make him innocent either. I swung around a cloverleaf onto the Skyway, accelerated to catch up with the breakneck traffic, and zoomed past dreary tenements toward the Loop's lofty skyscrapers. Within sight of a well-spaced arc of hovering jumbo jets, waiting permission to land, I turned onto the Kennedy Expressway toward O'Hare.

It was late afternoon when I pulled into the Beacon Hotel. I grabbed my suitcase and backpack to lug inside, reconsidered, and instead locked them together with my bulging dop kit inside the Toyota's trunk. I checked in, hustled to my room, snapped the deadbolt, braced a chair under the doorknob, and plopped down on the queen-sized bed. Was I really up to facing Zielsdorf? Only with another Monk at my side.

I showered and shaved and donned a brand-new pair of khaki slacks and a pink dress shirt. Rich would make the best wingman, I decided, but what if he hadn't escaped the drug raid? With Buddy's help I prayed he had. Would I ever be relieved to see Hoffman again in the flesh. Was I eager to hear what he had to say about the diary.

I stepped out into the corridor and twice tested the knob to make sure the room was locked. Downstairs, I emerged into a capacious atrium decorated with gigantic banana trees and a trickling fountain. The formaldehyde reek of a new carpet nauseated me. The third announcement on a tripod, listing the day's events read, "Det Q Reunion – Fogcutter Room." Were Peter and I really going to shake hands, exchange, "Long time no sees," and forget about the Timmendorfer Strand murders and his outrageous betrayal of my trust?

I was so distracted I nearly collided with Beth Dickinson. Attired in a snug, white dress, her lush, sable hair cascading to her trim waist, she looked dressed to kill.

Scott's wife gave me an ironic double take. "Did somebody die, Tommy?"

"I can't explain here," I said.

"So you want to tell me some other place? Wait, are you making a pass?"

Lacking the time and patience for such nonsense, I turned away, but she clutched my biceps. "You mean you really want to talk? I didn't think people did that anymore. Okay, guess what Scotty and I are up to? We're separating when we return to Columbus. He's already found me a shitty little apartment and hired strangers to take care of our kids. So what's new with you?"

"Have you spoken with Peter Zielsdorf yet?"

"Don't change the subject. What's the matter, Tommy?"

I sputtered.

"Are you drunk?" she asked.

"Sadly, no."

I excused myself and marched on with gritted teeth. Outside the door to an unused swimming pool, I found Scotty—thank God!—with an arm around a Rubenesque blonde, relishing his flirting. Flashing me a knowing grin, she greeted, "Toe-mahs."

"Hey, Bakken!" Scotty shouted. "Get yourself a drink, troop. No, make it two. I'll take a double Beefeaters G and T." He thrust his empty glass at me, the better to embrace the fetching babe, playfully twisting out of his grasp.

Grabbing me by the wrist, she said in perfect High German, "*Du hast mit mir doch getanzt, du Arschloch*—but you danced with me, you asshole."

I had?

Scotty took his cocktail glass back with a bloodshot wink and sauntered off.

Who in the devil might this woman be? She looked a few years my senior, here when all the Fräulein frequenting Club 69 had been younger. Yet her mouth was disturbingly familiar. God, no—chills ran up and down my spine. But if Peter was still alive, why couldn't Katja be, too? But what about her obituary in the Braunschweig newspaper?

"You look pale, Thomas," the woman told me. "Are you ill?"

"I danced with *you*?" I asked in disbelief. Jimi Hendrix's freaky guitar began to wail from inside the bar's double swinging doors.

"Sure!" she said. I had put on some weight myself with the passing years, and added poundage can distort a person's features. Her hair was the right shade of ashen-brown.

I squinted, blinked, and whispered, "Katja?"

"I'm Dagmar, silly!" she said, breaking into a giggle. "Karl-Heinz's sister! From Knittelstedt!"

I stared hard—thank God she was right. "What are you doing here?"

"We were invited," she said with a Midwestern American accent. "I'm married to John Jenkins. Shotgun you guys used to call him."

"Shotgun. Sure, the crazy gate guard—whoops, I'm sorry. We're not supposed to talk about our old Det Q jobs."

"I knew Johnny was a gate guard over there," she said with a good-natured chuckle. "Now he owns three carpet stores in the Waterloo, Iowa area. Three so far anyway."

I leaned against the wall to steady myself. I could hardly have been more relieved that she wasn't Katja. "I don't recall you going out with Shotgun in Knittelstedt," I muttered.

"It began after you Russian linguists left."

That statement jerked me on high alert. No civilian was supposed to know anything about our secret military specialties, least of all a Foreign National, even if Dagmar no longer was one. "I quit the Freie Universität," she said, "after East German and Soviet officers interrogated me on a train from West Berlin to Helmstedt. Then I got to know Johnny better at Club 69. After his discharge, we got married and moved to the States. I've been a housewife and mother here ever since."

Could this truly be Dagmar Schneider? And married to Shotgun of all people? The GI who came in a close second behind Umlaut for Det Q's biggest derelict, both of them regularly showing up at Club 69 in fatigues straight from the site and never leaving before bar time. I vividly recalled John Jenkins hanging from the iron girders and blushed. Not that I hadn't dangled up there like a monkey myself.

"Have you talked to Peter Zielsdorf yet?" she asked.

"No, not yet," I said, my heart suddenly in my throat.

"Peter's gotten so—oh, I don't know the word. Though he looks about the same. But then so do you, Thomas."

My forehead prickled at the prospect of meeting a man I had believed without the slightest doubt dead the past fifteen years. "He's not doing badly for himself, I hear."

"That's what I understand. Hey, go talk to Karl-Heinz. He's here, too."

"Your brother's here?"

"Yes! He's John's business partner and a US citizen like me. John does the selling, and my brother all of the purchasing and accounting. Karl recently remarried."

I was about to grill her about Peter, when I felt a tap on my shoulder. I spun around, braced for the long dreaded encounter with Zielsdorf, but it was only Burke. Will gave Dagmar a social kiss on the cheek and shook my hand with unusual vigor. "Not doing badly for himself? Such litotes, my good man. He's doing better than any of us. But would you expect anything less from 'our proud Prussian?'"

"Wh-what?" I stuttered.

"Hats off to Zielsdorf," Will went on. "My good man, how about Kasparov's new variation with the Gruenfeld?"

Suppressing panic, I flipped up my palms.

"I hope to demonstrate my own novel idea with Peter here this weekend. Catch you guys later." Will patted Mrs. Jenkins on the back and disappeared through the swinging doors. She excused herself and traipsed off to the bar as well.

A dark-haired bruiser thrust a beefy hand at me. "How ya doin', Tommy?" he greeted. "I see you've run into Dagmar."

I nodded, recognizing Shotgun when a broad smile stretched the unfamiliar chubbiness out of his cheeks. Though I had never known Johnny well, I was truly glad to see the guy. In fact, I was willing to stay out in the hall all night to remain near his brawny protection. I reluctantly accepted his invitation to join him at the bar, since I couldn't postpone the unavoidable forever. I took a deep breath and followed him into the dim room.

There in profile a guest resembled Peter, but when I got closer it turned out to be Fred Zimmermann, a ComTech from St. Paul. His Det Q section had seldom interacted with mine. Our gazes met, but neither of us felt inclined to speak.

"Tom Bakken, you old son of a bitch!" Whopper's voice called out, and a sinewy hand grabbed mine and squeezed hard. "Let me get you a drink. Bourbon, irish, or scotch?" When I hesitated, he pressed his paunch against the bar and hollered, "Barkeep, pour this man a double Johnny Walker on the rocks!"

I quaffed the fiery booze like lemonade.

Whopper thumped me on the back and moved on, so I slid down near broad-shouldered Jenkins. Where the hell was Rich? I prayed he hadn't gotten busted in North Carolina.

Once the highball's liquid courage kicked in, I ventured farther along the bar past conversations I wasn't tempted to join: "Good ECM can disable Exocets ... The human mind is the most complex relational database ... All of us spooks are weirdoes ... The future lies in Brilliant Stars and Brilliant Pebbles."

I spotted Dickinson across the room and hustled over.

"Bad ratio here, wouldn't you say, Bakken?" he said, grinning ear to ear. "Way too few women. Dagmar Jenkins sure looks delicious, if you like 'em ripe. I sure do. Say, guess what? Peter has finally figured out those three philosophical questions."

"What?"

"I just talked to Zielsdorf. Man, has the guy gotten his act together. Maybe he's too aloof now, but so much has happened to him since Det Q those days don't seem that important to him anymore. And he no longer drinks anything stronger than a wine cooler. Who could have predicted Peter of all people would end up this straight?"

"So what are the answers?

"Who are we? Homo sapiens. Where are we? On the planet earth. Why are we here? To advance the human race. That's it. Simple, huh? He answered them without a moment's deliberation. Probably because he's matured to the point where trying to figure out baffling crap seems like wanting to be depressed. Who cares if all this makes sense? Life is a goddamned ball, so what else matters but to relish it?"

I nodded. Though those replies sounded less like maturing than brain damage. The most penetrating mind I had ever met was satisfied with such glibness?

"What were you talking about with Dagmar?" Scott gave me a lecherous wink.

"Her marriage. Her brother. Life."

"Weren't you pretty darned interested in Dagmar over in Knittelstedt?"

I shrugged. The wisest move would be to confront Peter immediately and get it over with.

"Come on, Tom. You had a good six inches of interest in her from what I recall. Go for it, buddy." While Scotty prattled on about the virtues of zapping women with lusty thoughts and exuding pheromones, I scanned the room for Rich in vain.

"Have you seen Hoffman?" I asked.

He scowled and shook his head.

Dawn accosted us to rescue me from another of Scotty's eccentric monologues. I introduced what looked like a sixteen-year-old Asian girl going on thirty as Will's wife. Dickinson's jaw went slack.

She suggested a game of chess. I pleaded having already consumed too much booze, a big fat lie. "I'll give you white," she bargained.

"No thanks."

"Plus a pawn?"

"Maybe tomorrow afternoon. If I'm still here."

"Are you not staying both nights of the reunion?"

"Sure," I said, lying.

When Dickinson staggered off for a refill, Dawn told me, "I have tremendous news! William is going into his father's business in Seattle. No more nonsense about becoming a grand master. He is not that good at chess anyway. Now we can have children."

While she extolled their future grand life, I surveyed the room. Still no sign of Peter or Rich. When Dawn moved on, Pam Cook flirtatiously brushed my elbow and gave me a big "Howdy," even if she didn't recognize me. I couldn't spot her husband—our old company clerk—anywhere. Jim Fry, a former Trick Chief, came over to chat, and I learned that Sergeant Major Whitman and Master Sergeant Wilhelm were both Army lifers, while Jim was a civilian employed by the Defense Department and not at liberty to reveal the nature of his work.

"Star Wars?" I guessed.

"No, ferret satellites. But really, Tom, you remember what classified work is like. I can't even discuss it with my wife. And that's a problem for us. She says sometimes she wonders if she even knows me."

A blue-eyed brunette sidled up to him and kissed him full on the lips. "Charlotte, I'd like you to meet Tom, ah, Tom—"

"—Bakken," I said.

"We already met," she told me.

I couldn't place her familiar face.

"*Ich bin die Charlotte*," she said, pronouncing her name German style with three syllables instead of two. To wit, the Fräulein that Burke had screwed over. Little of her teenage prettiness had endured. "You were William's friend," she said without rancor.

"Yes, Will's and Rich Hoffman's and Scott Dickinson's."

"Don't bring up Will Burke," Jim begged.

"Forget about him, darling," his wife said. "I sure have."

"One of these days the bastard will get what's coming to him," Jim muttered.

"And you were Peter Zielsdorf's friend too, right?" she said, making me cringe. "I just spoke with him," she told her husband. "He was very curious about your job, so I told him the little I knew and said he'd have to ask you the rest. His voice sounds funny. Husky, I guess you call it in English. From an old throat injury. He went upstairs to get a camera, but said he'd be right back."

So the dreaded encounter wasn't far off. Where the hell was Hoffman?

"Chow time!" Umlaut bellowed. Upon command people abandoned the bar for the Formica-top tables, each set for eight places. Umlaut and Shotgun, as the chief organizers, had seated themselves up front, together with Jim and Charlotte. Still no sign of Zielsdorf. Or Hoffman. I hated seeing Beth Dickinson sitting so morosely among other sullen wives.

"Thomas!" Dickinson yelled from near the back alongside Will. I wound my way to their table and found them with two strangers—a balding, red-haired fellow in sunglasses, and a haggard, hollow-cheeked chap with a dark, greasy ducktail. Had these two really been at Det Q? I took the chair against the wall opposite the greaser and continued to scan the crowd for Peter.

"About time you got here, Bakken," the thinner stranger greeted with Hoffman's voice. Sans the beard of North Carolina or the moustache of the Army I had never seen him without.

"Glad you could make it, Rich," I commented coolly.

He giggled nervously. I bet he had quite a story to tell, but then so did I.

"Catch you later, Karl," Scott told the ginger-headed man. I watched in amazement as Dagmar's brother, the very person who had introduced Peter to Katja, thus unleashing untold havoc, trotted off, now as American as any of us. "Karl just got married again to the former Pam Cook," Scott explained.

We four sat without speaking, awaiting the one missing Monk. Up close, Will looked even worse than he had in Milwaukee, Scott and Rich, awkwardly situated elbow to elbow and keeping their gazes locked straight ahead, little better. I was grateful I couldn't see myself. Dickinson piped up, "Fred Zimmermann told me Peter's working on Star Wars software, Reagan's so-called Strategic Defense Initiative to end war forever."

"Bullshit," Rich snapped. "More like end the world forever. Only asshole technocrats think world peace is only the right technology away. No fucking way would Peter *ever* work on Star Wars. You know him better than that."

Scotty managed a weak smile. "I beg your pardon, Hoffman, but I'm just repeating what Zimm told me. He had a long chat here with Peter. I swear both of them are now working on Star Wars."

Rich rolled his eyes. Accusing once anti-establishment Peter of working on the Strategic Defense Initiative did seem slanderous. Like he had joined the ranks of the treads he had so despised. Yet to every indication this drastic change of heart had indeed taken place.

A Det Q veteran in the back corner stood up and took a flash photo of people at his table and then of other buddies nearby, and soon guys everywhere were standing and taking snapshots of each other. We four Monks, all without cameras, stayed glued to our seats.

When the servers finally showed up, everybody sat back down. "What's keeping Zielsdorf?" Will asked with a sigh. "I told him the Monks were going to eat together." Nudging Rich, he added, "Seriously, Hoffman, developing SDI is an honorable enterprise, and I'm proud to say Peter Zielsdorf is my friend."

"In Nazi Germany you'd have been proud to call Heydrich and Himmler your friends, you fascist, Burke. Weren't they great patriots though?"

"Please spare us such drivel, Hoffman. Your charge of fascism comes from the deepest of left fields."

"Horseshit. Man, we must be friends, Burke, or otherwise how could I stand to associate with a jerk like you?"

Will laughed heartily at Rich's repartee. He excused himself and headed across the room to accost a fellow near the door, who from our distance did vaguely resemble Peter. My God, could it really be him? A few minutes later Burke returned and reported, "Peter has already promised to eat with Zimmermann, but he'll stop by later."

A reprieve, in other words, one especially appreciated at least by me.

"Doesn't sound much like the old Peter we knew at the DLI and Det Q," Scott muttered.

"None of us are who we used to be!" Rich snarled. "You don't know jack shit about Zielsdorf, Dickinson!"

Scotty forced another lame grin. "Are you trying to pick a fight, Hoffman? Give me a break. What did I ever do to you?"

"You never respected me, asshole. But then how could you, as bourgeois and conventional as you've always been?"

Scotty looked stricken.

"Are you guys serious?" Will butted in. "Stop it. We're the Monks, remember?"

I was dying to hear the details of Hoffman's escape from the narc raid. "Have any trouble getting here, Rich?" was the best I could muster.

He met my pregnant gaze with a smirk. "Not too much. I left home so fast I was lucky I had time for a haircut."

"What about Sarah and the kids?"

"They're staying with family."

I nodded, having understood enough.

Moist-eyed Scott cleared his throat and said with a breaking voice, "Richard, I'm truly sorry. I never meant to disrespect you, and I sincerely regret giving you that impression. I never expected anyone else to live like me, especially not you guys. I'm just doing what my parents always wanted. I'm sorry to say it's not working out. Lately I can only stand my life when I'm partying, and I'm partying way too much. Have any of you talked to Beth yet?"

"I've never even met her!" Rich snapped.

"Come on, Rich. Forgive me. Okay, I wronged you way back when. Give me a chance to make amends."

"Okay," Rich said, relenting. "Do you know of a place to hole up a while where nobody could find me?"

"Definitely," Scotty replied. "You can stay in my northern Minnesota cabin as long as you like. I only use it summers. There's months worth of food in the cupboards and freezer."

Rich nodded with a pained smile. Scotty's apology lightened the mood among the other three Monks, if not me.

A trim gentleman with a balding crewcut and unfashionably narrow tie approached. "Hey, Jerry," tipsy Scotty gushed like a practiced salesman and even stood up to give the guy a hearty handshake. Gerald Murphy had to introduce himself before Rich and I recognized this particular old Army buddy. Not that I had ever really known the guy at Det Q. I couldn't recall his military specialty, but did remember that he collected stamps and coins, boring hobbies in my opinion.

To nobody's surprise, Murph had become a CPA, a dullish, though obviously essential, occupation. Unfortunately, Dickinson let his disdain toward this career choice show. In response we each were promptly handed a business card that read, "Gerald Murphy, Forensic Accountant, Federal Bureau of Investigation, Chicago Field Office." Okay, now I was impressed—and intimidated.

Plump waitresses served us reunion guests as much greasy fried chicken, instant mashed potatoes, lumpy gravy, thawed peas, and microwaved apple pie à la mode as desired. Umlaut and Whopper and Shotgun had arranged the meal on the cheap, all of it wholesome and hearty and one hundred percent American, even if as bland as Norwegian fare. The boring cuisine irked Will and Scotty, but they still politely downed it.

Unlike Hoffman and me, neither of us displaying much appetite. I suspected he had a lot to tell me about the diary. Dickinson joked about how innocuous our treads now seemed, the lot of them just more guys trying to make a living. "Remember all those inspections and that military courtesy crap," he said with a whinnying giggle. That Will did indeed. Scotty recounted Peter's obscene defacing of Captain Slater's parking sign at the DLI—twice. Soon Burke and Dickinson could hardly stop laughing they were so amusing each other, while neither Rich nor I cracked a smile. Hoffman kept glancing at the empty chair where Peter ought to have been sitting.

"Okay, I admit that was pretty gutsy on his part," Dickinson went on. "But still not a fraction so daring as the time he sneaked an audiotape away from the site."

What? Nobody ever did that. And why would they? Talk about an outrageous violation of security protocol.

Scotty proceeded to describe his most memorable SPETSNAZ broadcast ever. He and and Peter had just begun a mid inside the Green Room when they overheard a Soviet Special Forces officer cursing a blue streak in their earphones. Zielsdorf instantly hit the record button like the gunner that he always was. "Talk about colorful Russkie swearing," Scott went on. "This after their ops had cleaned up their act for months. 'You blankety-blanks mixed up the keys!' the officer screamed. "'Not these! Those! Sign off immediately! And don't come back up until you've straightened this crap out!"

"I don't see the humor," Will said.

"Wait, I'm not done," Scotty told him. "One obtuse Russian op, ignoring the officer, began to describe a tank underwater river crossing in progress, which triggered even worse swearing. All of which I found hysterical unlike Peter, who was acting like he was witnessing a mass murder in progress. Once this SPETSNAZ signal finally did go down as commanded, Zielsdorf nonchalantly proceeded to unspool the tape, lay it upon his desk, and thread a blank tape through to the empty reel. All without one word of explanation."

"Are you honestly going to take that snippet to the Scribe Room?" I asked him then in disbelief. Even it had been ages since the Soviets had mentioned a military exercise.

Zielsdorf not only didn't reply but refused to look at me. When I returned later from the latrine, the audiotape was nowhere in sight. Because he had indeed taken it to a transcriber, I assumed. Till I noticed it half-hidden inside his lunch bag. Did his sneaking home codeword material like this ever blow my mind. 'Now you see it, now you don't.'" More maddening giggling from Dickinson.

"Do you remember exactly when this took place?" I asked, my pulse pounding in my ears.

Scotty rubbed his chin. "Just before our big Fourth of July blowout in 1971," he replied.

So not the answer I wanted to hear. Because that was precisely when Peter's diary described tearing out a transcript of an intercept he had just scribbled down from memory and ripping it to shreds. Even worse, he had mentioned that tape inside his Knittelstedt rental and his crying need to destroy it.

Chapter Eleven

Dickinson's revelations so upset me I couldn't finish my slice of apple pie. My eyes even had temporary trouble focusing. Umlaut wobbled to his feet, clanked a fork against a water glass, and the hubbub died down. "I see everybody made it who could," he said. "Even Chicken Man."

A few laughed, though nobody at our table.

"I see ceiling-hugger monkeys from my ETS party."

This time dead silence. Rich eyed me warily. "Does anybody remember what a quad was?" Umlaut asked with a big grin, as though going over well, knowing the only real mistake an emcee can make is to appear ill at ease.

Another long, awkward pause till an attendee in back slurred, "A double double."

"That's right!" Umlaut crowed. "Four shots of moose juice."

Again no one laughed.

"Let me thank everyone here for coming," Umlaut gamely continued. "And my assistants for all their help." He took a deep breath and cleared his throat. "Well, let's get back to the real purpose of this reunion. Getting shit-faced together, just like old old times at Club 69. Go for it, guys. And will somebody take a dip in the swimming pool before this shindig ends? We paid extra for the damned thing, so use it."

When Umlaut sat back down, one person clapped, and then another, and a third, till soon most present politely joined in. "Gentlemen, please excuse me while I go get Zielsdorf," Will told us and hustled off. Hoffman buried his head in his hands.

I offered him some of the aspirin I always carried. He took a couple of pills and pocketed them.

"That Dagmar's something else, huh?" Scotty said, nodding toward Mrs. Jenkins two tables away. "I still can't believe she married Shotgun. You should have moved in on her faster at Det Q, Bakken, while she was still unattached. Or were you already tied up with Karen by then?"

In my agitation I couldn't even begin to respond. Scotty stumbled to his feet and shuffled off toward the bar, while I braced myself for the confrontation with Peter. What the hell was holding Will up?

Bleary-eyed Umlaut, ever the good host, now busily working the crowd across the room, accosted former Spec 6 Boudreau, the former supervisor of Det Q's Russkie lingies. As I watched our emcee gamely trying to engage the laconic man in conversation and failing, Boudreau's speculation fifteen years ago that Peter had written in his diary came to mind: "*What if our SPETSNAZ guys switched to double radio networks? One to punk us and another to conduct real business. And we've been listening to the wrong one.*"

I jolted to my feet. That was it! The explanation for Peter's baffling behavior back then! And the audiotape he had recorded, sneaked out of the site, and destroyed proved it. Because he had immediately understood the significance of the Soviet goof-up that shift. Spaced-out SPETSNAZ ops had mistakenly inserted keys for the worthwhile network into their punk network radios, which briefly allowed Scotty and Peter to listen in on their real business, like we had always done before their mysterious hiatus and change in transmission content.

"What's gotten into you, man?" Rich asked.

I plopped back down.

But why had the Russians bothered to create a second network? Because of the glossary! The special slang included in the copy Katja had provided them had revealed Det Q's ability to eavesdrop on SPETSNAZ transmissions. Peter instantly had recognized this that night, but out of self-preservation had kept this fact to himself, thus turning his earlier reckless, unwitting treason into the genuine thing. And from there it apparently hadn't been too big a leap for him to become the willing Soviet agent he now was to all appearances.

Umlaut plopped down in Burke's vacated chair. One glance at my empty glass and he signaled the waiter.

"No!" I snapped. "I've knocked back more than enough."

"Hey, if you're still conscious, troop, you haven't had too much to drink," he quipped.

I asked Umlaut whether he had spoken with Zielsdorf.

"Uh-huh."

"And his wife?"

"Yup, the Kraut, too. I think she's that same Fräulein he was seeing in Braunschweig."

"Who told you about Katja?" Rich snarled.

"I thought everybody knew about Petie's girlfriend. It was hard to overlook his shit-eating grins."

Umlaut soon moved on to gladhand other guests. I was dying to discuss everything I finally understood about Peter with Rich, but only in private. "Tommy," he said, "there's somebody you absolutely must see before you have it out with Zielsdorf."

"What?"

"Follow me. Now."

I got up and sidled through the festive mob after Hoffman toward the exit, both of us successfully avoiding entangling conversations. The music switched to Janis Joplin as we passed Scott, descending upon Dagmar. Her physical resemblance to Katja made me cringe.

A muscular grip on my shoulder halted us in our tracks. Umlaut pulled me up to a petite, short-haired blonde. "Angelika," he said, "I'd like you to meet two of Peter's best buddies in Knittelstedt—Tom Bakken and Rich Hoffman. Guys, this is Mrs. Peter Zielsdorf."

Was I ever relieved to see that she wasn't Katja. Angelika shook my hand limply, her poker face on the pretty side of plain poorly concealing her unease. Captain Slater joined us, nodding at Mrs. Zielsdorf, as if he knew her full well. "How's it going, Bakken?" he greeted with a hearty smile.

"Okay, Sir," I replied, lying. Our former CO was sporting the whitewalls and fit physique of an elite combat soldier.

"Don't 'sir' me anymore, Bakken," he said good-naturedly. "I'm a civilian now, working for the Defense Department. Your face is familiar," he told Rich, "but the name escapes me."

"Richard Hoffman," Rich mumbled.

Which obviously meant nothing to Slater. "You must have kept a pretty low profile at Det Q." Rich rolled his anxious eyes. When Slater grilled us about what we were doing for a living, Mrs. Zielsdorf's ears perked up. He was mildly amused to hear I taught at a small Ohio college, but laughed out loud when Rich said he was a farmer currently at loose ends. These replies visibly bored Angelika—till Umlaut asked Slater what he was doing for the Pentagon.

"Sorry, gentlemen, that's classified," he said in a charming tone none of us experienced once at Det Q.

Angelika excused herself to check on Peter. Ripping myself free of Rich's grasp, I pursued. Overtaking her, I blurted, "I was Peter's best friend in both Monterey and Knittelstedt. Which is why he entrusted his diary to me."

"A diary? What diary?" she said, looking horror-stricken.

So Peter hadn't told her about the journal either. Of course not. And not just because it described a torrid affair with another woman in lurid detail. "Ask Peter to explain," I said. "By the way, where is he right now?"

She glanced nervously over her shoulder toward the far end of the bar, where I spotted a tall fellow chatting with Fred Zimmermann. My God, it truly was Zielsdorf. No doubt about it. My stomach sank.

Hoffman grabbed my arm. "Come on, man. My friend's gotta leave." What a relief to let Rich drag me the hell away from there.

Karl-Heinz Schneider cut us off at the swinging doors with a big "Howdy" and firm American handshakes. "You fellas interested in a Cubs game tomorrow afternoon?" he asked. A Midwestern accent out of Karl's mouth sounded unreal, but it was Schneider all right. "We'll be back in plenty of time for the reunion cookout."

I glanced back toward Zielsdorf, now talking to Slater. The jaw, nose, forehead—no question about it, it was Peter. He had aged more gracefully than any of us.

"Come on," Rich begged, tugging at my sleeve.

"Let me talk to Karl a bit first," I said, holding my ground.

"My friend can't wait!" Rich insisted.

I promised Rich I'd join him in five minutes and told him to go ahead without me.

"Room 614," Hoffman whispered into my ear. "Make sure nobody is following. When you get there, only stop if the corridor is empty. Then barge right in without knocking. The door won't be locked." With that, he took off.

I explained to Karl that we already had a commitment for the next afternoon—a pure fabrication. He thanked me anyway and accosted another former GI from Det Q.

My precious target at long last in my sights, I homed in like a deadly missile. Never mind my resolve to confront the bastard together with another Monk. The closer I got, the less I liked what I saw. Feigning a friendly smile, peering coldly through glasses much thicker than before, Peter was soaking up everything our ex-CO was uttering.

Zielsdorf eyed me a couple of times, flashing a new, artificial grin, and of course recognizing me—how could he not?—without interrupting his current conversation. Like seeing his old roomie Thomas Bakken again was no big deal. Like I was just another acquaintance. Meanwhile, I had so much to tell him that I felt close to detonating. But what did he have to tell me? Apparently nada to judge from this nonchalance.

In a rage I shoved my way along the bar until I stood directly behind Slater and Zielsdorf. "We're really pleased with your work so far," our ex-CO told him. "Maybe I can land you the contract for Brilliant Pebbles, too."

"And I'll see what I can kick your direction," Peter replied in a hoarse whisper. That permanent laryngitis Will's wife had mentioned. But what was this disgusting sycophancy? Just the opposite of the proud Prussian I knew.

Leaning against the bar mere inches behind Peter's back, I eavesdropped on their discussion of military satellites that had to be classified. Though we had breached security guidelines similarly upon occasion in Knittelstedt. After talking freely at the site, it had seemed only natural to continue in the privacy of our apartments or at Club 69. Zielsdorf was proving himself a master at drawing Slater out by means of attentive listening and deft questioning. His diction was a beat slower than before, his sarcastic wit absent, but there still was that old Wisconsin accent.

Peter rested his elbows back against the bar beside me, and I studied him in profile. His posture was different now, too—more erect, more confident, more relaxed, as if finally at peace with himself and the world, as though he had finally become a calm, confident son of a bitch. It was uncanny how young he looked up close. Faint laugh lines and tiny wrinkles around the eyes, but no receding hair line, and not a trace of gray. Though the passing years had added some puffiness to most of our faces, his was still angular as a buck private's fresh out of Basic.

When he limped off to the men's room, I felt a powerful urge to pursue, but stayed put. Zielsdorf soon returned to the exact same spot, even though Slater had moved on.

Finally facing me, Peter said, "So how you doing, Tom Bakken?" Giving me the chilling impression he felt pleased with himself for recalling my name. We shook hands, his scar tissue cold and slippery to the touch.

"Fine, Peter," I replied. "You know, I'm quite surprised to see you here."

"Really? Oh, I wouldn't dream of missing this reunion. Who knows if there'll be another?" His grin was mirthless, like a shadow of the man I had known animating an empty shell. This new, shallower Peter seemed fully capable of murdering Katja and Breitenbach.

"I hear that you're at MIT." My entire body felt electrified by adrenaline.

"Yes, in Computer Science. It's a comfy mix of research and teaching that lets me travel on special projects."

Comfy? A most peculiar word coming from the least relaxed person I had ever met. "So where did you do grad school, if not UW-Madison?"

He hesitated, as if weighing the question's hidden intent, his smile shrinking a notch. "I earned my doctorate at Berkeley," he answered amiably. "Then accepted an assistant professorship at MIT, got tenure in due course, and have been teaching there since. The Institute and I enjoy an ideal relationship."

Peter's newfound cant and smarmy affability, both utter bullshit, made me ache for his old testiness. "I hear you're working on Star Wars software."

He scowled before grinning again like one of the guys. "Tom, you know better than to bring up classified stuff like that."

"That didn't keep you from talking about it with Slater. Or Zimmermann."

He bridled. "But that's different. We're all in the same business." His salesman smile tightened into a resolute, closed-mouthed smirk.

"What about the principle of need-to-know? Nobody in intelligence work shares any classified information that the other person doesn't absolutely require to do their job." Hey, I was arguing just like a tread.

"Well, that's the theory, Tom," he rasped. "But as you probably remember, in actual practice folks in the community routinely share resources with those working against our mutual foe."

"You mean the Soviet Union?"

"*Selbstverständlich*, as the Germans would say. Of course."

His use of Katja's favorite word only aggravated my fury. "Your views on the USSR seem to have changed a bit," I said, not bothering to conceal the sarcasm.

"Not really. I always knew it wanted to spread socialism across the world. The US as the bastion of capitalism has to be its mortal enemy. Hence conflict between the two systems is inevitable, and so we've got ourselves a Cold War."

"Who started the Cold War?"

He chuckled. "Hey, what is this, twenty questions? Another day, Bakken. A wise man once said there are two things a person should never argue about—politics and religion. A word to the wise is sufficient. So what line of work are you in?"

"Guess?"

"Teaching?" His grin was so unfeeling I could easily envision him strangling Katja.

"Yup," I said, glancing at the chintzy Timex on his wrist that he had won as Best Student at the DLI.

"Foreign languages and literature?"

"Close enough."

Flashing those ugly, artificial teeth, he told me, "Since the accident, my memory isn't what it used to be, especially about stuff that happened way back when. I hit my head so hard the doctors said I was lucky to survive. You've probably noticed my hands and permanent limp."

I glared at the scarred appendages, now as then still plenty strong enough to wring Katja's neck. Or bash in Breitenbach's skull. His slick fingertips could no longer leave prints, but in the moment I didn't realize its significance.

"In many ways," Peter went on, "my life didn't truly begin till that car crash. When you're that close to death, you finally sort out what's important and what's not. I'm a whole lot calmer and happier now."

"I've noticed. When exactly was this accident?"

"During grad school." His voice was getting hoarser.

"Where?"

"In California. Near San Francisco."

I stared at him, stunned to be seeing *the* Peter Zielsdorf in the flesh. His eyes wobbled behind thick lenses, as if underwater.

"So I hear you want the diary back?" I said.

He gave me a puzzled, nervous glance, but refused to lose his aplomb.

"Then you don't remember Katja either?"

That finally wiped the grin off his face. "Katja?"

"Katharina Wendt, your girlfriend in Germany. If you say you've forgotten her, you're a goddamned liar."

Managing only the thinnest of smiles, he replied, "Sure, I remember Katja. Have you heard from her lately?"

"Not too bloody likely! Why don't you just quit this fucking ignorant act. You and I both know full well what happened to her. So now the question is why did you do it? And what are you really doing at MIT?"

Peter leaned back against the bar and scratched his chin. He was about to reply, when Angelika leaned close, whispered something into his ear, and hustled off.

"Oh, yes, *that* old diary," he said ingratiatingly. "Sure. Say, would you mind showing it to me, Tom?" I absolutely detested this new unctuousness.

"Okay, I'll get it. Just stay put and I'll be right back."

"Angie and I'll be here a bit longer, but we won't be staying overnight. We'll be flying to Helsinki for a conference." How convenient, since the Finnish capital lay so near the Soviet Union he would no doubt slip across the border and consult with Russian handlers during the same trip. Oozing the charm of a practiced bon vivant, the traitor ordered himself a Perrier.

My dreaded duty no longer could wait. I excused myself, pleading nature's call, and slipped out into the lobby. I dropped a quarter into a pay phone and called the number on the business card I had in my wallet. The woman answering Jerry Murphy's number at the Chicago FBI Field Office connected me to a special agent on duty. I succinctly recounted the details of Peter's treason on behalf of the USSR and stressed the need to send colleagues to the Beacon Hotel as rapidly as possible.

I hung up and marched off to Rich's room, eager for the FBI to arrive and not caring whether they gunned the bastard down. Besides, that would be far more convenient for me than a trial, since my unwitting aiding and abetting of his espionage was much less likely to come up.

The gall of Peter to stand in front of me, acting this blasé after breaking into my home in Ohio. The gall to pretend not to remember Katja. Or to deny the diary's existence after personally handing most it to me and mailing the rest. He was an idiot to think I wouldn't have made myself copies.

But what still baffled was that if he had agreed to spy for the Soviets, why had it been necessary for him to kill Katja? Or had the Russians themselves killed her and Breitenbach on their own initiative to make sure Peter's future undercover work on their behalf would remain safe from exposure? Had they interrupted his suicide attempt and blackmailed him into working for them? Or had they persuaded him to willingly betray his country on their behalf? None of these possibilities made complete sense, no doubt because major pieces of the puzzle were still missing.

I burst out of the elevator and strode down the sixth-floor hall, Katja's face from fifteen years ago dancing before my eyes. My wrongdoing was minor next to what Peter had pulled, I kept telling myself. Yet by remaining his loyal friend the extent of my personal guilt was still appalling.

I knocked softly on room 614. Dead quiet inside. Too late I recalled Hoffman's instructions to walk right in. Suddenly the door flew open, and Rich yanked me inside.

"Damn it, man," he said. "I told you not to knock. And what took you so fricking long? Did you tell anyone where you were going?" Rich hadn't been this riled even during the North Carolina raid.

I assured him I hadn't.

The room was dark except for a night light near the door. Gradually, I made out a man seated at the far end by the window, peering outside around the edge of a closed curtain. He looked large and menacing enough to inflict bodily harm.

"I'll leave you two alone," Rich whispered. "Call the bar when you want me to return." With that, Hoffman left.

I flipped on a bathroom light and moved into its illumination. The stranger didn't bother to face my direction. I just stood there, listening to the muffled roar of the jets taking off and landing at nearby O'Hare. "Who are you?" I asked.

No answer.

"You have something to tell me?"

Two drunks staggered past out in the hall, one of them laughing just like Shotgun. A door opened across the way and slammed shut.

"Tommy," the man drawled, "you still walk like you expect to hit a patch of ice any step. It's that damned Norwegian in you. You were just a stitch walkin' across the parking lot today." The baritone voice sounded vaguely familiar, but I couldn't place it.

"Where do I know you from?" I said.

The man turned on a lamp beside his chair, and in profile I saw a bald, old geezer with a wizened face, checking the traffic outside. "You're too damned uptight about your center of gravity. Just let go. You ain't never gonna meet a decent woman otherwise. With that marriage you were in, you ain't hardly been married yet, so you have a lot of livin' to catch up on."

The accent was Appalachian. He looked my father's age.

"Cat got your tongue?" he went on. "Sorry 'bout all the shootin' at Rich's. Glad you got out all right." He dropped the curtain and faced me.

I let out a sigh and sat down on the couch opposite Buddy McCracken, wearing a too tight, tattered field jacket. Rich's I bet. Without a hat and clean-shaven, he looked even older than he had in North Carolina.

"Hi, Buddy," I greeted. "I can't thank you enough for saving me along with everybody else during the raid. I pray nobody was hurt. What is it you have to tell me?"

He stared at me long and hard, the thick, ill-fitting wire-rims blurring his eyes into blue-gray smudges. "Who do men say that I am?" he said, his accent suddenly Northern and no longer at all Appalachian.

"Are you going to speak in riddles?"

"Thomas, look at me," he growled. He grabbed an army baseball cap from a pocket and pulled it down on his head. Then took two plates of false teeth out of his shirt and slipped them into his mouth. Finally, he placed his hands alongside his cheeks and pulled back the wrinkled flesh until it was smooth. And he smiled.

"My God," I said, not believing my eyes. I started to shudder and then cry until I was sobbing uncontrollably.

"Yes, Thomas," he said in his own voice, "I can't be Buddy McCracken because he died shortly after childbirth in West Virginia over fifty years ago." The "o" of "ago" sounded long, pure, and Germanic—the way all of us Wisconsin natives pronounce it.

We both rose to our feet, and I jumped into his arms and embraced the real Peter Zielsdorf like the long lost brother I had never had. And like me, he wept, and without looking at each other we saw face to face.

Chapter Twelve

We sat back down, and he inundated me with information. The Zielsdorf I had met at the bar was a Soviet impostor, who with the help of plastic surgery and a faked car accident had taken over Peter's life after he had pretended to drown. At first, he had wanted me to publish the diary so that people would understand why he took his own life. Though once he had decided against committing suicide, he had wanted it published so that everyone would believe he was dead, even when he wasn't. That way he could begin a new life under a false identity with no fear that the KGB or GRU—or FBI—would ever try to find him. Thus he had followed Katja's plan to the letter without knowing she was playing it both ways—she not only wanted his death feigned so he could escape, but also so he could be replaced, thus saving him personally, while still accomplishing her spy mission. So when she impressed upon him that once safe in the States he had to avoid all contact with his former friends and haunts and live under a pseudonym, she was protecting both him and the double.

He didn't have any idea the fraud existed until Umlaut started organizing the reunion, and Rich learned from me that "Peter Zielsdorf" was teaching at MIT. All along he had assumed I hadn't made the diary public, since nobody knew anything about it. Then once he got wind of the impostor, there was no doubt of my suppressing it. Yes, he had called Scotty during my visit to Columbus. And he had stolen the diary original from my house, while I was taking the long way home from North Carolina.

"Why did you call Dickinson and ask about me?"

"For the same reason I eventually stole the diary from your place." He checked the parking lot again and removed the army baseball cap, now no longer resembling old Peter in the least.

"If you hadn't published it after all this time, I wanted it back. To make certain the document never saw the light of day."

"But publishing it now could very well expose the impostor and end his espionage mission."

Peter stared out the window with a wistful grin. "I can't afford to let the Soviets know I'm not dead. The Russians were ready to kill me once, and now they have even more reason to." As if he couldn't care less about the damage the double was doing.

"Katja tricked you to ensure their replacement's success."

"That and to save my life."

After she'd ruined it, I thought but didn't voice. "So who really killed Katja?" I asked. Try as I might, I wasn't convinced he hadn't done it himself for spoiling his life's big plans.

"The GRU," he said, thrusting his jaw forward. "The Russians strangled her to protect their impostor. And to avenge her disloyalty for foiling their kidnapping attempt in the Harz. If she hadn't gotten me started throwing rocks there to alert the West German border guards, my life would have been a whole lot simpler—and shorter. Just think how frustrated her comrades hiding nearby must have felt when the *Bundesgrenzschutz* led me away." Peter cackled.

"The Soviets knew how good I was at impersonating West Germans," he went on, "so they let me take the blame for her murder as Jost Schottenstein, the pseudonym I used when checking into our lodging. They certainly didn't want Peter Zielsdorf accused, not with the plans they had for him. The yearning to see my beloved one final time, even if very briefly, sent me back to the *Pension* after hiding my getaway clothes up the beach. To my horror I found 'Breitenbach' in our room wiping fingerprints and Katja lying lifeless with a ligature wound tightly around her neck. I recognized him as the guy with her in the Munich bar as well as the photographer in the woods. It wasn't hard to beat that Soviet bastard to death. For fifteen years one of my biggest regrets has been having to hurry with killing him." His voice tailed off.

"I don't remember everything that happened between my last blow and arriving at the beach," he resumed. "I do know I undressed near the water's edge and ran across the wet sand toward the ebbing tide to leave deep footprints. And waded in and swam out as far as I could, using the sealed plastic bag containing all my cash as a float. It wasn't too much trouble making it back to shore, not when I was furious enough to swim to Denmark. The Russians snatched up my suicide note and suitcase along with my IDs and wristwatch and used them to get their agent in place. So the West German *Polizei* never came close to figuring out they were looking for an American. It wasn't hard to slip out of the country as Reinhold Schmitt."

"Why did the GRU give you that legend?"

"No, Katja gave me Schmitt on her own."

"How do you know?"

"I know, Thomas. I knew her better than anybody. She saved me, even if she didn't save herself."

I struggled to absorb this tsunami of revelation. So the double's mission had succeeded only because I had kept the existence of the diary secret. Because if Peter had been publicly declared dead—even when he wasn't—the Soviets could never have replaced him. Thus my honorable motive—to save Peter's reputation—had compounded my wrongdoing beyond my wildest fears. To think I had been virtually paralyzed for years over so little beside the true enormity of my misdeeds.

"Once Katja persuaded her superiors that I would never cooperate with them no matter how much they blackmailed me," he said, "they chose to replace me. It didn't matter to them if they offed me or I did myself in. I'm sure they enjoyed nudging me closer to the edge. With my academic dreams in ruins, I was tottering on the brink, I admit. Katja convinced them I really was going to kill myself, thereby covering up my eventual escape. But then at the critical moment, staring death in the face, it seemed that life was too brief a candle in the eternal night to snuff out less than fully burned. I bet the bastards combed the beaches a good long while in a futile effort to seize my corpse before the West Germans stumbled upon it." He cackled at the thought of their frustration.

"I hung out in Amsterdam a few months, sleeping in a park with hippies from around the world and speaking broken English like a German. The Dutch never suspected I was a Yank. Then I flew KLM home as a German tourist and saw the sites in New York City, just as I had always dreamed of doing while growing up in tiny Chute Noire. From there it was easy to disappear."

"Why did Katja pick you out?"

He grimaced. "I used to be fairly good-looking, remember? Actually, Katja had little choice in the matter. At first, the Soviets wanted to know the reason for the sudden influx of Russian lingies at Det Q. Believe you me, I never told her one word about our stolen SPETSNAZ radio receiver. Thank goodness, showing her that glossary of vulgarity never harmed our secret intelligence mission."

Huh? In fact, that appalling blunder had ruined our Soviet Special Forces intercepts.

"Are you okay, Tom?" Peter asked.

I couldn't bring myself to explain. Though if our roles had been reversed, he wouldn't have left me wallowing in ignorance, would he? "Did you ever find that missing audiotape?" I began.

He threw me a nasty glare.

"I'm talking about the one Scotty saw you record one mid at the site and sneak back to your room. The tape proving our SPETSNAZ unit had created double radio networks. 'One to punk us and another to conduct genuine business,' as Boudreau phrased it in what we thought was wild speculation."

Talk about a flabbergasted expression on him.

"The Russkies really euchred us there," I went on. "After their month-long radio silence, the Soviet radio keys we had access to could only eavesdrop on the dummy network, the one without intelligence value. And never on their new parallel system that discussed genuine military operations. Except very briefly for you and Dickinson that one mid in early July 1971."

"What in the devil are you blathering on about?"

He sounded sincere. But how could he ever have forgotten something this significant? Okay, he hadn't had the chances to read and reread the diary these past fifteen years unlike me. And he had gone through hell just to survive, which undoubtedly had taken a toll on his recollection. Besides, what I was telling him hardly sounded plausible, even if it was the truth. Katja herself apparently never learned of the switch, probably because her handlers wanted to make sure she couldn't share this secret with Peter.

"Once they learned more about me from Katja," he continued, ignoring my shocking revelation, "they took a particular interest because of the position very high in American government they believed I could attain. When I turned out to be too stubborn for recruitment, they decided to replace me with a man they already had who resembled me. Since I didn't seem close to anyone, neither family nor friends, their scheme seemed safe from exposure. Just in case, the Soviets waited a whole year before letting their guy emerge in Berkeley after a fake car accident, the alleged injuries to his face and teeth in reality a plastic surgeon's handiwork to make him look as identical to me as possible.

"So Katja did risk her country's mission for you. If you'd been dead, no one would have ever found the impostor out."

My wreck of a friend nodded with a wistful grin.

"Why'd the Soviet risk coming to the reunion?" I asked.

"What risk? You believed he was Peter, and you were my roommate. Of course, his appearance would be different. But he still looks like Peter, he acts like Peter. In fact, he looks more like the Zielsdorf you knew than I do. Or Rich does Rich. And there was so much to be gained by his attending. Who knows what information he's getting from Slater and Zimmermann and the others? Maybe enough to compromise an entire new top-secret technology?"

"We have to stop him," I muttered.

"I'm planning on it."

I refrained from mentioning that the FBI was on the way, if not already inside the hotel. "What's Karl-Heinz doing here?"

"What are *you* doing here? He came as Dagmar Jenkins' brother and a former German we knew and hung out with in Knittelstedt. It's his reunion, too."

"How did he know Katja?"

"They were college pals, just like he said. Nothing else. He introduced me to her because she asked him to. And because he knew I was hunting for a girlfriend."

"You don't resent that?"

"She loved me, Thomas. Eventually. As I adored her. Every time I saw her—and I mean every time—my passion for her blazed anew. Without a doubt, she was the most attractive woman I have ever known. In my wildest fantasies, and you, Tommy, if anybody knows how wild they could get, I never once dreamed I'd find that perfect a lover."

I envisioned Katja as I had briefly seen her, Peter's description matching my own experience. But as much as I still loved him as a buddy and friend, I couldn't help but feel repulsed by this wretch sitting opposite me. "But she betrayed you," I insisted.

"No, she saved me."

"After she almost had you kidnapped, if not also killed."

Peter's cold-blooded glare was so chilling I shuddered to envision Breitenbach's battered corpse. "Okay, but only after trying to do her duty. And without ceasing to love me as much as I loved her. Because somewhere between recruiting me for her cause and working to replace me with a double, her love swelled to match mine. No, the only thing wrong with Katja was an accident of birth. She happened to be born into communism and grew up believing in it, just as every proper Soviet youngster should. Idealism came naturally to her, and how better to serve her nation than to help it win the Cold War? She did her job well until she met me. Then she figured out how to save both her mission and her lover, if not herself. My own solution was less clever. And less patriotic."

He paused to wipe his misty eyes before telling me how memories of all their blessed rendezvous filled his empty years with the Hare Krishnas. Not that he wasn't grateful that they took him in. He would never defend that religious cult, but he also refused to criticize it after giving him refuge, no questions asked. It was his own karma he had to live out, they said, and no one could absolve him of that.

"It was in a Hare Krishna temple in West Virginia, where I first learned a sense of serenity and oneness with the universe. But after three years, I realized the peace I had achieved through meditation was barely this side of death. I didn't want to spend the rest of my life balancing on the edge, happily gazing into the abyss like it was some kind of paradise. After leaving the Krishnas, I lived in places like Portland, Seattle, Phoenix, and Denver, doing various odd jobs, not unlike what I had done during high school to buy myself clothes. Stock boy, construction, factory work, whatever. Once somebody acted like they recognized me, but I lost him and left town on the spot, without even going back to the flophouse for my stuff."

I tried once more to convince him of the horrific damage showing Katja the glossary had done to Det Q's SPETSNAZ mission, but his self-deception on the topic was impenetrable. "How long have you been Buddy McCracken?"

"Since hooking up with Rich."

"Did meditation help you answer the three big questions?"

"Yes," he said, grinning repulsively.

"Well, what are they?"

"True friendship."

"That doesn't make any sense, Peter. The questions I meant were—what are we, where are we, and why are we here?"

"It makes more sense than anything else."

I pored over his drawn, lined face.

"Sorry to hear you're divorced, Thomas."

"Ours was an amicable dissolution. And inevitable it seems in retrospect, being mismatched from the beginning." Or was the problem that we were mirror images?

He asked where Karen was now, so I told him about her professorship in Grand Forks, North Dakota. "Peter, knowing I made it possible for a Soviet illegal to operate for fifteen years devastates me, but what I'm about to tell you—"

"—But don't you feel at least some sympathy for the schmuck at MIT impersonating me?" Peter interrupted. "I mean, give credit where credit is due. Aren't you impressed by his stunt? Of course, the guy can't be totally denying himself in acting out the role. It has to be somewhat natural for him, whoever he really is, or he wouldn't have succeeded this well. My guess is he's a German Soviet like Katja." He peeked behind the curtain at the parking lot again.

"So what are you going to do about the double?"

"Kill him, of course."

I flinched and wiped my sweaty brow. "What about turning him in?" I was pleading morality's cause, but I didn't truly want to convince him, did I? Because after everything I now knew I was guilty of, facing the authorities terrified me. Memories of Buddy's M-16 blasting away at Rich's farm echoed in my ears. He scared me then, just like he still scared me.

Peter guffawed. "The double's career was built on Katja's death. And today she will be avenged, whether she would have wanted it or not. Peter Zielsdorf's life is going to end tragically."

"But what will happen to the Soviet?"

"No, Tommy, you don't understand. He is Peter Zielsdorf now, not me. I'm Buddy McCracken. He's done a far better job of realizing me than I could have, given a similar chance, and I don't want to take that away from him—or from me. No, Peter Zielsdorf is going to die a distinguished MIT professor, his brilliant career cut short by an Appalachian madman."

He cackled at the prospect. "He took over my life, and now I'm going to take over his, stringing it together in everyone's minds into one continuous story. It'll make for an impressive biography. Assuming his reputation as my own, I'll die happy. Only you and Rich will know the difference, and you'll both keep your mouths shut, just like you did with the diary and Toddhunter's parking signs. All in all, I can't complain about how things have worked out, since I could have done so much worse. This is my chance to save my life in the most important sense, and I sure as hell am not going to waste it."

It took a minute for this outrageous plan to fully sink in. "But no one will know we were penetrated by a Soviet illegal?"

"You mean the treads won't know. It won't matter since the double will be dead."

"But somebody will have to figure out the damage he did. Otherwise, this might happen again. His death won't change that. They'll definitely want to interrogate him."

Peter waved off my objection.

"You could just leave with Rich and me, and let the false Peter continue to develop an even more dazzling reputation, which will redound in posterity's eyes to your benefit anyway." Or would that be even more immoral than simply killing the impostor and erasing all knowledge of his Soviet intelligence coup?

"No way."

Actually, that suggestion was no longer a choice. That phone call had already been made and would soon wreak havoc. The FBI would arrest the false Peter for espionage and expose his treason. Treason from our point of view, that is, since Russia would consider him a great patriot. Should I at least warn the real Peter? But if I did, wouldn't he interfere? I rubbed my burning eyes, debating which would be the wiser course.

If my arguments kept splashing off him, maybe I should just give up and let him do what he wanted. Besides, it was far more convenient for me if the illegal were eliminated before an interrogation. And didn't Peter deserve the Soviet's reputation?

"My whole life," he said, "from the first day of grade school, wearing my cousin's hand-me-down clothes, to my Russian speech at the DLI, I was driven by one thought—I'm more than I seem. And, by God, I was damned well going to prove it or die trying. Becoming high school valedictorian or Phi Beta Kappa junior year or graduating magna cum laude or winning the Commandant's Award—none of it was ever enough. Chagrin over how humbly I grew up was a hole so deep no pile of honors could fill it. It was never okay just being who I was, not when I was capable of so much more. But at the same time, by excelling wasn't I fulfilling my promise? I mean, I actually did all those things, didn't I?"

The phone rang. He let it jangle a while before ordering me to pick it up. "But don't identify yourself. And say Rich will be right back."

It was Hoffman, sounding panicky. Two men in gray suits had crashed the party and were asking around for me. Thank goodness, nobody knew where I had gone. Federal narcs was Rich's best guess as to their identity. Maybe somebody got my license plate number in North Carolina after all. "Meet me with Peter at my car. Forget about your fricking Toyota, because it's probably being watched. I'll buy you a new one." Rich hung up with a sharp click.

The party crashers of course were the FBI agents I had so stupidly summoned. Now that the real Peter had surfaced I no longer needed their help, but a card on the table was a card played. "Peter," I said, "our only hope is to leave immediately with Rich." Though now without any doubt I did want the false Peter silenced first.

"I'm not leaving while that bastard is still alive."

"But they'll arrest you."

"Not until it's too late for him, and then it won't matter. Besides if I'm caught, I won't admit who I really am." Dropping his Wisconsin accent, he drawled, "If I ain't Buddy McCracken, that don't mean I ain't still Appalachian."

"Peter, before you head downstairs, there's something very personal I need to confess. What I started to a bit ago. I'm really sorry I didn't tell you before Timmendorfer Strand. God help me if that would have prevented the tragedy there."

Peter pulled a snub-nosed revolver out of his field jacket and spun the chambers. "All I ever wanted was to go off somewhere with Katja and live."

"Forget about her," I said.

"So, Thomas, what is it you didn't tell me?"

"First, tell me how Katja really died."

"'Breitenbach' strangled her. I told you already."

"But the only evidence for that is your diary and what you say now. You admit yourself the diary ends in lies. How do I know where they begin?"

"The only lie in the entire document, as things turned out, is that I would drown myself. Every other word is the gospel truth. Trust me."

"But I can't, if you think the fake Peter's life is worth taking over. Because he's been stealing intelligence for the Soviets. He's betraying Star Wars to them. Yes, he must be stopped, but not by you. Let him be arrested and interrogated."

"You know, you saved my life in a key sense, too. Thanks to your discretion I will go down as a great success. Publishing the diary would have ruined everything. Thanks a million, buddy."

"Why did the GRU really want Katja dead?" I said.

"Because she knew I was to be replaced by a Soviet illegal, using my identity. Because she saved me from kidnapping in the Harz. Because she tried to play it both ways at the risk of ruining their grand scheme. How many reasons do you need? Why won't you believe me?"

"I don't understand why you don't despise her. Since she destroyed your life."

He peered out the window again. "If so, it was worth it. I've never been happier, never will be, never could be, than those brief months with Katja. Because of all the precious hours we spent together, I could never hate her."

I stared at him, trying to imagine the days and nights on the run that had left him looking this wretched at only our age.

"What makes a life worthwhile anyway?" he said dreamily. "For me, it's been the intensity of peak moments. An evening can make a month, a week a year, a year a lifetime. Without those, the humdrum mediocrity of day-in and day-out existence is like the vast, black emptiness bridging the blazing glory of the heavenly stars. Without those pinpoint flashes, there would only be solid darkness. Sure, she ruined my life, but she saved it, too. I have no regrets."

I glanced away from his grotesque grin.

"Thomas, where did we make the first wrong turn? Was it in Monterey? Or already when we failed to escape the draft by emigrating to Canada? Though that would have probably spoiled our lives, too."

"Katja ruined your life," I repeated, preparing him for my own confession.

"I've long since forgiven her, ever since I saw her lying there with glazed, unseeing eyes. In the bed we shared the last night of her life. Our lives. So tell me what you keep hinting at."

"Did you know that Katja saw somebody in Knittelstedt, while you were home on emergency leave?"

"She mentioned it. It was Will. At first, I thought it might be Dickinson, but he has principles. So it had to be Burke."

"Why couldn't it have been Rich or me?"

Peter cackled. "No, it was Will. And the bastard deserves to pay for the treachery with his damned life." He laid the revolver down on the table, leaving the barrel pointed at my chest.

"It wasn't Will," I muttered. "Katja was with me." Finally, I had admitted it. The prospect of Burke's life added to the rising toll on my conscience chased my hesitation.

Peter snorted. "How noble of you to lie for Burke's sake, but I don't believe you, Tommy."

"No, it really was me," I said, my voice breaking.

"Thomas, your acting skill surprises me."

"I'm not acting."

Averting his fierce glare, I added, "While you were back in Wisconsin, I was reading Pushkin's *Queen of Spades*, when someone knocked on my apartment door."

Peter picked up the revolver again.

"The knock was so tentative I knew it couldn't be you or Will or Scott. I guessed it was Rich. Dressed in T-shirt and underpants, I opened the door, and there stood a pretty blonde."

"*Bist du der Tom*?" she asked in familiar German and smiled. Are you Tom?

"*Ja*," I said, recognizing Katja from the Braunschweig train station. A long, clingy dress flattered her figure, as a shag haircut did her striking face. I slipped on a shirt and pants and invited her in. Every time I've reread your diary the past fifteen years I imagined her as she looked that evening. It wasn't hard to understand why you loved her so."

"Love her," Peter corrected, putting the gun back down on the table and crossing his arms. "Why did she come to you?"

"Because you had told her I was your best buddy and your only real friend."

"You were. You are. I gave you the diary, didn't I?"

"I told her I already knew she was your girlfriend. She proceeded to ask me everything imaginable about you, making it sound as if she wanted to be absolutely sure about your character before agreeing to marry you. My German wasn't always adequate, but she was patient, smiling kindly as I struggled with paraphrases to fill the gaps in my vocabulary. I explained where you were born and grew up and went to school and what your family was like—as much as you had told me anyway. Her rummaging in her purse several times while we spoke made me suspect she was taping me. But I didn't worry about it, since I was careful not to reveal anything classified."

"You simply told her whatever she wanted?"

"Well, not exactly. At first I wouldn't reveal a thing."

"What changed your mind?" He snatched the pistol back up and rested it across his thighs, aiming at my groin.

I glanced at the door and calculated there was no way I could distract him long enough to run that far. What insanity to be afraid of my best friend, but he was fully capable of pulling the trigger, wasn't he?

"She persuaded me," I said lamely. "Remember, I was very lonely. Even lonelier than you were before you met her."

"I bet she persuaded you. It's a good thing for her she's already dead. How did she persuade you? I want you to say it."

"Please don't ask me to spell it out."

"Oh, Tommy," he said, standing up, gun in hand, "there's only one way to end this all."

"Don't," I pleaded, unsure whether I was begging for my own life or the Soviet impostor's—or both.

"Goodbye, Thomas," he said, shifting the pistol to his left hand and extending his right. "Take care, buddy. And keep your mouth shut about Peter Zielsdorf. Like Toddhunter told us, nothing is more important than being security-conscious."

"I'll promise, if you'll forgive me for what I did with Katja."

He stared at his feet a while before nodding. I stood up and squeezed his hand, and we awkwardly hugged. He disappeared out the door, just as the phone rang again. "What the hell is keeping you assholes?" Rich shrieked in my ear. "Jesus Christ! Get to the parking lot in five minutes or I'm leaving without you!"

"Peter left to kill the Russian," I said and hung up.

Moments later, I shoved my way through the barroom doors and froze. Inside, guests were lounging about and listening to the Beatles' "Let It Be." Suddenly Dagmar's voice screeched, "He's got a gun!" followed by two explosions and screams. I pushed my way past people scrambling to flee toward the commotion and bumped into Angelika. I clutched her thin wrist, but she twisted herself free with a well-aimed, painful kick.

A man in a field jacket clawed away from outstretched arms and broke loose in a clumsy sprint. I stepped into Peter's path, but he bowled me over. "Get out of the way, Bakken," he bellowed, "or you'll get what you deserve, too!" He burst out the swinging doors into the corridor, where another shot rang out.

I picked myself up and limped outside. Two men in gray suits and hair short enough to satisfy Captain Toddhunter were leaning over Zielsdorf, sprawled on the floor, his right hand pressed against the spreading, dark circle on his upper chest.

"You should have dropped the weapon," the younger FBI agent told Peter.

"Shut up, George," his older partner said. He kicked Peter's snub-nosed revolver away from his free hand and snatched it up.

Peter smiled at the younger man, blood trickling out of the corner of his mouth. In a broad, Appalachian accent, he said, "Don't feel bad, buddy. I don't hold it against you."

I dropped to my knees alongside Zielsdorf. He pointedly met my gaze before closing his eyes and weakly grinning. Umlaut barged through the swinging doors, shouting, "Peter Zielsdorf's dead!" The real Peter's smile widened. Will stumbled past Umlaut, tears streaming down his cheeks.

The older agent sent his colleague into the bar, flashed a badge in my face too quickly to read, and rattled off Federal Bureau of Investigation blah-blah-blah. "Who is this man?" he snapped.

"Some drifter named Buddy McCracken," Rich piped up from behind us. "That's what he told me anyway."

"And who are you?" the agent demanded.

"Richard Hoffman from Boston, Massachusetts. I'm here for the army reunion. I ran into this dude in the lobby, panhandling for loose change. He seemed like he maybe wasn't playing with a full deck, but harmless enough."

The agent removed a wallet from Peter's pocket. Upside down, I read "Donald McCracken" on a North Carolina driver's license.

"It's so, so cold," Peter croaked. "The water's just freezing." A rattling came from his throat, his left hand slid away from the wound and flopped to the floor, his body went limp, and his skin turned ashen in a wave, starting from his forehead.

The younger agent popped back out of the bar. "Witnesses inside say your man shot a reunion guest dead with two bullets to the head. The victim's ID says he's Peter Zielsdorf, the guy Bakken told us about."

"This one's dead, too," the older agent said. Turning toward me, he snapped, "Did you know this man?" My kneeling over the body implied I did.

I shook my head.

"But, Tom," Umlaut said, "didn't the guy call you by name as he fled?"

"He called him Buddy," Will butted in. "I heard it quite distinctly." Burke, looking more upset than I had ever experienced, twisted his head to get a better view of the corpse. I had to suppress the urge to close Peter's glazed eyes. Rich bent down and gently did our dear friend this final favor.

"Are you Tom Bakken?" the older agent asked.

"Yes."

The emergency squad burst into the hall, and the driver swore like a drill instructor to learn they had gotten there too late. He cursed again when the agents ordered him not to touch the bodies until city police had finished processing the scene. While we waited, the two FBI agents grilled me about my relationship with the assailant.

Exaggerating my confusion, I haltingly explained that I had dropped to my knees next to "McCracken" because I had never seen a cadaver up close.

"Bullshit," the older agent said. "He didn't die immediately." Will gave both Rich and me puzzled glances, but said nothing. Dawn emerged from the bar and stepped into Burke's embrace.

Scotty stumbled through the swinging doors. "I can't believe it," he muttered. "Peter Zielsdorf's dead." Glancing at the body on the floor, he asked, "Who's this bum?"

"Donald McCracken," George told him. "The assailant."

While the crowd focused on the deceased, Scott sidled up to Hoffman and slipped a set of keys and a map into his pocket, and

Rich gave his onetime nemesis a shoulder hug. "So this joker here did it," Dickinson said, stepping alongside the corpse. He and Will distracted the agents with questions, while Rich retreated and exited, just as the Chicago police arrived.

"So where's this diary?" the older agent snapped.

"In my room," I said. "I mean, in my car."

"Get it."

My last sight ever of Peter was of him lying lifeless, faintly smiling, as if lost in a sweet dream. I turned away as uniformed cops began chalking an outline around his body.

George accompanied me down the long corridor and out into the parking lot toward my Toyota. I considered surrendering to him, but didn't have the courage. I opened the trunk of my Corolla and was groping in my backpack for a manila envelope, when the agent cried out and crumpled to the pavement. "Let's go!" Rich yelled, wielding a thermos bottle like a club. "I should have killed the bastard for shooting Zielsdorf! Why didn't Peter listen to me? We could have all gotten away!"

I grabbed my things and raced after Rich. To the muffled roar of O'Hare jets landing and taking off, we jumped into his Chevy beater and sped toward the Interstate.

Chapter Thirteen

Last September, Rich and I fled Chicago and hid out in Scotty's cabin here in northern Minnesota. At first, it was still tourist season, so a local general store was selling both major Windy City newspapers. I cut out every article from the *Sun-Times* and *Tribune* on the Beacon Hotel shootings and collected these in the same wrinkled envelope that for fifteen years has held the *Braunschweiger Zeitung* clippings on Katja's demise.

Both sources reported the senseless murder of Peter Zielsdorf, a prominent computer science professor at MIT, gunned down in the prime of life. They duly traced his meteoric rise from a humble beginning in tiny Chute Noire, Wisconsin, to a stellar academic career on the banks of the Charles River.

Significantly less space was devoted to his assailant. The *Sun-Times* described Donald McCracken as a drifter from Coon's Run, West Virginia, whereas the *Tribune* claimed his origin was unknown. Neither offered a motive for the killing and declined to speculate. It wasn't even clear whether the gunman had deliberately targeted Zielsdorf. They pronounced FBI Special Agent George Doughty a hero for thwarting the attacker's escape. The papers attributed Angelika Zielsdorf's flight from the scene and subsequent failure to make her whereabouts known to shock suffered upon witnessing her husband's brutal slaying.

The following week accounts closer to the truth appeared. The *Sun-Times* wrote that the FBI was investigating Zielsdorf for possible espionage on behalf of a foreign power. Two days later its rival stated that the Bureau had established firm evidence the deceased had been an active Soviet agent for well over a decade and declared his wife a fugitive from justice.

But Zielsdorf and McCracken weren't the only familiar names in the news. No, sirree. For the very first time since earning the honor roll at Madison East High School, Thomas Bakken made the papers, too, starting with a charge of assault and battery against an unnamed federal officer. Within days, the accusations grew to conspiracy to traffic in an illegal drug as a member of a North Carolina gang, accessory after the fact in an unsolved double murder in West Germany, and, to top it all, aiding and abetting domestic espionage on behalf of the Soviet Union.

As a youngster I had dreamed of one day achieving some measure of renown, not that I honestly expected it. But here, without even trying, I had become a household name, known coast to coast. Who could have ever imagined all those A's and B's would eventually lead to this infamy? But it wasn't just my life that was utterly wrecked. The real Peter's grand scheme to usurp the false Peter's glorious career upon the latter's death as his own was also thoroughly dashed.

October here was gorgeous. Rich and I finally quit worrying about anyone tracing us to our hideout. Will and Scotty paid separate visits and were told everything I am telling you. The evergreen firs and pines stayed true to their colors, while the white birches turned yellow. Flocks of American coots, Canadian geese, and mallard ducks rested on the cooling waters before continuing their journey south. By the first snowfall, the migrants were long gone, and leaves lay withering on the ground. The lake began glazing over in sheets so thin they melted in the afternoon sun—until one day the ice thickened enough to withstand the warming light and within a week grew strong enough to walk on.

It's almost Christmas now, and my parents and the staff at Northern Appalachian State must be losing hope that I will ever turn up. Forgive me, Mom, Dad, Karen. When you read this, I pray you will understand what I've had to do.

Hoffman finally left last weekend to take his chances linking up with Dwayne and Sarah and the rest of the family in Georgia. The cold was really bothering him—Scotty's fireplace never adequately warms this cabin—and he had come down with a deep cough he couldn't shake. If caught, his culpability should be far less than mine anyway, not that the law will likely ever get on his tail.

Rich begged me to join them and promised to find me something useful to do. But I'm not a chameleon like Zielsdorf. No, if anyone ever was, I am merely who I am and always have been. I don't belong anywhere so much as in these northern woods so similar to my ancestors' origin near the Swedish border of Norway. Nobody relishes a genuine winter like this more than me, the cool sunshine sparkling off the blinding water crystals, glistening across the earth like so many countless gems.

Every day of late I've been taking Scotty's firewood axe out onto the lake and hacking away at the same spot. Each time I don't get very far, but like history I'm making progress. When I finally break through, I'll widen the gap to the size of a manhole. Scotty won't mind sacrificing his andirons and tire chains to the bottom, not as a favor for an old buddy.

Though the first two charges against me are technically false, it is indeed my fault that Peter's sabotaging of Det Q's SPETSNAZ mission was never unmasked, that the Soviet double succeeded as a spy, and that Peter is now dead, and there is no consoling me.

So my only recourse—to salvage at least some of my dear friend's shattered reputation and maybe also a bit of my own—is to make the truth known in its naked fullness. Toward that end I've spent untold hours at this table inside Scotty's cabin, painstakingly composing this confession. Herewith I present my completed account of relevant events, along with Peter's diary.

What I'm leaving behind for others to read ought to save the essence of his life—as well as mine. Though our actions often resulted in evil, he was not fundamentally a bad man nor was I. Let someone else judge where we went astray. Remember that neither of us could see all the cards hidden in the hole. So many hands to play out, for better and worse, striving to stretch our luck, before the last lies exposed. Peter Zielsdorf was so not the man I long believed, but then neither was Thomas Bakken. What artful dodges indeed do we each employ to escape from the grim shadow of self-knowledge?

If my slate is written full, then it's high time to wipe it clean. I'm praying baptism isn't the only way water can wash away a person's sins. Of course no one will ever hear from my best buddy again nor will anybody from me. Like Peter, I'm going under.

Made in United States
Orlando, FL
04 February 2023

29543685R00192